To
Marry
a
Prince

Sophie Page is the author of several novels, and lives in London. Visit her at www.sophie-page.co.uk

SOPHIE PAGE

To Marry *a* Prince

arrow books

Published by Arrow Books 2011

1 3 5 7 9 10 8 6 4 2

First published in Great Britain in 2010 by
Arrow Books
Random House, 20 Vauxhall Bridge Road,
London SW1V 2SA

www.rbooks.co.uk

Addresses for companies within The Random House Group Limited can be
found at: www.randomhouse.co.uk/offices.htm

The Random House Group Limited Reg. No. 954009

A CIP catalogue record for this book
is available from the British Library

ISBN 97800990560456

The Random House Group Limited supports The Forest Stewardship
Council (FSC), the leading international forest certification organisation. All
our titles that are printed on Greenpeace approved FSC certified paper carry
the FSC logo. Our paper procurement policy can be found at
www.rbooks.co.uk/environment

Mixed Sources
Product group from well-managed
forests and other controlled sources
www.fsc.org   Cert no. TT-COC-002139
© 1996 Forest Stewardship Council
FSC

Typeset by SX Composing DTP, Rayleigh, Essex
Printed and bound in Great Britain by
CPI Bookmarque Ltd, Croydon, CR0 4TD

To my favourite authors,
thanks for all the fizz, fun
and friendship – especially
KF and EMR, you know why.

Britain

as it might have been . . .

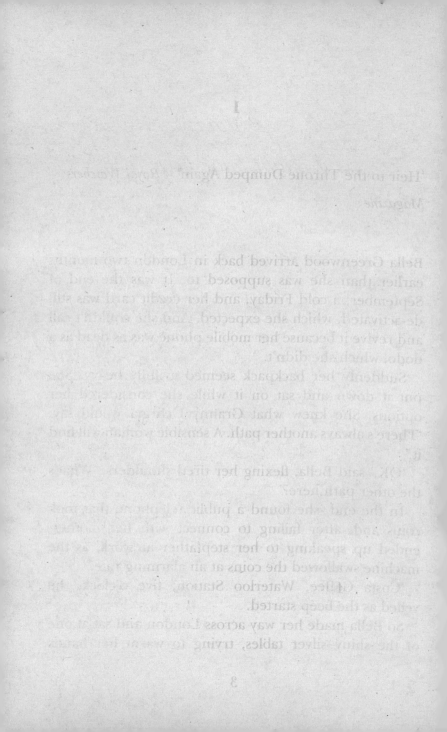

1

Heir to the Throne Dumped Again, Hello Reader
Magazine

Bella Greenwood arrived back in London two minutes earlier than she was supposed to. It was the end of September, a cold Friday, and her credit card was still de-activated, which she expected, and she couldn't call and revive it because her mobile phone was as dead as a dodo, which she didn't.

Suddenly her backpack seemed usually heavy. She put it down and sat on it while she considered her options. She knew what Grampa Clem would say. There's always another path. A sensible path, she'd find it.

Yes, said Bella, flexing her tired shoulders. Where's the other path, here?

In the end she found a public telephone that took coins, and, after failing to connect with her mother, ended up speaking to her stepfather, as, as the machine swallowed the coins at an alarming rate.

Coins. Office. Waterloo Station, five o'clock, he yelled as the beep started.

So Bella made her way across London and sat at one of the shiny silver tables, trying to warm her hands

3

1

'Heir to the Throne Dumped Again' – *Royal Watchers Magazine*

Bella Greenwood arrived back in London two months earlier than she was supposed to. It was the end of September, a cold Friday, and her credit card was still de-activated, which she expected. And she couldn't call and revive it because her mobile phone was as dead as a dodo, which she didn't.

Suddenly her backpack seemed awfully heavy. She put it down and sat on it while she considered her options. She knew what Granny Georgia would say: 'There's always another path. A sensible woman will find it.'

'OK,' said Bella, flexing her tired shoulders. 'What's the other path here?'

In the end, she found a public telephone that took coins and, after failing to connect with her mother, ended up speaking to her stepfather at work, as the machine swallowed the coins at an alarming rate.

'Costa Coffee, Waterloo Station, five o'clock,' he yelled as the beep started.

So Bella made her way across London and sat at one of the shiny silver tables, trying to warm her hands round a mug of coffee and scanning the commuter crowds for Kevin Bray's tall figure. But in the end he was nearly upon her before she caught sight of him.

'Look, Bella,' he said, plonking himself down in the chair opposite, 'it's good to see you, of course, but this weekend is just not on. Your mother's got people staying. Your room's occupied. I'm sorry.'

Bella had been travelling for four days by then. All she wanted Kevin to do, really, was pick up her backpack, shepherd her on to the train and take her back to the comfortable Hampshire villa where she could have a warm bath and climb into her bed and sleep for about a hundred years.

A hug would have been nice, too. But she was philosophical about that. Kevin was not a natural hugger and Bella had come into his life too late for him to adjust his habits. Kevin had many qualities that her natural father, H. T. Greenwood the explorer, lacked, most notably not being out of the country all the time. So Bella was reconciled to there being no hug.

But no bath, no bed, no monster sleep either? This couldn't be happening.

'Not on?' she echoed, bewildered. Jet lag always slowed her down.

Kevin could not quite meet her eyes. 'It's this Charity Ball tomorrow night. Your mother's on the Committee. Been working on it for months. We're taking a party, of course. The house is full. You know your mother.'

Yes, Bella knew what her mother was like. She fought down brain fog and interpreted. 'You mean, she doesn't want me home because she's partying with the movers

4

and shakers of Much Piddling in the Wold.'

Kevin was shocked. He was a nice man. 'Of course not. She wants you home. We both do. She can't wait to see you. Only—'

Bella sagged. 'Only not this weekend.'

'There's so much to do and the house, well, it's—'

'Full. You said.'

He winced. 'Sorry. If we'd only known. But we thought you were staying out on your island until after Christmas.'

'So did I,' said Bella, desolately. But her words were lost in the echoing station announcements and the stampede of Friday night commuters.

'You should have let us know sooner,' said her stepfather firmly. 'Call your mother on Sunday after the ball and she'll sort out a date for you to come down. You've got somewhere to stay?' And, before she could answer, 'You'll need some cash, I bet. Won't have had time to sort yourself out, if you only got in this afternoon.'

He had come prepared. He stuffed a wad of notes into Bella's hand and cast a harassed look at the departures board. It was clicking away, replacing lists of departed trains with those that would go any minute now.

'Look, I've got to go or I'll miss my train. Your mother sends her love. 'Bye.'

He kissed Bella's cheek awkwardly and stepped back, nearly stumbling over the corner of the backpack. He righted himself just before he had to see it, and strode off before she could protest.

Bella would have called after him, but a sudden yawn

nearly took her head off. And then he was gone in the crowd.

Her eyes burned with tiredness. She looked down at the notes in her hand. They were fifties, she saw, a big fat pin cushion of £50 notes. And then she realised – he must have given her enough money to pay for a hotel in London for the whole weekend.

The very thought of finding a hotel, checking in, *talking*, made her want to sink down on to the shiny floor of the concourse and go to sleep right where she was.

But she was a seasoned traveller now and she knew from experience, not just Granny Georgia's homilies, that you did not go to sleep until you were indoors and safe. If her old mobile had been working, she would have texted her best friend, Charlotte Hendred. But as it was, she had to start with the public telephone system again.

'Man is a problem-solving animal,' said Bella between her teeth.

She stripped one of her stepfather's £50 notes off the wad, stuffed the rest inside her bra and hauled her backpack on to her shoulders. She bought some chocolate, along with an expensive glossy magazine, so that the man on the till didn't mind giving her change for £50, and started the business of tracking down Lottie.

It didn't take long. Bella couldn't remember her mobile number but she knew the name of the big PR agency where her friend worked. She found the number and the switchboard found Lottie in seconds.

'Bella!' she squeaked. 'Where are you?'

'Waterloo.'

'Belgium?' said Lottie, bewildered. 'You've left the island?'

Bella choked with laughter. 'Waterloo Station. I'm home.'

Lottie squeaked quite a bit more at that. She was probably bouncing on her seat, thought Bella, warmed.

'Look, Lottie, it was all a bit last-minute and I haven't organised myself anywhere to stay—'

And Lottie, who had known Bella for ever, did not say, 'What about your mother's place? Where's your father? Can't you stay with your brother and his wife?' She said, 'Great. Crash *chez moi*. Can't wait to catch up. In fact, I'm closing my laptop even as we speak. I'll be home in half an hour. Race you.'

So Bella blew some more of her stepfather's cash on a taxi to the Pimlico flat and got her hug from Lottie, followed by the promise of several bottles of wine and a blissful shower.

'I've made up your bed. Now tell all,' said Lottie as Bella padded out of the bathroom, wrapped in a towel, with her blonde hair dark and dripping.

The wine bottle was already open on the low coffee table. Lottie poured two generous glasses as Bella sank into the deep sofa with a sigh of pure bliss.

'This is so good. I feel clean for the first time in days. Hell, no. For the first time in *months*. I'm sorry to dump myself on you—'

Lottie waved that away. 'Garbage,' she said briskly. 'Couldn't be better. The harpy I used to share with moved out last month to be with the Man of Her

Dreams . . . poor sod. I was thinking I ought to rent out her room. But I don't really fancy living with another stranger, not after The Harpy. So I didn't get round to it. And now you're here.' She raised her glass in a silent toast. 'Sometimes the Lord provides.'

Bella laughed and raised her glass in return.

'Lottie Hendred, you're a star.'

'Stay as long as you want.' Lottie curled up in the armchair and tucked her bare toes under the skirts of her exotic Eastern robe.

'Lovely idea but I'm not sure I can afford to.'

Lottie raised her perfectly arched eyebrows. 'Explain?'

'Well, to be honest, Lottie, I've got to get a job. Fast.'

Lottie's brown eyes were shrewd. 'Island job didn't materialise, then?'

Bella shook her head. 'Go on. Say it. Everyone else will. Say "I told you so".'

Lottie was indignant. 'I *never* say I told you so. Anyway, what did I know?'

'But you never trusted Francis.'

'I thought,' said Lottie carefully, 'that be-my-unpaid-assistant-for-a-year-and-I'll-give-you-a-job didn't sound much of a deal. Or, well, terribly reliable.'

'You were right,' said Bella gloomily.

'Want to talk about it?'

Bella shrugged. She swirled her wine, staring into its ruby surface as if she were seeing something very different from reflected firelight and the pleasant room.

'There wasn't a job?' ventured Lottie at last.

Bella came back into the present. 'Oh, there was a job all right. One job. And about twenty of us that Francis had offered it to.'

Lottie sat bolt upright and her wine spilled. 'Blimey. The man is a real operator,' she said with respect. '*Twenty?*'

Bella forced a smile. 'Not all at the same time. They came and went – usually when they found the job was counting fish. I lasted longer than pretty much everyone else.'

'Um – why?'

'You know me, Lottie. Never know when I'm beaten.' There was an edge to Bella's voice. 'Besides, they got me teaching the kids in the school a bit. Made me feel like I was doing something real.'

'Better than counting bloody fish anyway,' said Lottie with feeling.

Bella drained her glass and reached for the bottle. 'Ain't that the truth? Pissed off Francis, too,' she added with satisfaction. 'I was supposed to be there to run his errands, not work with the villagers.' She topped up Lottie's wine as well. 'Boils on the bum to Francis Don!'

Lottie's eyes gleamed. 'I'll drink to that.'

They both did, glasses solemnly raised.

'So what do you do next?'

Bella shook her head. 'I honestly don't know.' She stretched. 'Don't get me wrong. I'm glad I went. I learned a lot. But – well, I don't think I'm really a born ecologist. I like people more than fish.'

'Thank God for that, at least.'

'I thought I might do a course on teaching English as

9

a Foreign Language. I seemed to be quite good at it. But I've got all these debts and my father will disown me if I don't start earning. So it's the temp agency for me tomorrow.'

Lottie looked at her carefully. 'I thought you said you'd input your last invoice when we left college?'

Bella pulled a face. 'I know. But needs must. Besides, I have a sentimental desire to see a paycheque again.'

'Fair enough. But wait until Monday. I've got an invitation to a Fab-U-Louse party tomorrow night, and you've just gotta come too.'

'Great,' said Bella, and suddenly cracked a massive yawn. 'Oops. Sorry.'

'I'll give you a hot water bottle,' said Lottie. 'The heating has been off in that room for weeks. Come on, you. Sleepy time.'

And Bella staggered off to clean her teeth before falling into bed and sleeping for fourteen hours straight.

She woke to find Lottie had gone out, leaving two messages on the table in the tiny kitchen.

The first was vintage Lottie Hendred: *V. posh party tonight, pick a dress, any dress*.

The other was a phone message. *Robopop rang in case you were here. He says don't call your mother too early on Sunday. Pillock*.

Lottie really did not need to add that last word, thought Bella wryly. Lottie had never liked Kevin. Bella was always telling Lottie that her mother's obsession with climbing the social heights of the Local History Society and the Ladies' Golf Section was not his fault. Lottie had never believed her but Bella knew her mother. Turning over Kevin's message, she could almost hear her mother saying it.

Don't call too early? Don't call too *early*? Gee, thanks, Mum.

Suddenly, gloriously, Bella was so angry she knew exactly what she was going to do. She was not going to raid Lottie's wardrobe, though they had cheerfully borrowed from each other for three years at university and even before that. But today Bella was going to splurge Kevin's conscience money on a dress and pretty, crazy shoes and she was going to go to that posh party and dance until morning, or possibly the morning after.

Don't call too early? She was going to party so hard she wouldn't be able to call her mother for a *week*.

Of course, it didn't work out like that. For one thing, she needed more than party wear, as Lottie, returning from the Saturday grocery shop, told her crisply. For ten months Bella had lived in shorts and tee-shirt or diving gear. She had no clothes to wrap herself up in against the chill breezes of a London autumn; and she soon realised that her much-washed underwear was about to disintegrate.

'Besides,' said Lottie, sitting on Bella's bed and surveying the contents of the backpack critically, 'your hair is like straw. I just have to look at it and I smell seaweed.'

'Don't mention seaweed. We had it for dinner twice a week.'

Lottie was appalled. 'You're joking, right?'

11

Bella shook her head, her eyes dancing.

Lottie moaned.

'It was a very healthy life-style. Out in the fresh air, bags of exercise, healthy diet—'

'*Seaweed?*'

Bella grinned. 'I said healthy, not tasty. Seaweed is full of minerals.'

Lottie shuddered. 'And what does it taste like?'

'Oh, pants,' said Bella matter-of-factly. 'But when you're hungry you'll eat anything. And it really is nutritionally good value.'

'You were hungry?'

'Um, yes.'

'Well, no wonder you look so terrible.'

'Do I?' Startled, Bella peered at herself in her predecessor's massive mirror.

What she saw was not *that* bad. OK, the blonde hair was a haystack and her hands were a bit rough by Lottie's Metropolitan PR Industry standard. But she had a faint golden tan from working under the tropical sun and her eyes sparkled. She'd certainly lost that puffy, pasty look she'd had when she left England last November.

She decided to take a stand. 'I think I look pretty good, actually. I've got cheekbones, for the first time in my life.'

'Huh. That's not all you've got. I could cut myself on those shoulderblades.'

'What?'

'Look at yourself,' begged Lottie. She took Bella and turned her round, so that she could see over her own

12

shoulder into the mirror. 'You've got a backbone like a kipper.

'Bloody, bloody Francis!' she spat, her eyes bright. 'He manipulated you, ran you ragged. Then on top of that he went and *starved* you.'

Bella put an arm round her friend's shoulders and hugged her.

'Don't worry, Lotts. Give me a week in the same town as Maison Paul's chocolate doughnuts and I'll be back to the pudding you know and love.'

Lottie fished for a tissue but said tartly, 'Well, I certainly hope so. And I'll book you an appointment with Carlos, too. He'll have a heart attack when he sees your hair.'

'OK,' said Bella peaceably.

'*And* you need to reactivate your cellphone. Gotta keep in touch.'

Peaceable was one thing. Doormat was another. 'You know, you've got very bossy.'

'Bossy? Nonsense. I'm a decisive manager,' corrected Lottie loftily. She fled as Bella threw a pillow at her. 'And get your nails done,' wafted back from the sitting room.

So Bella went out and bought everything from the skin up, including a party dress for tonight, and a woolly hat, scarf and gloves for immediate use. A nice guy in the phone shop tried hard to get her mobile working again but in the end he had to give up. He wanted to sell her the latest one but her credit card was still in suspension until she rang them up and told them she was back in the country and her mother's maiden name. So she reluctantly shook her head at an all-singing, all-dancing Formula 1 of a phone and settled for a plain old replacement. The shop guy sympathised with her credit card hiccup and threw in a pink and glittery clip-on cover for the new phone, as consolation. He even transferred the SIM card for her, and handed it over with a flourish.

Bella went back to the flat in triumph.

She found Lottie wedged into a corner of the kitchen, waiting for the microwave to ping while leafing through a thick, glossy magazine. She looked up as Bella came in.

'Hi there. Did you buy this copy of *Mondaine*?'

Bella put down her carrier bags and unwound the new woolly scarf. 'Yup. I had to break into a fifty-pound note at Waterloo last night. It was the most expensive mag I could find.'

Lottie nodded enthusiastically. 'I'll bet. We take it at work, but I never get to see it. People pounce on it as soon as it comes in. Have you looked at this piece on the Top Ten Eligibles? Just gorgeous.'

'The men or the article?'

'Both.' The microwave pinged and Lottie removed a frothing mug of hot chocolate. 'Do you want one?'

Bella didn't really, but she said yes to be sociable. She looked at *Mondaine*'s gallery of gorgeous guys for the same reason. Shedding the cherry red hat and gloves, she fluffed out her hair and peered over Lottie's shoulder.

'Who's that?'

'Milo Crane. From *Si Fy the Movie*.'

Bella looked blank.

'You must have heard of him. He's the newest hottie on the block, ever since the movie came out.'

'Haven't seen it. Don't forget, I was fifty miles away from the nearest internet connection, Lottie. TV and films didn't figure at all.'

Lottie shuddered. 'Unbelievable. Well, who *do* you know out of this lot?'

The photographs were works of art: a lithe fast bowler stretching up to a cloudless sky; the newest software billionaire, endearingly scruffy, staring blankly at a screen where his company's share price was rocketing; Richard, Prince of Wales at some ceremony, looking startlingly handsome in a scarlet uniform that any one of his ancestors of the last three centuries could have worn, gleaming gold-embellished sword and all.

'All of them except Milo,' said Bella, somewhat reassured.

Lottie put her head on one side. 'Fabulous photo of the Prince, don't you think?'

Bella considered. He looked eager and determined. 'Full of va-va-voom,' she conceded. 'But you'd want to stand well clear of that sword.'

Lottie choked. 'I suppose so. But he's still mega-fanciable.'

'If you say so.' The microwave pinged and Bella took out her own hot chocolate.

'Don't you think so?'

Bella shrugged. 'Royals in military fancy dress don't

15

do it for me. I overdosed on *The Prisoner of Zenda* when I was a kid. Sorry. Don't forget, I'm the daughter of a fully paid up anti-monarchist.'

'Oh, but—' Lottie started to say, then changed her mind.

'What?'

'Oh, nothing.'

'I know that look. It isn't nothing. Spit it out.'

'You wouldn't actually be nasty to Prince Richard, would you, Bella? I mean, if you came across him somewhere?'

She sounded so worried that Bella was touched. 'Don't worry, Lotts. I'm not that far gone. I wasn't nasty to Francis and, as you pointed out, he starved me. Quite apart from breaking his promises, the toad. Hell, I won't even swear at Carlos if he turns my hair green again.'

At that, Lottie looked really alarmed. 'No, don't. You have no idea the favour he's doing you, fitting you in at all. He said it was for old times' sake but, make no mistake, Carlos can pick and choose his clients these days. So play nice, Bella, please. For me?'

So, an hour later, Bella was siting in a very smart grey-and-lavender-decorated salon and not so much as murmuring a protest while Carlos, Lottie's long-time friend and increasingly fashionable hairdresser, lectured her on Letting Her Hair Go and the Importance of Conditioner. He plastered her hair with something that smelled of apricots, wrapped it in a towel, and left her to leaf through a bunch of celebrity

16

magazines. Unlike *Mondaine,* these were full of people she didn't know. With their orange tans and day-glo teeth, the various celebrities had been photographed at buzzy parties and premières in London, Hollywood and the South of France. Bella didn't know their names, their faces, or what they were famous for.

'I don't even recognise the names of the dress designers any more,' she sighed. 'Have I been gone so long?'

'Much too long, doll,' said Carlos, flicking her hair. 'This is going to take months of work.'

'Well, see what you can do for today. Lottie's taking me to a party tonight.'

'Ah-ha. A party.' His eyes lit up at the challenge and he began to mutter to himself.

Realising that her participation was not required, Bella turned to *Sherlock,* the satirical magazine that her father always bought, with its wicked cartoons and sly comment on politicians and media figures. Though even there, many of the names were new to her. It was almost a relief to find a piece on the Royal Family. At least *they* were still the same, even if *Sherlock* didn't think much of them. The magazine was running a spoof advertisement for *The Royal Pantomime or Snow White's Escape,* starring a flashing-eyed brunette called Deborah as Snow White, with the King and his family as the Seven Dwarfs. Bella had never heard of brunette Deborah either.

'I think I just lost a year of my life,' she told Carlos ruefully.

He peered over her shoulder at a cartoon of the

three youngest dwarfs tap dancing. Their faces were recognisably those of Prince George, Princess Eleanor, and the heir to the throne, Prince Richard. *Dim, Ditzy and Dull were excited,* read the caption. Carlos grinned.

'Poor bastard. Every time a girl dumps him, it's all over the tabloids. And now *Sherlock* is calling him Dull. That's got to hurt. It'll stick, too.'

'I suppose so,' said Bella, not much interested in the PR problems of the King's eldest son.

But the other people in the salon didn't agree.

'Who said she dumped him?' said the grey-haired woman on Bella's right indignantly.

'She's dating someone else,' Carlos pointed out.

'So? Maybe Prince Richard dumped *her*.'

'Why would he do that? The woman's hot, hot, hot.'

'And now she's dating someone else. That's fast. What if the Prince found out she was a slapper and gave her the boot?'

Carlos was unconvinced. 'Why wouldn't he say so? I would.'

The grey-haired woman sniffed. 'Because *he's* a gentleman.'

Carlos snorted.

'I think he looks lovely,' said one of the junior hairdressers dreamily. 'Dark and brooding, like he's got a secret sorrow.'

She put a magazine on Bella's knee, open at a black-and-white photograph of an unsmiling Prince Richard.

'Very nice,' Bella said without interest. 'What about my hair?'

18

'But don't you think he looks sad . . . underneath?'

Bella glanced down at the photograph again. It wasn't a party shot, like the others, but a studio portrait with the subject looking straight at the camera. Hooded eyes, mouth like a steel trap, cheekbones to make a Renaissance painter do a jig with delight.

'Secret? Maybe. Sad? Nah, not a chance. He's got a General's scarlet uniform at home and a nice bright shiny sword to play with.'

The grey-haired woman said, 'But things like that are just for show, dear. He could still be sad, you know.'

'What's he got to be sad about? He's rich and good-looking and he knows what he's going to do with his life.' None of which applied to Bella just at this moment, though she did not actually say so.

'Well, he has just lost the delicious Deborah,' said Carlos thoughtfully. 'No matter who ended it, or how serious it really was, that's always a bummer.'

But Bella didn't want to think about ending affairs. Of course, it hadn't exactly been an affair with Francis. Nowhere near. Right from the start they'd agreed – well, he'd announced and she'd agreed, of course she had – that they couldn't do anything about their attraction to each other while they were working so closely. It would de-stabilise the team. It wouldn't be fair, Francis had said, looking noble and handsome and terribly responsible, to *anybody*. She thought now: how many others had he said that to? Half of them? All twenty? She flinched. How could she have been so naive? How could she? She groaned in spirit.

She found they were all looking at her, surprised, and

realised that she had actually groaned aloud. Somehow it was the last straw.

'What about my *hair?*' she yelled. 'Come on, you idle crimpers. Don't just stand there wittering. Work your magic.'

So they all went back to the important stuff. And Carlos piled her blonde shoulder-length hair on to the top of her head, leaving some feathery tendrils to caress her long neck.

I just hope it's clean, thought Bella, uneasily aware that a couple of long showers might not have been enough to clear away the grime of ten water-restricted months spent living in a tent.

But everyone else told her she looked lovely. And Bella had to admit that the soft, artistically untidy style, had turned her wide-eyed and feminine. She hadn't felt feminine in a long, long time.

She kissed Carlos as she left. 'Thank you. You're a miracle worker.'

'But of course. Haven't I always said so?' But he was pleased, she could see.

So was Lottie on coming into Bella's room to check that her instructions had been carried out.

'Well, at least no one's going to mistake you for a Shetland pony now.'

'*What?*'

Lottie grinned. 'I *told* you, this party is *über*-posh. Very smart people, deep into the horsey set. The way you were looking this morning, they'd have fed you a carrot and showed you to the stables.'

And, quite suddenly, Bella started to laugh. In fact,

she laughed so much she jabbed the mascara wand in her eye and had to start again.

'Oh, Lotts, I do love you,' she said, when she could speak. 'Gosh, it's good to be home.'

2

'Trees in Tubs Make Your Party Swing' – *Mondaine*
Magazine

Lottie called a minicab to take them to the party.
Conscious of her own jobless state, Bella protested at the
extravagance. But her friend was adamant.

'These shoes are meant for dancing, not pounding
the London Underground,' she said firmly. 'You'll
thank me later. Besides, it's cold out there.'

That was undoubtedly true. Reluctant to spend her
remaining cash on a stellar outfit, Bella had in the end
found a pretty dress in an Oxfam shop, one of the better
ones in Soho that sold nearly perfect vintage clothes,
rather than size 20 tee-shirts from George. It was
vaguely Ossie Clarke in a heavy, midnight blue crepe.
The neckline plunged into a deep V, a bit risqué she
had thought, but it also had long sleeves that gathered
at the wrist with a row of tiny buttons and it swirled
nicely when she walked. But it was almost certainly a
retiree from the summer. It was not warm.

'Odd but stylish. You look like Greta Garbo,' said
Lottie, deciding it would do.

She insisted on dusting Bella's skin with gold glitter.

'You've got the perfect tan. Light, real and everywhere. Make it work for you,' she instructed.

She also lent Bella a full length suede coat with a big fake-fur collar, along with a sparkly gold bag. They checked the contents of their bags together, just as they used to do when they were eighteen.

'Lippy, perfume, hankie.'

'Check.'

'Phone.'

'Check.'

'Keys.'

'Check. No, I left them in the kitchen—' Bella dived to retrieve them.

Lottie was patient. 'OK, that's it. Except for running away money, of course.'

Their eyes met. It was Bella's Granny Georgia, a Southern Belle of the old school, who had taught them that: never go to a party without your running away money tucked into your underwear. Ladies didn't make a fuss but they were always prepared. If their gentleman escort wanted to stay too late at the party or had a little too much to drink, a lady quietly and discreetly made other arrangements and kept the cash to do so about her person at all times. Men, said Granny Georgia, momentarily less ladylike, Never Thought of That.

Bella chuckled. 'I've got enough cash to get me home.'

Lottie clicked her fingers. 'That reminds me, you'll need the minicab company's card.' She dived into the hall drawer and with a flourish produced a dog-eared bit of pasteboard. 'Put this number into your phone *now*.'

23

Bella complied. And while she was at it, she checked her incoming messages. No, nothing from her mother, so no surprise there. Her father hadn't got back to her either, but he was probably up a mountain somewhere. And she knew Granny Georgia was in Brazil saving the rain forest until Christmas. But she was a bit hurt that her brother Neill hadn't even bothered to leave her a message.

Lottie was oblivious. 'I have an account. You won't have to pay cash. Just say Hendred Associates.'

'Hendred *Associates*?'

'Well, I'm not going to be working for someone else all my life. Establish the brand early and keep it cooking,' said Lottie blithely.

But later, in the back of the minicab, she said more soberly, 'Tonight I'm sort of on duty, Bella. Networking stuff. I may even have to go on somewhere. I'm sorry, on your first weekend home. But I can't get out of it. Will that be OK?'

'Fine,' said Bella, who was beginning to feel the effects of a day's unaccustomed shopping, on top of the jet lag. 'I'll probably push off earlyish anyway. What do we do? Should I text you when I want to leave?'

'Good plan. And we can spend all tomorrow together.'

'Sure. So who are the people giving this party?'

'My boss. The Big Boss, I mean. Not my team leader.'

'Coo,' said Bella, impressed and just a bit wistful. 'Your career must be really whooshing along.'

Lottie snorted. 'Career, nothing. This is pay-back for personal services.'

24

'*What?*'

'Whoops! Sounds bad, doesn't it? Memo to self: don't say that to my mother. Actually, his idiot Number Three Son came into the agency for work experience in the summer. I was the one who drew the short straw and had to mentor the little toe-rag. Believe me, that family owe me.'

'Ah.'

'The party will be OK, though. Big Cheese is pretty much the last word in contemporary PR. He doesn't do anything but work, but his wife is into charities and the arts and all sorts of groovy stuff. The kids aren't all bad, either. And their parties are legendary. There should be some interesting people there. You'll have a good time. Promise.'

She was right.

The party didn't seem unduly posh, in spite of what Lottie had said. It was in a very smart house, though, in a very smart part of town, with some amazing artwork on the walls. But it all seemed friendly and casual, with dancing in a big, darkened room in the basement and people talking in every other room in the house, except the kitchen. Some were even sitting on the stairs.

Bella didn't know anyone but it didn't matter. She danced a bit, and talked a bit, and drank more than she had in nearly a year. The Oxfam dress fitted in nicely, neither too showy nor too casual, and the new shoes, not much more than sparkly gold straps atop four-inch heels, attracted enough envy to make Bella's spirits fly. She had a great time until about three hours into the party when she suddenly realised that her head was ringing and she could not feel her feet any more.

'Air,' she said, and fought her way up the darkened stairs from the basement to the ground floor, where French windows opened on to a handsome terrace.

But it looked as if someone was giving a speech out there and Bella hesitated. Seeing this, one of the circulating waiters took her by the elbow and directed her through a small doorway. She supposed he thought she wanted to go outside to smoke and shook her head to tell him she didn't. But then she saw that the door led into a small courtyard, a small *empty* courtyard, and she thought: Lottie's right. Sometimes the Lord provides.

She slipped outside.

It was utterly quiet. That was the first thing that struck her. In every room in the house there had been music – fierce, danceable rhythms in the basement; discreet string quartets to converse over in the reception rooms; cool clarinets on the stairs. Now for the first time there was silence. Not even the rumble of distant traffic disturbed the midnight air.

Bella wandered out into the silent darkness. Her heels clipped on the flagstones. The courtyard was open to the sky but it was not cold. A large pale plate of a moon hung in a gun-metal sky, playing hide and seek with billowing clouds, but not a breath of wind stirred the branches of a tall ornamental fig tree in the middle of the courtyard. Someone had wound a string of lights through it. They were shaped like little Chinese lanterns, and the shadows they cast were as still as a painting.

A ironwork table was tucked into one corner, surrounded by fragrant trees in stone pots – a lemon tree, an orange with the fruit nearly ripe, breathing an elusive sweetness into the air, and great wooden tubs of golden-leaved Mexican Choisya, smelling of basil. There was a half-drunk glass of champagne standing on the table, and the guttering remains of a flower-pot candle. Patio chairs were pushed back, as if the people sitting there had left in a hurry.

Bella looked around. But no, the shadowy courtyard seemed deserted. She let herself sink on to one of the vacated seats and found the reason for the astonishing warmth of the little outdoor space: a tall patio heater was lurking among the greenery, like an apologetic butler robot. She laughed a little and patted its conical steel base. It was pleasantly warm to the touch. She felt herself relax as she hadn't for – how long? Days? Weeks, maybe?

She fished around in the borrowed bag and pulled out the unfamiliar phone. Leaning forward into the pool of wavering light, she managed to see the buttons well enough to send Lottie a text: *Running out of steam, will call cab. U?*

A text came back almost at once: *BBL.*

Bella clutched her head. BBL? What did that mean? Oh, hell, less than a year ago she had used this stuff all the time. How could she have forgotten?

The dying candle flickered briefly and she jumped, remembering. Oh, yes. Be back later. Lottie was telling her to go on home and not wait for her. Well, that was a relief.

Bella dialled the minicab service, who told her apologetically that it would be forty minutes, and yes, they knew where to come; they had the address from Ms Hendred's earlier booking.

'Thank God for that,' said Bella with feeling. 'I didn't think of that. I'd have had to go and ask someone for the postcode. You're a star.'

The minicab company clerk was quietly pleased. He said she was welcome.

'Thank you. Forty minutes, then. I'll be ready.'

She cut the call and re-checked her messages. No, nothing new had come in. Well, it was a Saturday night. People don't start texting unexpectedly returning sisters on a Saturday night, do they? They're out enjoying themselves.

Bella stretched a bit. Then, as she was alone, she thrust her legs out in front of her and wiggled her feet. The strappy shoes were sex incarnate but they were tough on feet that had spent ten months in flip-flops. Bella rotated her ankles in opposite directions and sighed with pleasure.

And then three things happened.

The candle flame suddenly shot up like a rocket and died.

Bella jumped several inches into the air in a sort of dolphin arc and fell back on the very edge of the little patio chair.

The chair recoiled and then lurched past the point of no return. Even the solid ironwork table rocked a bit as, in pure instinct, Bella threw out a hand to save herself. All that she managed, however, was to grab hold of a fistful of the ivy that clad the brick wall to her right. The ivy came away from the wall, descending as rapidly as she did.

'*Shi-i-it!*' gasped Bella, in free fall.

Plant containers, big and small, tumbled around her in a hail of leaves and twigs. She heard them fall and at least one smashed, unmistakably. She came to rest in a mass of tangled ivy, with one arm around the base of a bay tree.

Silence fell, except for the tinkling of pottery shards on the flagstones. Bella lay there, stunned, her eyes closed.

Eventually she got her breath back and opened her eyes.

'Oh, no,' she said aloud, in horror

It was like the path of a hurricane, she thought. Devastation! Quite apart from the curtain of ivy which she had clawed off the wall, every single shrub she could see in the dark was either lurching at a drunken angle or missing branches. She struggled to sit up, but had got herself hemmed in by displaced urns and fallen foliage. She could not see where the shadows ended and the plants began but there was no mistaking the pressure of solid objects against her back, her knees, her feet, even her stomach. And there seemed to be nowhere to put her hands, to give herself purchase. And when she did finally wiggle up a little, so that her back was against the stripped wall, she found that the spiky heels on her shoes made it impossible for her to plant her feet side by side and simply heave herself upright.

'I'm trapped,' she said, in disbelief. 'Come on, think, woman. Think!'

She had a go at releasing the strap of her right shoe. Between the awkward angle and the romantic shadows, she couldn't really see what was going on, but tendrils of ivy seemed to have wrapped themselves round and locked the shoe to her foot tighter than any buckle would have managed.

'What I need is a Swiss Army knife. Oh, boy, am I in trouble.'

It seemed there was only one thing left to do. She would have to surrender what was left of her dignity and crawl out of the fallen foliage on all fours, hoping that sheer body weight and her forward momentum would snap the bloody ivy. Well, thank God no one had been there to see the disaster at least.

And then an arm, in a silken sleeve as pale and perfect as the moon, pushed aside the fallen plants.

'No Swiss Army knife, I'm afraid. And I don't know where they keep the gardening tools. But may I offer a hand?' said a voice. It was trying very hard not to laugh.

Bella jumped again and in pure reflex kicked the bay tree. A mistake in strappy shoes. The pain was excruciating.

'Ow!' Instinctively, she made to rub her stubbed toe. But she still couldn't reach, for pots and plants.

What she did manage to do, however, was to set all the plant life in motion again. Specifically, the bay tree. It started to tip sideways slowly, like a drunken judge.

Bella pushed herself away as far as she was able, which was not very far at all. 'Oh, *no* . . .'

Silk Shirt, however, was there first. He arrested the bay tree before it fell on top of her, and returned it to the upright position. Then he walked round her carefully, picked the thing up, mighty planter and all, and moved it out of the way.

He turned back to her then. 'I think you'd better get out of there.'

'I'm trying,' said Bella between her teeth. She was tearing at the ivy that had wound itself round her ankle. But the more fiercely she tore, the faster she seemed to be caught. 'This damned stuff won't let me go.'

'Let's have a look.'

He hunkered down and considered her foot. From where she lay sprawled she saw that he had springy dark hair. And she was right, that shirt was silk. Nothing else had that sheen. Pearly white silk, as pure as snow, and here she was, looking like a compost heap. It was enough to make a girl weep.

'Have I got twigs in my hair?' she asked.

But he was concentrating on her feet. 'Hmm. You're certainly tied in pretty tight. Wonder if this ivy is carnivorous?'

'Thank you for that thought.'

'No problem.'

He slid a finger under one of the tendrils and Bella yelped, as much from surprise as the tightening around her ankle. He looked up quickly and she had the impression of dark, laughing eyes and a determined expression.

'No help for it. In the absence of a knife, I shall have to tear it off with my teeth.'

31

He was *serious?*

He was serious. He bent his head.

Bella felt his breath on her ankle and went into a spasm of embarrassment. Without the bay tree to prevent it now, her foot kicked out freely. She got her rescuer under the chin, making him sit down abruptly, and followed it up by knocking out the National Grid. Well, that's what it felt like. With a sound somewhere between a fizz and a pop, all the Chinese lanterns in the fig tree went out, along with all sorts of discreet lighting along the walls that she hadn't even been aware of. They were plunged into total darkness, except for the moon.

'Hell's teeth,' said Silk Shirt blankly.

And then he began to laugh, as if he couldn't help himself.

'What have I *done?*' whispered Bella, appalled.

'No harm done. I'm fine,' he said, when he could speak.

'You may be. Look at this courtyard. I've wrecked it. And now I've fused the lights.' Her voice rose to a wail of guilt.

That set him off again, uncontrollably. She could hear him hauling noisy gulps of air into his lungs, as if trying to get control of himself, but his shoulders shook and so did the plants around them.

'It's not funny!' she yelled, hating him.

He got hold of himself at last. 'Yes, it is. Even though you kicked me in the chin and now I think I've bust a rib laughing.' He gave another hiccup. 'Oh, God, when that bay tree started to topple—'

32

'All right, all right,' said Bella before he went off again. 'I guess it did look quite amusing from where you were standing. But I'm the one causing death and destruction here. I feel terrible.'

'Nothing that can't be fixed,' he said comfortingly. 'Don't worry about it.'

'That's easy for you to say. You didn't do it. And it's not your plant collection. At least—' he had said he didn't know where they kept the gardening tools. But did very rich men and their families do their own gardening? There was probably an under-gardener who looked after the courtyard. He was too young to be the Big Boss and too old to be idiot Number Three Son. But he could still be Number One Son or Number Two. 'Oh God. Do you live here?' she asked, wincing.

At least it stopped him laughing. 'What?'

She said rapidly, 'I'm sorry, I'm sorry . . . I'm not a gatecrasher, honest. I'm Charlotte Hendred's Plus One. She said it would be OK.'

She could feel him staring at her in the darkness. But he said nothing.

'Charlotte Hendred? Tall redhead? Walks as if she's on springs?'

'Oh, that Charlotte,' he said, but absently. It seemed as if he were debating something with himself. 'Don't worry, I'm just another guest like you. You don't need to apologise to me.'

'Phew, that's a relief.' Bella hadn't realised, but she had been holding her breath. 'Though, actually, you're wrong. I'm pretty certain that I *do* need to apologise to you.'

There was a pause.

'Why?' His voice was almost wary.

'Well, I kicked you in the head, didn't I?'

He gave a hoot of startled laughter. 'You did at that. I'd forgotten.'

'Very chivalrous,' she said, starting to feel better. 'Thank you.'

'Undeserved. A chivalrous man wouldn't have left you lying on the floor in the grip of Hell's Ivy. Hang on. Let's see if a key will cut it.'

He knelt down and put a strong hand across her foot, holding it steady. She knew it was the only thing he could do but the warmth of his palm on her exposed ankle felt amazingly intimate. And *right*, somehow, as if she had known him all her life.

Bella stared into the darkness but, as far as she could tell, he did not feel the same reaction at all. He was simply a competent man doing what was necessary. She felt the coldness of a key against her bare skin, followed by a gentle sawing motion. First one, then more of her ivy bindings fell away. She could not see but she felt them go. She flexed her foot, made to stand up. But . . .

'No. Stay still for the moment. I can't see properly. I might not have got it all. If you try to get up before I've cleared the stuff, you could break your ankle.'

'Or a few more pots,' said Bella dryly.

He laid his hand, palm down, on her foot, as if he were calming a nervous animal, and she felt his touch right through to the top of her head.

'Don't worry about that. I'll make sure you don't break any more stuff. Trust me.'

He was as good as his word. As soon as he had freed her from the ivy to his satisfaction, he said, 'Try now,' and kept an arm like a vice round her as she clambered upright, not very steadily.

But as soon as she was upright, her right leg turned out to have all the strength of cotton wool and she would have fallen off her heels if she hadn't grabbed his arm and held on.

'Sorry. Stupid. Pins and needles.'

'I'm not surprised. Take your time.'

He kept his arm round her. Bella was grateful. She felt strangely shaky.

He seemed to guess. 'Look, you'd better sit down. You could probably do with a drink, too.'

She shook her head, half laughing. 'I lost my champagne a long time ago.'

'I didn't. You can have mine.'

He steered her through the shadowed paths between tall banana plants and bushy sweet-leaved citrus trees. He must have eyes like a cat, thought Bella, torn between gratitude and annoyance with herself.

He clearly knew where he was going, even if he didn't live here. He steered her round a semi-circular stone wall, saying briefly, 'Fountain at three o'clock,' before locating a deeply cushioned wickerwork sofa.

'There you go.'

Bella sank bonelessly into the cushions. She shook her head. 'I don't know what's wrong with me. I've been dealing with creepy-crawlies and tropical storms and stuff for nearly a year.'

'I'm impressed,' he said nicely.

Bella shook her head. 'No, you're not. Why should you be? It's just – I mean, I don't normally go all wimbly like this.'

'Maybe you don't often destroy your host's landscape gardening like this?'

'You're laughing at me again.'

'Yes. Do you mind?'

Bella shook her head. Then realised he probably couldn't see it and said, 'No, not really. Anyway, I guess you're entitled. After I kicked you.'

'That's very fair of you.' There was a smile in his voice. 'How are you feeling now?'

Bella thought about it. 'A bit odd, to be honest.'

'I'll get you that champagne.'

He made his way sure-footedly through the dark maze that was the courtyard. She listened but did not hear so much as a pot scrape or a branch snap in his wake. When he returned, she accepted the glass of wine gratefully, but sighed.

'I wish I could do that.'

He was amused. 'Do what?'

'Navigate my way round these plants without sounding like a herd of buffalo. I'm afraid I'm one of the world's bumpers.'

'Bumpers?' he said blankly.

'That's what my father used to call me. "Let's hope Bella doesn't want to be an actress," he used to say. "She'd always be bumping into the furniture and breaking the crockery."'

'Did you want to be an actress, then?' He sounded intrigued.

36

Bella drank some more champagne. It was good. The bubbles seemed to act on her like water on a drooping daisy. She straightened, feeling chirpier by the minute

'Good God, no. I hate being on show. Curdles my insides. But I wish I wasn't so clumsy.'

'Would it help you with the creepy crawlies and the tropical storms?'

She took another mouthful of champagne, then another and another. Yes, bubbles were definitely energising. 'There you go, laughing at me again.'

'Do you mind?'

'No. I think I quite like it.'

'Thank you,' he said gravely.

He sat down on the sofa beside her. Bella shivered.

'Are you cold?'

'No.' She looked up at the sky. The clouds were still scudding across the moon but she felt as warm as toast. 'You know, three . . . no, four . . . nights ago, I walked down a beach at night and there were so many stars you couldn't have put a hand between them. And here there isn't one.'

'So why are you here, not there?'

'Ah. That's a long story.'

He settled back among the cushions. 'Well, I'm not going anywhere.'

She sank back too, clutching the champagne flute against her. 'Nothing's ever as good or as bad as you expect, is it?'

'That's a bit sweeping. Sometimes it takes a while to find out how good or bad something has been.'

He had a wonderful voice, she thought, deep and dark and thoughtful. Merlin would have a voice like that. Shame he didn't know what he was talking about.

'You're wrong. You know at once when a thing is wrong. I did. I just didn't—'

'Didn't?' he prompted.

'Oh, all right,' said Bella, annoyed. In the darkness, it didn't seem so bad to say it aloud. 'I didn't want to admit it, all right? I went out to the island convinced I was going to get close to nature, save the planet and find my place in the universe.'

'And you didn't?'

'Nope. Nowhere near.'

'Tough,' was all he said.

But she had the feeling that he understood.

'Waste of time, feeling sorry for yourself.'

'You are so right. But was this island of yours all bad?'

She thought about it. 'I suppose not,' she admitted. 'I learned a few things.'

'Like what?'

'One . . .' She ticked them off on her fingers. Or, at least, she started to tick them off on her fingers, but that made her glass tilt alarmingly, nearly spilling champagne. So she stopped. 'See what I mean?' she said, side-tracked. 'Clumsy.' Champagne had slopped on to the back of her hand and she licked it up. 'Waste not, want not.'

'Mmm.' He sounded a bit distracted. He cleared his throat. 'You were going to tell me what you learned?'

'Oh, that. Well, lots of things. The nutritional value of red seaweed. That wind in the palm trees sounds like

38

rain on a corrugated-iron roof and it breaks your heart when it isn't. That counting fish is really boring when you do it every day. That people tell you something is adventurous when it's really just hot and dirty.'

'Ah.'

'And also,' said Bella loudly, 'that I'm not very brave. So here's to the stars and equatorial fish stocks! I hope they're very happy, but I'm not going back.'

And then, to her own surprise, she began to cry.

Silk Shirt coped surprisingly well. He didn't say everything would look better in the morning like Lottie would have, or that she'd change her mind when she thought about the importance of the work, like Francis Don had, in their last, vituperative exchange. He took her glass away from her – Bella resisted but he pointed out that it was empty, so in the end she let it go – and put an arm round her, and drew her against his shoulder, and let her weep it out. He would probably even have produced a handkerchief, but she had one tucked into her watch strap under one long blue sleeve, so she was spared that indignity, at least.

'I thought it'd be all right when I got home. But it isn't. I'm *cold*. The magazines are full of people I don't know. My mother's much too busy running a Charity Ball to have me home . . .' She ran out of voice and blew her nose hard.

'Bummer,' was all he said.

But she had the feeling that he knew what she was talking about. It steadied her.

She drew a long sigh. 'Yes, but I didn't belong on the island, either. I'll miss the children in the village. Some

39

of the people. But that awful knowing I'd been a gullible idiot . . . and everyone else knowing it, too . . . that was the pits.'

He sat very still. She sniffed, and straightened the handkerchief that she could barely see, folding it and folding it, corner to corner, in her absorption. She had a huge urge to tell *someone* the whole sorry story.

'The trouble was, a man I respected basically did a con job on me. It took me too long to recognise it and a whole lot longer to admit it. But that's the truth. And that hurts, you know?'

He hugged her a bit closer. 'Yes, I know. Been there.'

'I mean, if he'd said, "Come and help out; we've got no money, so we live on rich kids doing work experience," that would have been fair. That would have been the truth. But he spun me this big line about what a valuable researcher I was, and how I could make all the difference, and he said he would make sure I got a real job at the end of it. When all he wanted was someone to count bloody *fish*.' Her voice rose. 'I don't even like fish.'

'I can see that one would go off them.'

Bella's head reared up. 'Are you laughing at me again?' she said suspiciously.

'Maybe a little.' He tucked a tumbling strand of blonde hair behind her ear.

She relaxed back against his shoulder again. 'You know, I don't feel quite real. Not here. Not there. It's like I'm a character walking through other people's dreams. When they wake up, I'll disappear. Pffft!' She clicked her fingers. She had to have three goes at it but she managed it in the end. 'Pffft!' she said again, pleased. She peered up at him in the darkness. 'Does that sound weird?'

'It sounds as if it's time I got you home.'

But Bella was on another tack entirely. 'Are you an actor?'

'Good heavens, where did that come from?'

'The voice . . . Wonderful warm voice.'

'You know, I'd be really flattered if you weren't slurring your words,' he said, shifting her. 'Come along, Dream Girl.'

'I know. You're a psychiatrist.'

'Why on earth . . .?'

'You ask really good questions and then you listen.'

'Oh, yes, I listen all right,' he said. 'It's about the only thing I do.'

'Well, you're very good at it,' Bella told him. 'Very, very, very good.' She snuggled into his shoulder.

'Oh, no. You can't go to sleep here. On your feet, Dream Girl. You've got a home to go to, and it's time I took you there.'

He hauled her upright and got her across the courtyard. But as soon as he opened the door into the house, the lights switched her brain into gear again, and she looked at her watch in horror.

'The minicab! They'll be here any minute, asking for Hendred Associates. I said I'd be waiting for them. Where did I leave my *coat*?'

'Ah, the car. It is for you,' said one of the passing waiters. 'They are waiting outside. Your coat, it is on the rack in the breakfast room. I show you.'

Bella dashed off to get it but when she shot back to

41

retrieve Lottie's borrowed bag from the courtyard, there was no sign of Silk Shirt. She did look, but the cab was waiting and she could not see anyone the right height or wearing a pearl-white silk shirt. So she had to go without saying goodbye to him.

Just as well, she thought grimly. Panic banished the effects of the champagne. Now Bella was remembering, rather too vividly, how she had curled up against his shoulder and told him the story of her life.

She said a distracted goodbye to her hostess and fell gratefully into the back of the minicab. She told herself she was just tired. She told herself she was over-reacting.

But there was a cold voice in the back of her head, like a headmistress giving an end-of-term report. Change everyone around her . . . change time zones . . . change continents . . . Isabella Greenwood still makes an utter fool of herself.

AAAAARGH!

'When is a Date not a Date?' – *Tube Talk*

Bella woke the next morning with a mouth like the inside of a sandpit. She groaned and rolled over, muttering. But the taste wouldn't go away.

Eventually she hauled herself up on one elbow and peered at the bedside clock. But even closing one eye, she couldn't stop the figures dancing in and out of focus. She fell back with a thump – and something scratched her ear.

'Eeeugh!' she yelled, forgetting she was no longer on the island.

She leaped out of bed and looked round wildly for something to hit the bug with. If it was a bug. She had horrid images of scorpions and poisonous centipedes . . .

It was only when she was looming over the pillow, with a copy of the heaviest Harry Potter she could grab from the bookcase raised high above her head, that all the bits of her brain clicked back into place. *Of course*. She was not on the island: no tent, no cooking pots, no wonky table with sheets of data stacked high on it. And this was a real bed, too. She was in Lottie's spare room and the most lethal thing in it was the dodgy hair dryer.

Bella lowered Harry, feeling a fool.

Still, even if Pimlico was scorpion-free, something had bitten her. With well-practised caution, she pulled back the covers.

And stopped, appalled.

It looked as if someone had emptied the contents of one of Granny Georgia's pot-pourri jars over it, exactly where Bella had been sleeping. There were bits of powder-dry leaves, mixed in with twigs and, frankly, earth. A green stain across the bottom sheet ended in a half-crushed bay leaf. Where her head had lain, the pillow was peppered with a brownish-grey dust. It was all made worse by unmistakable smears of last night's lippy and a sad bit of sparkle.

'Yuck,' said Bella from the heart.

The bedroom door opened and Lottie wandered in, yawning. She was wearing an oversized teddy bear tee-shirt that reached down to her knees, and pink socks. 'You screamed, miss?' she said amiably.

Bella shuffled a bit. 'Er – I thought a scorpion had got into bed with me. I *was* half-asleep.'

Lottie narrowed her eyes at her. 'Have you been reading science fiction again?'

Bella shook her head. 'No. Worse than that.' There was no help for it. She would have to come clean. 'I – er – sort of fell into bed last night without taking my make-up off and . . .' She stood aside, letting the state of the sheets speak for her.

Lottie stared and her mouth fell open. 'That's not all you didn't take off, from the look of it. Is that mud?'

'No. Or rather, well, yes, I suppose it is.'

Lottie closed her mouth, opened it again, shook her head, closed her mouth and sat down rather hard on the end of the bed.

'Why?'

'Um – you could say I had an accident.'

'I can see that. If Carlos saw your hair now, he would slit his throat. Or possibly yours.'

Conscience-stricken, Bella put up a hand to her hair. A couple of pins fell out. So did a withered ivy leaf and rather a lot of dust. She turned to look in her predecessor's mirror and recoiled. She had gone to bed in her underwear. She had a wide smear of dirt on her right cheek. Nothing at all survived of Carlos's work of art. Where there had been an artless cascade of feathery blonde locks, there was now a lopsided mess of pins, garden detritus and, possibly, wildlife.

She prodded it, cautiously. 'Do you think there could be a centipede in there?'

Lottie moaned.

'I know. I know. I go to the ball dressed up like a million dollars and come home looking like Fungus the Bogeyman. I didn't do it on purpose. These things just happen to me.'

Lottie closed her eyes. 'It's too early for this,' she said. 'I need coffee. And water. Lots of water. You can tell me what happened, but not until I've rehydrated.'

She padded out of the door.

'Mud,' Bella heard her complain as she stomped off

towards the kitchen. 'I take her to the smartest party *ever* and she finds mud.'

Bella showered and washed her hair. And when she saw the silt in the bottom of the shower tray, she got right back in and washed her hair again. Emerging pink and a bit soapy-eyed, she pulled on her new underwear, drainpipe jeans, crisp cotton shirt and a cashmere jumper which she had picked up from the Oxfam shop the day before. Then she went into the kitchen, still rubbing her hair with the towel.

Lottie was slumped over a carton of orange juice at the breakfast bar, flipping through texts on her telephone.

Bella thought: I used to do that too, every morning. And when I was shopping, and when I was waiting for Lottie to meet me at a club. Why does it feel so strange now?

Aloud she said, 'Anything interesting?'

Lottie huffed. 'No. Dammit.'

Bella poured herself some juice but pulled a face as soon as she tasted it.

'Water,' said Lottie, recognising the signs. 'Your taste-buds will be all over the place until you've rebalanced your water table.'

'You make me sound like farmland.'

'And you're surprised? After the stunt you pulled last night? *Mud!* I ask you!'

Bella flung up her hands. 'OK. OK. I'm sorry. I'll change the sheets.'

Lottie shrugged. 'You're sleeping in them. Up to you.'

Lottie was not usually grumpy, not even the morning after a heavy night. Bella reached a glass off the shelf above the counter top and filled it from the cold tap. Then she pulled out one of the high stools and sat down at the bar next to her.

'What's wrong, Lotts?'

Lottie pushed back her hair and gave a watery sniff. 'I thought I'd nailed a contract last night. But not a peep out of the bastard this morning.' She looked at her watch. 'Make that this afternoon. And I really *worked* at that pitch.'

'Maybe he's saving it up for working hours,' suggested Bella. 'He'll call you on Monday.'

Lottie gave her a pitying look. 'Billionaires' working hours are twenty-four seven. They don't wait till Monday. If he was interested, he would have called. No, I've blown it.'

She got up and opened the fridge, staring at its contents moodily. 'No milk. No fresh coffee. Oh, well, it will have to be fizz.'

She hauled out a bottle of Cava and clawed ineffectually at the black foil over the cork.

'Let me.'

Bella took it away from her and removed the foil and restraining wire from the cork. Texting might feel strange but opening champagne came back to her as naturally as breathing. She tilted the bottle at forty-five degrees, held the cork firmly and turned the bottle until the cork gave a little. Bella applied pressure to ease the transition and eventually removed it with no more than a ladylike hiss from the wine.

Lottie silently held out two glasses. 'You've always been good at that. No bangs, no spills. It's super-cool. I suppose Georgia taught you how to do it?'

'Nope. My grandmother doesn't think a lady should open her own wine bottles. A lady ought to sit prettily while a Big Strong Man makes a prat of himself spraying champagne everywhere.'

'There's a very nasty side to your grandmother,' said Lottie, with admiration. 'Seems a waste though.'

Bella thought about it. 'Actually, Georgia once told me when she was pissed that men were only good for two things: opening wine bottles and emptying mouse traps. And then she said cats were more rewarding and alcohol was overrated.'

Lottie gave a snort of laughter. 'She was wrong.' She waved her glass. 'Come on, start pouring.'

Bella did, but shook her head at the other glass that Lottie pushed towards her.

'Not for me, thank you. You're right, I need to acclimatise, I think. I only had a couple of glasses last night and it made me really weird.'

Lottie flumped back on to her high stool. 'Ah-ha! This is where you tell all about the mud. Come on then, give.'

Bella leaned against the door and gave her an edited version of the Great Ivy Disaster, dwelling on the unreasonable number of plants in the courtyard and skirting lightly round the rescue activities of Silk Shirt.

But Lottie was no fool. 'You're looking shifty. There was a man, wasn't there?'

Bella shook her head. 'No, there wasn't. I fell into the ivy all on my own.' Well, it was the truth, she told herself. Silk Shirt had not appeared until she was already on the floor.

Lottie stared at her for a moment like a Junior Inquisitor with something to prove. Then she seemed to get bored. 'If you say so. So – apart from attacking the ornamental plants, did you have a good time?'

'Yeah, it was great. Good music, great dance space. *Fabulous* art. It was lovely to dance again. I talked to some nice people, too.'

'But . . .?'

Bella shifted her shoulders uncomfortably. 'Oh, I don't know. I just sort of overdosed on people, somehow. All of a sudden I felt I couldn't hear for everyone talking, could hardly breathe for all the bodies. So that's when I went out into that courtyard place.'

Lottie was picking at a '3 for the Price of 2' sticker on the juice carton. She did not look at Bella. 'And you didn't enjoy that?'

'Apart from making a spectacle of myself, you mean?' said Bella bitterly.

Lottie glanced up then. Her eyes gleamed with triumph. 'See? I *knew* there was a man. You can't hide anything from me.'

'Oh, rats.'

Lottie waited.

Eventually Bella sighed. 'OK. Somebody came along and dug me out of the compost heap. He was very nice and I was – well, a bit drunk and soppy, to be honest.'

'Did you make a pass at him?'

'No, I did not,' said Bella, outraged.

'Then you didn't make a spectacle of yourself,' said Lottie cheerfully.

Bella shook her head in disbelief. 'You know, you have a very black-and-white view of life.'

'Just being practical.'

'Huh?'

'I know you. If you'd made a pass at him, you'd want to avoid seeing him again. Depending on who else he knows, that could be very limiting. You've got a social life to revive prontissimo. The Christmas party season is coming. What's his name?'

Bella glared. 'We didn't exchange business cards.'

Lottie pursed her lips. 'He didn't tell you his name? Not a good sign. Did he ask yours?'

'Look,' said Bella crisply, 'he got me up, dusted me down, waved me goodbye. No big deal.'

'If you say so.'

'I say so. Now – are you going to climb into that fizz until it meets over the top of your head, or can I take you out for a burger?'

Lottie said she couldn't face a burger and she didn't really want to go out. She wanted to slob around in sweatpants and read the papers. But if Bella was offering to cook her famous Eggs Benedict, she, Lottie, wouldn't say no.

Bella recognised an olive branch when she saw it. 'I'll go and get the necessary.'

Lottie pushed off to shower and Bella slid the end of a spoon into the neck of the Cava bottle and put it back in the fridge. Then she made a careful list of all the things she would need for Eggs Benedict plus the other essentials that Lottie had somehow let get away from her, like milk and coffee, grabbed her friend's coat again and went out.

It was a bright golden day and the low sun hit Bella straight between the eyes. Dazzled, she raced to the corner shop, promising herself that she would unearth her sunglasses before she came out into this light again. She came back with a stripy plastic bag full of food and a copy of every newspaper that the shop sold. By that time, Lottie was dressed and in a much better temper.

Bella cooked and they had a companionable afternoon brunch in the kitchen, before tucking themselves up in front of the fire and dividing the newspapers between them, sharing the good bits. From time to time Lottie would also read out some snippet about the current scene that she thought Bella ought to catch up with. Eventually daylight disappeared, leaving only the firelight and the glow of a table lamp in the corner of the room.

Lottie cast the last bit of newspaper on to the floor, yawned, and said, 'You can't beat a lazy Sunday with an old mate. What do you want to do this evening? Telly, a movie or a DVD?'

Bella looked up from the last colour supplement she was leafing through. 'Whatever. Don't ask me to make decisions.'

'DVD then. Something with a happy ending.'

'Sounds great. I suppose I ought to call my mother, too. This should be late enough for her.'

Lottie gave a crack of laughter. 'Too right, even if she danced till dawn.'

'She'll probably have an early night, though. So I'd better move sharpish before the window of opportunity snaps shut.'

Bella went to retrieve her shiny new mobile from her beside table. Then remembered she had put it in the bag Lottie had lent her last night. After turning over all the various piles of clothes in her room, she found the bag under the bed.

She took it back into the living room. 'Sorry, Lotts, I forgot. I should have given this back to you this morning.' She emptied it out and retrieved her lipgloss, the cab company's card, her running away money, even a scrunched-up handkerchief.

There was no phone.

'Oh, hell! I must have lost it.'

Lottie was calm. 'Problem of being plastered in a new place,' she said tolerantly. 'Walk me through what you did when you came home last night.'

They went to the front door and did the whole action-rewind thing. It was no help. Bella had not put the phone down on the hall table, with her keys. She had not left it tucked into the pocket of Lottie's coat. She had not even taken it into the bathroom with her and put it in the bathroom cabinet, which Lottie said that she herself had done several times.

'Damn. It's got all my numbers in it,' said Bella, furious with herself.

'OK. When did you last use it? I mean, you called the minicab, right? What did you do after that?'

Bella bent her mind to the problem. Her memory was hazy but she was almost certain that she had called the cab before Silk Shirt appeared. 'I suppose I might have left it on the table in the courtyard,' she said doubtfully.

'That's easy then. I'll call them.'

'Actually, they might be miffed. I did leave a bit of a mess in the courtyard,' said Bella uneasily.

'Well, I don't suppose they'll have dusted for fingerprints. If they ask, I'll just deny all knowledge. I'll call. You have another look in the bedroom.'

But their hosts had not found a phone. And, even though Bella stripped the bed back to the undersheet, it was nowhere in her bedroom. Then Lottie called the minicab company, while Bella, reminded, put fresh sheets on the bed and hovered up the twiggy fallout.

The minicab company hadn't found it either but the car Bella had taken home was presently on another job. They promised to check and call back if they found it.

'Only one thing for it,' said Lottie. 'We call your phone and see if someone answers.'

She did.

And someone did.

'Hello? Who is this? I think . . . What?' Pause. 'Er, no, not me. It's my friend's phone. Maybe you should talk to her.'

Lottie handed the phone across to Bella with a very odd expression on her face. She went into the kitchen, closing the door behind her ostentatiously.

'Hello?' said Bella, puzzled.

'Who is this?'

Even through a cheap mobile's tinny reception, Bella knew those dark brown tones. She looked down at her

53

bare toes and saw they were curling into the rug with appreciation.

'Um – me.' It came out in a squeak. She cleared her throat, tried to imagine a gargle, tried to imagine she was speaking slowly and clearly to someone who didn't understand English very well, and tried again. 'I mean, Bella Greenwood. We met last night and you've got my phone. Hello.'

'I thought it was probably yours.' Oh, yes, it was him all right, that hint of laughter in the smoky voice. Her toes wriggled.

'Er – really? Why?'

'Pink and sparkly, covered in ivy, just a bit battered.'

'Oh.'

'It's a compliment,' he assured her. 'How many people do you know whose mobile phone is completely unmistakable?'

Bella cheered up a little. 'Well, if you put it like that—'

'I do. Now,' he said briskly, 'how are we going to get it back to you?'

'Are you in London? Could I possibly collect it?'

There was a silence. She thought: damn, I shouldn't have said that. He'll think I'm angling for a date. And now he's trying to let me down lightly. Ouch!

She went into delete mode. 'From your office, maybe? I mean, we don't have to meet in person. I could just drop in, if you left it with Reception. If you have a reception desk, that is. Or you could have it couriered to me here. I'd pay, of course. Can you tell them to collect the cost from me . . .' Oh, God, she was burbling.

But he interrupted. 'Do you jog?'

'What?'

'Jog. Run. Exercise.'

'Oh, *jog*. No.'

'Ah.' He seemed to be thinking. 'Look, do you know Battersea Park?'

'I suppose so,' she said, puzzled.

'I'll be running there tomorrow morning. Meet me on the bridge over the lake at . . . . let's say, ten to eight.'

'Bridge over the lake. Right.' Bella couldn't remember a bridge and had only the haziest recollection of a lake. But there had to be a map somewhere that showed it.

'I've got a really full schedule tomorrow. I may not be able to wait, if you're not there.'

Bella stiffened. 'Wouldn't it be simpler just to put the phone in the post?' she said frostily.

'But then I wouldn't get to see you again,' he said, redeeming himself a bit. 'No, let's try to meet up tomorrow. If we don't manage to meet, then I'll have it sent round. Give me the address.'

She did and he rang off. Bella took the phone back to Lottie.

'Thanks.'

'Asked your address this time, did he?'

'I thought you weren't listening.'

Lottie gave a naughty grin. 'Didn't need to. Dream Girl.'

'*What?*'

'That's what he called me when he thought I was you.'

Bella could feel herself blush, and glared at her friend. But Lottie was unrepentant. She looked knowing. 'So where's he taking you?'

'He isn't,' snapped Bella, and banged off to call her mother, without telling Lottie one single thing more.

Lottie wasn't a morning person. She still hadn't surfaced by the time Bella let herself out of the flat the next day. So she didn't have to lie about where she was going. She wasn't sure that she *would* have lied, if Lottie had been up and feeling nosy. But she was really glad that she didn't have to decide.

It was a crisp morning, with a heavy dew making the grass sparkle in the garden squares. But when the sun came up, it was dazzling, hitting her straight between the eyes again. After yesterday, though, she had come prepared. She fished sunglasses out of the pocket of her borrowed coat and marched stoutly over Chelsea Bridge.

It took her longer to get to the park than she had expected and the bridge wasn't easy to find once she got there. It turned out to be reached via a smallish path, overhung by evergreens. By the time she finally found it, her watch said it was after eight. So maybe he wouldn't still be there, she thought, remembering his warning. Her first instinct was to break into a run.

Then she thought of another of Georgia's maxims: a lady may be late but she is *never* rushed. Bella laughed out loud and slowed down, thinking: what the hell? He's probably gone. And if he hasn't – well, given the disasters when we met, I'm not rushing up all pink and panting the second time he sees me. Granny Georgia, she felt, would be proud.

But still she strode out briskly. And when she arrived, he was there.

Or, at least, she thought it was him. Bella couldn't be absolutely sure. Tall man, running on the spot, navy blue jogging pants and hooded sweatshirt, wearing wrap-around shades. She frowned, trying to impose a silk shirt and wicked laughter on that lithe figure in the early morning sun. Was it? Wasn't it?

And then he saw her and she had her answer. He broke into a great grin and jogged down the path to meet her.

'You made it!'

'Hi,' said Bella. Now they were face to face she found she felt awkward. Did they shake hands? Kiss on the cheek? High five?

He had no such hesitation. He gave her a big hug.

'Nrrgh,' said Bella, winded. Though it wasn't just the bear hug that was making her breathless.

He steadied her – for which she was grateful; her head was definitely swimming a bit – and let her go.

It didn't make any difference. Even through Lottie's coat and woolly gloves, his touch made her tingle. Bella shivered involuntarily.

'You're cold. Come on, let's walk.'

She fell into step beside him. Actually, that was a bit of an overstatement. He strode out and she kept up by means of a sort of skip step every few paces. She was not a short woman but he was so much taller that he naturally outpaced her. It wasn't comfortable.

'When did you find your phone had gone?'

She told him about Lottie and retracing her steps through the flat. She didn't tell him Lottie was not going to forget him calling her 'Dream Girl'. After all, this could be the last time they met, he might never call her that again, so it wouldn't matter, would it?

'And how are you? No ill effects?'

'From the champagne or the low-flying pot plants?' And Bella told him about her morning-after scorpion scare.

He laughed so hard he actually stopped walking for a moment.

Grateful, so did she. He'd set a punishing pace and she had been racing along even before that. She was aware of the beginnings of a stitch in her side.

'You're a joy,' he said when he could speak. 'A total joy. I've never met anyone like you.'

'Just accident-prone.'

'*Creatively* accident-prone. You must have a very rich inner life. Scorpions!' And he was off again, laughing helplessly.

'Well, until about five days ago, scorpions were a clear and present danger for me,' Bella pointed out.

'I'd forgotten that. Has it been difficult for you, readjusting?'

They had started to walk again.

'Not difficult exactly. But – well, I keep feeling I'm out of step, you know? I looked at a magazine in the hairdresser's and didn't know half the celebrities in it. I mean, I just didn't recognise them.'

'You're a celebrity watcher?' He sounded incredulous.

'Not particularly. But they're everywhere, aren't

58

they? If you watch TV or read a newspaper, anyway. And, for nearly a year, I haven't.'

'Oh, right. Culture shock.'

'And how! I've got out of the habit of living with lots of people. I nearly freaked when I went shopping on Saturday. And as for the party . . . that's why I retreated into the courtyard. All those people were doing my head in.'

'Sounds reasonable to me.'

'Yes, well—' Bella felt suddenly shy. She'd told him all about making a prat of herself over *Francis,* for heaven's sake. As if he were an agony aunt, instead of a sexy guy at a party. 'You were very kind.'

He stopped. 'Kind? No. Call it fellow feeling.'

She searched his face. He seemed to mean it but . . .

'Why?' she said doubtfully. 'Have you done the year away thing?'

'No. Or rather, yes, I do it all the time. I travel a lot, you see. Abroad, mostly. When I come back, everyone expects me to get off the plane and start right on trucking, like nothing's happened. Because, of course, nothing has – to them.'

He travelled a lot? Banker? International lawyer?

Before she could ask, he said, 'It's disorienting. Well, it disorients me. And it can make you feel really lonely.'

'Lonely,' she echoed. 'Yes. Yes, that's it.'

'You're not the person they knew, that's the trouble.'

'Ain't that the truth? A year ago, I'd have shopped till I dropped. And danced all night.'

He grinned and started to walk .'It will come back. People don't change fundamentally.'

'Do you think?' She was doubtful. 'Never?'

'Not in my experience.'

It didn't sound like that experience had been good. Bella looked at him sharply, but those massive shades hid his expression and he didn't say anything more.

'Well, I hope I at least get my phone habit back,' she said brightly. 'Lottie never moves without hers.'

'Oh. Yes.' He rummaged in the pocket of his hooded jacket. 'Here you are.'

In the morning sun, the phone looked very sparkly and *very* pink.

'Thank you,' said Bella, faintly embarrassed. 'I hunted everywhere for that yesterday.'

'I was starting to think that you'd written it off.'

'No way.' She was horrified. 'My life is in that phone. Or, at least, my life up to ten months ago.'

'So why did it take you so long to call?' he asked curiously.

She almost said: because I had to call my mother and I didn't want to think about it. But you don't have conversations like that at 8.30 in the morning while striding round a public park. So she said vaguely, 'Oh, life started happening.'

Through the autumn trees she could see a brisk breeze ruffling the waters of the lake. They were walking through an overgrown part of the park and a man in a tweed cap and Barbour was peering through the bushes at the ducks on the lake, stamping his feet and slapping his gloved hands together. His breath was like a puff of smoke in the cold air. So was Bella's, when she looked.

She pointed out, 'Isn't there a café by the lake? We could get a coffee.'

'Won't be open yet,' he said firmly, though she had the impression that he would have said no anyway. 'We just need to step out briskly. That'll warm you up.'

And she was back to a straight choice between trotting to match his pace or breaking into a hop, skip and a jump to catch up with him every few yards. It was not conducive to conversation. And that stitch in her side was threatening again. She stopped dead.

'Look,' she said to his back, 'I told you, I don't jog. What's the point of tearing round the place like this? Can't we go somewhere and just, well, talk a bit?'

He turned those mask-like shades on her for a thoughtful moment. Then he said, 'Talk? OK. Let's go this way.'

Coffee, thought Bella. Maybe even hot buttered toast. She worked hard not to dribble at the prospect.

He turned out of the overgrown path, past a grove of what looked like giant banana plants, towards a big, open ride with a Dickensian lamp-post on one corner. There were more people here: mothers taking children to school and walking dogs at the same time; purposeful joggers; and even more purposeful people walking as part of their journey to work. You could tell them by the briefcases, headphones and grim jawlines. A couple of rollerbladers swooshed past, too fast for Bella to make out whether they had briefcases or, worse, school uniforms.

'Here,' he said.

And, grabbing her hand, he ran her through the

61

pushchairs and dog walkers, up the long path, into the middle of the big central circle and then up the steps of the large, deserted bandstand.

The bandstand?

He dropped her hand and strode over to the wrought-iron railing, beaming. Bella took her sunglasses off and stared at him in disbelief.

He turned. 'What?' he said, plainly surprised. 'You wanted to talk. You said you did.'

'Not,' said Bella with restraint, 'to an assembled multitude. You look as if you're about to make a speech.'

'What do you mean?'

She gestured helplessly. A group of women with pushchairs stood talking at the end of one of the paths. The man with the flat cap was reading a park notice. Half a dozen rollerbladers were doing circuits of the bandstand, whooping and cheering each other on. A spaniel lolloped after them, barking, its curly ears flying wide. Bella swung round, watching it all until it made her dizzy, and then she fell back against the ironwork balustrade beside him. If he'd rung a handbell, she thought, they'd all have gathered round and listened.

'I was sort of hoping for a table in a corner somewhere and something hot to drink.'

He didn't seem to hear. He was drumming his fingers on the ironwork, scanning the park as if trying to commit it to memory.

'I like this place. It's so full of life. People going about their own business, in the same way as they have for a couple of hundred years. Reminds me of pictures in our old children's books in the nursery.'

62

Nursery? thought Bella. Sounded a bit grand. Or possibly grand-in-the-past, fallen-on-hard-times way, like Granny Georgia. Though Silk Shirt didn't look as if he had a problem paying his clothes bill. On the other hand, she herself had gone to that party looking like a million dollars and it was all borrowed or second-hand from Oxfam.

She said abruptly, 'Who *are* you?'

He looked down at her then. He seemed startled.

At once, she was flustered. 'I mean, where do I write my thank you note for returning my phone?'

'Oh, that. Don't worry about it. I'm just glad to have got it back to you.' He added wickedly, 'In fact, very glad. My friends were starting to comment on my having a pink phone that I kept checking.'

Did that mean he had *wanted* her to call? *Wanted* to meet her again? Bella looked at him doubtfully. She had to narrow her eyes against the low sun. He did not take off his shades. It was hopeless. She could not read him.

And he still had not told her his name. Lottie was probably right. The man probably fancied a mild flirtation; an assignation that couldn't get too heavy. Oh, well. No harm done, and at least she'd got her phone.

'Well, I ought to be getting back,' said Bella. She held out her hand. 'Thank you for the seek-and-rescue service. My phone buddies and I are very grateful. Not to mention my mother.'

He ignored her hand. 'You're going?' He sounded amazed.

Well, damn it, what did he expect, when he told her nothing and didn't let her have so much as a hot drink?

63

'Needs must,' said Bella, with a determined smile. 'I've got to see an agency about a job, and then I have to pick up my real life again.'

'I—'

'Yes?'

'Yes, of course, you must go. Your real life.' Suddenly he wasn't so difficult to read at all. He sounded bleak and disappointed.

'It's been nice knowing you,' said Bella, softening a little.

He shook his head.

'Well, goodbye.'

And she ran off down the steps of the bandstand and out towards the main eastern gate of the park as fast as she decently could.

He did not come after her.

4

Anthea of Jodie's Jobs was glad to see Bella.

'Christmas temping, is it?' she asked, after giving her a hug, calling up her file and providing her with some warm, stewed coffee from the bubbling machine.

Bella held her hands round the cup gratefully. 'Actually, I was looking for something a bit longer term than that.'

She ran through everything she had done since the last time Anthea took her details.

Anthea sucked her Biro. 'To be honest, we don't get a lot of call for fish counters. How urgently do you need a job?'

Bella had checked her bank balance that morning. 'Today would be good.'

'Ah. I see.' Anthea's fingers flickered over the keyboard as she talked. 'Well, Christmas temping hasn't started yet. But I could do you a stand-in receptionist at a dentist's. He's a bit of a bastard, actually, so a lot of the girls won't go back. But if you're desperate . . .'

'What sort of bastard?'

Anthea read aloud off the screen, '"Smarmy to the

65

rich clients. Bullying to the staff. Has been known to throw things."' She peered at Bella. 'You could go and see him today, start tomorrow, if you like.'

Bella pulled a face. But it was gainful employment and faster than she could have hoped. 'How much?'

Anthea told her.

Bella was surprised. 'That's not bad.'

'Pig's Premium,' said Anthea, and they both laughed.

'I'll do it. Give me the address.'

The dentist's consulting rooms were in a smart Belgravia house and they were in a shambles. A harassed woman was trying to talk on the phone, deal with a new appointment for a bad-tempered client and take a credit-card payment at the same time. Bella stood quietly by and watched until, eventually, she was done.

Then she stepped forward and introduced herself. The woman nearly wept with relief. As it turned out, she was the wife of one of the partners, helping out because The Man, as she called him, had sworn at the temporary receptionist on Friday and the girl had told him he could stuff his job.

'You're a godsend,' she told Bella. 'I didn't dare hope they'd get a replacement so quickly. Of course, you'll have to see The Man first. He insists on that. But I'm sure it's just a formality. I'll show you to the waiting room.'

But the phone started ringing again. So Bella found her own way to a luxurious room full of squashy sofas and tables holding glossy magazines. It could have been the drawing room in a country-house hotel, she thought, smiling at a nervous small boy in school uniform and by-passing the glossies for a pile of today's newspapers.

The Man kept her waiting for ages. Otherwise, she would never have read the gossip column in the *Daily Despatch*. And when she did, she sat bolt upright, feeling sick. It was only a snippet:

> What does a chap do when a girl dumps his big brother? Takes him on the town to forget.
>
> Prince George is a regular at Mayfair's supersmart Funky Bôite. But it was the first time regulars had seen the Prince of Wales there. Looks like he was having a good time.

But it was the blurry photograph beside the gossip item that made Bella feel as if the world had just turned flat and she was sliding off it. Half a dozen people were pictured dancing. One of them was waving a champagne bottle over his head. In the forefront was a blonde in a backless black dress, glancing over her shoulder at the camera while her partner's eyes gleamed.

Bella knew those eyes; knew the way they looked as if they were laughing even when the rest of his face was still. Come to think of it, she even knew the silken sheen of that shirt sleeve.

It was *him*.

The Prince of Wales? And she had blurted out her problems to him! Left him to return her naff pink phone! Not *recognised* him!

What a fool he must think her. What a blind, blank fool. And he had seemed so kind. Damn it, she had even *told* him he was kind, this morning. *Thanked* him for mopping her up on Saturday night. When all the time he was holding out on her, pretending to be someone else. And had gone straight on from that party to a backless blonde at the Funky Bôite. There was no doubting that Backless knew who he was.

Had he told her about the mad girl he'd met at the party? God, maybe he'd even had a bet with her or the others at the club. 'I met this blonde bimbo tonight who couldn't see straight enough to recognise me. How much says I can string her along a bit more, if I wear my sunglasses and keep her on the move?'

Bella writhed with embarrassment. But it was worse even than that. It *hurt*. In his way, he had done as much of a con job on her as Francis had. Only with Francis it had all been about vanity and getting his work done for him. With Richard – bloody Prince bloody Richard – it had been a deliberate deception.

And he had seemed so . . . honest. She'd thought there was an attraction between them. When he'd said that about fellow feeling this morning, she'd thought it was something they shared.

Well, that would teach her not to go reading too much into a few words that meant nothing. She thought: I am never telling anyone about this, not even Lottie, and I am going to forget it. I *am!*

68

She was polite but crisp with her prospective employer. It cowed him into signing her up without any attempt to bully her. Bella barely noticed.

When Lottie rang, she didn't answer. In fact, she didn't answer any call except her mother's. She took that, chatted briefly and arranged to visit next weekend. But when her mother said anxiously, 'Darling, are you all right? You don't sound it,' she just said, 'Bit busy right now. Gotta go.'

She didn't want to go back to the flat. Instead, she walked for hours: Harrods, warmly scented and blessedly anonymous; Hyde Park, bright and chilly, with a wind making waves dance on the Serpentine; Oxford Street; the luxury shops of Mayfair; Piccadilly, the Haymarket. By the time she got to Trafalgar Square, she was chilled to the bone and exhausted. She fled into the National Gallery and went round three galleries without taking in a single painting.

This is ridiculous, she thought. I only met the man once. Well, twice, if you count this morning. He *can't* do this to me. Pull yourself together, Bella. Answer your phone calls. Tell Anthea you've taken the job. Get on with real life. No bones broken, as Georgia would say.

She found a small café and took a latte to a table in the corner. She pulled out her phone – she was starting to really hate the pink sparkly thing – and worked her way through the messages. There was one number she didn't recognise. It had called several times.

Could it be him?

Nah, not a chance.

She was just about to text Anthea when the phone rang. The unknown number. Bella's heart lurched.

'Yes?'

'Can we talk?' said a voice she recognised.

To her horror, her eyes filled with sudden tears. What was happening to her?

'No, we can't,' she said nastily. And cut the call.

She dropped the phone on the table top and rummaged for a hankie. She couldn't find one, so she blew her nose hard on one of the café's paper napkins instead. Georgia would have called it sordid and Georgia would have been right, she thought.

The phone rang again. She glared at it. But in the end she answered.

'What?'

'You know, then.' He sounded chastened

'Know? What do I know? I just saw your photo in the *Despatch* and I know who you are, if that's what you mean.'

He groaned. 'Hell!'

'But I don't know why you wanted to play games like that. It's not honourable and it's not *kind*.' Her voice shook. She wasn't going to let him hear her crying. In fact, she *wasn't* going to cry. She cut the call fast.

And stocked up on café paper napkins.

She even managed to drink some of the latte before he rang again.

'Bella, don't hang up,' he said as soon as she answered.

'How do you know my name's Bella?'

'You told me yesterday when I rang.'

'Oh.' That took the wind out of her sails a bit.

'Look, I've handled this badly, I admit.'

'Oh, I don't know.' She sounded brittle and sophisticated, she thought. Also very angry. 'I think you handled it very well. Kept the girl distracted, avoided giving her your name, even when she asked. And she *still* didn't twig what a liar you are.'

That stung him. 'I didn't lie!'

'Yes, you bloody did,' she yelled. 'And you know it.'

This time she not only cut the call, she threw the phone at the café wall, where it broke into bits.

Well, at least it gave her something to do. She went to buy a replacement, a smartphone this time. She'd got a job now.

It rang as soon as the chip was in place.

'Ignore it,' she told the startled salesman. 'A nuisance caller.'

She stamped home to the flat, the phone going every few minutes. Setting her teeth, she vowed to sign up to a new company the next day. But she didn't turn it off, and when it stopped ringing she felt even worse somehow. She even checked the new device to make sure that she had not inadvertently pressed the silent button on the unfamiliar keypad. But she hadn't. He had just given up.

Well, that was a good thing, wasn't it?

Lottie was still at work when Bella got back. The flat felt empty and alien and she realised that the heating had not yet come on. It took a bit of a hunt but she found the controls and punched the override. Pretty soon, the place felt homey again, especially after she'd turned on the radio. She got out of her going-to-work clothes, lost the heels and padded round the flat in jeans and a sweater. She had just made herself a large mug of tea when the entry phone rang.

'Hello?'

'Bella?'

She dropped the mug of tea. It crashed on to the polished pine floor and broke into a dozen pieces. Hot tea soaked into her socks, making her jump.

'Ouch!'

'Bella? Can I come in?'

She was dancing on the spot, trying to avoid the scalding liquid and the shards, as she plucked at the wettest sock.

'Dammit.'

His voice grew urgent. 'Bella, what's wrong?'

Distracted, she pushed the entry button and heard the long buzz as the outer door opened.

She got one sock off and threw it into the corner, but she was still hopping and pulling when there were loud footsteps, as if someone had run up the stairs, followed by a thundering on the front door of the flat.

'Bella! What's happening? Let me in.'

She hopped up to the door and threw it open. Or at least she tried to. She had not allowed for being bent nearly double, hauling at the sock on her left foot. She recoiled and sat down hard. Among the shattered china, as it happened.

'Oof,' she said. Followed by, 'Oo-ow.'

'Bella . . .' He shouldered his way in, looking wildly round, and stopped dead as he saw her sitting on the

72

floor, nursing her foot, a wet and now blood-smeared sock draped over her shoulder like a waiter's napkin. 'What on earth . . . ?'

'I've hurt my foot,' said Bella in a small voice.

He shook his head as if to clear it. 'What? Why? *How?*'

'I dropped my mug. Spilled the tea and trod in it. Broke the mug and sat on it. I think –' her voice started to rise '– I'm bleeding.'

He didn't need any further explanation. He scooped her up, kicking the door shut behind him, and carried her into the sitting room, where he deposited her on the oldest, shabbiest sofa.

'Show me.'

Cautiously, Bella withdrew the pressure from the side of her foot. That revealed a wedge-shaped cut, tailing off into a long shallow scratch. He inspected it like a pro.

'That needs cleaning. There could be glass in the wound.'

She sniffed a bit. 'Ceramic. With forget-me-nots on.' Her voice wobbled.

He looked up at her then. It was the heart-stopping smile she remembered. How could he be such a lying toe-rag and have a smile like that? It wasn't fair.

'OK. Forget-me-not ceramic. It still needs to be fished out. Hot water? First-aid box?'

Bella was starting to feel faint. She directed him to the bathroom but denied all knowledge of any first-aid supplies. He went and she fell back among the lumpy cushions, nursing her foot. She didn't want to look at it again. There was a purply-white flap of flesh that made her feel quite sick.

Fortunately, he was not so squeamish. He came back with a soap dish full of warm water, a fistful of Lottie's eye make-up remover pads and a tube of antiseptic cream.

'Let's see if gangrene has set in,' he said cheerfully, brushing her hand away.

Bella leaned forward, peering in spite of herself.

'It looks gross.'

'Then don't look.'

She sat back hastily and averted her eyes while he mopped in a brisk, no-nonsense fashion that somehow didn't hurt as much as it ought to. When he'd finished, he pressed an eye make-up pad to the side of her foot and said, 'Hold it there. You don't have to look. Just keep pressing hard so it doesn't start bleeding again.'

He disappeared into the bathroom and returned with a handful of serious-looking packets and a roll of bandage. Bella stared.

'I'd say that either your flat-mate is a hypochondriac or she dates rugby players. Hold this.'

She took the roll of bandage while he ripped open one of the smaller packets.

'Here we are. Sterilised pad. Brilliant. You can take your hand away now.'

She did and braced herself for a fountain of blood. But the gash only oozed a bit.

He slapped the pad on to it, wound the crepe bandage around her foot like a professional, and stood back with a flourish.

'I should stay there for a bit, if I were you. Keep the pressure off. If you stand up it will start to bleed again.'

74

'Thank you,' said Bella.

She could see he was pleased with himself and she was genuinely grateful. On the other hand, he was still a lying toe-rag who'd had no compunction about making a fool of her. He had no *right* to tell her what to do, even if it was for her own good.

He cocked an eyebrow. 'Still annoyed with me?'

She sat up, furious all over again. 'Annoyed? *Annoyed?* Annoyed doesn't begin to cover it. What you did was unforgivable.'

He backed away, blinking.

'Would you really call it unforgivable?' he demurred.

'I just did. What's more, I mean it.'

'I can see that. But – look, give me a chance to explain?'

But she swept on. Anger was better than weeping. His duplicity still hurt more than she wanted to think about.

'I thought I knew every lousy trick in the book that you guys play on women. But this is a new one, even for me and my friends.'

He looked serious. 'You've told your friends?'

That made her even madder. 'Oh, yes, that gets you, doesn't it? What if one of my friends goes and tells the *Daily Shag*? You – you – you *wart poultice.*'

He blinked. Just for a moment, Bella thought she saw his mouth start to lift at the corner. She reared up against the battered corner of the sofa.

'Don't you dare laugh at me! Don't you dare.'

At once he was serious again. 'Not laughing. Not laughing. If your friends have told the *Daily Shag*—' his voice shook for a moment but he got control of it with admirable speed '—it's no more than I deserve. I'll tell my office to admit everything and issue an abject apology.'

She relaxed. 'Well, they haven't. Though it would serve you right if they did.'

'They haven't? How do you know?'

'Because I haven't told anyone,' she snapped. 'I didn't find out myself until this afternoon. Then I saw your photo in a paper in the dentist's waiting room and realised you were a sodding prince as well as a total . . .' Words failed her.

'Wart poultice?' he offered, straight-faced.

'Con man,' she said coldly.

'I know.' He sat down in the shabby old armchair on the other side of the fireplace and clasped his hands between his knees. 'I'm truly sorry. I don't know what came over me. I've never done anything like that before.'

'Huh!'

'No, I mean it. Ask anyone. Not me at all. My brother George now, it's exactly the sort of thing he loves. Does all the time. He's been known to dress up in a gorilla suit and sell kisses at a hen night. But me – no. I'm the boring, well-behaved one.'

'Not,' said Bella between her teeth, 'from where I'm sitting.'

He sighed. 'No. I can see that. I really am sorry.'

'So you've said.'

'Look – can I explain?'

'I don't know. Can you?'

'I don't know. But I can try.' He looked into yesterday's ashes. 'When you didn't know who I was – really didn't know, I mean, weren't just playing some game you thought was cute – I felt as if I'd been given a present. Everyone always knows who I am. So they're polite and a bit careful. Or challenging, sometimes. Or flirtatious. I know how to put them at their ease. Or deflect hostility. Or blank the predatory vamp. Oh, boy do I know how to do *that*.' For a moment he sounded bitter.

Bella was aware of a sneaking sympathy for him. She repressed it. He deserved to suffer a lot more yet before she forgave him. *If* she forgave him.

'I never tried to vamp you,' she said hotly.

He looked up then. 'No. Exactly. You were just sweet and all tied up with your own problems.'

She stiffened. 'Are you saying I'm self-obsessed?'

He smiled. 'No, you just had your own priorities. And I wasn't one of them. You have no idea what that was like. I felt like a horse galloping into a field after spending its life walking round and round a paddock.'

'Really?' She was sceptical.

He ran his hands through his hair. 'Look, everyone around me thinks I'm so important, and it's not good to be the person for whom everything is done, around whom everything is planned. They treat me like a national monument. And then, on Saturday, as far as you were concerned I was just a guy who happened by. It was a new experience for me.'

'I – see.' It made sense in a weird way.

'I didn't want to give that up. Can you understand that?'

'I suppose so. But it still doesn't explain why you

77

went on playing Mr Nobody this morning. That was horrid.'

He flushed. 'I know.'

'I even asked who you were, for God's sake.'

'I know,' he said miserably. 'But I don't usually have to tell people who I am. I couldn't find the words somehow. And while I was floundering, you ran off.'

'Hmm.' That made sense, she thought, softening.

'I knew I'd done it wrong as soon as you did. You looked so – hurt.'

Bella flinched and hardened herself again. 'So why didn't you come after me and put it right? Tell me who you were, at least?'

'I wanted to. But, well, there was my security man watching. And God knows who else. You might not have recognised me but there are plenty of people who do, all the time.'

'Recognise you?' She gave a hoot of derision. 'How the hell would they recognise you under a hoodie and shades? You looked like a CIA assassin.'

'Really?' He sounded flattered.

'Not a very good assassin.'

'Oh, well, that's me in my place,' he said resignedly.

In spite of herself, she gave a faint giggle.

He looked up hopefully. 'Bella, please. I know I've been all sorts of an idiot and you have every right to kick me out and never see me again. But – can we start again? Please?'

She thought about it. 'Start again?'

'As if we'd just met.'

'Saturday never happened?'

His eyes lit with that secret laughter. 'I don't want to go that far. You looked very fetching among the flower-pots. Say this morning never happened.'

'Ah.' She thought about it. 'Proper introductions?'

'If you want. The Hamiltons could ask us both to dinner . . .'

She waved that aside. 'I don't mean references and people you know setting it up with people I know. I mean you telling me who you are, what you do and what you want. And then giving me a phone number, like people do. If you want to.'

He looked dazed. 'I want to,' he said in a sort of strangled croak.

'OK then. Let's see how it goes. Hello. I'm Bella Greenwood.' She held out her hand.

He took it. But instead of shaking it politely, he stood up and went down on one knee in front of the sofa, holding her hand between both of his.

Oh, my Lord, she thought, startled.

'I'm Richard. I'm heir to the British throne. I saw you across a moonlit courtyard and I couldn't wait to meet you.'

WOW! she thought.

Aloud she said, 'You are nuts. You know that?'

'You can't say things like that to the heir to the throne,' he said calmly.

And kissed her hand. Very gently, but it was a real kiss all the same. She felt it through her skin and down to her bones, and it damn nearly stopped her heart.

'You are going seriously OTT,' she said in a breathless, scolding voice.

'You told me to tell you what I want,' he said in an injured voice.

'I said proper introductions,' she hissed, seriously flustered.

'Well, all right, if you insist. But if you want to curtsey, you'll have to stand up.'

'Curtsey? No way.'

'You are quite right. You shouldn't put any weight on that foot yet. Not for hours. In fact, I think—'

Abruptly he stopped kneeling beside her and plonked himself down on the sofa. 'Budge up.'

She did, eyeing him warily. He put one arm along the saggy old back and leaned forward, looking down into her eyes. His, she saw, were brown and very, very amused.

'I think you should lie back and—'

'If you tell me to lie back and think of England, I shall deck you,' snarled Bella, finding herself a lot deeper among the cushions than she had expected.

He smiled. 'No, you won't.'

And kissed her.

And there was a yell as the front door opened and Lottie skidded on spilled tea and the ruins of her forget-me-not-mug.

Richard let Bella go rather slowly. 'There.'

She swallowed. 'You took advantage of me.'

'Yup.'

'Oh, God. And now Lottie's home.'

'Charlotte thing? Good.' He stood up.

'Good? _Good_? Have you no sense of timing?'

But he was already in the small hall. Bella heard him

say, 'Charlotte Hendred? You won't remember me, but we met at the Hamiltons' several months ago. I wonder if you would do me the immense kindness of introducing me to your friend, Miss Greenwood.'

There were glugging sounds from the hallway. Bella sympathised. The man was a swine, with a very nasty sense of humour.

She struggled off the sofa and limped over to the door of the sitting room. She was very much afraid that her hair was a mess and her cheeks were pink. Lottie would recognise the signs of a woman who had just been comprehensively kissed. But there wasn't a thing Bella could do about it.

'Um . . . hi, Lottie. Richard –' she glared at him '– is teasing you. We met on Saturday.'

'But we weren't properly introduced,' he said imperturbably. 'Miss Hendred?'

Lottie looked from one to the other of them, and shrugged.

'Your Royal Highness, may I present Miss Isabella Greenwood, a childhood friend and currently my flat-mate.'

Bella's chin rose. 'I told you. No curtseying.'

His eyes laughed. 'OK. What about a date? A proper date, where I pick you up, take you to dinner and bring you home again?'

Bella was so taken aback she could only mouth, like a goldfish, but no words came out.

He stood there, all courteous attention, waiting for an answer.

Eventually she managed a wordless 'squee' noise,

like a demented dentist's drill, and he inclined his head.

'Thank you. Tomorrow? Eight o'clock?'

She squeaked again.

He clicked his fingers. 'Phone number. You wanted me to give it to you. But I think you have it on your phone already. Lots and lots of times, in fact. Call me if you want to change the plans. Otherwise I'll see you here tomorrow at eight.'

He came over and looked down at her, half laughing and wholly purposeful. Bella swallowed. But he didn't kiss her. Instead he touched one hand to her scarlet cheek. Which was worse, somehow; wonderful but worse.

'Take care of that foot,' he said softly. 'I'll see you tomorrow.'

'Um, yes.'

He inclined his head to Lottie. 'Miss Hendred. A great pleasure.'

He left.

The front door closed gently behind him. The two friends stared at each other, Bella hot and confused, Lottie looking as if she'd been sandbagged.

Lottie recovered first. She gave a huge grin and punched the air.

'Woo-hoo! You pulled the Prince!'

5

'Are First Dates Always Difficult?' – *Tube Talk*

It was just as well, Bella thought, that she was starting a new job or she would have spent the day in a fever of 'what ifs' and 'should-I-have-saids'. As it was, she had her first trial of strength with the bullying dentist and forgot for at least an hour that she was going out on a first date with the most unlikely man in the world.

When she arrived, early as she always did, the harassed woman of the day before was waiting for her in the cubby hole they called an office. She presented Bella with notes in a range of handwriting and legibility. And fled.

It did not take her long to work out that the appointments system was a mess, the staff roster worse, and the outstanding queries on bills, orders and even lost property went back months. The filing was laughable. But Bella had not spent the best part of a year counting fish for nothing. If there was one thing she knew how to do, it was organise data. She made a list of the jobs to be done and consulted a friendly hygienist on what to do first.

'Get the appointments straight,' said Anya with feeling.

'The best receptionist we ever had used to telephone people the day before to remind them. These days I get at least one missed appointment a day, sometimes more.'

'Right,' said Bella, bringing appointments to the top of her list.

Anya leaned over the counter watching her. 'Nice idea, but you'll never make it stick. Mulligan the Magnificent will come steaming out and make you drop everything to do something he wants.'

She was right. Between checking patients in, directing them to the waiting room, making out their bills and taking payments, Bella straightened out appointments for the next day. Two patients said they'd changed their appointment; one had a broken leg and was in hospital, the others were grateful. She had two left to go when Mulligan appeared at her desk.

'You're not supposed to make phone calls,' he told her disagreeably.

'They're phone calls to patients.'

'Well, you should ask me first.'

Bella just looked at him.

He started to bluster. She sat there with her hands folded and listened.

When he finished she said, 'I have established that you have three appointments tomorrow where patients will be unable to turn up, Anya has two cancellations and Mr Page has one.'

'What?'

Silently she swung the screen round so he could see.

'Ridiculous! Patients are so irresponsible. Bill them anyway.'

'Difficult to do that when it's our fault. Two have already rebooked, but someone here forgot to take out the original appointment.'

There was a stand-off.

'Then book someone else in,' he snapped at last.

Bella gave him a sweet smile. 'You mean, you give me permission to make a phone call or two?'

If he'd been a horse he would have thrown back his head and neighed with frustration.

'Bastard,' said Anya with satisfaction, emerging from the hygienist's suite. 'Well done, you.'

So Bella went home, cautiously pleased, and when Lottie asked, 'How was your day?' said, 'First round to me.'

'First round?'

'There will be others. I've worked for the Mulligans of this world before.'

'You'll handle it,' said Lottie. 'Now what are you wearing tonight?'

Bella had been thinking about that and had worked out a strategy. 'Nothing too fancy,' she said firmly. 'First dates are a minefield. I want to feel comfortable. I did buy some shoes at lunch-time though.'

Lottie approved the cute patent T-bars she had picked up but was disappointed by her refusal to dress up in full party fig. But in the end she sighed and agreed that Bella was probably right.

'But no jeans,' she warned. 'You don't know where he's taking you and some places don't let in people wearing jeans.'

Bella raised an eyebrow.

'OK, they'd probably let the Prince of Wales in. But you'd have everyone staring, like one of those horrible Bateman cartoons. *The Woman Who Wore Jeans at Club Exclusive*. You'd hate it.'

So when Richard arrived, Bella was ready in a pair of waist-hugging cigarette pants over an old silk camisole top of Lottie's. She had found a short, fitted blazer on her Oxfam trawl. It was covered in a spray of small black beads and was one of those classic vintage numbers that managed to look both chic and casual all at once.

'Actually, I like it,' said Lottie, inspecting her critically. 'Not coming from a charity shop would have been a real bonus. But you'll definitely do.'

She even allowed Bella out with only the minimum of make-up, on the grounds that her Indian Ocean tan was as good as anything that came in a bottle.

'Jewellery?'

But Bella had none. She'd not taken any to the island with her and she was still living out of her backpack, with a few supplements. 'I'll pick up all my stuff at the weekend,' she promised.

Lottie was desperate to lend her some pearl earrings but Bella hooted with laughter and told her to get real.

'I'm not a Jane Austen heroine. Pearls are for historical novels and grandmothers.'

'Well, you need something. Otherwise you'll look as if you're going for a working lunch or something.'

'In this jacket?'

Lottie admitted it would be a bit sparkly for the office but they settled on a pair of golden chandelier earrings from Lottie's extensive bauble collection, just to add a sparkle or two more.

First dates always have their awkward moments and Bella braced herself. But Richard was perfectly at ease from the moment she opened the door to him. He kissed her on both cheeks, quite naturally, and flapped a cheerful hand at a hovering Lottie, saying, 'Do you mind if we push off now? I've parked a bit adventurously.'

'Sure,' said Bella, surprised but obliging. ''Bye, Lotts.'

He held the door open for her and grinned at Lottie. 'See you later.'

Which very neatly established that he would be back tonight and so would Bella.

She told him so as they went down the stairs. 'God, you're smooth.'

He looked down at her, one eyebrow raised. 'That sounds as if you don't approve.'

She shook her head. 'Not at all. It will be a new experience.'

He was right about his parking. He was nearly blocking a garage entrance and the front wheels were definitely on a double yellow line.

'Anti-social,' he said ruefully. 'But I'd been round three times and there was nowhere else. And I didn't expect to be long. Thank you for being ready to go.'

'You're welcome.

The car was an unremarkable saloon. No Royal Standard, no fancy number plates, Bella was relieved to see. Richard held the door open for her and she got in. He slid into the driving seat and they were off.

He drove down to the Embankment and turned west along the river. So he wasn't taking her into town then.

'Where are we going?'

'Small restaurant, run by a man I know. I hope you like it. Later you shall tell me all the things you like to eat, where you like to go, what you enjoy doing. But tonight I had to guess.'

'Great. I love surprises.'

She was taken aback all the same. When he passed up on Mayfair, she braced herself for some Michelin-starred foodie's paradise in a smart village. But the restaurant was in an outer suburb, in a set of arches under a railway line. It had candles set on old sherry barrels in the bar area, and red-checked tablecloths.

The greeter at the door seemed to know him. 'Mr Clark. Table for two. This way.'

'Mr Clark?' said Bella, when they were seated.

He pulled a face. 'My brother George's idea of a joke. Kent Clark. Superman backwards.'

'So are you always Mr Clark when you go out on the razz?'

'Sometimes.'

The waiter brought them two menu cards and Bella saw the food was Spanish.

'What would you like to drink? Sherry is the house speciality but you can have a cocktail or proper champagne, not just Spanish fizz, if you'd rather.'

'My grandmother drinks sherry. I don't think I've ever tried it. Deal me in.'

It was the start of a wonderful evening, low-key and

88

very friendly. Maybe first dates didn't have to be so fraught after all, she thought. Plate after plate of exotic tapas was put on the table, along with wonderful crusty bread. She and Richard swapped tastes and dipped their bread in the same earthenware dishes of sardines, and oil and olives, and wonderful oniony potato cakes, and, of course, paella. She got olive oil on her chin. Richard blotted it for her, and it was like a caress. The food was so delicious that when the patron chef emerged from the kitchen to tour the tables, Bella could genuinely tell him the paella was the best she'd ever tasted. He beamed.

Richard was equally pleased. 'OK. That's a good start. You like Spanish food. What else? Thai? Italian? Tell me.'

Bella thought about it. 'I'm pretty much of an omnivore. I don't like squid because of the idea of it or okra because it's slimy. Oh, and I wouldn't want to eat hare because they dance. But that's about it, I think.'

He nodded gravely. 'I'll bear that in mind. And where are your favourite places?'

'Depends. I like the Downs in the early morning when the sun's coming up, you know, and the dew is sparkling on the fields. And I like ruins like Minster Lovell and Warkworth Castle.'

He stared.

'What?'

'Ruins.' He shook his head.

'*What?*'

His shoulders began to shake. 'I meant,' he said when he could speak, 'where do you like to go for entertainment? I was thinking of where we go next. Along the lines of clubbing and so forth. Food. Dancing. Maybe ten-pin bowling at a pinch. Ruins is a new one.'

'Oh, I *see*.' Bella was rueful. 'Well, I've never been much of dancer. I've got two left feet and I tend to flail with drink taken.'

'I wasn't thinking of competitive ballroom activity,' he assured her.

'Oh, well, in that case,' she said, relieved, 'I can stomp around on the dance floor like anyone else, I suppose. Before I went away, I used to go clubbing with the girls every few weeks or so.'

He stared at her, fascinated. 'But you prefer ruins really?'

'I think I do,' she said reflectively. 'Is that odd?'

'You're a romantic,' he said on a note of discovery. 'Who'd have guessed?'

'No,' she said, revolted. 'Practical twenty-first-century woman, me.'

And started telling him about her new job. He laughed at the idea of her being paid a Pig's Premium because the boss was so vile.

She shrugged. 'I can handle him.'

'I don't doubt it.'

'Well, I've handled worse. And if I stuck the island for ten months, I can manage Dentist Hell. At least there's a going home time when I can see friends and read books.'

'The island was real hell, then?'

'Not all of it. But I went because I was sort of stuck on the guy who was running it and he turned out to be—'

90

'A pig?'

She thought about Francis, noble and disorganised and just a bit too sure of his charm.

'No not a pig. But, well, shallow. You know? With an enormous appetite for being waited on, preferably well-larded with breathless admiration. I got tired of saying, "Francis, you're so clever."'

He winced. 'Poor guy.'

'Not poor guy at all,' said Bella robustly. 'He keeps sending me texts saying he can understand why I've had a crisis. But when I come to my senses I'm welcome back, and anyway he will always be there for me.'

'There's something wrong with that?' said Richard cautiously

Bella was scornful. 'It's code for, "Come back and sort out the files." I told you, Francis is high-maintenance. Never logged any data himself since the day he found he could get his devoted students to do it for him.'

'Ah.'

'What?'

'You're very clear-sighted, aren't you? Not quite so much a dyed-in-the-wool romantic as I thought.'

'I told you, I'm not romantic.'

'Wanna bet?'

But Bella backed away from that one. This might be the most relaxed first date she had ever been on, but there was a look in his eyes that was not relaxed at all. And if there was one thing an unromantic, sensible woman did *not* want to do, it was mess up her life by falling for an unavailable man. And they didn't come

91

much more unavailable than the heir to the throne.

She said lightly, 'You'd lose your money. Don't forget, I lived on a tropical island – and counted fish.'

'There is that.' He leaned forward. 'So what next for you? I assume Frankenstein the Dentist is only a – er – stop gap.'

Bella was drinking Rioja at the time and nearly choked. 'That is a very bad pun,' she said reproachfully, when she got her breath back.

He looked wounded. 'I thought it was rather good for the spur of the moment.'

'Well, maybe,' she allowed. 'And, yes, I'm looking for a proper job, too. But that will take time.'

'What sort of job? Something adventurous?'

She sighed. 'I think I'm off adventure. I like being clean too much. And keeping in touch with people. My father will drum me out of the Greenwood family.'

'Really? Why?'

'He's an explorer. Arctic wastes, deserts, Mongol plains. As long as it's remote, uncomfortable and deserted, he's in seventh heaven. His mother, my Granny Georgia, is an ecologist, who keeps popping off up the Amazon to save the rain forest.'

Richard was not interested in Georgia, though. He sat bolt upright. 'Greenwood? You're not H. T. Greenwood's daughter?'

'Yes,' said Bella sadly.

Hitherto Richard had seemed quite perfect. But she had seen that look before on the keen-eyed groupies who came to her father's lectures. Who would have thought the Prince of Wales was a fan of old Finn's?

'He's an inspiration,' said Richard in hushed tones, confirming it.

Bella sighed, torn between pride, loyalty, and a bedrock desire not to lie to this man. 'Hector Toby Greenwood. Known as Phineas, because he ran away and went round the world when he was supposed to be at school. Yes, that's the Daddy. He has his moments.'

Richard studied her for a moment. And then he surprised her. 'Hard act to live up to?'

She felt warmed. 'Yes, that's it exactly. My brother Neill refused to try. Told everyone he was a homebody and wanted to teach. Finn never argued, to be fair. Never tried to talk him out of it, not even when he said he didn't want an exciting gap year travelling, just wanted to get on with his life.'

'So you were the one left carrying the Greenwood banner?'

Bella was struck by this. 'I've never thought of it like that. You could be right.'

'I know I'm right. Welcome to the club.'

But Bella was still thinking about the Greenwood inheritance. 'Do you know, I was even named after a nineteenth-century explorer.'

He shook his head. 'I don't believe it. There was never an explorer called Bella. What's your real name? Augustus?'

'You're wrong there. Isabella Bird was the first female fellow of the Royal Geographical Society.

'Never heard of her.'

'You've missed a good thing,' said Bella with enthusiasm. 'She was a phenomenon. Half the time she reclined on a couch or stayed at home with Mama and did good works. And the other half she would pack her bags and go travelling. After Mama died, she went round the world. She was passionate about horses and rode all through the Wild West in the days when it still was wild. Possibly had an affair with a Davy Crockett type and maybe another one in Japan with her translator, who was less than half her age. She went to Persia, Ladakh, Tibet, Hawaii, all round the States. Wrote some pretty good books. My father always says she was an anti-colonialist and bent Gladstone's ear about it.'

Bella stopped dead, suddenly realising where her enthusiasm had led her.

'Er . . . I probably ought to tell you. I mean, it's not going to matter, you'll probably never meet him, but my father is a conviction Republican. Doesn't hold with monarchy. Or empire. But mostly he just hates kings and queens.'

Richard stared at her for an unnerving minute. She had the impression of his brain working very fast to process a lot of new information. He said slowly, 'You mean, he wouldn't approve of me.'

'Probably not. No.'

'I see.'

'Nothing personal,' she added hurriedly.

He nodded. She could still sense his brain racing. 'So you're not going to tell him you're seeing me?'

That sounded underhand somehow. 'Well, I don't see him very often, and he's not a great one for writing. The subject probably won't come up.'

'Don't see him? How come?'

94

She explained about her parents' divorce and moving to Hampshire with stepfather Kevin.

'But you still try to keep up the Greenwood traditions?'

'Yes, I suppose so. I was sort of always Daddy's girl.'

'Ah. Do you ever travel with your father?'

She was shocked. 'Good heavens, no. He wouldn't have me. You need full survival training to go anywhere with Finn. Not to mention the patience of a saint, an orderly mind, and a determination to Stick to the Plan. Finn tends to be impetuous.'

Suddenly Richard was amused. '*Very* clear-sighted,' he murmured.

She was conscience-stricken. 'Do I sound mean?'

He shook his head. 'Beautifully honest.'

'Oh. Good. I think.'

'Good, definitely.' He paused. 'So you're Daddy's girl but you're not going to tell him about me?'

Bella looked down at her plate. This was the crunch then. The point in each first date when you had to decide whether there was going to be a second one.

She swallowed. 'I've been away a long time and I'm still a bit disoriented. I need to find my feet again. Get a job, see where I'm going. I'm not looking for a full on relationship—'

He sat very still. 'So thank you for a nice evening and goodbye?'

NO, screamed something inside her.

'Does it have to be so black-and-white? Can't we just enjoy each other's company and see where it goes?'

He looked at her for a long, unnerving minute.

'I mean, do *you* usually rush off to tell your parents every time you meet a new girlfriend?'

'I'm twenty-nine years old. I don't often tell my parents anything. Anyway, there are plenty of people to do it for me. Starting with the Press.'

'Oh.' She hadn't thought of that. 'Of course. Like that piece in the *Despatch* on Monday. That's when I first recognised you, actually.'

He pulled a face. 'Well, at least we had two days when I was just me.'

'Hmm.' She was remembering the blonde in the backless dress. 'Who was the girl you left with?'

'Chloe Lenane. Our families have known each other for ever. Her aunt is one of my mother's ladies-in-waiting. She's like another sister.'

He raised a hand and a waiter materialised beside them. 'Would you like anything more? A brandy? Coffee? Something sticky?'

She didn't care. But she knew the evening wasn't ending yet. 'Anything.'

'Madeira for my guest,' he said to the waiter. 'Black coffee for me.'

When the man had gone Richard leaned back. 'Do you know what has been really different about tonight?'

She shook her head.

'You haven't once said, "So what is it like being Royal?"'

'I've talked all about myself,' said Bella, instantly conscience-stricken.

'You're missing the point. You answered my questions. You asked some of your own. As if this was just like any other date you've ever been on.'

She was puzzled. 'So? How else—?'

'Don't get me wrong. I like it. I just don't think it's ever happened to me before. But there's this bloody great elephant in the room and you're refusing to see it.'

'What?'

He leaned forward. His voice was low and intense when he answered. 'OK. Tonight's an ordinary date for you. Do you know how much management and sheer fucking ingenuity went into delivering it?'

She shook her head, open-mouthed.

He ticked off the points on his fingers. 'Rented car. Not rented by me, obviously. A friend of my security guy is the name on the ticket. I left wearing his jacket and flat cap.'

Suddenly Bella remembered the man in the park, with his all-weather coat and cap, standing in the cold sun.

'You brought him to Battersea Park with you, didn't you?'

'Strictly speaking, he brought me. Drove me there and back. Kept an eye out for the paparazzi all the time we were there.'

'Oh.'

'You wanted to know why I was togged up like a Hollywood assassin on Monday. Well, that's the answer. So there wouldn't be any pictorial evidence.'

Suddenly she felt completely out of her depth.

'Look, Bella, people recognise me. They take photos of me on their cellphones. I don't have a private life.

And if you and I try to have a let's-see-where-this-takes-us deal, you won't either.'

The waiter brought their drinks.

At once Richard sat back, smiling again and talking about a movie.

But the moment the waiter had gone, he said in a low voice. 'I could only take you out this evening because there was nothing in the diary. I've given the staff the night off. Ian is sitting in my flat, watching my television and pretending he's me. But if anything blows up and someone comes to find me, he's toast. His career's gone. And the Press and possibly the security forces will start looking for the woman I spent the evening with. Do you see?'

'I – never thought,' she answered in a small voice.

'Well, think now.'

Bella stared at him, all the lovely laughter and intimacy gone. She didn't know what to say.

He gave a tired smile. 'It's OK. You don't have to say anything. I can see you're not a paparazzi sort of girl. I always knew it really. Don't worry about it. No harm done.'

She could have cried.

He drove her home in silence.

When they got there she said, 'Why don't I just jump out here? You'll never find a parking place and—'

'I took you out, I'll see you home.'

Bella recognised finality when she heard it. She didn't argue.

It was chilly now, with autumn taking hold. She was shaking so much, she couldn't get the key in the lock.

98

For a while he stood beside her on the front steps, hands in the pockets of his coat. But eventually he took the keys from her gently and unlocked the door himself.

She thought he would say goodbye then. She even turned to him for a good-night kiss. But he held on to the keys and they both went upstairs.

The flat had that indefinable air of being deserted. It was silent and not quite in darkness. There was a low light from the sitting room and, when they went in, they found the fire glowing and a tray of unlit candles on the mantelpiece.

'Oh, *Lottie!*' said Bella.

But Richard knelt and lit the candles, then put the tray on the table beside the armchair. He added another log to the fire, for good measure. Bella took his coat and discarded her own jacket.

'A drink? More coffee?'

He shook his head. 'I'm fine.'

But he didn't go. And Bella didn't want him to. She went over and put her arms round his waist, leaning her head against his shoulder. He put his arms round her.

She did not know how long they stood there in the semi-darkness, just holding each other. How could it hurt this much to say goodbye, when they'd only just met? It was ridiculous. But Bella still didn't let him go.

It was he who moved first.

'Bella—'

'Don't go.'

She was nearly voiceless but he heard.

'Oh, love.' He sounded shaken.

She kissed him with a sort of fury. For a moment, just

a moment, he responded totally. Then he let her go and stepped away.

She could not believe it. Reached for him. 'Why not? What does it matter, one night, in the scheme of things . . .'

'*Don't.*' It came out like a pistol shot.

And stopped her dead

He ran a hand through his hair. He was breathing like a marathon runner, she saw.

'You made a good decision tonight, Bella. Don't complicate it.'

He was going, reaching blindly for his coat as he went, not looking back. She said his name in a disbelieving whisper. But all she heard was the front door opening and closing behind him.

6

'Friends, Parents and the Art of Breaking Up' – *Girl*
About Town

It was not a good week. A dozen times a day Bella was
on the brink of calling Richard. A dozen times a day she
cut the call just before it started to ring. One day she
would be too late, she thought. And where would that
leave her? Would he even answer?

Meanwhile she seemed to see his picture everywhere
– in a new batch of glossy magazines that came into the
surgery, in the free paper *Tube Talk* which she bought
on the way to work in the morning, in the *Daily Despatch*
and other newspapers. From hardly noticing the Royal
Family, she seemed to be reading about them all the
time.

Queen Jane launched a ship; King Henry opened an
exhibition of early machinery in a waterworks dating
from the Industrial Revolution; Prince Richard gave a
speech at a degree ceremony in a college of further
education. On Thursday all three of them went to the
opera. It was Wagner. The King looked as if he had
been dragged there and was suffering, but Queen Jane
was graciousness itself, not a hair out of place and her
regal tiara glittering. Richard, in the regulation tuxedo,

looked quiet and a little tired. Bella found herself stroking his face on the printed page.

As soon as she realised, she snatched her hand away. Fool. *Fool.*

From Richard himself there was no word. Well, she didn't expect it.

Lottie was an angel. She must have taken a change of clothes for the morning when she left the flat on the night of the date because she did not come back for breakfast. But she did ring the next morning.

'How are you? Hung over?'

'A bit.' Bella wasn't, but it was as good an excuse as any. She had not slept much and she had dark circles under her eyes. Make-up had been a major undertaking that morning and she had stopped off on the way to work to buy herself a new phial of Touche Éclat.

'Where did he take you?'

'Oh, a little place he knew. You won't know it.'

'Did people recognise him?'

'Not that I noticed.'

'Bella, are you OK?'

She started to say, 'I'm fine,' then thought better of it. 'No, I'm not actually, Lotts. But can we talk about it later?'

Lottie drew in a sharp breath. 'What did the bastard do?'

She was always ready to go to war for a friend, Bella remembered. It was kind of comforting. But she had to be stopped.

'Nothing. He didn't do anything. Look, Lotts, I can't

102

talk about it. Not now. Please?' Her voice cracked on the last word.

'Ah. All right. See you tonight then?'

'Yes.'

Lottie must have left work early because she was waiting when Bella got home, with the fire blazing and a delicious smell wafting from the kitchen along with the mellow tones of Christian Tabouré.

'Moroccan stew,' said Lottie. 'It won't be done for ages. Have a bath. Soak away the day. Help yourself to the Roman bath oil. Then come and have a drink.'

Bella did. When she emerged, she found that Lottie had left a package on her bed, wrapped in silver tissue paper. She ripped it open and discovered a floor-length kimono in softest sapphire silk. She put it on at once and went out to the sitting room, feeling distinctly weepy.

'Oh, Lottie, you are so kind. It's gorgeous.'

Lottie was curled up on the sofa with her feet tucked under a cushion, reading. She looked up, discarding her novel. 'I knew it was your colour as soon as I saw it. Gosh, I wish I was a blonde.'

Bella blinked her damp eyelashes. 'You could be if you wanted. I'm sure Carlos would love the challenge.'

Lottie shook her head sadly. 'Carlos wouldn't hear of it. Says I've got the wrong skin tone. He lets me have gold highlights sometimes.'

'Do you want a drink? I still make a mean Margarita. Or there's wine.'

'What I'd really like is tea,' Bella confessed.

'You shall have it.'

'You're a star.'

Lottie stood up and plumped the pillow, waving Bella on to the sofa. 'Go on, cuddle up and toast your toes. I'll put a brew on and stir the stew a bit. Back in a jiffy.'

She returned with a glass of wine, a dish of olives and Bella's tea in a Snoopy mug. Accepting it reminded Bella that she needed to confess to her breakage.

'I owe you a mug. I'll get you a new one tomorrow.'

Lottie shrugged. 'Mugs come and they go. Don't worry about it.'

She flung herself down on the armchair and rested her feet on the smart brass fender, watching Bella sip her tea.

'How is it?'

'Blissful.'

'How was your day?'

Bella made a face. 'I've had better.'

'I can imagine.' Lottie hesitated. 'Want to talk about it?'

'We went on one date. What's to talk about?'

'You looking like you've gone ten rounds with Lord Voldemort, for a start.'

Bella shifted her shoulders. 'Probably too many changes all coming on top of each other. Or, like my mother would say, me making a fuss about nothing.'

Lottie snorted.

Bella shook her head. 'No, she'd be right in this instance. Richard and I . . .' She swallowed. It was the first time she had said it like that, coupling their names together. 'Richard and I didn't even know each other.'

Lottie sucked her teeth. 'That wasn't how it looked last night.'

'Then looks were deceiving.'

'And he called you his Dream Girl.'

'That was just a silly joke.'

'People who share jokes know each other. I rest my case, m'lud.'

Bella smiled unwillingly. 'You're too clever for me. OK, there was something.'

'Not enough?'

Bella put the mug down and hugged a cushion to herself. 'I don't know. I suppose I'd been drifting along rather. I mean, I didn't know he was a blasted Prince for so long, I'd never really taken it in. I was just thinking we could go out a bit, see if we liked each other, that sort of thing. But he said it wouldn't work. He said he was public property.'

'Ah. I wondered if it was something like that.'

Bella nodded. 'I suppose you think I'm an idiot.' She was used to Lottie's robust opinions.

'No, I don't,' her friend said, surprising her. She laughed at Bella's expression. 'Don't forget, I'm in PR. I've seen a lot of people get hit by celebrity. It's fine for people who have some skill, or role, or talent or something. But if you're just famous for being famous, it can be a terrible curse. Especially if you don't enjoy people staring at you and asking you intrusive questions. And you're not really a girl for the spotlight, are you? You're always bouncing off things.'

Bella had to admit it.

'Shame, though. He seemed a real sweetheart.'

105

'Yes,' said Bella sadly. 'Yes.'

Lottie didn't mention him again. For the rest of the week she talked about her work, the contract she had failed to nail and the next one she had in her sights, and about easing Bella back into a social life. Bella did her best to respond in kind. But she begged off the social life until she had collected some of her things from her old room at her mother's house.

She went down on Friday night after work. She had bought herself a little weekend bag by then. She knew her mother would not appreciate the backpack. She wouldn't like most of Bella's charity-shop clothes either. Fortunately the new silk kimono ought to hit the spot.

Kevin met her at the station, which surprised Bella, and when they got home, her mother flung open the front door and seized her in her arms, which surprised her even more.

'Let me look at you. You've lost weight. But your skin looks good, and I love your hair.'

I do wish that the first thing she did when she saw me wasn't always to make an inventory of my personal assets, thought Bella, sighing inwardly.

Aloud she said, 'Lottie sent me to her hairdresser, Carlos. Do you remember him from uni? Lottie says he's going to be very successful.'

Her mother feathered Bella's newly trimmed blonde locks against the light. 'Well, he's done a lovely job on you,' she said approvingly. 'Come in, darling. Come in. You know the Nevilles and the Jackson-Smythes . . .'

It set the tone for the weekend. There were to be

guests for every meal, and even more for drinks before the meals. Janet had always been hospitable but since she'd married Kevin she seemed to have grown absolutely feverish about it, thought Bella. It was as if a meal didn't really happen unless there was an outside witness to it, preferably with a title and an important job in the City.

But there was no doubt her mother was struggling to be proud of her this weekend. She introduced Bella to everyone as 'my clever ecologist daughter, so like my mother-in-law'. Since Janet and Georgia had always got on, in a mutually uncomprehending sort of way, there was no hidden putdown in that.

Not so Janet's references to Finn. She always told people it had been an amicable divorce and she certainly never stopped him seeing the children. But Bella remembered the tears and her mother's white cold face when her father had first announced that he was leaving. He needed to be free, he'd said. He had to go where the wind blew him round the world, not keep checking in with mortgage payments and Parent Teacher meetings.

'There was never another woman,' Janet would tell people lightly. 'He left me for a yak.'

And, indeed, Finn's next expedition, before the divorce was even final, had been to Mongolia. So people would laugh and say he was incorrigible. But Bella knew that it had hurt Janet horribly when it happened and it hurt still. She and her mother were not on the same wavelength and they never would be, but there are some things you can't avoid knowing if you're part of a family. And would never say aloud, of course.

'Have you spoken to your father?' Janet asked on Saturday morning.

They were in the local town, doing some mother and daughter bonding in Janet's favourite dress shop.

'No. I sent him a text when I got back and I've tried a couple of emails but he hasn't called to me. I suppose he's somewhere out of range.'

'Patagonia,' said Janet, who always knew what her ex-husband was doing. 'Georgia said they might meet up somewhere before she comes back to London. She's coming for Christmas by the way.'

'Oh, that's nice. Will Neill and Val be here too?'

Janet's face closed. 'I've no idea. Neill is being very difficult at the moment.'

'Really? It's not just me he's avoiding, then,' said Bella, relieved. She had been hurt by Neill's failure to reply to her messages.

Janet sniffed. 'I suspect he's been talking to his father. Finn would never make up his mind about Christmas either. But now you're back, you'll be coming, won't you? Unless you're going back to that island?'

'No, Ma. That's finished.'

'Good.' Janet patted Bella's shoulder awkwardly, as if she were afraid of offending her. 'I mean, you said it was a dead end, didn't you? Do you want to talk to Kevin about a job? I know he'd like to help.'

'No, thanks, Ma. I've got a job to tide me over and the long-term career search is in hand.'

'You're such a capable girl,' said her mother involuntarily. 'I wish I'd been more like you when I was your age.'

Bella stared. 'You're one of the most capable woman I know. You're always organising things.'

'Not when I was your age. Wouldn't say boo to a goose. Your father used to say—' Janet stopped abruptly. 'Well, that's ancient history. Now, what about me buying you something smart for those interviews? And some good warm trousers, so you can walk round the golf course with me tomorrow.'

Normally Bella would have said no, she had been buying her own clothes since she was fourteen and anyway they never liked the same things. But this time, something made her say, 'Yes, thank you, Ma. That would be great.'

Janet flushed. 'Really?'

She looked so surprised that Bella felt a flicker of compunction. She gave her mother a quick, awkward hug.

So Janet presented her with an outfit for a cold-but-smart day in the country with the wealthy middle-aged, plus a discreetly expensive business suit for interviews. And then there was The Frock. For Christmas parties and special occasions, said Janet, though Bella thought it made her look like a middle-aged golf wife on the prowl. All of them made Bella feel mildly depressed. Janet, however, was delighted.

'You have lost a lot of weight. Wish I could,' she congratulated her daughter.

But actually Bella was a bit shocked to discover how much thinner she was than when she had left. All her trousers were so loose she could stuff a cushion down the front of them and a couple of pairs actually wouldn't stay up any more. Shirts flapped and her smartest party dress was unwearable because she kept moving around inside the boned bodice.

'Bella's gone down two sizes,' Janet told her Saturday night guests, plainly delighted.

Bella soon understood why. They all congratulated Janet as if this were the highest maternal achievement. But Kevin, who never commented on his wife or step-daughter's appearance, said it didn't suit Bella, she was looking ill. And when she came to pack her clothes to take back with her to London, it disconcerted her to find how few of them still fitted.

She knew she had lost weight on the island. Everyone did. They were racing around so much and there was often not quite enough food to go round. But the emails said they all started going back to normal the moment they got home. Whereas she . . . She looked at herself in the mirror. Could she have lost *more* weight over this last crazy week? She had been eating, hadn't she?

But, thinking about it, she realised that she hadn't, or not much, not since her dinner with Lottie. She was never hungry at breakfast. At lunch-time she walked round, glad to get out into the air and move after the confines of her cubby hole. Bella tried but she couldn't remember buying herself so much as a sandwich for lunch. In the evening, she could only be bothered to eat if Lottie was there.

Could her stepfather be right? Bella felt a flicker of alarm. Lottie's older sister had had a bout of anorexia in her teens and she always said that it crept up on her. She'd started losing weight, everyone admired her, so she decided to lose more. And then she couldn't stop.

I'm not a teenager, thought Bella. That's not going to happen to me. I am in charge of my life. But she might have to take care to remember to eat, for a while.

The possibility did not even occur to her mother, though. 'You can't be too thin,' she laughed.

They were at Janet's golf club by then, where her buddies from the Ladies' Section were frankly envious. They'd never had much time for Bella before. It was mutual, though Bella tried not to let it show, out of a sort of exasperated affection for her mother. They either interogatted her or offered advice on man-catching so explicit that it made Bella wince, which she tried to hide. But they were experts in diets.

'Wish my daughter could lose a few pounds. You look like a model, darling,' said the Social Secretary, her eyes snapping.

How could you say 'darling' and make it sound like 'ratface'? The woman looked like a witch, too, with a thin scarlet mouth and expressionless Botoxed face. Bella was not impressed. But her mother preened, so she bit back a sharp retort. The husband of the Botoxed one had been knighted in the last New Year's Honours, and Janet was dying to get them to come to her next drinks party.

'She must be in love,' said the Captain of the Ladies' Section. She was wealthy singleton with a racy past and an eye for other people's husbands. Bella often thought that the others only forgave her because of her mansion on the hill and her top-of-the-range Mercedes convertible. 'That makes the pounds fly away, I always find.'

Everyone laughed sycophantically, though no one was really amused, thought Bella. The thin ones didn't like the reminder that they didn't have lovers and the fat ones didn't want to remember that they weren't thin.

I want to get out of here.

But Bella made the effort and laughed too, though she was starting to feel stifled. It often happened when she was with her mother's friends.

'Have you got a boyfriend, Bella?' said the witch queen.

'No,' she said.

'Yes,' said her mother loudly. She gave that trill of artificial laughter that always made Bella want to put her head under a cushion until she stopped. 'Of course, her lovely Francis will be abroad for a while yet.'

The Ladies' Section knew marketing when they saw it.

'Broke up, did you?'

'No,' said Bella. Well, you couldn't break up if you were never an item anyway, could you?

Her mother relaxed visibly. The daughter's boyfriend was a very important status symbol in the Ladies' Section. Bella started to count the hours before she could decently leave.

Her mother tried to persuade her to stay until Monday morning. 'You know how dreadful Sunday trains are, Bella. You might just as well stay the night. You can go up with Kevin on the train tomorrow and then straight into work.'

But Bella felt that if she stayed any longer she would scream. 'I've got all those clothes to take back,' she said. 'Don't want to haul them through the rush hour. Besides, I want to get myself sorted before the start of the working week.'

Her mother argued but her stepfather came to her rescue.

'Let the girl do what makes her comfortable. We'll see her soon.'

And on the way to the station he said, 'Don't want to pry. None of my business. But you know you can always come home, don't you? If your plans don't work out. Or anything.'

And when he took her bags out of the car he said hesitantly, 'All right for money?'

Even though he wasn't a touchy feely sort of step-father, Bella hugged him then.

'I'm fine, Kevin. Really. Don't worry about me.'

'We do. Can't help it,' he said gruffly, pink-cheeked but pleased. 'Look after yourself. And don't forget, there's always your old room, if you need it.'

But when she settled down into her seat on the train, it felt like being let out of prison. It was a slow, Sunday afternoon train, meandering through the darkening countryside. Eventually it got too dark to see anything but the inside of the carriage reflected in the windows. Bella pulled out her phone and checked her messages. There were several from old friends, hearing that she was back and wanting to meet, and one from Neill, at last. Oddly cagey, she thought. No invitation to visit still, but at least he said he'd be up in London next week and maybe they could have a coffee, if he could fit it in. This was so unlike him that Bella was worried.

But then there was a text from a number she knew and she forgot about Neill, friends, everything.

Call me.

Bella sat bolt upright. It had been sent yesterday evening. There were other missed calls, and then a message on her voice mail.

'Bella, where are you? Can we talk?'

Without giving herself time to think, she pressed the Call button.

He picked up at once. 'Bella.' He sounded amazingly relieved.

'Hi,' she said cautiously.

'Where are you?'

'On a train.'

'Oh.' He clearly didn't expect that. 'Why? Where? What's happening? Are you taking off again?' He was uncharacteristically distracted.

'I spent the weekend with my mother. I'm heading back to London now.'

'Oh. Right. Look – I know what I said. But I can't stop thinking about you. Do you think we could, well, give it another go? Your way? Not telling anyone, trying to keep it quiet. I mean, it's worth a try.'

She couldn't speak.

' Isn't it? Bella . . . Bella, are you there?'

She swallowed hard. 'Yes, I'm here. And, yes, it's worth a try.'

'Thank God,' he said quietly.

She was astonished. 'What?'

114

'What train are you on? Which station are you coming in to? I want to meet you.'

It sounded like heaven. She gave him the details. She even braced herself for curious glances and even, maybe, someone catching them with a phone camera.

But she needn't have worried. Waterloo on Sunday afternoon was as empty as she had ever seen it. And the untidy man slouching towards her in scuffed jeans and a grubby Batman tee-shirt didn't attract a second glance from anyone.

Bella wheeled the big suitcase through the barrier and walked straight into his arms. He held her as if he would never let her go.

7

'Unexpected Delights in Décor' – *Mondaine Magazine*

He took her hand and walked her out to the South Bank. There were swags of lights looped along the Embankment on the other side of the river. They went to the parapet and stood there, arms round each other. Trains rumbled across Hungerford Bridge above them and the dark water rippled and surged around its struts.

'It's like fairyland. All those lights. I've never seen this before. Or never noticed.'

'Nor me,' said Richard, rubbing his chin against the top of her head.

'I've missed you.'

He groaned. 'Me too.'

'I couldn't wait to get away from my mother today. Just because some silly woman at her club said I must be in love.'

His arms tightened and for a moment he said nothing at all.

'I've been moping around like an idiot.'

'I've been snarling at everyone. Poor Ian thinks I'm losing my mind.'

'Ian the security man?'

'Ian the provider of anonymous cars and multiple alibis,' he said, that note of laughter back in his voice at last. 'You're going to have to meet him.'

She rubbed her face against his jacket. 'So we're not going to be entirely secret then.'

He kissed her. 'We're going to need a couple of co-conspirators, I think. Your Lottie will have to know anyway. Do you mind?'

'Mind Lotts knowing? Of course not. She's my best friend. Anyway, she'd smell a rat if I suddenly went round beaming from ear to ear without telling her why.'

'Are you? Beaming from ear to ear?'

'What do you think? Just look at me!'

They kissed for a lot longer this time.

In the end he raised his head and said shakily, 'We'd better walk or this will get out of hand.'

'Goody.'

'Walk, woman. Walk.'

They did, for at least a couple of steps. Then he stopped and turned her in towards him and they kissed again. In spite of the cold, Bella felt as warm as toast, all yielding and open. She was really glad that Lottie had given her that sapphire kimono, she thought. What to wear in bed wasn't a problem but it was hard to keep the magic going if you had to prowl round in cast-off clothes afterwards.

Sapphire kimono!

She hauled herself away from him with a yelp.

'I had a bloody *suitcase*. Where is it? What have I done with it? Did I walk away and leave it on Waterloo Station?'

He dropped his arms and looked round. 'No. No, I had it. Ah, it's there.'

He sprinted back to the place where they had leaned against the wall looking out across the water. The suitcase still stood there, its handle pulled up. It looked like a small, abandoned alien, hunched and reproachful.

He dragged it back to her, bubbling with laughter. 'Think we got a bit carried away. If we'd left the thing much longer someone would have reported it and the police would have come along and blown it up. Maybe we ought to get inside before we cause a major incident.'

'Sounds good to me.'

He placed the suitcase in front of them and fished out his phone. 'Ian, we're on the South Bank. Can you pick us up by the National Theatre? Usual place.' A pause while Ian clearly asked a question. And Richard, looking at her, answered him. 'No. Everything's perfect. Just perfect.'

They went to a house in a village off the M40 somewhere. Ian drove with Richard sitting beside him.

He murmured an apology about that but Bella said, 'Just as well. Don't know how much longer I can keep my hands off you,' and he gave a squawk of laughter and thrust her into the back seat without ceremony.

Ian, very sensibly, pretended not to hear.

Once they were on their way, Richard swung round to talk to her. 'This is a secret, right? Not just because of you and me. Ian's job is to keep me safe from assassins and people who throw paint. He's not my driver and it is not part of his duties to fix me up with bolt holes.'

Ian grinned. 'You're welcome.'

'Yes, and I'm very grateful. But this is the last time.'

Bella mimed a kiss and watched with deep satisfaction the way Richard's eyes kindled.

'I'll take charge of the bolt hole aspect, shall I?' she said sweetly.

'Probably easier,' said Ian. 'His Highness has credit cards in – er – pen names. But these things always get out. And, if I may make a suggestion, probably best not to make a habit of going anywhere too often. Even if the press don't sniff it out, you can never be too careful with the general public.'

'Thank you. I'll bear that in mind.'

Richard looked irritated. 'I don't like leaving it to you.'

'Good for you to have someone else in charge. I bet you get your own way all the time.'

But both Richard and Ian laughed noisily at this idea. Ian said, 'The Prince is a slave to his diary.'

'Which reminds me,' Richard said. 'I'll put a copy on a memory stick for you. It won't change much between now and Christmas, at least.'

'Thank you. I think. So where are we going now?'

Richard said, 'House belonging to a friend of Ian's who's away. We have to be extra careful with this one. It could be traced back.'

'How careful is extra careful? No lights? No flushing the loo in case the neighbours hear?'

Richard's eyes danced. 'I don't think we have to be that self-denying. Just not answering the door will do.'

But Ian said, 'Actually, no lights on in the front of the place would be a good idea.'

'See?' said Bella. 'I'm a natural at this undercover stuff.' And stuck her tongue out at Richard naughtily, just so she could watch his eyes kindle all over again. 'You are *so* rewarding,' she murmured, as Ian looked over his shoulder and pulled out into the fast lane on the motorway.

Richard's expression promised revenge. She wriggled in happy anticipation.

The house was a tiny detached stone cottage next to an untidy farm entrance, off a single-track lane with high hedges. Ian drove in off the road, parked out of sight in the lee of a privet hedge and they all got out.

'Couldn't be better,' said Richard.

But Ian was not happy. 'This place is a kidnapper's wet dream. Let me book you into the pub.'

But Richard waved the idea away. 'You know the guy. I know the guy. Nobody followed us. Relax.'

'But—'

'Ian?'

'Yes?'

'Go inside and check it out. Do whatever you must. Then push off to the pub and don't come back till morning.'

Ian threw his hands up. 'Whatever you say, boss.'

The moment he'd disappeared into the house, Richard and Bella went into each other's arms, kissing frantically.

'You're a dirty rotten tease,' he said

'Would you say rotten? I thought I was quite good.'

'God, I want you.'

'Glad to hear it.'

Ian came back. He approached them with caution and a certain amount of throat-clearing.

'No problem. The back door is rotten, so anyone could kick it in. I suggest you lock the door from the kitchen to the rest of the house. Everything else looks fine. And keep your pager with you at all times.'

'Yus, h'officer.'

'I'll take the food in and then I'll be at the pub. It's a quarter of a mile further on. I can be here in three minutes, if you call.'

'We won't. And we'll take the food in,' said Richard firmly. 'You push off and have fun.'

'Likewise,' said Ian. Heard what he'd said, clearly wished he hadn't, slapped the key into Richard's hand and left in disarray.

If he'd looked in his rear-view mirror he would have seen his delinquent charges hopping about, clutching their sides with mirth.

Richard wouldn't let Bella help unload.

'This is Man's Work,' he said, inflating his chest and beating it King Kong-style. But, rather to her surprise, he got her case, a carrier bag of food from Marks and Spencer and his own overnight bag indoors in record time.

He closed the door, locked it, pulled the rusty old curtain draught excluder across it and said softly, 'Come here, you wicked tease. You've been taunting me for fifty-seven miles. Now you pay.'

'Promises, promises.'

121

But neither of them could hold out any longer. Richard just about managed to shrug off his coat before Bella jumped at him, hauling at his sweater and shirt so that she could get her hands on his skin, kissing his throat, his ear, the hard jaw and soft hair. And then she reached his mouth.

She found the button at the top of his jeans.

'Jesus!'

She leaned back in his arms. She was breathless and every nerve quivered. But she was still ready to challenge him.

'Oh, sorry, do you want to unpack first?'

'AAAARGH!' he shouted, and went into full King Kong mode.

He picked her up and thundered up the narrow stairs, so that they shook. He hesitated, briefly, at the top.

'Not the front,' Bella managed. 'Ian said. Nothing facing the road.'

So Richard plunged into the back bedroom and they fell together on to the bed, their clothes coming off in a tangle and falling where they were thrown.

A long lovely time later, Bella lay with her head against his shoulder and his arm wrapped round her, holding her close. She considered the strange shapes in the moonlit room.

'Is that your shirt on the the lampshade? Heck, is it even a lampshade?'

'As far as I remember, he said sleepily, 'my shirt is somewhere on the stairs.'

'Umm . . .' She wriggled, remembering. 'Think you could be right. So what's that?'

He didn't open his eyes. 'No idea.'

She pummelled his ribs. 'You could at least look.'

He opened one eye. Then the other. 'No idea – hey, that's not clothes. That's a cat.'

'It can't be a cat.'

'I can see whiskers,' he said, really interested now.

He got out of bed – when had they got under the covers? – and, after carefully drawing the curtains together, put on the light.

'Ow . . . ow!' said Bella, pulling a pillow over her head to cover her eyes.

'It *is* a cat,' Richard said triumphantly.

She pushed the pillow away, to see him reach up – he was so tall, he could lay the palm of his hand flat against the low ceiling – and carefully remove something from the wildly swinging light fitting.

'There,' he said, lobbing it on to the bed.

Bella prodded it cautiously. But the fur was definitely fake and it felt more like a limp cushion than anything that had ever been alive.

'I think you'll find,' said Richard in the tones of a connoisseur, 'that it's a nightdress case. Probably hand-made.'

'You're joking. Aren't you?'

'Nope.'

Bella picked the thing up cautiously and shook it out. He was right. It was made of orange-coloured fake fur, with limp, stubby paws and pipe-cleaner whiskers. On one side these were bent out of shape. Richard took it away from her and straightened the whiskers briskly. Then he turned it upside down and parted the fur to reveal a pouch where someone was supposed to install their night attire.

'There. You see?'

He flipped it back and made pouncey movements over the covers towards her. The cat had a louche, piratical expression.

'It's winking at me,' said Bella, affronted.

'Can you blame it?'

He took it away from her and put it on top of the wardrobe.

'How did you know it was a nightdress case?' she said, suspiciously.

'It goes with the job. When you've opened as many school Bring and Buy sales as I have, you get to know the product.'

He kissed her casually. It was breathtakingly possessive.

He thinks we belong together, she thought, startled.

'Hungry?'

She yawned and stretched. 'Mmm. 'S'pose so.'

'I could eat a giraffe,' he announced cheerfully. 'I'll go and see what Ian has brought us.'

He thundered off downstairs.

Bella got out of bed more slowly and patted the covers, as if they were the blanket on a friendly horse. There was distinct chill in the air but, with nothing obvious to wrap herself in, she ran downstairs too. She flipped open her case, dragged out the sapphire kimono, and padded barefoot into the kitchen.

Richard was in the kitchen. He had found his trousers at some point on the journey and was standing, be-trousered but bare-chested, at the kitchen table, unpacking the Marks and Sparks bag.

Bella went up to him and put her arms round his waist. 'What have you found?'

He picked up her hand and kissed her knuckles absently. 'It's a real boy's bag, I'm afraid. Everything for the microwave. How do you feel about pizza?'

She kissed his shoulderblade and watched the muscles twitch responsively. 'Whatever.'

The kitchen spanned the width of the house. It had a sagging sofa at one end, covered in a hand-knitted throw, beside an open fire. This, Bella saw, was already laid.

'Do you think we can light it?'

'Of course,' said Richard, puzzled.

'That means we have to clear it out and re-lay it before we leave,' she said warningly.

'Naturally.'

'Well, have you ever done it before?'

'How hard can it be?'

'It's a skill,' said Bella, who had lived with open fires several times in her life and never got the hang of them.

He waved a lordly – no, princely – hand and announced, 'If we can't work out how it's done, we'll Google it.'

She was sceptical. 'If you say so, dear.'

He kissed her quickly. 'Trust me. I'm not as useless as I look.'

She shivered voluptuously. 'Not useless at all.'

His eyes darkened. 'Now look. Do you want feeding or don't you?'

'Yes,' she said hurriedly, retreating behind the table. 'Yes, you're hungry and I was telling myself only today that I need to remember to eat. So break out your pizza.'

But Ian had provided red wine and olives and garlic bread and various cold meats as well.

So Richard lit the fire and Bella pulled cushions off the sofa and every chair in the place and made a nest in front of the flames. She found glasses and plates and even a corkscrew – though Richard said he knew how to open a bottle of wine with just a key, a trick he had learned from his obligatory stint in the Navy – and they ate nibbles and pizza in front of a friendly blaze.

He was, she found, surprisingly good at knowing when to feed the fire to keep it crackling away merrily.

'Norman castles run in the family,' he said lightly. 'I once met a World War II veteran who told me that life was so hard when he was child that he had ice on the inside of his bedroom window in winter. I didn't like to say that there's still ice on the inside of mine in Scotland.'

Bella was appalled. 'But why?'

'Tradition. And living in a Listed Building that is also an Ancient Monument. And it's character-forming, allegedly.'

She was oddly moved. 'It's not all joy being a prince, is it?'

He kissed her nose. 'It's not all joy being an ecologist counting fish either. Into each life a little rain must fall. Shall I put on another pizza? Artichoke or American Hot?'

'Hot.'

When he brought it back, she nibbled at a slice, partly to be companionable, partly to soak up the wine, which was truly delicious.

'Ian's taste in wine is better than his food,' she said idly. 'Next time I'll cook for you.'

'I'll hold you to that.'

She held up the glass of wine so that the firelight played through it, turning it ruby red.

'What's your best memory?'

'What?'

'You must have a good memory. A place you go to when everything else is shite.'

He raised himself on one elbow, staring at her curiously. 'Sounds as if you have one, at least. Tell?'

Bella smiled reminiscently. 'My grandmother Georgia's birthday one year. You will –' she corrected herself '– may like my grandmother Georgia. She made us all go for a huge walk, so my parents couldn't argue. And then my brother and I got to recite things she'd taught us. Neill had "Lord Lundy" but she said I was too young for politics, so I had to do a bit of *Winnie-the-Pooh*. She's a tough cookie, my grandmother.'

'And . . .?'

'My mother laughed and so did my father and they both said we were wonderful and my father took photographs. And then I knocked over some sodding enormous Chinese urn with a massive spiky plant in it and they all laughed even harder.'

'Was this when your father told you not to be an actress?'

She was momentarily side-tracked. 'Did I tell you that? I'd forgotten.'

'I hadn't,' he said, his mouth full of pepperoni pizza.

'And then my grandmother said it was too late to go home and everyone had had too much to drink to drive, and we all stayed the night in this little pub. Wales, I think it was. They only had three rooms, so my brother and I had to share. And he decided that I was too little to be left up there on my own while they all had grown-up dinner, so he came and read me a story. It was something he was learning at school. Might have been Dickens. I don't know. I just remember falling asleep to this exciting story and the grown-ups talking away downstairs as if they liked each other. There were oak beams in the ceiling and creaky floors and the smell of furniture polish and summer . . .'

She stopped.

'Am I making sense?'

His eyes were warm. 'Lots of sense.'

She held up the glass again, looking at him through the firelit wine. 'Your turn.'

He put his wine glass down and stretched out, looking into the fire.

'A good memory? My first climb, I suppose.'

It was so unexpected, she lowered the glass and stared at him blankly.

He was rueful. 'I got into terrible trouble. For the first time ever.'

She was even more confused. 'Your best memory is getting into trouble?'

'No, of course not. Especially as everyone else involved was carpeted too. I never wanted to get anyone into trouble. But I suffered from congenital good behaviour. Still do, I suppose. And it was such a great feeling.'

She was intrigued. 'How old were you?'

'Oh, I don't know. Eleven, twelve. Not old enough or strong enough, anyway. But I've always liked climbing things. And this father of a school friend said that if I was going to climb anyway, I'd better learn how to do it properly.'

'You *climb*?'

'Anything that goes up high enough,' he said serenely. 'Rocks. Mountains. Masts. I'm a reasonable sailor but that's always the best part of it for me, climbing the mast in a brisk wind. There are several good walls in assorted palaces, too. I've been up most of 'em. But you never forget that first climb, when you actually get to the top and don't give up. I scrambled up this bit of scree in Skye. I remember standing on the top with my head in the clouds. It felt as if I could do *anything*.'

'Good heavens.'

He picked up his wine again and slugged it back, looking into the fire, as logs shifted and fell apart.

'You know what's really sad? When most people feel like that, they say they feel like a king.'

'So?'

A muscle was working in his jaw. Bella wanted to reach out and calm it, but somehow she thought that this was something he needed to tell himself, not her.

'Well?' she prompted gently.

'My father's been King most of my life. I don't think he's ever felt like that. And neither will I when—' He broke off. 'Hell. We're not supposed to be talking about bloody families. I want to know about *you*.'

Bella punched a couple of cushions, and took the glass away from him. She set it down carefully on the hearth.

'My pleasure. Let me introduce you to my very smart new kimono. Gift of my friend Lottie. For some reason they've put a ducky little tassel on the belt.' She folded his fingers round the tassel. 'Got it?'

'Got it,' he said gravely, leaning over her and starting to pull the silk sash very, very slowly.

'Well done,' she said, approving and just a little breathless.

'Mmmm?'

She felt hot and cold, between the flames and the shadows; weak as water under his hands – and, at the same time, the most powerful force in the world.

She smelled wood smoke and wine, with a side order of garlic bread. The old cushions felt heavenly. The intensity in his eyes was dazzling. It felt so right to be here, in this place, at this moment.

They stopped talking.

8

'Can You Keep a Secret?' – *Girl About Town*

It was the start of the strangest two weeks of her life. Basically she felt she was living two lives. There was the Bella who was picking up the strands of her old life, seeing friends, working at the dentist's surgery, meeting her brother for a drink.

And there was the Bella who took Richard's phone calls and made dates to meet him which got cancelled at the last minute.

Lottie, the only one who knew, shook her head. 'He's got you on a string.'

'He can't help it,' said Bella defensively. 'His father isn't well. Richard's taking up the slack. And I can't call him. He's always in a meeting or on his way somewhere. Surrounded by people anyway. So he can't talk, not properly. He has to phone me when he's alone. Well, he does if we want to keep it secret.'

Lottie sniffed. 'Which leaves him calling all the shots.'

'Yes, but that wasn't his choice,' Bella said candidly. 'He was willing to take our chances with people finding out. I was the one who wanted to keep it, well, private.'

Lottie shook her head over this lunacy. 'Why on earth?'

'I thought it would be easier to back away from, if it didn't work out. You know the idea. Keep it casual and nobody gets hurt.'

'This is *casual*?'

Bella stiffened. 'We're not committed or anything.'

'You could have fooled me,' muttered Lottie into the fridge.

'Neither of us has made any promises,' Bella told the back of her head, loudly and clearly.

Lottie took out her breakfast orange juice. 'OK, OK. Keep your hair on. You're both fancy-free. You can each date anyone you like.'

Bella glared.

'No, I thought you didn't mean that,' said Lottie with satisfaction. 'Oh, go to work and give someone else hell. I need to put on a happy face.'

But, even if her flat-mate disapproved, at least Bella could *talk* to Lottie about Richard. With everyone else, she had to remember not to mention him. What was worse, she couldn't talk about anywhere they'd been together in case it invited questions and she let something slip. It made for some silent coffee breaks.

'This thing is changing my character,' she told Richard when they snatched half an hour in a bookshop café in Piccadilly.

'Mine too,' he said cheerfully. 'Until I met you, I'd never gone out in disguise before.' Today he was wearing jeans and a lopsided baseball cap along with

132

Clark Kent spectacles with no lenses in them.

She leaned forward and straightened the baseball cap. 'Your own mother wouldn't know you.'

'I know. I'm getting good at this. The secret is to look like a nerd. Nobody looks at nerds twice.'

She grinned. 'Greater love hath no man, than he will dress up as a nerd for his lady.'

He made a face. 'Not just dress up. I'm playing hide and seek with my security patrol too. And those guys are *trained*.'

That hadn't occurred to Bella. She said in quick alarm, 'You're not putting yourself in danger?'

'Nah. I'm just being a bit less amenable than usual. It gets us half-hours like these while they scamper round looking for me.'

But Bella was still worried.

He touched her cheek reassuringly. 'It's good for them. A couple of those guys had written me off as a pussycat. Now they know different.'

'But—'

'Hey, they were due a challenge.'

She stared at him for a long moment and made a discovery. 'You're enjoying it.'

'Too right.' He caught himself. 'Though, of course, I'm only doing it for you.'

'I feel truly cherished,' said Bella with irony.

'So you should.' Even though he was teasing, the warmth in his eyes was like a caress.

She laughed and conceded him the point. And after he had slipped away, back to business-as-usual, she carried that look with her all day.

It was turning out to be more difficult to see each other than Bella could ever have imagined. 'It's the time of year,' Richard said. 'People go mad, trying to shoehorn in a Royal event before Christmas. One day I'm in London in the morning, Cornwall for lunch and Manchester for dinner in the evening. Crazy. It will be better in the New Year.'

'You were going to let me see your diary,' Bella reminded him. They were curled round each other on Lottie's sofa, drinking hot chocolate and half watching an old Audrey Hepburn movie.

He was surprised. 'I thought Ian had already sent it to you. I'll get it sorted tomorrow.'

Lottie came in from work then, tired but pleased with the way her evening PR event had gone. Richard untangled himself and stood up, courteously. Bella turned off the television.

'No, don't do that,' said Lottie, kicking off her shoes and padding across to the fire. 'Finish your film. I'm beat. I'll just fall into bed.'

But she was so obviously cold and hyped up that Bella insisted on making her some hot chocolate too while Richard built up the fire so that Lottie could toast her toes.

'I have to be going soon anyway,' he said with regret. 'Early start tomorrow. I'm on board ship for breakfast.'

Lottie shuddered and held her hands to the blaze. 'Rather you than me.'

'It'll be fine. The only problem is sorting out time for Bella and me to be together.'

'He's very inventive,' Bella remarked, bringing in

134

Lottie's hot chocolate. 'He escapes from his minders and comes dressed as a nerd. So far we've met in a bank, a bookshop, and on the main concourse at St Pancras Station. And nobody has given us a second glance.'

'People see what they expect to see,' Lottie agreed.

But later, when Richard had gone, she said, 'I have an idea. Do you know which evening receptions he's going to? Say, striking distance of London?'

Bella didn't. But Ian did eventually disgorge Richard's official programme.

'Poor lamb, first of all he has to go to endless drinks receptions. Then he goes on to dinners and gets made speeches at,' she told Lottie.

'Hmm. Can you still do silver service?'

When they were students, they had both earned extra dosh from moonlighting as waitresses at weddings and directors' lunches. Bella said now, 'I suppose so. Why?'

'Because I think you ought to tell Anthea that you're available for some evening work.'

'What? Why? I'm not short of money—'

Lottie sighed patiently. 'There's no reason for Richard to be the only one who's inventive. You get yourself on to the caterers' waitress roster and surprise him. Ta da!'

Bella thought about it. 'That's not a bad idea, Lotts.'

'Although you'd have to get clearance to work at Royal dos, I suppose.'

'I'll ask Ian,' said Bella, more and more intrigued by the idea.

The security officer thought it was a hoot and put her in touch with a terrifying woman who provided stand-in

135

footmen and butlers for big Palace occasions. With Christmas coming up, Ellen Catering would be looking for extra occasional staff, she said, and with a Royal security officer as one referee, Bella was a godsend. Could she also provide three other references, including one from a minister of the cloth and one from a JP? Bella did. Nothing happened.

In fact, it took so long that she had almost forgotten the wheeze. Then one night in November, she got a phone call out of the blue. Would she be available that night to serve at a reception at the Landscape Gallery? Their staff had been struck by 'flu and Lottie had mentioned that Ms Greenwood might be available.

Bella consulted the coded notes she had transcribed into her own diary and saw that Richard would be going to the reception before dinner with the gallery's director. Realistically there was not much chance of seeing him, still less managing to talk to him, she knew. Still, at least they would be in the same room and, if she got lucky, she could wave across the room at him. They had developed a series of rather good secret agents' hand signals.

'Fine,' she said. 'Where and when?'

They told her. Also, could she provide her own black trousers and shoes, as flat as possible? They would give her their uniform steward's jacket, but she would need something black to wear underneath it.

Bella swapped duties with another receptionist and left work early to race home and bundle her supplies together. She did not have time to get out to the caterer's West London headquarters, but turned up at the tradesmen's entrance of the gallery as arranged.

The kitchen was in the state of controlled ferment that Bella recognised from her student years. She slotted in with the ease of long practice. The only thing that surprised her was that her steward's jacket turned out to be quite sexy, white with black piping, nipped in at the waist and rather low-cut.

'Not ideal. White shows every mark and people will spill things,' said the organiser briskly. 'But the laundry didn't get our black uniforms back in time. So we're down to our summer yacht club rig. Oh, well, at least the presence of Royalty should stop a food fight breaking out.'

It was a huge party, nearly a thousand guests, Bella calculated. It spilled over five galleries and two floors and out on to a heated terrace. She was run off her feet, carrying large silver trays of canapés to the furthest corners of the room, fending off hungry guests until she got to her appointed station. As she expected, she did not get so much as a sniff of the Royal party.

'You're good,' said the organiser, impressed. 'Take this through to the Woodley Gallery. It's for the directors' party. Make sure the ravening hordes don't strip it bare before you get there.'

'That means it's the hypoallergenic tray for the Big Wigs,' one of the other waitresses told her, looking harassed. 'Sir Brian Woodley is the guy who gave the money for this new gallery, and he can't eat eggs, dairy, nuts . . . God knows what else. All that worrying over his billions, I guess. Who'd be rich? Good luck!'

Bella got the tray through the crowds and was

directed to the official party. The speeches were over and they were standing in front of a picture of a cliff overlooking a stormy sea. She moved quietly among them, concentrating on keeping the big tray level and trying to identify the food-challenged benefactor, when she heard a strangled sound to her left.

Looking round, she saw Richard staring at her.

Staring? Glaring, more like, completely ignoring the VIP who was talking to him, and narrowing his eyes at her as if she and her canapés would poison him.

She recoiled. Her tray tilted dangerously.

'Whoops,' said one of the VIPs, restoring it to the horizontal.

'I'm so sorry,' murmured Bella, tearing her eyes away from Richard.

He looked furious. She had never thought of that and was completely taken aback. So she concentrated so hard on what she was doing that it *hurt*.

Nobody else seemed to notice or to blame her for the near accident. Indeed, she got a kind word from the director and a nod of appreciation from the egg-allergic benefactor. But Bella could only be thankful when the tray was cleared and she could race back to the kitchen.

Only, as she approached the staircase – 'One moment,' said a voice behind her.

She turned. It was Richard, still furious, she could see, but hiding it well under a layer of courtesy as he shed his attendant VIP with smiling charm and strode over to her, through the crowd. She flattened herself against the wall, in the hopes that he wanted to get past her. But no such luck.

'Can you get me another of those anchovy pastries?' he said loudly.

'Y-y-yes, of course.'

'Sir.'

'Wh-what?'

He said under his breath, 'You call me "Sir". Or people will notice.' But for once his eyes weren't smiling when he said it.

What was wrong?

'Of course, Sir,' said Bella, confused.

'Well, jump to it then.'

She jumped.

The kitchen was impressed. 'Hey, His Royalness likes our anchovy straws,' said the organiser. 'Nibbles by Royal Appointment, no less.'

The chef put a fresh batch into the oven and Bella took a smaller tray on a quick circuit of the nearest room, to be back as soon as the anchovy straws were cooked.

Fifteen minutes later, she was weaving her way through the guests on the big staircase again, this time carrying a small basket of warm savoury pastries, looking for Richard. When she finally saw him, he was standing firmly in front of a set of three paintings, listening to a guide, or it might even be the artist, hold forth to the director's party.

Bella hesitated. As if he could feel her eyes on him, Richard looked up and made one of their hand signals, acknowledging her and pointing towards the far end of the screen. It was so fleeting that nobody could have been certain that he did it, or not unless they were watching him closely.

He was a born conspirator, thought Bella, somewhat reassured. She must remember to tell him so.

She eased her way through the crowd. There was a respectful distance between the director's party and everyone else, which resulted in even tighter bunching at the margins. Several times she lost sight of Richard altogether and by the time she got to the edge of the screen, he and his host and fellow guests had moved on. She hovered, not sure whether she was meant to follow them or not. But even as she stood there undecided, she saw Richard's head turn and he was retracing his steps. He did not look up – he was frowning down at the catalogue – but he made a gesture which just *might* have been a signal to retreat behind the screen

Oh, hell, thought Bella. Still, what have I got to lose?

She backed round it, and found herself in a narrow space, full of chairs and signboards. She nearly backed out again, only almost immediately Richard was with her.

'Quick.' He put one hand over her shoulder and did something complicated to a wall-mounted console she had not noticed. A bit of wall slid away behind her. 'Inside.'

Bella backed, predictably stumbling a little. She caught hold of him to steady herself and stood there, blinking, as the wall closed again behind him. It left them in darkness except for the street lights beyond the uncurtained windows. Richard's breathing was thunderous.

They appeared to be in a small boardroom. Just at the moment, it was a dumping ground, not only for chairs but for stepladders, paint pots and, unmistakably, dust sheets. It smelled of turpentine.

'Gosh. They only just got the place finished in time, didn't they?' Bella said brightly.

But Richard was not interested in the gallery's refurbishment issues.

He towered over her like an avenging angel. 'Just what the hell do you think you're doing?'

Before she could answer, he drove her back against the baize-covered boardroom table and was kissing the life out of her.

When at last Bella got her breath back – *some* of her breath back – he was kissing her neck, her hair, her temples, and muttering. She swallowed hard.

'Um—'

'You're crazy,' he whispered urgently. 'You know that? Mad as a Cornish cat. This party is crawling with photographers, journalists of all persuasions, not to mention a whole bunch of people who would sell their granny for a name check in the gossip columns. And you waltz in, looking like something out of a 1940s musical, and expect to get *away* with it?'

'Nobody looks at waiters.'

His laugh was half a groan. 'They look at perky waitresses dressed like cabin boys. *Sexy* cabin boys.'

'Oh.'

'I just bet there's half a dozen dirty old men out there who already have your picture on their phone.' He flipped open her mess jacket and did some complicated breathing into her cleavage. 'God, you're gorgeous,' he said, muffled.

141

Bella's head went back and her toes started to do that curling-for-the-carpet thing again.

'Is this wise?' Her voice came out high and breathless.

'Nope.' He was laughing, intent, and there was no way he was letting her go.

She was wracked with pleasure. 'What if someone comes in?'

'Your problem,' he said smugly, not raising his head. 'I don't care.'

She gave an involuntary gasp of pleasure. 'Don't *do* that.'

He did lift his head then. 'Don't you like it?'

'That's not the point.'

'Thought so,' he said with satisfaction, and went back to driving her quietly out of her mind.

Bella stuffed her knuckles in her mouth and concentrated on not screaming the roof off. Then various irritating fastenings began to give and her concentration became even more focused. They toppled sideways, Richard laughing like a maniac. She felt a shoe fall away, then her trousers and suddenly he wasn't laughing any more and neither was she, as they pulled at each other's clothes almost desperately.

A bit – a tiny and diminishing bit – of her brain said: *I don't do things like this. And nor does he!*

But her body wasn't having any truck with that. There was that moment of total completion as he slid inside her and then they were off on a crazy ride and she stopped thinking at all.

She floated gently back to earth to find he had collapsed on top of her, his mouth against the naked

142

skin of her armpit. Naked? How did she get naked? She smelled warm skin and freshly laundered cotton and shampoo. Or was it aftershave? And, distantly, the whiff of new paint. She moistened her lips and discovered she was tasting champagne that she had never drunk.

'Oh, Lord,' she said, as her brain came tiptoeing timidly back into consciousness.

He stirred. His tumbled hair was soft against her sensitised breast. Bella shivered involuntarily.

'Whaaa?'

She began to push at him. 'We need to move. We've got clothes to find.'

At once he was alert. He sprang to his feet, only to trip over his own trousers and stagger, hobbled, to the boardroom table. He held on to it like a drunk in a Western saloon.

'Jesus!'

Bella could not help herself. She started to laugh and couldn't stop, lying on the carpet convulsed and helpless.

He looked down at her, sprawled and giggling. He ran a hand through his wild hair. A slow smile dawned.

'You are disgracefully tempting—'

And then the worst imaginable thing happened. A door that neither of them had been aware of opened at the far end of the room.

He dropped like a stone to the carpet and rolled under the table. Bella hauled up her trousers and grabbed her jacket, trying to wriggle deeper into the shadows and join him. She found that she had picked up a carpet burn.

'*Ouch!*'

She shut up at once. But was it too late? She could not see anyone for the piles of chairs and the big table. But that door was definitely still open. She held her breath, aware that Richard, too, was hardly breathing. His hand felt for her across the carpet and she realised that he was sitting with his knees up, his back against the table leg. He gathered her against him, comfortingly, and they braced themselves for discovery as Bella buttoned her steward's jacket.

A hectoring voice said, 'This looks terrible. If Sir Brian asks, you'll just have to say that the paint is still wet. We'll have to keep it locked. We can't have Royalty coming in here.'

'Too late,' muttered Richard into Bella's hair.

She started to shake again, with agonising, silent laughter.

The bossy person went out and closed the door decisively. Silence and shadows reigned again.

'Oh – my – God,' said Bella on a long, shaky breath.

Richard was stuffing his beautiful shirt back into his trousers. 'Too right,' he said with feeling.

She thumped back against the piled chairs with a great sigh of relief.

'I thought we were for it.'

'Yup. Me too.'

But he didn't sound as worried at the thought as she would have expected. Instead, he sounded positively tranquil. Even pleased with himself.

'What happened to that terminal good behaviour syndrome?'

He laughed. 'I must be getting over it at last.'

He stood up, shaking out his jacket, and held his hand down to help her up. She took it and came lightly to her feet.

Trying for normality, she said, 'That was unexpected.' Her voice did not sound like her own.

'Tell me about it.'

Richard's hair was all over the place. Her fault, Bella realised. She tried to restore order to it, without much success.

He caught her hand and carried it to his lips, kissing the palm. 'Why didn't you *tell* me what you were going to do? Do you know what I felt when I saw you?'

'Yup. I think that was pretty clear.'

'You were damned lucky I kept my cool.'

She wriggled a little, appreciatively. 'Not that cool.'

He shook his head, laughing. 'Call it a slow burn, then.' He shot his cuffs. 'Have you any idea how far outside my comfort zone this is?'

Bella was indignant. 'And whose fault is that?'

'Mine. Mine.'

'If you hadn't jumped on me . . .'

'Stop it,' he said, not laughing now.

She widened her eyes, innocently.

'And you can stop looking like that, too. I have three hours of speeches, compliments, and landscape art to get through. I need Zen, not—'

'Not—?'

'Not an inner eye full of you looking, well, like that.'

Bella raised an eyebrow.

'OK. OK.' He re-buttoned the offending mess jacket

145

and straightened it over her hips. His hands lingered, as if they had a will of their own. But he said, '*No!*' and put her away from him with resolution. 'I have places to go, people to be bored by. This has gone far enough. I am leaving *now*.'

Just before he pressed the button to slide the door open, he turned and said as if it were desperately important, 'I need to be with you tonight. Will Lottie be OK with that?'

'I'll sort it,' said Bella, dazed.

'Of course,' said Lottie, when she called.

She didn't ask any more and Bella didn't volunteer any confidences. But they had known each other a long time.

'I think I'll stay over at Katy's. We're going to a movie and it will be easier.'

So they had the flat and the night to themselves. And they didn't talk about the diary, or the dangers of being found out, or friends, or family, or anything but the moment and what they wanted next.

It was their last night together for nearly two weeks. There were no more evenings in front of Lottie's fire, not even curtailed ones. They spoke during snatched moments on the phone, several times a day. Although they went on to radio silence, at Bella's request, when her mother came up to Town for a day of exhibitions, shopping and pampering.

'I can't face standing next to her and talking to you on the phone,' Bella told Richard frankly. 'She'd be over the moon if she knew. I couldn't bear it. I know that. But *not* telling her feels so underhand, somehow.'

'I can relate to that. OK, silent running on Thursday. We can have a nice long call after midnight to make up for it.'

They did. But in all that time they only met face to face twice: once in a sandwich shop, with Richard disguised in jeans and a Millwall supporter's scarf; once at a literacy fund-raiser for which Lottie's company was doing the PR. Richard was guest of honour, of course, very princely in tuxedo and all the trappings, monogrammed cuff links included. He and Bella had a sedate dance. She did her usual trick of falling over her feet. He managed to stay looking regally courteous and kept her at a decent distance, but a muscle worked in his cheek, and she knew it was no easier for him than for her.

'This is torture,' Bella muttered.

'I know. I'm sorry. You've been very patient. And at least we've got dinner next week.'

'A whole evening! Do you think you can stick to it this time?'

'Definitely. I've told everyone on my staff that nobody, *nobody*, interferes with my night off. If they try to put anything in my diary that evening, I'll send them all on an endurance team-building exercise in Sutherland in December.'

Bella laughed up at him. 'That should scare them.'

His arm tightened. 'Too right.' He looked down at her searchingly. 'How are you doing, my love?

'Fine. Great. I'm seeing Neill tomorrow. He's come

147

up to London for some teachers' bash and we're having a quick meal before he gets the train home.'

'Sorry I can't meet him.'

Bella shifted uncomfortably. She was coming to realise that Richard didn't understand why she didn't want to tell her family. He was fine with keeping their relationship secret from the media. But it was increasingly obvious that he minded not telling his own family, especially his brother George. And he'd said more than once that he would like to meet various members of her family. He didn't press it but it was there, undiscussed, like so much of this relationship.

She said now, 'Maybe some day.'

'I'll hold you to that.'

Bella thought he probably would. God, this thing was going so *fast*.

She said defiantly, 'Anyway, you haven't got a window to meet anyone new for months. Don't forget I've seen the diary.'

He laughed. 'Have you studied it so closely?'

'Ian more or less told me to eat it after I'd read it, so I thought I'd better. You know I've only got hard copy? He refused to let me have a memory stick. Said I might lose it.'

'He's a careful man.'

She harrumphed. 'He went on as if it were a state secret.'

He laughed aloud. 'Bits of it probably are state secrets.'

'Oh, God, I keep forgetting.'

He looked as if he wanted to kiss her. 'Carry on forgetting. I like it.'

So Bella went to meet her brother next day wearing a big fat smile that she could not get rid of, no matter what she did.

Waiting for her in their favourite Covent Garden wine bar, Neill, not normally the most observant of men, saw it at once. 'You look cheerful.'

'I am.' She hugged him.

He raised an eyebrow. 'Do I need to congratulate you?'

At once she was wary. 'What? Why? What have you heard?'

'Francis proposed, has he?'

'*What*?'

'Ma thinks that you've left the island so Francis would miss you, see the error of his ways and propose.'

Bella snorted. 'Ma is delusional,' she said, settling herself on a tall stool and inspecting the cocktail list. 'Francis is history. Except for whiny texts when he can't find something, of course. And even those are tailing off.'

She could feel her brother studying her. 'And that's OK?'

She shrugged. 'I get pissed off when I have to give him a step-by-step guide to find something for the fifth time. Apart from that, no problems.'

Neill looked relieved. 'I'm glad. I mean, I know he does good work and everything. But he really is a pompous prick.'

Bella agreed cordially.

'But Ma was so sure you had a thing for him.'

'I did for a while,' Bella admitted. 'I grew out of it.

149

Have you tried any of these nineteen twenties cocktails?'

He shook his head.

She considered. 'What do I feel like? A Side Car ? A White Lady? Or what about a Perfect Lady? That sounds like me. And it's got peach in it.'

He hooted. 'A Perfect Lady? *You*?'

Bella was oddly put out. 'Oh, come on, Neill. I'm not that bad.'

'You're not bad at all,' he said affectionately. 'You're great. You're just not a lady.'

'Ouch.'

'Good thing, too. Ladies are a pain in the butt,' said Neill with unusual bitterness. 'Always poking and prying, and showing off to each other, and telling you what to do.'

This was serious. Bella put down the cocktail card.

'What's wrong, Neill?'

He shifted his shoulders irritably. 'Don't you start. Ma has been at me ever since I told her Val and I weren't coming for Christmas.'

'Er – yes. She said something about that.'

'I just bet she did.'

'She seemed to think you'd been talking to Finn. She said it was all his fault?'

He laughed but it didn't sound amused. 'Tell me about it. Val and I want to stay in our own home for Christmas, so it has to be somebody's fault. What can I say? From Ma's perspective, Finn's the usual suspect.'

Bella said cautiously, 'Doesn't sound like him.'

'Too right. When did our father ever notice Christmas?'

150

There was that new note of bitterness again. Neill rubbed his face and Bella realised how tired he looked, not just tired after a heavy day's conferencing, but bone tired, as if he'd been carrying something for too long and had just suddenly ground to a halt.

Feeling even more worried, she said, 'Has something happened?'

He gave her a stricken look and his eyes filled suddenly. Horrified, Bella realised that she had hit paydirt. And that was exactly the moment that the barman came up to take their order.

'Perfect Lady,' she said at random. 'And a Brandy Alexander for my brother.' Because that was what he had liked years ago, before he was married. 'We'll sit over there in that alcove. Can you bring them over?'

'Sure thing,' said the barman easily.

Bella grabbed up their coats and Neill's briefcase and herded her brother towards the secluded table. The wine bar was in an old cellar and its brickwork walls were supported by numberless arches, providing alcoves that gave an illusion of privacy. She dived for one of the smallest. It was clearly designed for lovers, with a little candle flickering in a glass holder and a fresh posy on the polished table, but that couldn't be helped.

Neill sank down on to the old settle and blew his nose hard.

'Sorry about that,' he said, plainly embarrassed. 'Been a long day.'

'Stuff has obviously been going on while I've been away. Come on, give.'

He leaned back and closed his eyes. 'OK. I s'pose I've got to tell someone.'

Bella felt a cold clutch in her stomach. 'There's something wrong between you and Val?' They had always seemed so in love, so good for each other, the successful businesswoman and Bella's gentle, laid-back brother.

He opened his eyes. 'You're not to tell anyone else, right? Particularly not Ma. Promise?'

'I promise.'

That was when the dam broke. 'It's like I can't do anything right. She's angry all the time. When she gets home, if I talk to her, I'm insensitive because after a fourteen-hour day she is too exhausted to make conversation, just to amuse me. And if I don't talk to her, I'm taking her for granted. Or ignoring her. Or being petty and spiteful . . . I tell you, Bella, I'm lost.'

She was appalled. 'What started it? Something must have.'

He looked wretched. 'Val lost a baby,' he said baldly.

'Oh, Neill, no. I'm so sorry.'

'I didn't realise it would be so bad. I mean, we'd only just found out she was pregnant. It wasn't planned or anything. In fact, Val wasn't very keen at first. She said it was the wrong time in her career. But then we both got used to the idea and, well, it's exciting, isn't it? So we had about a week of talking through plans and thinking about baby names and, then she had this bad cramp and – well, it happened.'

Bella took his hand. Neill looked surprised. They were not a demonstrative family. But he seemed to appreciate it and did not draw away.

'At first, Val was great. Very practical, you know? The doctor said there was nothing wrong with her, it was just one of those things, no reason why we couldn't have other children. And she said that was good to know and she was glad she hadn't told anyone. She went back to work at once.' He looked at Bella wretchedly. 'That was the only time I did *anything*. I did say, "Stay at home, take a few days to recover." But Val was so *sure* she could handle it. And so I didn't argue.'

'It would take a strong man to argue with Val,' said Bella, who was fond of her sister-in-law but careful around her.

'I should have been strong,' said Neill, even more wretched.

'So what are you going to do? Counselling?'

He shook his head. 'I suggested that. Val won't hear of it. She says it's our business, nobody else's. She says it's just because she's overworked at the moment and we'll come through this.'

It didn't sound like it to Bella. 'But?' she prompted.

'Sundays are hell,' Neill burst out. 'I can cope most of the week. I have lesson plans and marking and Val leaves early and more often than not it's nearly midnight when she gets home. So we're not together that much. But Sundays are a battlefield.' He gave a short unamused laugh. 'That's what I was talking to Finn about, to be honest.'

'You were asking for advice about marriage from *Finn?*'

'Good God, no. I was after advice on weekend adventure activities. Something where I'd have to do

153

lots of training. Something to keep me out of the house all Sunday, basically.'

Bella was silenced.

'Oh, well, I suppose we'll sort it out somehow. People do, don't they?'

Their parents hadn't, thought Bella. She did not say so but she could see from Neill's expression that he was thinking the same thing.

They had a subdued meal, and when the time came to part Bella felt so tender of him that she saw him to the mainline station. At the barrier she hugged him hard, as if he were going off on some long and terrible voyage and stood watching him stomp off down the platform until he boarded the train.

Bella felt very cold, going back to Lottie's flat. Cold and lonely. The Underground was harshly lit and everyone else in the carriage seemed to be part of a couple, holding hands or cuddled up together against the world. The flat was dark and empty. She remembered: Lottie was working again tonight. Just like Richard, she thought. He was at a gala concert in Leeds, followed by some sort of reception. He would not be answering his phone.

But suddenly Bella desperately needed to speak to him. So she didn't text but left a voice mail.

'Saw my brother. Things aren't good. When you get a moment, I'd like to, well, hear a friendly voice, really.' She tried to pull herself together. 'Hope the music was good.'

It wasn't worth lighting the freshly laid log fire. So she put on the small electric fire to boost the central heating and huddled over it in the dark, too sad to read or even to go to bed.

She did not know how long she sat there in the half-dark before the phone rang. She checked the number and felt better at once.

'Hello, Richard.'

'Hello, lovely. Tell me everything.'

She did. Well, some of it. Some of it was Neill's private business, of course, and Val's.

'But when I looked at him, I could see all those years of awfulness when Finn and my mother were married. I could see it all starting up again with Neill and Val. And I knew he did too. He looked so forlorn, Richard. I wanted to make it better. And I couldn't.'

There was a short pause. Then, 'Where are you?' he asked.

'In the flat,' said Bella, surprised.

'Where's Lottie?'

'Doing a product launch in Birmingham.'

'So she won't be back tonight?'

Bella looked at her watch. 'Shouldn't think so. Not now.'

'Blast!' He sounded worried.

She hastened to reassure him. 'Don't get me wrong. I don't want to talk to Lottie. If she were here, I'd be curled up in my room. I don't want to talk to anyone. Except you.'

There was an odd silence. For a moment she thought she'd lost the signal.

'Richard? Are you still there?'

He said decisively, 'Right. Don't go to bed. I'll be there as soon as I can.'

155

'What?'

'I don't want you to be on your own,' he said simply. 'Not feeling like this.'

'Oh, Richard.'

'I'll call you as soon as I have an ETA.' And he rang off.

Bella felt so much better after that, she actually roused herself enough to make a cup of tea. She turned on the table lamps in the sitting room and then went into the kitchen and did the washing up from breakfast.

And then Richard called back.

'Two hours.'

She nearly dropped the toast rack she was de-crumbing. 'That's impossible.'

He sounded angry, though not with her. 'No, it isn't. I might be a horrible boyfriend in the support department and too far away when you need me, but at least I have access to helicopters. See you later.'

He cut the call before she could argue.

'Wow,' said Bella, sitting down slowly on the sofa. She felt as if someone had sandbagged her when she wasn't looking. She felt muzzy-headed and she couldn't seem to breathe properly. 'Did he say he was my boyfriend?'

She decided to light the fire after all.

When he arrived she flew to the front door and walked into his arms. They stayed there for ages, just hugging in the dark little hallway.

'Thank you,' she said at last in a muffled voice.

'Thank you,' he said, kissing her hair.

'What? Why?' she asked, honestly puzzled. 'I mean, I throw a wobbly and you thank me? What for?'

'For calling me.'

She pushed herself away from him a little and stared up at his face. He seemed very serious.

She said uncertainly, 'I don't think I understand.'

'OK. What about this? For wanting me with you.'

Bella had that breathless, sandbagged feeling again.

Keeping his arm round her, he walked her back into the sitting room. The fire was blazing cheerfully. It felt like home.

She said so.

The arm round her tightened like a vice.

But all Richard said was, 'Right.'

9

'The Good Boyfriend Guide' – *Girl About Town*

The night was wonderful. Next morning was not.

For one thing, they both overslept. They had talked until later than late, until there was no more traffic outside in the street and the other flats were silent. And then they didn't talk at all. By the time they fell asleep neither of them was thinking about anything as mundane as alarm calls.

Bella awoke to find Richard hopping and swearing at the end of the bed. It reminded her of the crazy moments at the gallery.

'Hello, handsome,' she said, putting her hands behind her head and watching with pleasure.

He ignored that. 'We should have set an alarm call,' he snapped.

Even then, she didn't scent danger. Maybe she was too relaxed, looking round the small bedroom that resembled a war zone. There was a pillow on the window sill, where it had clearly been flung, and the duvet was hopelessly tangled. Various garments, male and female, lay along the floor like a paper trail.

Richard fell to his knees, turning over the detritus

with increasing impatience. 'I've lost a bloody sock.'

Bella looked at his naked shoulders with appreciation. He had a beautiful spine, she thought. 'I've got news for you. You haven't found your shirt either.'

'Try not to be stupid.' He sounded seriously put out.

She blinked, trying to clear her head. 'Where did you take it off? The sock, I mean.'

'How the hell do I know?'

His face appeared over the side of the bed. His hair was tousled and he had a distinct morning shadow. He looked gorgeous – and very bad-tempered.

'Retrace your steps?' suggested Bella lovingly.

One glance at his expression was enough to tell her that teasing him was not a good idea this morning.

'No. Right. Cancel that suggestion. I'll look in the sitting room.'

She swung her legs out of bed and searched round for something to wear. The flat was distinctly chilly. Or maybe it was his expression. She couldn't remember where she'd put her sapphire kimono and it didn't seem worth hunting for it, so she pulled on the tee-shirt she normally slept in and padded out to look for his clothes.

She didn't find the sock, but she did collect his white dress shirt from where it had fallen on to the log basket. She shook it to get rid of the wood shavings and looked round for the rest. His overcoat was hung tidily over the back of a chair but his jacket was in a heap behind the sofa. She shook that out too. There was a lot of fluff and old crisps behind that sofa.

An anguished roar came from the bedroom. 'Where's my sodding *phone*?'

Bella trailed round the room but could not see it on any of the tables or bookcases or even the floor. She was just investigating the mantelpiece when Richard appeared in the doorway, wearing one sock and shoe. He was carrying the other shoe.

'No sock. No phone. Why aren't you looking? Why are you staring in the mirror? This is *important*.'

Bella was beginning to feel she'd had enough of this. 'I'm looking along the mantelpiece for your phone,' she said frostily.

'Why would I put it on the blasted mantelpiece? It'll be in my jacket pocket.'

He held out an imperious hand for the article of clothing.

Bella was outraged. 'Call me Jeeves, why don't you?' she snapped, handing it over.

He held the jacket up on one finger and went through the pockets without success. 'Damn! What did you do with it? Did you turn it upside down?'

'Oh, sure, I shook it out of the window.'

He yelled, 'Will you stop being a facetious idiot and help me look?'

They glared at each other.

Then he turned away. 'Oh, it's hopeless. Do whatever you want.'

He started moving stuff around the crowded sitting room in a haphazard way but with increasing desperation.

In spite of her mounting indignation, Bella could see there was a problem.

'It might have fallen out of the pocket, I suppose.'

'That's what I *said* . . .'

She cast his shirt aside and dived over the back of the sofa like a pearl fisher heading into the deeps. She lay flat on the floor and started to wriggle her arm under the sofa, groping about for alien objects. In quick succession she found a lipstick, a small plastic bottle of mineral water, half-empty, and a paperback. She lobbed all of them over the top of the sofa.

'What are you doing?' he said impatiently. 'Your housekeeping can wait. I need—'

'Hang on.'

Her fingers had encountered the edge of something small, flat and hard. It was just out of reach. Concentrating, Bella closing her eyes and stretched the very furthest she could manage. 'Ow-ow-ow . . .' She felt the sofa move under the pressure and grabbed. 'Got it!'

She rolled on to her back, clutching the phone to her, and looked up, only to find Richard standing at her feet, looking anything but grateful.

'Why didn't you ask me to move the sofa?'

She ignored that. 'Look, here it is.'

She scrambled up, flushed with triumph. The little phone had not gathered as much fluff and crumbs as the paperback but it was grimy. Richard took it from her. He shook out the jacket and draped it carefully over the back of an upright chair. Then he produced a pristine handkerchief from the pocket of his dress trousers and wiped the screen.

'Thank you,' she prompted.

But he was already calling someone. 'Davis? A car. Soon as possible. No, not Battersea. Let's think. Outside

Mozart's House on Ebury Street. Do you know that? Call me when you're five minutes away.' He shut it off. 'Shirt.' And held out his hand.

Quite suddenly Bella's temper broke free. She put her hands on her hips.

'Oh, yes. Very Royal.'

That startled him. 'What?'

She clicked her fingers. 'Jacket! Shirt! Phone! Car! Now!' The last word came out as a shout.

'And your point is?'

'Real people say thank you. Please, even. *Real* people don't bark out orders like a dalek.'

'I'm sorry. Thank you.' But it didn't sound as if he meant it.

She shouted, 'Don't think you can snap your fingers at me, sunshine. I'm not paid to take your crap.'

He stiffened. 'What do you mean by that?' Icicles hung from every syllable.

'There are two of us late here,' Bella hissed. 'But does that matter to you? No, of course not. My *first* duty is to help Your Royalness get dressed and then go scrambling around under sooty sofas after your phone . . .'

'You do not understand.' Every word came out like machine-gun fire. 'You have no idea what my life is like.'

'Not sure that I want to.' And she clicked her fingers mockingly. 'Do this! Do that! Jump! Jump! Jump!'

His face went a dull red. 'I have no choice,' he yelled. 'I am who I am. I do what I have to do. That means I am never late. *Never*. Can you understand

162

that? People look up to me and I have to be there. I *have* to.'

'Fine. Then stop shouting at me and go.'

He gave her a look full of fury and seized up his jacket without a word.

'And don't come back,' Bella shouted.

She stamped off to the bedroom. She dragged clean clothes out of the closet, muttering to herself, and took them off to the bathroom, without saying goodbye. She was cleaning her teeth when she heard the front door slam.

'*Bastard*,' she told the bathroom mirror.

Then she sat down on the loo and howled her eyes out. So after that she had to wash her face all over again and was even later for work. It was no consolation at all that nobody had even noticed she was missing, as she told Lottie later that evening.

'That's a tribute to your fabulous new system,' Lottie said. 'Everybody did what they had to do because it was all up on the screen for them. And you'd put it there. Result!'

Bella smiled reluctantly. 'You mean I've just organised myself out of a job?'

'So what? You always said it was temporary,' said Lottie, refusing to sympathise. 'Give Anthea another call.'

'I keep texting her. She never gets back to me.'

'Then go and sit in her office until she does the business.'

'Yes, I was thinking I'd probably have to go round there,' agreed Bella. 'Boring.'

'But necessary. Don't worry, you'll get a job in ecology soon. Now tell me all about Neill.'

Bella chose her words carefully. 'He's fine. Looking for a hobby, I think. His career's going well but he wants to get out into the fresh air. He told me he'd been asking Finn for suggestions.'

'Fund-raising,' said Lottie at once. 'I can use him. Give me his number.' And, as a second thought, 'Where is it he's based?'

'Dorset.'

Lottie was pleased. 'Thought so. Devon would be better but Dorset will do. I've got just the thing for him. Teamwork, lots of physical exercise, fantastic scenery and free beer. And all for a good cause.'

She looked so pleased with herself that Bella hadn't the heart to discourage her. She thought it sounded a bit too much like organised games for a man who worked all day in a school. But she handed over her brother's phone number and listened with respect to Lottie selling it to him.

'I'm looking for volunteers to row a Viking longship over Easter next year. For charity. Some mad designer has built an authentic boat. There's a group already committed but they haven't got enough oarsmen. They'll train you but you have to be willing to put in the time. Good fun and it's *very* educational.'

Clearly, Neill didn't even struggle.

Lottie put the phone down and did a little victory dance round the kitchen. 'Sold. One Viking warrior signed on the dotted line. I've already got three sponsors for various bits of it. *And* a celebrity, because

164

Milo Crane will be over here making an action movie at Easter and he wants an opportunity to show off his muscles. And now I'm getting the Vikings. God, I'm good.'

'Congratulations.'

Lottie stopped dancing and looked at Bella in concern. 'You haven't still got the hump about being late for work? Look, you're young. You have a life. It happens. Don't let some dentist in a temper spoil the night before.'

Bella stiffened. 'What do you mean, the night before?'

Lottie didn't answer for a minute. Then she said awkwardly, 'Look, I wasn't snooping, honest. But the sitting room was all higgledy-piggledy when I got in. So I just did a bit of tidying up. And I found—' She sighed and rummaged behind the coffee-maker. 'Look, here it is. I was going to leave it somewhere in your room. But – well, there's no use pretending I haven't seen it. Here.' She thrust a piece of black silk ribbon into Bella's hands.

At first Bella didn't understand. Then she shook it out and saw what it was: two black fish-shapes joined by a thin band. Richard's bow tie! She felt herself blushing until even her ears were hot.

'Where did you find it?'

'On the floor. It was under a cushion.'

'Also on the floor?'

'Yes.'

'I'm sorry.'

'Don't be. You pay half the rent. You're entitled to throw the cushions around. And have anyone you want to stay the night.'

But Bella knew all about flat-sharing etiquette. 'I'm really sorry, Lotts. I should have cleared it with you first. Only, it was a spur-of-the-moment thing, very late, you were away . . . I just didn't think. But I should still have called.'

'We'd all have got a nasty shock if I'd come home early and walked in on you,' Lottie said with feeling. 'Just let me know next time, OK?'

Bella didn't say so, but she didn't think that there was going to be a next time. Richard had not only gone off in a temper that morning, he hadn't tried to call her all day. And she wasn't even sure that she wanted him to. One moment he was calling himself her boyfriend, as if it was obvious, an agreed thing between them. (Just to remember him saying it made her shiver, half excited, half dreading all the implications for the future.) The next moment, he was ordering her about and being scathing about the quality of their housekeeping. She hadn't liked him very much this morning. For the first time she had felt that he wasn't on her side and it had been a shock, especially after their closeness of the night before. It was very confusing.

'I don't want another complicated relationship,' she said now, half to herself.

Lottie laughed merrily. 'Show me a relationship that isn't complicated, Bel. You'll get used to it.'

But the next day she brought home a copy of *Royal Watchers Magazine* and a fistful of printouts of online gossip pieces. Lottie threw them on to the coffee table dramatically.

They showed various photographs of Richard coming

166

out of a nightclub with his arm round a tanned beauty. In spite of the chill of the November night, the woman's most substantial item of clothing was her earrings, Bella noted.

'The bastard's got a bimbo,' Lottie spat.

Bella picked up the longest article and read it quickly.

'This was last night,' she said slowly. 'That explains why he didn't call.'

'I see he found another bow tie,' snarled Lottie. She kicked the end of the sofa, then rubbed her foot. 'I wonder if he left that one behind, too.'

Bella winced. 'The Honourable Chloe Lenane,' she read. 'That was the women he told me about. He said she was like another sister.'

Lottie sniffed. 'Yeah, OK, he probably played with her in the nursery. The woman's an aristocrat with an A-level in advanced flower arranging. But that sure doesn't look like a sister to me.'

Bella studied the photographs. The blonde mane was expensively streaked; also artfully tangled to look as if the woman had only just got out of bed and it wouldn't take much to persuade her to get back into it. Maybe it was the way the flashing cameras had caught her, maybe it was the heavy black eyeliner, or, just maybe, the Honourable Chloe was as high as a kite. In spite of her fixed smile, she seemed dazed and bewildered, clinging on to Richard's black-clad arm like a life belt.

Richard himself was quite unreadable. He appeared comfortable with his arm round Chloe but he was neither waving to the cameras nor murmuring intimately into her ear.

'She doesn't look his type,' Bella said involuntarily. *He said he was my boyfriend.*

'You think not? She's got a pulse.'

'Why are you so angry, Lottie? I thought you liked him.'

'So did I. How wrong can you be? The rat.'

Bella swallowed. 'What have you heard? Have you any reason to think they're an item?'

Lottie flung herself down on the sofa, her arms extended along the cushions. 'Honestly, Bel, I haven't a clue. Our tame celeb watcher at work says that the smart money has been on him marrying her all along. The families have known each other for ever.'

'Who marries someone because the families get along? Get real, Lottie.'

'Yes, but even *Royalty Watchers* has her on the list of Top Ten possibles. Number eight, I think.'

'Oh.'

Lottie looked wretched suddenly. 'I'm really sorry, Bel. I didn't know before or I'd have warned you. He seemed a nice guy. I thought you could trust him.'

To her own surprise, Bella heard herself say, 'I think he is.'

Lottie stared at her in amazement.

'This photo doesn't have to mean anything. He told me once that he was public property. If he goes out with friends, he's bound to be photographed with one woman or another, isn't he? If I don't want that to happen, I ought to be ready to go out with him myself. In public.'

Lottie shook her red head in despair. 'Hey, I'm all for

168

giving the man the benefit of the doubt. But that's going too far!'

Bella said slowly, 'You can only go with your gut, right? My gut says he's always been straight with me.'

Lottie gave up. 'Heaven help you, Bella Greenwood, you're in love with the man.'

10

'Breaking Up, Making Up' – *Girl About Town*

Bella spent a restless night. The scary thing was that she was almost certain that Lottie was right. It came as a nasty shock.

She hadn't been in love with anyone since the actor who played Romeo when she went to Stratford with a school trip. Not *in love*. She'd had good boyfriends and bad boyfriends. She'd gone out with guys who were so keen on her, it seemed she couldn't turn round without treading on them; and others who managed to slot her in once a week between their careers and their squash, rugby, golf and stamp-collecting. There had been relationships which ran out of steam over months and relationships which flared up like a firework and died in a week. She'd been more serious about Francis than about anyone else. Now she thought about it, she had been dazzled by his reputation in their small circle and even thought they might have a future together. But she had never said to herself that she was in love with him.

He doesn't make my toes curl.

Oh, hell. That was the worst reason in the world for

seeing someone. No substance to it at all and it could be dreadfully deceptive.

Yes, but Francis had been a deceiver, too, in his own mean, egotistical way, and he was totally free from the toe-curling factor.

I don't think Richard is a deceiver. But why hasn't he called me?

What am I going to do if he doesn't? And what the *hell* am I going to do if he does?

However, next day she was too busy to think about Richard or anyone else for that matter. The evil dentist fired his senior hygienist, after a long-running fight about supplies, and the other hygienists all walked out on the spot. Bella spent the whole morning on the phone rearranging appointments. Her employer wanted her to work over her lunch hour as well, but she was determined to see Anthea and refused.

It was as well she did. The moment she went in, one of Anthea's assistants leaped up and almost hugged her.

'Bella! Oh, it's good to see you. Anthea's been trying to contact you all week. She's got the absolutely right job for you . . . number two at a tree conservation charity. Wait right there and I'll get you the job spec. Anthea will have finished with her client by the time you've looked through it.'

Anthea herself was less effusive. 'Don't you ever answer your phone? Oh, well, never mind, you're here now. Don't move from that seat until I've got you an interview.'

Bella left the agency with an appointment to see the

charity's director and chairman that evening and clear evidence that her phone was not reliable. In fact, when she looked at the memory, she saw that she had not received or sent texts for several days.

She could not get to the phone shop until the evening but the friendly assistant recognised her and her new phone and was only too happy to sort it out.

'It's a design fault. It happens when you press . . .' He showed her the exact key sequence to be avoided and Bella told him he was brilliant. It was more difficult to undo, apparently, but eventually he found a way through the walls and barriers and up flickered a great list of unanswered texts.

On the bus down Piccadilly, she ran through them, skipping over Anthea's, Neill's and her mother's.

Yes, there it was. At 10.18 yesterday morning Richard had texted: *I'm an arse. Forgive?*

Bella pressed the phone to her heart. So he hadn't been ignoring her. He hadn't stayed angry and imperious. He *was* the man she'd thought he was.

He'd texted eight times in all during the day, and another six today. She didn't have time to read them all because the bus had reached Green Park and she had to get off. She was meeting her potential employers at the Ritz for a drink. But the texts she had read grew increasingly frantic. She almost danced along the wet, cold pavements and into the fabulous hotel.

An hour later she emerged with a new job.

She could have gone home, of course, told Lottie and taken her out to celebrate. She would do that, of course she would. Later. First she *had* to read the rest of

Richard's messages. It wouldn't wait until she got back to the Pimlico flat.

So Bella found a coffee shop, bought a coffee she didn't want and tucked herself into a corner table so she could go through them in order.

He knew he had been horrible as soon as he left, he said. But he had been preoccupied about how to keep her name and address from his security officer. The reliable Ian had not been on duty. She had known that Richard didn't get on as well with any of his other minders, but it sounded as if he really disliked this particular guy. It had obviously been a really full day, too, and his team had had to scramble to try and reschedule things all the way. He had known they would, as soon as he realised how late he had slept. He was sorry he had taken his temper out on Bella. What could he do to apologise?

There followed a series of increasingly lunatic treats by means of which he hoped to lure her back, starting with star-gazing on the South Downs and ending with diamond earrings of her choice.

Bella grinned and composed her answer to this last with care.

Downs cold. Earrings also. Write me a sonnet. P.S. Not ignoring you, phone not working.

She drank some of the luke-warm latte and went through the other texts. Anthea's added nothing to what she had said today, so Bella deleted them. Neill, on the other hand, had clearly wished he'd not unloaded his troubles in the wine bar. Bella wasn't to take it too seriously, he texted. He'd been tired and it had been a tough week. He and Val were fine really, just fine, and Bella wasn't to worry about him. His later texts about the Viking longboat were a lot less stilted and more believable. He was clearly going to have the time of his life as a Viking oarsman. Bella decided that Lottie was a genius and texted her to tell her so.

Her phone pinged and she saw Richard had replied. Eagerly she opened the message.

Sonnet too long. Settle for a haiku? P.S. Bad phone!

Bella laughed aloud.

Haiku too short. Offers?

She started to work her way through her mother's texts. Janet had never really embraced the idea of texting brevity. She wrote in paragraphs, more or less as the ideas poured out of her brain. There had been times when it made Bella feel seasick, as if she were trying to stand upright on a surfboard, with the waves getting bigger and faster underneath her. This time, however, it just stirred her conscience.

Janet was worried that there was something Bella wasn't telling her. She knew that children need their privacy and she didn't want to pry but she didn't want Bella to feel that she had to carry everything on her own, either. No matter what happened, no matter what Bella had done – she said this several times in ten different messages – there was always a home for her with Janet and Kevin. They would always be there for her. Kevin would be delighted to help her find a job, or to fund her course if she wanted to re-train. Janet would do anything Bella wanted. Anything.

The last text was a killer: *I know we've never had a lot in common. Sometimes I feel I don't know you at all. But I have this feeling that you're on the edge of something huge. Don't shut me out, Bella. I'm your mother and I love you. I want to help.*

You know me better than you think, Ma. Better than I know myself, maybe. I didn't know I was on the edge of something huge until last night.

But true as that was, it didn't help her reply to her mother.

There was another ping. She looked. Richard again.

Quatrain? (4 lines). Can I see you this evening?

She snorted. *I know it's 4 lines, smug sod. Octet (8 lines) minimum acceptable.*

His reply came back so fast, she suspected he'd guessed what she would say.

A triolet? What about this evening?

She laughed aloud.

OK, you got me. What's a triolet?

She was drinking coffee when his reply pinged back. She nearly choked as she read it.

If you meet me this evening, I can tell you all about triolets.

She could just hear him saying it.

There was no doubt what she would do really. It was just a question of how long she was going to make him persuade her.

And then she thought: I'm on the edge of something huge. This is no time to play games. So she didn't.

When and where?

Almost as soon as she'd sent it, her phone rang. It was Richard.

'Are we OK?'

'I don't know,' Bella said honestly. 'I hope so.'

She heard him give a long, relieved sigh.

'You are a wonderful woman. And we really can meet?'

'Yes.'

'Where are you?'

'About five hundred yards from the Ritz. I just got me a real job.'

'Brilliant.' His voice was warm. 'Tell me all about it when I see you.'

'Which will be where?'

'Take a cab to the Chelsea Embankment. I'll see you by the dolphin statue at the foot of the Albert Bridge.'

'OK. When?'

He was plainly astonished. 'Now, of course.'

He was waiting for her. He made a lonely figure, standing by the statue as cars came to a stop at the traffic lights or swooshed past along the river road, speeding home. There was hardly anyone else about, just a couple of people hurrying over the bridge. They were hunched against the cold, anxious to get home. An edging of fairy lights picked out the struts and pretty gothic towers of the bridge, turning it magical. But everyone shot past, intent on their own affairs. It was, she realised, a good place to meet if you didn't want anyone to notice.

Richard was wearing an old fisherman's navy jacket with toggles on the front and an obviously torn pocket, stamping his feet against the cold. As she climbed out of the taxi Bella almost didn't recognise him for a moment. Almost.

He was looking across the river and didn't see her as she crossed the road. She hesitated. Last time they'd met she had run into his arms. But that didn't feel right this time, and anyway it needed to be mutual. She cleared her throat.

'Um—'

He turned.

She said the first thing that came into her head. It was idiotic. 'I've never seen you wear a jacket like that before.'

'I borrowed it. Don't you like it?'

'Borrowed it from whom?'

'Well, more inherited it really. I don't have to wear it again if you don't care for it.'

'*Inherited* it?'

His voice was warm with laughter. 'Come and see.'

He held out his hand. She took it. And, as simply as that, everything was all right again.

He walked her along beside the dark river, their hands entwined. Eventually they came to a collection of houseboats, bobbing gently on the tide.

'This way.'

Stunned, Bella followed him down on to the dock and then a walkway over the water. It all seemed very domestic. There were even garden planters on some of the decks. There were lights on in a couple of the boats but mostly they seemed dark. It didn't seem the place for a restaurant, even a super-discreet one. She said so.

'You're right. Not another restaurant. Tonight I'm cooking.'

'You have a houseboat?' She couldn't believe it.

'A share in one. Here we are.'

It was one of the smaller boats. At first Bella thought it was in darkness too, but as he led the way on deck, she saw that there was a sort of porch light above a door. He opened it and held out his hand to her again.

'Welcome aboard – and mind the step. We go down the companionway and then we're home.'

It was like stepping into another universe. The companionway was not much more than a spruced-up wooden stepladder at a sixty-degree angle, painted white. She stopped halfway down, looking round, trying to get her bearings.

It was more like a large friendly wooden tunnel than a boat. There were soft lights at waist-height set into the walls and skylights set in the ceiling. To her right, at the end of the narrow space, she saw a small kitchen, clearly already in use, with vegetables waiting on a chopping block. Between cupboards and the companionway, there was a table, old and well polished, with a motley set of bentwood and bar-room chairs set round it. Bella counted nine. To her left there was built-in seating, a beaten-up armchair that had clearly seen better days and a small desk. There seemed to be bookcases in every corner that could be found, but everything was wonderfully neat.

'This is yours?'

He beamed with pride.

'Like I said, I share it. My godfather left it to me and all his other godchildren when he died. We decided to keep it on. We run it between us. It's a bolt hole very few people know about. None of my family has ever been here but I love it. Come and talk to me while I cook. You can even have a seat.'

He pulled out a tall folding stool and set it for her with some ceremony. He gave her a glass of wine and returned to his interrupted cooking. Bella watched, fascinated.

'I didn't have you down as a cook.'

He flashed her a smile. 'You had me down as a useless Royal who couldn't even dress himself.'

She blushed but said with spirit, 'Can you blame me?'

'Not after my last performance, no. I'm sorry about that.'

'Yes, you said. It's forgotten.'

He put down his knife briefly, leaned forward and kissed the tip of her nose. But he did it, she noticed, rather carefully, as if he wasn't *quite* sure how she would take it. Well, good.

'You're a forgiving woman.' It wasn't quite a question, but he wasn't absolutely sure of himself, she saw.

But Bella was more shaken by that casual caress than she wanted to admit, or even to think about. So she just said, 'Aren't I just?' and dived into her red wine.

Richard went back to slicing courgettes. He was very fast.

She said curiously, 'Have you trained or something?'

He smiled. 'Imagine you're a child, in a draughty castle you don't really know, which is full of adults being terribly serious. It's too wet to play outside and people keep telling you not to run around or disturb your parents because they're sad. Your nanny is looking after the little ones and says a big boy like you ought to be able to keep himself amused. What would you do?'

'Run away to sea,' said Bella flippantly.

'Right. I ran to the kitchen. And a wonderful ex-army chef, who had no stupid ideas about keeping small boys away from knives, taught me how to chop vegetables and pluck and draw a pheasant.'

He diced carrots, with equal expertise. Then onions, with no sign of eye-watering.

'The skills have stayed with you, then.'

'When I start something, I like to finish it. And do it properly, too.'

'I can see that.' She sipped her wine. 'When was this grim time?'

'When my grandfather died. My grandfather the King.'

'Oh.'

He took chicken thighs out of the fridge and dusted them lightly with seasoned cornflour.

As he worked, he said, 'When girls ask what it's like being a prince, of course, I don't know, because I don't know what it's like *not* to be one. But I do know what it's like suddenly to realise you're King. I watched it happen that week. I was nine. I saw it all. My mother went on doing what she always does: looking on the bright side, being constructive, doing the next thing. My father – froze.'

It was a desolate little world he was describing. Bella had a sudden vision of the isolated nine-year-old and his grieving, overwhelmed parents.

180

'Was it unexpected? And were they close, your father and your grandfather?'

He didn't answer, turning on the small oven and putting a casserole dish in it to warm. Then he poured oil into a pan and heated it up. When the oil was smoking, he picked up the chicken joints and placed them carefully in the pan. Minimum splatter, Bella noticed. He was right: what he did, he did properly. More than that, he did it with attention to detail and precision. Bella did not cook much, but whenever she did something like this she regularly coated every flat surface with a fine spray of oil or fat. She looked at him with increasing respect.

But had she overstepped some Royal boundary by asking about his father?

She said hastily, 'Don't answer that if I shouldn't have asked. Sorry, I was just interested.'

He turned away from the food and took both her hands in his.

'You can ask anything you like,' he said with surprising intensity. 'Anything. Whenever you want.'

'OK,' she said slowly. 'But I don't want you to think you have to answer. I mean, not if it's private or some deep family secret or something.'

Richard turned back to the pan, adjusting the heat, cooking tongs at the ready, concentrating on the food.

He said levelly, 'It's no secret. My grandfather was a bully and a bigot. He had all the vices and a low boredom threshold. Which meant he made everyone's life hell, just because he could. Everyone who was able to avoid him, did. That included my father. My mother

181

was particularly good at arranging our lives so that there was minimum opportunity to see the old bastard. My mother has honed dutiful busyness to an art form.'

There was something in his voice that made Bella sit up and pay very close attention suddenly.

He sent her an odd, almost shamefaced look.

'You know the first time we met? When you fell into the foliage and I pulled you out?'

She nodded.

'You must have forgotten but you said something that night that I really recognised.'

'Me?' She couldn't think what it was.

'You said, "My mother's much too busy running a Charity Ball to have me home." My mother has never organised a charity do in her life. But, well, my brother and sister and I, we always knew where we were in the priority list: after King, country, Parliament, Prime Minister. And probably a few favourite charities. In that order.'

Bella was stunned. The Queen was always supposed to be the perfect mother. The King was said to be eccentric and distant but not the Queen, never. She did not know what to say.

Fortunately, Richard did not wait for an answer. 'Of course, even my mother couldn't get round a direct command from the King. So we had to go sometimes. And when he died, she lost all her options. We all did.'

'Oh, love.' Bella was appalled. She slid off the stool and rubbed his back in futile but heartfelt solidarity.

He leaned back into her touch while he carried on cooking.

'Worse for my father. I think now that he was probably terrified that he was going to turn out like the old man, once he was King. I've noticed that the nastiest thing you can say to him is, "You're just like your father." Sometimes one of the elderly relatives does it and he goes into a brown study for days.'

She said, 'I thought you were the perfect family. No divorces. No mistresses. No scandals.'

'No scandals? My brother George? Riding a motorbike through the centre of Bristol, dressed as a banana?'

Bella spluttered. 'Must have missed that one.'

'Oh yes, it probably happened while you were off on your island. The paparazzi shadowed him for weeks after that, hoping for an encore.'

She gurgled. 'Well, OK then. No *major* scandals.'

'You can be dysfunctional and keep it quiet, you know.'

The chicken was done to his satisfaction. He removed the joints, turned down the gas and fed the vegetables into the warm pan. At one point he splashed some wine over them. At another he added a dribble of this, a pinch of that, and a lot of fresh tarragon. The room began to smell heavenly. He tasted.

'Not quite. What do you think?' He offered her a teaspoon. She swirled the sauce round her tastebuds. 'Tastes wonderful to me.'

'Not enough bite. Hand me that lemon.'

She did. He chopped it in half and squeezed it over the vegetable goo, filtering the pips through the fingers of his other hand.

'Taste now.'

She did, closing her eyes. 'Yummy.'

'It will be.' He slapped the chicken back into the pan and spooned the vegetables on top. Then he got the casserole dish out of the oven, tipped the entire contents of the pan into it, and shot it back. He adjusted the temperature and the timer.

And then he washed up!

Bella stared, astounded.

'You must be the perfect man. If that was me, I'd be sitting down with a large glass of something, patting myself on the back, and leaving the dishes for later.'

Richard laughed. 'In a galley you wash up as you go. No room to do anything else. But sitting down with a large glass is good too.'

When he'd returned the work surface to pristine condition, he took her hand, another glass and the bottle of wine, and took them all to the other end of the room. It was chillier away from the cooker and Bella shivered involuntarily. He switched on a serviceable electric fire which she hadn't noticed before, and then contrived a nest of cushions for her in the built-in couch.

He topped up her glass and flung himself back in the battered old armchair, looking at her with such affectionate pleasure that Bella hardly recognised him. Nobody had ever looked at her like that, as if they had been given a prize. She felt warm and flattered and flustered and strangely humble at the same time. But she hadn't a clue what to do next. So she cuddled down into her cushions and did nothing.

Eventually he gave a long sigh of satisfaction. 'This is nice.'

'Mmmm. You said it was your godfather's boat?'

He smiled lazily. 'Strictly you should say her about a boat. He lived here for years. This is still pretty much all his stuff – the campaign desk, the books, the furniture. We put in a new galley because the old stuff was dangerous, and we replaced the skylights with modern, double-glazed ones that are easy to open. But otherwise, it's the same.'

'Isn't that a bit creepy?'

He gave a shout of laughter. 'That's my Bella. Tell the truth and shame the devil. Yes, it could be creepy in theory. In practice it isn't because he wasn't that sort of man. He taught me to sail and how to do stuff. Actually, he was the one who gave me your father's books.' He looked round. 'They're all here somewhere.'

'It doesn't feel like a mausoleum,' she admitted. 'But even so, why keep it?'

He was rueful. 'We'd all had fun here with him. And also, there was Ship's Cat.'

'What?'

'He had this massive tabby mouser called Ship's Cat. Great character but very territorial. So we agreed, all five of the godchildren, that we would share the boat until Ship's Cat pegged out.'

You kept a houseboat for a cat?

'Yes. Why?' He cocked an eyebrow.

'But houseboats have to be lived in, don't they? I mean, kept warm and dry and the pipes working and stuff.'

'Good practical thinking,' he said approvingly. 'Absolutely right. Sometimes one of us lives here.

185

Sometimes we have a tenant. At least three books have been written here.'

'And the cat?'

'Lived a full and happy life and died a couple of years ago, aged twenty. Actually Chloe was living here then and she took it backwards and forwards to the vet's for several months. I was surprised, but she stuck to it.'

Chloe. Ah.

'I saw the photograph in the papers of you with her. Lottie said she didn't think Chloe looked very sisterly.' She let the remark hang.

But he didn't get indignant. Instead, he frowned, looking troubled. 'I know what she means. Chloe is a bit of a mess, frankly. Starts things and doesn't finish them. She can get a bit, let's say, fixated. She ran with a bad crowd for a while when she was younger. I'm certain there were drugs involved. But we don't say so because she is the niece of my mother's oldest lady-in-waiting and it would be Bad Form.'

'But you don't mind sharing a boat with her?'

'She behaves herself on board. One of my fellow godchildren is a tough lady soldier who'd scalp her if she didn't. Anyway, she genuinely loved our godfather. It's been OK so far, anyway. Which is a relief, because we'd all be sad to sell the old girl. We've got used to her. I like it here.'

More than like, she thought, seeing him laze in the armchair with his long legs stretched out before him. You're basking. You love this place.

It was gorgeous to see him looking so happy.

Suddenly, she knew the answer to the question that had tormented her last night. Lottie was right!

Bella pushed the cushions aside, slipped off the couch and knelt beside him with her arms round him.

'I love you,' she said.

11

'Telling the Parents . . .' – *Girl About Town*

Richard didn't seem to think it was quite the earth-shattering revelation that Bella did. He was very nice, of course – those beautiful manners again – and he kissed her as if he meant it. But he didn't leap to his feet and beat his chest in jungle triumph. Nor did he seem very surprised, unlike Bella.

She was about to point this out when the damned timer went off and their supper was ready. Frustrated, she felt they had only had half the conversation. It was like waiting for the other shoe to drop.

But Richard didn't seem to feel like that. Over food, they drifted away from declarations of love. He told her about a security officer he wasn't keen on, the nightclub he'd been photographed in, the crazy diary of the next few days. Bella told him about Lottie's idea of turning Neill into a Viking oarsman.

Richard snorted with laughter. 'I know you said he needed to get out more. But rape and pillage seems to be taking it a bit far.'

'Neill is not a natural pillager. They won't corrupt him!'

She told him about her new job. 'It's my sort of charity, saving woodland and replacing trees. They want me to reorganise their admin system, which I can do standing on my head. But what they *really* want me to do is evaluate project proposals, drawing on my experience in the field.'

'And that's the bit that has got you excited,' he said, seeing the glint in her eye.

Remembering the island and all the supplies that Francis was sure they could cope without until the next consignment arrived, Bella's eyes narrowed to slits of pure venom. 'Oh, yes. After ten months with the fragrant Francis, I can tell a waffler at fifty paces. They say things like "I'm a big-picture man", and "I concentrate on objectives, not operational minutiae". They think it's a waste of their valuable energy actually to spend any time with the researchers on the ground. Francis always used to—'

'Since you mention Francis—'

She flipped back to the present with a jump. 'Yes?'

'I haven't asked before. But how close exactly were you? I mean, ten months on a tropical island . . .'

'You mean, the moon, the stars, the virgin beach, the turquoise sea?'

'Yes, I suppose I do.' He didn't look very happy about it.

Bella leaned across the table and put her hand over his. 'They didn't stand a chance. In London, I was starry-eyed about Francis, I admit it. He was the big cheese and he was very flattering to me and, well, he talked a good story.'

189

A look of amusement dawned. 'Our Gallant Leader Syndrome?'

'Exactly. Francis is big on Inspiration. As long as he's doing the inspiring, of course.'

Richard choked.

'His feet of clay showed the first day. The very first *day*. He was supposed to have organised chemical toilets to be brought in by sea. He forgot.'

'Ah. Not a good move.'

'After that, well, I can't say the scales fell from my eyes. I mean, he still had the charisma. But, well, he didn't quite seem so irresistible somehow. It just all wound down rather sadly.'

'I'm not surprised. Nothing like propinquity and poor sanitation for showing a man in his true colours. So you didn't . . . er . . .'

She shook her head. 'We didn't sleep together, no.'

'I'm glad,' he said simply.

'So am I.' She leaned back and watched him for a while. Then said 'And what about your ex? Almost the first day I got back, I was reading that someone had dumped you.'

One of the nice things about Richard was that he didn't shy away from the suggestion he'd been dumped. He nodded. 'You mean Debs.'

Bella didn't remember the woman's name but she recited what she could remember of the article.

'Yes, that would be Debs.' He thought about it. 'That's not an easy one. At first, Debs was great. She never got uptight. Didn't mind being on display.'

Bella winced. One in the eye for me, she thought.

190

Richard did not notice. 'She even laughed at the photographers when they ran down the street after us. Used to joke with them. She was so relaxed. As you know, I'm not very. I was crazy about her.'

Bella sat very still. He was crazy about her. Well, of course, there was going to have been someone. Of course, there was. He was twenty-nine, not a kid. But she felt angry and resentful and hurt and she wanted to kick Debs so hard she disappeared off the planet. It took her a while but she worked it out in the end: she was jealous. It was stupid, but there it was.

Richard was oblivious, still wrestling with the problem of Debs who had dumped him

'You know me, Bella. I've always been a bit dull. Never late for receptions. Read my briefing, remember it.'

Bella's eyes narrowed. 'Is this the genetic good behaviour myth again? The one you peddled before jumping my bones in the middle of a major reception?'

He had the grace to flush faintly, though he looked pleased at the same time. 'That was rather out of character for me.'

'Hmph.'

'Even you have to admit that I don't have a lot of pizazz. Debs had pizzazz.'

'You dated her for her *pizzazz*?' Bella was incredulous.

'What can I tell you? I'm a man. I'm shallow!'

'You're also winding me up,' said Bella, not deceived. 'What really went wrong? If you want to tell me, of course,' she added conscientiously.

Richard stopped grinning. 'Have you heard of the

idea of the starter marriage? Well, that's what I would have been for Debs. She probably didn't know it, of course. But I watched what her friends did and she was on the same track. Big engagement party. Big, *big* wedding. Lots of gadding about and flirting with the cameras. And then the wife does her thing and the husband does his, and after a couple of years in the limelight they're both ready to move on to someone else. I was so determined I didn't want a dynastic marriage like my parents that it took me a while to see that there are other sorts of marriage that won't do for me either. Debs's sort, for instance.'

'So she *didn't* dump you?'

'Yes and no. She did. But she wasn't the woman for me and I knew it before she did. So I just went on not asking her to marry me until she got tired and gave me the push.'

'I see.'

Bella said nothing more.

But later, when they were walking back to Lottie's flat along the river, with the clouds scudding over Battersea Park, exposing and veiling a nibbled-cheese moon, she said thoughtfully, 'You know, Debs probably did you a favour and Francis did the same for me – patronising twerp! In fact, when someone stops him buggering up perfectly good research projects, he will undoubtedly make himself a fortune as a motivational speaker.'

Richard stopped dead, flung back his head and roared with laughter.

'You're lethal,' he said. 'I love you too.'

And that was when Bella realised what she had been

waiting for. Not the jungle chest-beating, not the exclamations of delight and astonishment. The vow returned.

She thought: I've never felt so right before.

Not that it was dramatic or even very romantic. Richard gave her a quick hug, but said, 'We'd better keep walking or you'll get cold. There's snow in the air, I think.'

So instead of wandering hand in hand under the London stars, they marched briskly up from the river along Chelsea Bridge Road, past the well-lit, fashionable shops of Pimlico Road, then Orange Square and Mozart's statue, heading towards the flat.

Only there was display in a shop window that caught Bella's eye. 'What's that?'

She went over to it. Richard did not resist following.

It was a Christmas special in an interior design shop. In the window there was a family of mechanical polar bears, rather good ones with liquorice allsort eyes and huge powerful feet, their slab heads nodding. There were four of them, a mother, father and two cubs, one batting the other back into line. It was kitsch but at the same time, immensely appealing.

Richard peered down at Bella. 'Are you crying?'

'I like the little ones,' she said, in a muffled voice.

'You *are* crying. You old softie.'

Bella sniffed unromantically. 'Well, you said you loved me. I think it just caught up with me.'

He said in a shaken voice, 'Oh, Bella, my darling. Don't cry, my love. Don't cry.'

And they did kiss then, properly. They stood in front

of the spotlit window and the first snowflakes drifted down and neither of them noticed.

People came out of the restaurant opposite, stopped, peered, then stared. They put their heads together, muttering. Then one of them brought out a phone and took a picture, took several. The group went off, bunched together to look at the tiny screen, chattering excitedly.

Bella and Richard didn't notice that either.

Eventually, Richard raised his head and cupped her cheek in his gloved hand. He was breathing hard. Bella, dizzy and swaying, felt she would never remember how to breathe again.

'Come on. Home.'

They ran back to the flat hand in hand.

Lottie looked up when they went into the sitting room. She was sitting on the sofa with her laptop on her knee. She looked uneasy.

'Hi,' she said. 'Have a nice time?'

Bella nodded. 'I got the job,' she said in a voice that said her cup of happiness was running over.

Lottie seemed oddly distracted. 'The job? Oh, the forest charity. Good for you. When do you start?'

'Second of January they think. They're sending me the contract tomorrow.'

'Excellent.' Lottie looked back at the screen. It kept beeping. 'Um . . . where did you go tonight?'

'We dined at home,' said Bella, taking off her coat and twirling round happily.

But Richard was watching Lottie, a frown between his brows. 'Something wrong?'

'That depends.'

'On what?'

'On whether you two want to go public.'

Bella stopped twirling. 'What? Why?'

'You're on Twitter,' said Lottie brutally. 'You know how fast these viral things go? I reckon global in fifteen or twenty minutes.'

Bella went cold. 'No-o-o.' It was a wail.

Richard kept his cool. 'Someone saw us? Recognised us?'

'They're not sure.' Lottie turned the laptop round and gave it to him. 'See for yourself.'

He sat down on the sofa beside her and considered it gravely. 'Ah, I see.'

There were three photos. Two of them could just have been any couple kissing. The third had Richard raising his head, three-quarter face to the camera. The back lighting of the polar bear window display gave the picture dramatic shadows. Unfortunately these only served to intensify his distinctive profile.

He sighed heavily. 'My damned Coburg nose. There's not much chance of convincing people there's been a mistake, is there?'

'Look at the tweets,' Lottie suggested. 'Plenty of doubters. You could always deny it.' She stared hard at Bella. 'Depends how much you're prepared to lie.'

Richard read them fast. 'Yes, I see,' he said without expression. He looked up at Bella. 'I think this one is your call, darling. Have a read, then tell me what you want to do.' He stood up to make room for her.

She sat down and tried to focus on the messages. The

limit on characters meant that many were so compressed she couldn't understand them. But others were clear enough. Diners in London had seen Prince Richard (or was it?) kissing an unknown blonde/local barmaid/Australian ladies' golf champion/any one of several soap and movie stars.

'Golf champion?' said Bella, seizing on the one thing that didn't matter.

Richard raked one hand through his hair. 'I danced with her at a Sports Personality bash. The photo's on my file, that's all. I barely know the woman.' He sighed. 'I'd better check in with my office.'

He pulled out his phone and Bella realised that he must have had it switched off all evening. As soon as he turned it on, it rang. He looked at the caller's name and sighed; then answered, with his usual dutiful calm.

'Hello Monty . . . Yes, I've heard . . . No, I don't think that's necessary. I will work on a statement with you tomorrow . . . *Tomorrow*, Monty. You can come and see me at eight. I'll even give you breakfast.'

The moment he cut the call his phone rang again. He looked at the screen and groaned.

'Hello, Mother . . . Yes, so I hear. I'm surprised you have, though. I didn't know you were on Twitter . . . Oh, Lady Pansy told you, did she? Don't see her as a typical Twitterer either.'

There was silence, while he listened to what was clearly a vehement maternal lecture.

'I'm not being evasive, Mother. I just haven't made my mind up yet. Be assured that when I do you'll be the first to know . . . What? No, not tonight. I'm talking to my Press Secretary tomorrow about the options. And can I just point out that this is not life and death, or even a bad case of measles? Yes, we'll clear any statement with Father. And you, of course.'

Another, shorter harangue.

Richard stiffened. Suddenly his voice turned icy. 'Very well, Mother. Thank you. I will bear that in mind. Good night.'

He nearly shattered the phone when he pressed the Call End button. As soon as the thing started to ring again, he said, 'Oh, *shit*,' and switched it off entirely.

Bella went to him.

'We're in the soup, aren't we?'

Lottie said hurriedly, 'Don't mind me. I'll go and . . . and . . . And tidy something.'

But Bella said, 'No, don't go, Lotts. You're good at this PR stuff. Richard, it's OK if Lottie stays, isn't it?'

He said with sudden bitterness, 'You probably ought to have your own Press Team and a lawyer to boot. Of course Lottie must stay.'

Bella pulled herself together. 'Then take your coat off and let's talk. Lottie, can you think what you would advise us—'

'You,' said Richard swiftly. 'This has to be *your* decision.'

Bella did not argue. 'OK. What would you advise me to do, Lottie? Think about it. I'm going to make a pot of strong coffee and then we can sit down and talk. We need to agree a strategy.'

'Cool,' said Lottie, clearly relieved.

But Richard looked surprised.

'Don't worry about her,' Lottie said kindly, leading him to the sofa. 'That is one seriously together woman. You're in safe hands. Trust me on this.'

Bella came back with a cafetière of maximum-strength medium roast, three mugs and two litres of semi-skimmed milk. Richard took his black. He swigged half a mug in one go. It was the only sign of agitation he betrayed.

'I wish I smoked,' said Lottie, who was less controlled than the Prince of Wales.

However, her summing up of the situation was masterly.

'You have three options, Bella. First of all, you don't have to say a thing. The photo is clearly Richard but it's not so clear of you. You've done a good job of keeping below the radar so far. None of the Royal watchers have ever heard of you. You can keep your mouth shut and ride out the story.'

She paused, looking from one to the other of them.

'Of course, that means you'll have to stop seeing each other. The story's out there now and the Press are going to keep after Richard until they find the answer to the secret of his mystery companion.'

Richard said swiftly, '*An* answer. I doubt if they'd ever be able to identify you for sure, Bella.'

'But I don't want to stop seeing you,' she said. 'That's a no-brainer.'

He gave her such a blinding smile that for a moment she couldn't think of anything else.

'Right,' said Lottie. 'Then here are your other options. You can lie. You can stay silent and hope it all goes away. Or you can 'fess up. All of these depend on Richard's co-operation.'

'Of course,' he said. 'Bella never asked for this. I got her into it. I'll do, say, confirm, whatever she's happiest with.' He spoke direct to Lottie, not looking at Bella.

Lottie nodded. 'Thank you.' She turned to her friend. 'The first thing you have to remember is once you've told a story, there's no going back. You can fudge and finesse or you can downright lie. But if you decide not to come clean, you have to keep on lying. Do you want to do that? From experience, I know it can be done. But often it's more painful than telling the truth and it certainly goes on for longer. The tabloids have scented a story and they will dig and keep on digging after it.'

Richard said quietly, 'She's right.'

Lottie looked straight at Bella, serious-faced. 'If you want to kill this story, my best advice is tell the truth – yes, it was you – and don't elaborate. Don't answer questions. No second press release. Certainly no exclusive to *Royal Watchers* or the *Daily Despatch*. Just shut up. Remember, you've done nothing wrong. You're both unattached.'

Bella nodded.

'Eventually he'll date someone else and the Press will lose interest.'

Richard flinched but said nothing.

Lottie went on. 'Of course, you could just keep your head down. You probably wouldn't be found out. There are only four people who know – we three and Richard's security officer. You could keep schtum and leave it to his Press Office to handle.'

Richard said quietly, 'It's what they're paid for. You don't need to be involved. You wouldn't have been if I were anybody else. If I weren't—'

'Public property,' said Bella softly. She tried to take his hand but he seemed to be lost in thought and didn't respond.

Lottie said crisply, 'Of course, if the Press Secretary admits it was Richard and doesn't give up the name of the lady, the nastier rags will imply that it was a one-night stand and she was probably – er – professional.'

Bella was aghast. '*What?* They wouldn't . . .'

Lottie shrugged. 'Whatever sells their paper.'

Bella looked at Richard.

He spread his hands, in answer to her silent question. 'I don't know. I suppose they might. But that's my problem.'

Lottie said, 'And then we come to the fourth option.'

Bella sat up very straight. 'There's a fourth? I thought you said there were only three?'

'Three b then,' said Lottie impatiently. 'Tell the *whole* truth. Whatever that is. Be prepared for further questions. Answer them. And keep on answering them as long as the relationship lasts.'

She sat back, looking at them expectantly. Richard got up.

Bella said to his back, 'If you say it's my call one more time, I will *scream*.'

'Be fair, Bella. What else can he say? He's had the

paparazzi shadowing him all his adult life. He knows the score. He can cope. Can you?' Lottie asked.

Bella ignored her. She stood up and went to Richard. 'You said you loved me.'

He didn't turn round. 'Yes. Of course I love you. I would do anything . . . But if we tell the world we're seeing each other, you'll become public property too. You never wanted that. You said you didn't.'

'I know I did. But that was before.'

'Before I said I loved you?' He sounded tired. 'Pu-lease.'

'Before I knew you properly.'

He turned round then, looking oddly uncertain. 'What?'

She said simply, 'You learned to cope without selling your soul. So will I.'

Richard searched her face. 'Bella, think about this. Are you sure?'

He looked so drawn she wanted to put her arms round him. 'Are you?'

'Me? Oh, yes,' he said, quite as if it didn't matter, as if that were a given. 'I was sure the moment I saw you.'

There was complete silence.

'Oh,' Bella said on a long note of wonder.

He searched her face. What he saw there seemed to reassure him. His shoulders came down from under his ears and the tension lines round his mouth eased. He took her hands and swung them a little. His eyes were starting to smile again, she saw, and her heart turned over.

He drew in a long breath. 'Well,' he said. 'Well.'

'That's settled then.' Bella sounded a little breathless but brisk. 'Press statement says we're going out together.'

His fingers tightened. 'Yes.'

'Well, thank God for that!' Lottie said. 'Now, look, you'll need to tell your nearest and dearest, along with anything you want or don't want them to say. *Someone* will go to them for a comment, as sure as eggs is eggs. And you really ought to do that before you issue the press release.'

Richard couldn't stop looking at Bella. 'I'm afraid she's right,' he said. 'The Palace machine will handle my family. But what about yours?'

Bella groaned. 'Oh, great! My mother will burst with joy and my father will never speak to me again.'

'I'm sorry?' said Richard, startled.

'He's an anti-monarchist. I *told* you.'

'I didn't realise he was that bad. He'd actually break off communication because you've gone over to the enemy? That's impressive.' Richard brightened suddenly. 'Actually, I'll get to meet him now, won't I? Great. Maybe I can talk him round.'

'Don't count on it,' said Bella. She was making a list. 'Mother and Kevin. Finn. Neill. Granny Georgia.' She looked at her watch. 'I'll text them now and speak to them properly in the morning.'

'Don't forget the people at work,' Lottie instructed her. 'And you'll need to update your Facebook page. I'd advise you to change the settings or you'll get all sorts of nutters leaving stuff on there. Now let's work out what you're going to tell everyone.'

'Er – one thing,' said Richard. 'My mother wants to meet you.'

'Yes, of course, we'll organise a date.'

'I mean tomorrow.' He looked at his watch. 'Make that today. As soon as possible. She said lunch.'

Bella and Lottie exchanged alarmed glances.

'My mother,' he said dryly, 'is a warm and wonderful human being and a miracle of organisation and tact. But she doesn't like being blind-sided. She's not pleased with me for not telling her about you.'

Bella gulped. 'I shall tell her that was because I asked you not to,' she said bravely. 'But please – not lunch. I have to work tomorrow. Life has to stay as normal as possible or I'll lose myself.' There was an edge of panic in her voice.

Richard was unperturbed. 'Fine by me.'

It was Lottie who said wisely, 'You don't want the first thing you do as Richard's acknowledged girlfriend to be a head-to-head standoff with his mother. Quite apart from the fact that she's Queen of England, the mother of every son in the world would hate you for that.'

Bella's jaw set. 'I'm *not* turning my life upside down.'

'No need to. Negotiate, Bel, negotiate. Richard . . . suggestions?'

He thought. 'I'll speak to her in the morning. Tell her you feel you have to talk to your own parents first. She's not unreasonable – when she's not spitting mad. I'll sort something out.'

They worked out a list of who would tell what to whom, when.

When they had finished Lottie stretched and stood

up. 'That was a good night's work,' she said with satisfaction. 'I'm going to bed now. If I were you, Richard, I'd stay the night. It's too late for anything else. But your choice.'

With which tactful invitation, she wandered off.

He stayed.

This time they both remembered to set an alarm call. So the next morning Bella waved Richard off then rang her stepfather. It was 7.15 and Kevin was on the train, already on his way to work. He had not read her text of the night before, which was par for the course. Kevin did not like mobile phones and used them as little as possible. Bella told him the bare facts, as she, Lottie and Richard had worked out last night.

Kevin took it calmly. 'That's very good news, my dear. He sounds a fine young man. Time you had some fun . . . Your mother? She's got a hairdresser's appointment this morning, so she'll be up in half an hour or so, I'd say.'

Janet had not read her text either. So when Bella eventually spoke to her, a few minutes after 8, her mother was inclined to think it was a joke.

'It's true, Ma. I met him at a party and we've seen each other quite a few times since. Last night somebody got a photo of us together and now it's all over the internet. His office will issue a press release later today.'

But Janet still refused to believe her.

Finally Bella gave up. 'OK, Ma. Have it your way. But if you Google "Prince Richard" plus "Rumour", you'll see the photo. I'll email you the press release when it comes out. Call me if you want to talk about anything.'

Her father texted: *Disbelief here. Where are your principles?*

To which Bella replied immediately: *YOUR principles, Phineas Fogg.*

Granny Georgia texted: *I look forward to meeting him. Back on Christmas Eve.*

Bella went to work.

At 9 Richard's office sent her a copy of the draft press release for her approval. She approved. At 9.20 Richard rang.

'It's gone.' She could hear that he was in the car. 'I'm saying to anyone who asks that it's a private matter and I'm not giving any interviews.'

'Where are you going?'

'Municipal swimming baths. I'm opening them. Followed by a diving display and races between first-year swimmers of all ages. Followed by lunch with the Mayor.'

'Wow! Rock on.'

He laughed. 'You?'

'About to tell the evil dentist and his cohorts that when they see the papers at lunch-time, yes, it's me.'

'Good luck.'

'They won't care,' said Bella, surprised.

But she was wrong. After she'd sent a brief email round the system, she was astonished by the messages of good-will she got in reply. The hygienists bought her a Groucho Marx mask, complete with glasses and cigar, for getting out of buildings unnoticed. Everyone seemed to be pleased for her. Bella was touched.

Janet, once she grasped that Bella had not been winding her up after all, was uncontrollable. She phoned continually, wanting details, strategies. When could they meet him? When could she tell the Golf Club ladies?

'Ma, we've just told the world. The Golf Club ladies will know.'

'But they'll ask me about him. What can I say?'

Bella controlled a flicker of alarm. 'As little as possible. Just say you haven't met him yet but I'm bringing him to meet you and Kevin before Christmas.'

'They'll want to know if you're getting engaged . . .'

They would want to know, Bella noticed. Not Janet.

'There's no question of that,' she said firmly. 'And you can tell them I said so.'

'. . . and then Meeting Them' – *Girl About Town*

In the end, Richard's office and the Queen's negotiated a late supper that very evening, after she had returned from a recital given by a prize-winning string quartet at the Royal College of Music.

The prospect flung Bella into an uncharacteristic panic. 'What do I *wear*?' she wailed.

Lottie was astonished. She had never heard her friend in such a stew. Without ever appearing to be much interested in clothes, Bella had acquired her own style over the years and usually carried it off with a certain flair.

'What's the fuss about? You're the coolest woman I know,' Lottie told her now.

But at the prospect of meeting her boyfriend's mother for the first time, Bella had lost all self-confidence. Bad advance publicity didn't help. Nor did the Royal sniffiness which she had decided was a cast-iron certainty

'Calm down,' said Lottie. 'Let's both take the afternoon off, for a start.' She told work that she needed to take some time at home to work through ideas for a campaign, and left the office early.

'Well, it's true,' she said defiantly, when Bella raised an eyebrow. 'I just didn't say it was a campaign we were going to be paid for. Now let's go through your wardrobe and mine.'

Lottie was a chameleon, with a wide range of clients and an even wider range of friends. She had three wardrobes. Bella only had one and she couldn't think of a single item that would be suitable.

Bella tried on every single dress in Lottie's wardrobe from an irregular black and white print – 'Ascot,' said Lottie fondly; 'Makes me look like a Dalmatian,' said Bella, not even bothering to do up the zip at the back— to a classic Little Scarlet Dress – 'Very little. Much too scarlet,' said Bella with regret.

Eventually they could not see Lottie's bed for the tumble of silks and chiffons and jersey and . . .

'It's hopeless,' said Bella, nearly in tears. 'I'm just not comfortable in your clothes. And the only thing that I have that's remotely formal is the ghastly suit my mother bought me.'

'Go and put it on,' urged Lottie. 'It might be better than you think.

But when Bella came back, she gave a low whistle and shook her head. 'Holy cow! Pure Stepford Wife. Get it off, get it off . . . I can't bear to look at it.'

They went and sat glumly on the end of Bella's bed, inspecting her clothes.

'Of course,' said Lottie thoughtfully, after a while, 'it doesn't have to be a dress. I mean, this is an informal supper, right? We're not talking tiara and orders. You've always got the Ginger Rogers Cocktail Look.'

208

In a trip round Greenwich Market one Sunday, Bella had discovered a vintage pair of very wide-legged black silk trousers. They looked dreadful on the stall, but she had been certain they had promise. After a little love and attention, they had proved to be very stylish. Now she tried them on and at once they felt right, especially when she added her cute T-bar heels. But neither Lottie nor Bella had a jacket that worked with them.

'What they need,' said Bella, turning this way and that in front of the mirror, 'is a very simple white silk shirt.'

Lottie bounced to her feet. 'And I know exactly where you can get one.'

As a redhead, Lottie only ever wore cream rather than white, but she had bought a wonderful tailored silk shirt from one of Carlos's other clients only last week. As soon as Bella tried it on, she agreed the shape was perfect. The boutique still had one in white. Bella returned triumphant.

'It makes me feel like myself,' she told her friend, with a great sigh of relief.

'That's what you need. Now,' Lottie advanced with a determined expression, 'pearl earrings. I don't want to hear a word about Lady Golfers or Jane Austen. This is a classic look.'

And when she had them on, Bella had to agree. Even so, she held her breath in case Richard staggered back, saying, 'You cannot call on the Queen wearing trousers.'

But he arrived early and wanted to leave at once.

'My father gets out of the classical stuff if he can, so he'll be at home anyway. We can see him first.'

'He's not having dinner with us?' said Bella, surprised.

Richard shrugged. 'He likes his routine. He never eats late. How's your day been?'

'No problem so far. I didn't answer calls from anyone I didn't know. A couple of journos left messages on my voice mail. My mother's told the Golf Club and wants to show you off to them as soon as possible. My grandmother wants to check you out. My father is still fulminating. Could be worse.'

'Not bad at all,' he agreed.

This time he was driving a powerful black car, with a dashboard like a rocket ship's. The policemen on the gate at the Palace clearly recognised it. They swung open the doors and raised their hands as he drove through. He gave them a friendly wave.

He drove into an inner courtyard and parked close to a covered walkway. It was starting to snow again. They left footprints behind as they ran for shelter.

Richard took her hand. 'Stick close to me. This place is a rabbit warren.'

He was right. They went into an eighteenth-century bit, all wooden floors and polished banisters, through a service corridor that might once have led to kitchens which now seemed to be office accommodation, and then up and down so many little half-staircases that Bella's head started to spin. But then the portraits got grander and marble columns started to appear.

'The public rooms, with thrones and so forth, for investitures, dinners, and occasions of national importance,' Richard said conscientiously. 'Lots of pictures of battles and men in uniform.' He stopped in front of one epauletted grandee.

'Leopold, the Prince Consort. It's his fault I have this damn' great nose. He's wearing the uniform of a British Field Marshal.' He studied Leopold with some affection. 'In fact, he really was a soldier, so he was more entitled to wear uniform than most of the other old mountebanks. He fought against Napoleon for the Tsar, though he was rather keen on the French before Napoleon decided on world domination. It was always said that he brought a touch of French style to the court, balancing the excesses of George IV.'

It sounded as if he were talking about a friend. Bella wondered what it would be like to know your ancestors in such detail. She didn't know anything about any of hers, beyond her grandmothers. She said so.

'It's easy enough to find out if you're interested. I've been to several Family History centres. Fascinating places.'

'I might do that one day,' said Bella, not meaning it.

He took her up another staircase and down a corridor. Bella had half expected flunkeys in knee breeches, or at least maids, to be flitting about. But the only people to be seen were on the walls. The portraits were smaller here, though, and there were more women.

'Queen Charlotte by Watts, 1850 or so. She got plump like her father and rather sententious, but she was very racy in her day . . . had several flings as a teenager . . . but Leopold seems to have calmed her down.' Richard moved on. 'Her daughter Virginia, also by Watts. She was rather dreamy and poetic but she knew her own mind. Defied her mother, turned down a Danish prince to marry an American and went to live in Charleston.'

'My grandmother comes from Charleston. Well, she did forty years ago. Then she met my grandfather and went travelling with him, and they came back to England when he retired.'

'She's the one who wants to check me out?'

'Yes. You'll have to be on your best behaviour, too. She has Standards, my grandmother.'

'I'll do my best. Only one left?'

'Yes. I hardly remember my mother's mother.'

'I have the full complement, God help me. My father's mother lives in a castle in Wales, where she Encourages the Arts and breeds Siamese cats. And my mother's mother has hobbies that include younger men and roulette.'

'Goodness!'

It didn't sound as if he liked either of them very much. Bella bit her lip. She adored Granny Georgia and hoped Richard would do the same. But it didn't sound hopeful.

'Here we are. My father's apartments.'

There were servants here, though not the crowd she'd expected and not a pair of knee breeches in sight. A pleasant man in a neat grey suit took her coat, and another, very dignified, told them they were expected.

He led the way to another set of doors and knocked before entering.

'The Prince of Wales, Your Majesty.'

This is not happening, thought Bella suddenly. This is just *unreal*.

But Richard held her hand tight and they went in.

It was quite a small room really, though it had large Georgian windows with theatrical curtaining and a lot of gold tassels. There were several glass cases containing substantial models of trains, and all the furniture was antique and beautifully polished. But apart from that it was quite homelike, Bella thought.

The King stood up from a chair by the fire where he had been reading. He shook hands politely and asked if they had known each other long. But Bella did not feel that he was really interested. His eyes kept sliding towards his book. He offered them a drink but seemed relieved when they both refused. He took Bella over to one of the glass cases in the corner, which enclosed some sort of structure with two huge wheels and a lot of moving parts. She had no idea what it was or was designed to do, and admitted her ignorance.

The King beamed. 'It's the engine of HMS *Sphinx*, a revolutionary steam paddleboat of the mid-nineteenth century. Designed by John Penn. The original is in the Institute of Mechanical Engineering here in London. He became their President, you know. Are you familiar with the Institute?'

Bella had to admit she wasn't.

'Pity. Pity. Ver' good place. Ver' good. Sometimes go to lectures there. They are building our future, Miss Greenwood. Engineers always find solutions.'

He showed her a couple of the train after that, and Bella couldn't dredge up any more intelligent comments on them, either. She thought he was glad when they left.

Though Richard said, 'He took to you,' sounding surprised.

Bella was doubtful. 'Really?'

'Yes, really. He talked. He showed you the models. Normally, it's painful introducing him to new people. But he liked you. He will be a lot more relaxed next time, now that he knows you. You'll see.'

He said a courteous goodbye to the King's servants and they walked to his mother's apartments. There were a lot more signs of life in this corridor.

Richard said uncomfortably, 'Look, there's a protocol which might help with my mother. *She* gets to start the conversations.'

'I don't understand?'

He stopped striding down the red-carpeted corridor and drew Bella into a window embrasure. One of the men standing at the next door started forward, but Richard shook his head and the man fell back.

'Do you know about Fanny Burney?'

'Who?'

'Fanny Burney – eighteenth-century novelist, daughter of the Master of the King's Music. Anyway, she did her time at Court because the Queen wanted conversation.' He seemed to be searching his memory. 'She told Fanny that she had great difficulty in getting any conversation because she commonly not only always had to choose the subject, but also entirely support it. And the form hasn't changed since. The Queen picks the topic. Got it?'

'Got it,' said Bella.

'Just for tonight, until she's got over her bate. Normally, she's fine.'

'I'm sure she is.' Bella could feel her heart sinking lower by the minute. To disguise it, she said brightly, 'Did Fanny enjoy her time at Court?'

Richard was matter-of-fact. 'Hated every minute.'

Bella glared. 'Thank you very much for the encouragement.'

He squeezed her fingers. 'You'll be fine. Remember, you're not going out with my mother. You're going out with me.'

But either Queen Jane had got over her ill humour or else she was very good indeed at hiding her real feelings. She could not have been more welcoming.

'My dear, what a pleasure,' she said, kissing Bella on the cheek. 'Richard never tells us what he is doing, so it is a great relief to find that he has a private life.'

Richard stood like a rock and said nothing.

The Queen's rooms were charming, with great bowls of flowers in every corner and some fine modern paintings. Not a hint of gold tasselling or steam engines, thought Bella. And the Queen didn't mention her husband, though she did say that the evening's music had been very modern and she was glad to be home.

'We'll eat at once. You must be very hungry. We're in the small salon . . . quite informal.'

She led the way to a dining room where, as far as Bella could see, places had been set for at least four courses.

'Now, tell me where you met my son.'

215

So Bella told her and the Queen laughed a good deal at the story of the collapsing ivy.

'I'm glad Richard had the good sense to stay and rescue you. Do you find you have a lot in common?'

'Bella is Finn Greenwood's daughter, Mother. She's very adventurous.'

The Queen looked worried. 'Oh, dear. Do you sail, my dear?'

'I'm afraid not.'

'Then don't let my son persuade you to try it. He has been wanting to go ocean racing since he was a child. And of course it's out of the question.'

'Is it? Why?'

The Queen bit her lip and did not answer.

It was left to Richard to say with heavy irony, 'The safety of the heir to the throne must be assured at all times. Isn't that right, Mother?' To Bella it sounded as if he were quoting an official document.

The Queen clearly thought the same. 'That's not quite fair, Richard. Your father and I obviously don't want you to put yourself in danger.'

He sighed and said tonelessly, 'Of course.'

She turned to Bella and said, a bit too brightly, 'What do you do, my dear?'

So Bella explained about her research into fish in the Indian Ocean and her new job in forestry research.

'And what are you doing now? Spending time at home with your parents?'

Here we go, thought Bella. Dirty linen, one pile, on the table now, quick smart.

She said, 'No, Ma'am. I'm living in London with a

216

friend and doing a temporary job. My parents are divorced.'

'Oh, *dear*,' said the Queen. And to Bella's surprise went on, 'Was that very difficult for you? Broken homes can be so disorienting for the young.'

Bella said, 'Actually, I never really felt I had my feet on the ground until my mother married my stepfather. He's a solid citizen, which my father isn't, and more importantly he is always there when my mother needs him. My father is just as likely to be up a mountain or in the middle of the desert somewhere.'

The Queen leaned forward. 'How interesting. Didn't you miss your father?'

'If your father's an explorer, you kind of get used to it.'

'Yes, I suppose you do. I hadn't thought of that. And are you an explorer too?'

'I wanted to be,' admitted Bella. 'but I don't think I have the temperament somehow.'

The Queen smiled at her suddenly. It was a real smile, full of fun and a sort of intimacy. Briefly, she looked very like Richard, Bella realised, startled. She found herself smiling back, without reservation.

'I think you are a wise young woman. I look forward to getting to know you better.'

In spite of all the courses, the meal moved along briskly. Bella couldn't face cheese or the delicious-looking chestnut and meringue pudding, and was starting to look hopefully at Richard for a signal that he was OK to go when the Queen rose to her feet.

'Let us go and tidy ourselves, my dear.'

Richard stood up. 'Oh for God's sake, Mother.'

The Queen raised elegantly shaped eyebrows. 'Language, dear.'

He waved that aside. 'Hasn't this charade gone on long enough?'

The Queen stiffened. 'Charade?' she said icily.

Very like Richard, thought Bella.

He gestured widely. '*Quite informal?* Three different wine glasses and four courses for a simple supper? What are you playing at . . . putting Bella in her place right from the start?'

'Richard!' The Queen sounded genuinely shocked.

He said to Bella, 'Don't be fooled by this "We are so pleased that Richard has a private life" guff. The last time I had a private life and made the mistake of introducing my girlfriend to the family, my mother told her that she was my "little rebellion", and I would get over it. Isn't that right, Mother?'

The Queen looked away, as if he had not spoken.

'Come, Bella.'

He was almost savage. 'Are you seriously going to leave me to port and cigars on my own? Get real.'

'Bella and I want some girl time alone, dear. If you don't want port and cigars, get them to make you a chocolate milk shake,' flashed his mother. 'It's about your age group.'

And she swept out. Bella looked at him in alarm, but he just jerked his head to send her after his mother and sank back into his chair. Bella bundled after the Queen.

She found Queen Jane had retired – there was no other word – to a beautifully appointed boudoir, with mirrors and soft lights and cushioned window seats plus three loos and half a dozen hand basins. The Queen was sitting in an exquisite little tub chair, blowing her nose rather hard. The air was heady with the scent of many perfumes.

Bella sat down on the edge of the window seat and waited.

'Oh, he makes me so mad sometimes,' said the Queen. 'I know it's not easy being Prince of Wales and I try to help. But he just bites my head off.'

She blew her nose one more time and then blotted carefully under her eyes for good measure.

'I'm sorry you saw that. Normally we don't fight in front of other people. I suppose I was just so worried when I saw all the nastiness all over the web.'

Bella was surprised. 'I didn't see much nastiness. People were curious, of course. But it all seemed quite kindly.'

'They were saying he was – well, let's not talk about it. A dear friend showed me some messages that you may not have come across. And just as well.' She patted Bella's hand. 'Now, listen. Richard won't like me saying this, but you're going to need some help. The Press was bad enough in the old days, but now, with the web and all those social networking sites, it's just out of control. I think you need a mentor, someone you can call any time that you have a problem.'

'Thank you,' said Bella. 'But my flat-mate is in PR and she's been pretty good at guiding me up to now.'

Queen Jane looked relieved. 'Oh, that's good. So there's really only protocol to worry about.'

Bella was non-committal.

The Queen laughed. 'I see Richard has been telling you what he thinks of protocol. I don't blame him, really. It must seem very artificial to your generation. But it eases the wheels with a lot of people of different ages and from different cultures, if you just tell them what the rules are.'

'I suppose I can see that.'

'Good. I will ask a good friend of mine to call you and talk you through it. Lady Pansy helped me when I came here as a bride. She's utterly reliable and very kind. You will like her.'

The Queen stood up, went to the mirror, fluffed up her hair and tidied her make-up.

'I'm glad we've had this talk. I do want you to feel that I am on your side. Shall we go back and see whether Richard has murdered someone?'

He was in the Queen's drawing room, pacing. The coffee tray was brought in. Both he and Bella refused a cup, but they sat dutifully making conversation about books and the weather until the Queen had finished hers. Then Richard leaped to his feet and they said their goodbyes and were gone.

On their way to the car, he said, 'Have you had enough of me tonight?'

Bella gave him naughty look. 'What do you think?'

At once he lost his impatient frown and bellowed with laughter. 'Thank God for you, Bella Greenwood,' he said when he could speak. 'You might just turn me human again. Right. Where? Back to the flat or my pad?'

'The Palace?' she said doubtfully.

'God, no. I hate the Museum. My flat is in Camelford House. George and Nell both have apartments there, and so has my grandmother for when she leaves Wales and comes to London. But we don't interfere with each other and you won't see them. Fancy it?'

'Yes!'

'Good.'

13

'Can this Last?' – *Royal Watchers Magazine*

The entrance to Camelford House was more forbidding than the Palace's, with huge blank black gates. But once inside, it felt a lot smaller and a great deal friendlier. The gates opened as soon as Richard's car approached and closed noiselessly behind it, as a security officer came out of the small guard house to check them in.

'Good evening, Sir. I don't have a guest on my list for tonight, Sir.'

'Spur of the moment, Fred. Bella meet Fred, who keeps the bad men out. Fred, this is my lady, Bella Greenwood. I've no doubt you know all about her by now.'

Fred smiled. 'Very nice to meet you, miss. I'll add Ms Greenwood to the Approved Visitors List, shall I, Sir?'

'You bet. Good night, Fred.'

'Good night, Sir. Miss.'

Richard drove round a corner into a sort of square formed by an substantial eighteenth-century house, a small Jacobean block, and what looked like a nineteenth-century school house, its front covered in ivy.

'You'll need to check in with Security whenever you come here, if you're not with me. If I'm not around, just poke your head though the guard-house door and the guys will sign you in. You'll need keys, too. I'll organise that.'

He led the way into what Bella was privately thinking of as the school house. Inside it was warmer and more comfortable than the Palace. The ceilings were lower and the art was less warlike. There was even an elevator, with gilded bars and a leather-covered bench seat around three sides of it. Richard flung open the doors for her.

'You must take a ride in Gertrude. Don't look down if you get vertigo, but Gertrude is a work of art. They wanted to put in something modern and silent that opened straight into my apartment, but I said no. She's part of my childhood, Gertrude.'

He patted the leather seat as if it were a friendly dog and swung the hands of a floor indicator as big as a grandfather clock face. Gertrude clanked into life and juddered sedately to the top floor.

Richard's apartment was a shock. Bella had seen him in someone else's cottage, in Lottie's flat and in the shared houseboat. All those places were friendly, book-filled, cosy. This flat was enormous. The main room ran the entire length of the building, as far as she could see, with a pale blond-wood floor and minimalist furniture: deep ivory-coloured sofas surrounded a low wooden table inlaid with an intricate pattern of pale woods. There was a cocktail cabinet at one end, currently closed up to reveal its flowing Art Deco lines, and a

223

floor-to-ceiling bookcase at the other. No flowers or knick-knacks here, but a spotlit alcove housing a beautiful urn, the colour of the sunlit stone of the Acropolis, and a huge painting occupying the whole of one wall. At first glance it looked like a black-and-white architectural study of a ruined castle in the middle of a mediaeval town. But the longer you looked at it, the more you saw anomalies: tiny touches of colour, staircases that couldn't possibly exist, hints of people just out of sight, a shoe, a drifting scarf.

'That,' said Bella, staring, 'is amazing.'

He stood beside her and looked too. 'I never tire of it. Every time, I see something different.' He put an arm round her. 'The Palace is full of *stuff*. People are always giving you things and some of my ancestors were avid collectors, too. And you never throw anything away, on principle, in case the next generation would like it. So my mother lives in an upmarket junk yard and tries to hide it with flowers. I didn't want that.'

'You haven't got it. This is beautiful.'

There were windows all along another wall. She went to them and saw that they looked out across lawns to another building.

'Is that part of Camelford House too?'

He shook his head. 'Government building.'

'So you're in this great big place all on your own?'

His eyes started to dance in the way she loved; the way they hadn't for too long. He took her hand and pulled her towards him.

'Not,' he said, 'tonight.'

*

224

It was a good start but things went wrong almost immediately.

Richard had to leave to take a flight to Edinburgh the next morning, so he left before Bella did. And no one had told her that she had to sign out when she left Camelford House. So in the middle of the day she got a frantic phone call from someone in Richard's entourage of the day, asking her to call the Guard House. She did, and a meticulous functionary insisted that she come back *at once* and sign out. She would do well to apologise to the Officer of the Watch as well, he said. Bella suspected that he was the Officer of the Watch. But she remembered that these were people whom Richard saw every day, and liked, so she complied.

Then she had a call from someone who described himself as working in the King's private office. Please would she give him her date of birth, her social security number and her passport number? Also her parents' and her stepfather's. And, in future, would she remember that it was not permitted to stay overnight in a Royal residence without three days' prior notice?

'They're not exactly making you feel welcome, are they?' said Lottie, hearing Bella's side of that particular conversation.

'I know. It's odd. Both the King and Queen Jane were very nice to me.'

But she rounded up the passport numbers, as instructed.

'You know, I think you ought to check with Richard,' said Lottie. 'I mean, it's odd. Maybe Wormtongue doesn't work for the King at all. What's his name?'

'Madoc . . . Julian Madoc.'

'Well, find out if Mr Madoc is legit before you send him anything.'

So for once Bella called Richard. He answered immediately.

'How's Day Two of being the First Girlfriend going?'

'Odd actually.' And she told him about the messages she'd had from the Palace.

He exploded. 'Bloody Madoc! Officious little toad! Know what he's doing, don't you? He's trying to get you positively vetted.'

Bella gasped, coughed and couldn't stop laughing. 'Sounds a bit agricultural and rather nasty.'

But Richard wasn't amused. 'It's security clearance for people who have to read government secrets. How dare he? How *dare* he?'

But Bella was still bubbling with mirth. She went into a very bad Russian accent. 'I am Olga the Beautiful Spy. You will tell me all your secrets.'

Richard laughed reluctantly. 'Yes, very funny. But Madoc needs kicking. I shall speak to my father. What else has the House of Horrors thrown at you today, my love?'

She told him about the Officer of the Watch and her decision to grovel without protest. 'I look on it as an investment in future good-will.'

He groaned. 'And I thought it would be the Press that were the problem!'

'Well, I'll probably do better now. Your mother is providing me with a mentor.'

'A what?'

'A mentor. You know, someone who's already done something and guides the faltering footsteps of a new recruit.'

'Hell's teeth,' he said blankly. 'The woman's got a mind like a corkscrew. Has she really wished one of my old girlfriends on to you?'

Bella giggled at the idea. 'I don't think so. She's called Lady Pansy, and when she called me this morning she sounded like Celia Johnson. Must be a good seventy-five.'

'Oh, Pansy.' He sounded more relaxed. 'She's harmless. She'll probably give you long lectures about orders of precedence and teach you how to curtsey.'

'Coo-er.'

This time Richard laughed as if he really meant it. 'I love you,' he said before ringing off. 'Dream Girl.'

Lady Pansy didn't give Bella lectures on orders of precedence. She gave her a booklet, bound in shiny Royal blue, with the Royal coat-of-arms on the front and gold lettering. And a book on protocol at the Court of St James's, revised edition, and a book on the Royal Families of Europe, plus a ring binder about the organisation of the Royal Household (London) with the internal telephone numbers of, as far as Bella could see, everything and everyone from the King's Private Office to the Head Groom.

'Just a few memory joggers,' she said sweetly. For Lady Pansy was very sweet indeed.

Bella found her way to a sitting room off a back staircase in the Palace for, as she thought, a friendly chat, and came away feeling as if she had gone ten rounds with the Cookie Monster.

The woman who had summoned her was tall and rangy, with a profile like a horse's and a lacquered backcombed helmet of beautifully tinted grey-brown hair that would, thought Bella, have withstood a Force 10 gale. She was elegantly dressed in a dark blue dress and short jacket worn with a triple string of pearls, matching pearl earrings, and a pair of well-polished shoes. So far, so Golfing Ladies. Except that Lady Pansy smiled all the time and never stopped talking. She did not so much gush as swirl like the tide. She was, in short, unstoppable.

She also called Bella 'dear' a lot. It set Bella's teeth on edge.

'I have known the dear Queen since she came here as a bride. And the Dowager Queen before her. Indeed, I was brought up with His Majesty's father. My own father was what is called an Equerry. You will find out about the Court in here.' And she added another tome to Bella's extensive pile.

'Thank you.'

'Of course, I have retired now. The King has very kindly given me a little Grace and Favour apartment in Hampton Court but I come in to the Palace most days, to give what service I can. Old habits die hard.' She had a tinkling laugh, that didn't sit very well with the horse-like teeth or a strident upper-class voice that could have stripped paint.

'I suppose they must,' murmured Bella.

'Royal service is my inheritance. I am very proud to

228

serve. I have my little corner here,' Lady Pansy explained, indicating a sitting room the size of a suburban house, full of eighteenth-century furniture and a goodish collection of porcelain. 'And I am always available to help new people who join the Court with any little pieces of advice that I can. Just ask me anything you like, dear. My card. My phone number.'

She gave Bella two small pasteboard cards, one simply inscribed with Lady Pansy's name in flowing gold script, one more businesslike with phone and fax numbers but no email address.

'You will find it all bewildering at first,' instructed Lady Pansy. 'But I shall be here to guide you. You may call on me at any time. I suggest we meet regularly.'

Taking a surreptitious glance at her watch, Bella realised that the interview had already taken two hours. Her discussions with Lady Pansy, she resolved, would henceforward take place on the telephone. But she murmured more grateful thanks. And Lady Pansy launched into a terrifying account of the hounding she could expect from the Press.

Bella finally staggered out with two cloth bags full of books and papers, three hours after she'd gone into the Palace.

She went straight back to the flat and lay down in the sitting room, in blessed, blessed silence.

'Thank God I took the day off,' she told Lottie that evening. 'The woman made my head ring – and scared the wits out of me. She made me think the journalists and photographers would be knee-deep outside the flat. But there wasn't one.'

As it turned out, the Press were relatively uninterested in Bella. There were a couple of pointed questions asked of Richard at his next public appearance, but he evaded them neatly. And a single photographer turned up outside Bella's office. But that was it.

'Of course, you're not one of the candidates to become his Princess,' explained Lady Pansy on the telephone. 'The serious Royal correspondents know that and won't waste their time. But the riff-raff can be intrusive. When would you like to call on me this week?'

'Thank you, but I think I will save that pleasure for when the riff-raff get worse,' said Bella, and put the phone down before Lady Pansy could object.

Lottie, however, agreed with the courtier.

'There's a lot of celebrity action at the moment,' she said darkly. 'You wait till the dead zone between Christmas and New Year. That's when we'll get all the pieces about "Isabella Greenwood, Is She Right for Our Prince?"'

'So what?' said Bella, who had just come off the phone with Richard and was still basking in his 'Good night, Dream Girl'. 'I've got my love to keep me warm. I can handle it.'

She and Lottie were both wrong.

The trouble started when an undercover freelance journalist approached Bella's mother in Town. Of course, she didn't say she was a journalist. She said she'd heard the news about Bella and the Prince of Wales, and just had to stop and tell Janet how pleased she was. And then she switched on her mini tape recorder and let Janet burble.

Bella's mother didn't say anything untruthful. She said that they hadn't met Prince Richard yet but hoped to soon. She also said they were very much looking forward to meeting the King and Queen – at this point, reading the article, Bella put her arms over her head and groaned loudly – and that she hoped to invite Queen Jane, a noted amateur golfer, to a round at her own club. Yes, she agreed, it would be lovely if Bella and Richard got married. Following your heart was so important. Only then the journalist asked if she thought that the family would object, and Janet got completely the wrong end of the stick. Her ex-husband, she said, could keep his silly opinions to himself and not jeopardise his daughter's happiness. Who cared whether he thought the monarchy should be abolished or not? He was never in the country anyway.

It went round the wires in seconds. The next day a journalist turned up in Cambridge, asking about Finn's behaviour when he was an undergraduate there. Someone found an incendiary article he had written as a student coming back from Paris, praising the French événements of 1968. A man he had fallen out with badly on his Pamirs expedition sold a highly coloured account of Finn's alleged anarchist ravings while they were in the mountains together.

The headlines were grim. 'Prince Woos Revolutionary's Daughter' was the mildest of them. 'Trotskyist Totty in the Palace' screamed the *Daily Despatch*.

Julian Madoc rang Bella and asked her for a list of all

the clubs and societies she had ever joined, particularly any political ones. He was, he said in a smug voice, commanded by the King to ask. Lady Pansy said it was most unfortunate and that Bella should issue a statement, distancing herself from her father.

'Can't do that,' said Lottie the guru. 'Turns you into a sneaky little traitor, letting your dad down.'

'I wasn't going to do it,' said Bella, more bewildered than anything else.

Richard was furious. A television interviewer stuck a microphone in his face at a Christmas Fair and he lost his cool. 'I am a great admirer of Finn Greenwood's work,' he told a reporter icily. 'I have read all his books. It will be a privilege to meet him.'

'Prince Turns Anarchist' trumpeted the *Daily Despatch*.

'Oh, dear,' said Lady Pansy, worried. 'Maybe you ought not to see each other. Just for a bit, you know. Until all this dies down.'

But Bella was starting to get annoyed too. 'The trouble is, people who buy the *Despatch* can't read. They probably thought it said Anti-Christ,' she said tartly.

And somehow that got out into the Press too. There were rumblings that the First Girlfriend was too big for her boots. Not being Royal or even aristocratic and sneering at the reading abilities of good working people.

'Now I'm not only a Trot, I'm toffee-nosed,' she told Richard, trying to make a joke of it. But it was starting to hurt.

She did not go to any official functions with him, and when they went to the same parties they arrived and left separately. It seemed to her that now they had acknowledged that they were seeing each other, they saw less of each other than they had when it was only in snatched, secret moments.

'I know,' said Richard. They were in his flat again, curled up together on the huge sofa after a long walk and a lazy evening with a DVD. 'It's like there's a conspiracy to keep us apart.'

Bella propped herself up on one elbow. 'Do you think . . .?' But at once they both shook their heads. 'Nah. Why would anyone bother?'

'If I have the choice between cock-up and conspiracy, I go for cock-up every time,' said Richard. 'We need to spend time together, private time, that everyone knows about. I can't get away for Christmas, but I could do the Saturday after next if your mother invited me. And you could come to Scotland for the New Year.'

'Do you think that's wise? Lady Pansy said maybe we should cool it.'

'Pansy's an old worryguts,' said Richard disrespect-fully. 'I'm not feeling like cooling anything.'

He kissed Bella long and pleasurably to illustrate his point. After a long, complicated interlude, she could only agree with him.

'Right,' he said later, lying half-naked and wholly relaxed on his priceless Chinese carpet. 'That's agreed then. You square your parents. I'll tell mine.'

Thirty-six hours entertaining the Prince of Wales on her own territory was all Janet Bray had ever dreamed of. She paraded him round the Golf Club and he behaved, as Bella told him later with heartfelt appreciation, like a complete star. He laughed at all their golf stories, even producing a couple of his own. He admired their charitable fund-raising, expressed interest in the club's upcoming centenary – and spent long cold hours on the fairway playing a round with Kevin and smiling for the local paper, the curious, and children who came along hoping that the Prince of Wales would be in armour, or at least have a sword. His smile never faltered. Nobody would ever have guessed that he wasn't riveted by golf and golfers or delighted with his day's entertainment.

'You're really good at this, aren't you?' Bella said, walking beside him back to the clubhouse, her gloved hand tucked into the crook of his arm.

'It's my job,' he said.

Janet's stock had soared with the Ladies' Section.

'Good to meet the boyfriend that our Bella said she didn't have,' said the witch-faced Social Secretary, making certain that she was the first to shake Richard's hand when they reached the clubhouse. Her husband's new knighthood, as she had pointed out in the Ladies' Cloakroom, gave her precedence.

'It is a great treat to be here with her,' said Richard, retrieving his hand and flexing it out of sight. The Lady Social Secretary's Botox did not seem to have frozen her iron grip. 'Such a privilege to meet family friends.'

Janet sent him a look of utter devotion and he smiled back at her.

'Hope you'll be here for the Spring Dance,' said the Captain of the Ladies' Section. She had changed out of her golfing clothes into a snazzy cocktail number, and was giving it lots of cleavage and flashing eyes.

'It sounds delightful,' Richard assured her, avoiding the cleavage like a professional.

'Do you play darts?' said Janet, with an indignant look at the Mercedes-driving houri, and swept him off to the Ladies' Bar, where he had a very jolly time allowing himself to lose by not too much in matches against the Junior Mums until Janet relented and took them home for dinner.

She had wanted to invite her usual complement of guests but Bella had begged her not to.

'Let it just be us, Ma, just this once? Ask Neill and Val, if you like. But nobody else.'

Janet was disappointed. 'But I was going to hire a butler.'

'No-o-o-o.'

It was a cry of anguish.

'But it must be what he's used to?'

Bella sat her down in the kitchen and took both her hands. 'Ma. This is me. Forget him. *Me.* If he were anyone else, would you hire a butler? Did you hire a butler when Neill brought Val home?'

'No,' said Janet, struck.

'Well, then. Just treat him like you treated Val. *Please.* I just want us to be normal for once.'

'You're a funny girl,' said Janet, succumbing to her desperate tone. 'But if that's what you want, darling, of course.'

So supper was for the six of them. Neill and Val had driven over from Dorset, but after a good meal and plenty of wine they would not be driving back again. Which made redundant the nice problem of whether

Janet should allow Richard and Bella to sleep together under her roof. The Brays had two fully appointed guest rooms, with en suite showers. Neill and Val would have one. Bella the other. There was also a box room which doubled as Janet's sewing room and was fully of spooky dressmaker's dummies and rolls of fabric. And there was Kevin's study.

Kevin, who had given silent thanks to be relieved of the burden of a butler, was enough of a traditionalist to suggest that you couldn't put the Prince of Wales on a couch in the study.

'Bella could go on the couch?' mused Janet doubtfully.

'Don't think he'd like that. Not very chivalrous.'

So Janet had given in and Richard was to share Bella's room and en suite shower room.

'Thanks,' she muttered to Kevin, as she passed him in the hallway. 'We owe you.'

It turned into a fun party. In the end Neill pushed a coffee table into the middle of the floor and taught them all how to row to Viking rhythm. Kevin threw himself into the part, roaring out what he swore were Anglo-Saxon incantations. Even Val joined in, looking happier and more at home than Bella had ever seen her.

And when they all said good night, Richard kissed Janet's cheek with genuine affection.

'I like your mother,' he told Bella, sitting on the end of the bed to take his socks off. 'She's scared but she's still in there, punching her weight.'

Bella was sliding out of the dress her mother had bought her last month, but paused on hearing that.

Janet had been so pleased to see her in it that Bella completely forgot the thing made her look like a middle-aged golf wife.

'What do you mean, she's scared? What has she got to be scared of? Kevin takes care of everything.'

'No, he doesn't,' said Richard. 'He can't take care of her getting things wrong, being ignored, becoming a laughing stock.'

Bella dismissed that, half angry at the idea. 'Don't be ridiculous.'

But hadn't her mother said, 'I wish I were competent like you'?

'I told you, love. This is my job. I meet people who are scared of doing or saying the wrong thing all the time. And, believe me, Janet's a bad case. She's terrified.'

'Nonsense.'

'Didn't you see her when we were all playing Vikings this evening? She was never quite sure whether she was doing the right thing by joining in. Not sure we wanted her. Not sure she wasn't pushing in and spoiling it. Wondering whether she ought to be making coffee while the rest of us did what people like us do?'

Bella sat down on her side of the bed. 'No!' she said. But not because she still disbelieved him. 'Oh, poor Ma.'

Richard turned and gathered her up into his arms, as if he knew she needed comforting. 'She's like her daughter. She's brave. She took a chance and joined in.'

'You're quite a psychologist, aren't you?' she said slowly.

But he shook his head. 'I'm not anything. I just know what I see.'

237

Bella leaned against him, muzzy from wine and the pent-up anxieties of the last weeks. 'And you're kind. So very kind.'

He let her go, flipped down her bra strap and said in quite another voice, 'Also a half-trained Viking and randy as hell. Get your clothes off, woman.'

14

'What's your worst New Year Ever?' – *Tube Talk*

It was their last chance to be alone together in the run-up to Christmas.

Ian said he couldn't give Bella the updated diary pages. She suspected that was Wormtongue's doing. But she didn't sneak on him to Richard. For one thing it seemed feeble. For another, Richard was desperately busy, rushing about all over the country and out of it. She knew that because she saw pictures of him in the papers and on the News.

He did a good-will trip to New York, with a bunch of industrialists in tow, and sent her a text from the dance floor of Bar Bahia: *I'm boogieing for Britain here. Where are you when I need you?*

She laughed and texted back: *Ready to boogie any time*.

It was really late by then, the small hours in London, and Bella knew she should have been asleep. Instead she was sitting cross-legged on her bed, with a pashmina shawl round her shoulders and thick ski socks on her feet, trying to sort out some files for the evil dentist. Work was becoming increasingly busy as people dashed in to sort out their dental problems before the holidays.

She wanted to get the whole system indexed and in perfect order before she left on Christmas Eve. There would be no handover period with her successor.

Bella had rented a car and would be picking up Granny Georgia at the airport before driving the two of them and Lottie down to the New Forest for Christmas. Bella would spend the rest of Christmas week with Janet and Kevin, before heading north to Drummon House, the Royal residence on the edge of the Highlands, for the New Year.

She was not looking forward to the New Year.

On Richard's advice, Bella had braced herself for another Little Talk with Lady Pansy in advance of the invitation. It was an afternoon gig and Lady Pansy had served up a terrifying list of traditions and customs for the New Year, along with China tea in cups of porcelain so thin that their contents were cold before the first sip. Bella liked builder's tea with a good slug of milk, or Earl Grey if she was pushed. She nearly gagged at the smoky, herbal stuff that Lady Pansy favoured. It was, as she told Lottie afterwards, somehow slimy and sharp at the same time.

'Vomitorious,' said Lottie, repelled.

'Tell me about it. And then she went on for ever about the Family Traditions and how they had been spending New Year there since 1839 or something. I tell you, Lotts, my head began to spin.'

'I'm not surprised. The woman sounds a complete pill.'

'I don't think she means to be. She's very gentle and pleasant. I think she's doing her best to turn me into a good little courtier in the time available. But my family hasn't done anything since 1839, and I can't get worked up about traditions unless they have some point to them.'

Lottie grinned. 'That's my girl. Red Finn would be proud of you.'

Bella groaned. 'Don't talk to me about my father. I think he's deliberately trying to make things worse. He was threatening to write to the *Despatch* about Royalty grinding the faces of the poor in the dust, the last time we spoke.'

'One thing I'll say for Finn – he's consistent.'

'So is Lady Pansy,' said Bella, returning to her original grievance. 'Just look at that.' She flung a bulky envelope on to the kitchen table.

Lottie turned it over curiously. It had the Royal monogram on the back and weighed a ton.

'What's this?'

'Briefing,' said Bella in a voice of doom.

'Briefing? For the New Year party?'

'Yes.'

'For *two days?*'

'Yes.'

'The woman's mad,'said Lottie, with conviction. 'Nobody reads briefing of more than a page. What's in all this bumf, for God's sake?'

'Protocol. When you get up. When you eat breakfast. Where you eat breakfast. Where you're expected to be at all times of the day. How to curtsey. How to drink the loyal toast. Did you know that *some* people are allowed to say "The King, God bless him"? Not very many. Most people are expected to say "The King" and shut the fuck up.'

Lottie boggled.

'Then there's the Ball. Instructions on what to wear, skirt length (and fullness of), shoes.'

'*Shoes?*'

'Soft-soled Princess pumps are preferred,' read Bella out loud. 'Oh, God, it's like I've fallen through a wormhole into another universe. Individually the words make sense but I don't know what they mean when you put them together like that.'

She soon found out. Lady Pansy, it transpired, had taken the initiative. First off a small box arrived from a Scottish footwear manufacturer, containing shoes that were more like unstructured ballet slippers. They were light and pretty but too big for Bella's feet.

'Why doesn't the woman bloody *ask?*' fumed Bella, phoning the company. She was horrified to find that Lady Pansy had blagged them out of the company for free, as a gift to the Prince of Wales. 'They are nothing to do with the Prince,' said Bella tightly, down the phone to the Highlands. 'Please send me an invoice. Yes, for both sizes. I shall be paying.'

But that wasn't the only thing that Lady Pansy had ordered to turn Bella into a halfway decent guest at the Royal Family's New Year house party. A large, flat box also arrived.

Lottie and Bella surveyed it cautiously. 'It looks like one of those old-fashioned laundry boxes my grandmother used to have,' said Bella.

They opened it. Inside was a ball dress.

'That's a ball dress and a half,' said Lottie, extracting it from loads of tissue paper, an expression of fascinated horror on her face.

It was shiny. And very, very full. The material was so rigid, the thing could have stood up on its own, but it had a stiff underskirt anyway, just in case. It was patterned in huge vertical stripes of purple, turquoise, midnight blue and cerise. When Bella put it on, it turned out to have sleeves puffed to such bloated proportions she would have to go through doors sideways.

It was beyond dreadful.

'But it ticks all the sodding boxes,' said Bella, beginning to gibber. 'No slits, no bare upper arms, full-length, full skirt, not black. AAAAARGH!'

Lottie was studying Lady P's briefing. '"Tiaras may be worn." Wonder if she's going to send you one of those, too?'

But Lady P's initiative had worn itself out with The Striped Horror. 'Stripes,' she said, when Bella rang to query the purchase, 'are Very Slimming. And puffed sleeves are so youthful. The Queen,' she added as a clincher, 'agrees with me.'

Bella put the phone down, defeated.

But Lottie was made of sterner stuff. 'Look, there could be a misunderstanding. Hope on, hope ever. Take a dress of your own as well.'

Bella looked at The Horror with loathing. 'I don't have anything that meets the criteria. I've got to do Scottish dancing in the thing. *Me*. You know me and dancing. I wish I was dead.'

Lottie was sobered.

243

'Lady P has sent over instructions on how to dance Scottish reels. There are bits on the footwork and bits on the arm gestures. Only gentlemen raise their arms above their heads in the Highland Schottische, whatever that is. There's no namby-pamby gender equality on a Highland dance floor, I'll have you know. And there are even bloody road maps on the dances themselves!'

'Bella,' said Lottie very quietly, 'I'm sorry, but I think you're going barmy.'

'So do I.'

'Dances don't have road maps.'

'Scottish dances do. It's deeply depressing.'

Of course Richard, bopping away for King and Country in Bar Bahia didn't know that. He texted: *We'll boogie in the New Year*.

To which Bella replied: *Wanna bet?*

Almost immediately her phone rang.

'What is it, sweetheart? You're not getting cold feet about coming to Drummon?'

'Not cold feet, no. But I haven't got time to do the necessary homework.'

'Sorry, I missed that. Did you say homework?'

'Yes.'

She could hear the latin rhythms in the club behind him.

'Don't follow.'

She told him about Lady Pansy's package. 'The dress makes me feel ill to look at. And the dance instructions are like preparation for an Outward Bound course,' she said in horror, 'with crossword puzzles and charades thrown in. I may run away to sea.'

244

'Nah. Not you. You're not a runner.'

'I could be. How the hell do you make an arch without raising your arms above your head?'

'Ah, the Reels,' he said, enlightened. 'Look, forget all that. I'll make sure you only dance with me or guys who know what they're doing.'

'Hmm,' said Bella, unconvinced.

'Trust me. Just close your eyes and I'll drive. I came reeling out of the womb.'

'Oh, God.'

'Don't worry, Dream Girl. I'll get you through it.'

'You'll need to,' she said grumpily. But she felt better for talking to him.

The week before Christmas was mad, with lots of parties at which she saw people she hadn't heard from for ages. Some of them knew she was seeing the Prince of Wales but very few of them cared. Very few of them, Bella thought with a little chill, expected it to last.

By lunch-time on Christmas Eve the shops were empty and the London streets nearly deserted. There was a fine fall of rain but it was too warm to turn to snow. Both girls stowed their overnight cases and presents in the back seat of the rented car, leaving the boot free for Georgia's international luggage, and went off to Heathrow to meet her flight. She was coming via Madrid.

Georgia strolled out through Passport Control looking, as she always did, a miracle of understated elegance. She was wearing slim jeans, cowboy boots, a fringed alpaca jacket and a pearl-white poloneck sweater. Her nut-brown hair was shoulder-length, drawn back at the neck with a thin band. Her hair shone. Her eyes sparkled. She looked like a million dollars and totally in control of her world.

'Who travels for twenty-four hours in a white poloneck?' said Lottie in awe.

'She changed in the ladies, after she landed,' said Bella, who had travelled with her grandmother and knew her strategy.

They surged forward and embraced her.

'You look wonderful,' Georgia told them both impartially.

Bella took charge of her case and led the way to the car park.

'Did you have a good flight?'

'Her grandmother was wheeling the smallest possible carry-on case.

'I had a good book. The flight passed.' She shrugged. 'Now tell me about you two. Bella has a young man and a new job, I know. Lottie, what about you? Still enjoying London?'

Most of the traffic had gone by the time they got on to the M3. So they had a straight run, in a light grey drizzle, with Lottie talking about her job, very amusingly, and Georgia asking all the right questions, just as she always did, in her soft Southern drawl.

They delivered Lottie to the Hendreds, had a cup of tea and a mince pie there, and drove on to Janet and Kevin's.

'Now,' said Georgia, as Bella pulled out of the Hendreds' drive, 'tell me about him. I can't get any sense out of either of your parents. How long have you known him?'

'Not long at all.' Bella gave her a rapid outline of events to date.

'Hmm. No, you're right. That's fast.' It was interesting. When she was thinking aloud, Georgia's Southern drawl became more pronounced. It was, decided Bella, very attractive – calm and somehow poised.

'I wish I were poised,' she said involuntarily.

Her grandmother looked at her quickly. 'That's an interesting word. Does he make you feel inadequate? Socially, maybe?'

'He doesn't but, well—' She described the New Year's briefing package.

Georgia's sculpted lips tightened perceptibly. 'How discourteous. Who did you say this person is?'

'Lady Pansy. She's Queen Jane's right-hand woman, as far as I can see. Been with her for ever.'

Georgia drummed her fingers thoughtfully. 'That suggests she has no life of her own,' she drawled. 'You need to watch these loyal retainers. They can become very gothic in their devotion.'

Bella laughed heartily. 'Not Lady Pansy! If she weren't so elegant you'd say she was a horse.'

'Horses are very gothic,' said Georgia obstinately. 'You watch her. And watch your back around her.'

Of course she didn't say any of that in front of Janet and Kevin. Georgia's idea of good behaviour demanded a high degree of forbearance, as well as refraining from giving advice in public or arguing either. So when Janet started to complain about Finn baiting the newspapers with his antipathy to the monarch, Georgia just smiled faintly and drifted away to somewhere more congenial.

But she did take Bella on one side and say, 'Are you really worried about spending the New Year with Richard's family?'

'No-o-o.' But in the end it all poured out: the dancing-by-numbers Bella had never done before, The Striped Horror, the pumps.

Georgia laughed. 'My dear child! You just need a posh frock.'

'I've got one,' said Bella gloomily. 'And how.'

'No. One you like and feel comfortable in. Look, you may not care for the idea, but I have a lot of my own frocks stored in London. We still just about made a debut in my day. Why don't we see if there's anything that you suitable among them? We're quite similar. I think the size will be about right. They may be a little short, but if you have complicated dancing to face, that is hardly a fault.'

Bella agreed, but without much hope.

She spent an edgy Christmas, sustained mainly by Richard's phone calls from various places in the world where British forces were serving. No wonder Ian had kept the diary from her, thought Bella, watching the TV News to see Richard jump lightly from a helicopter on to the deck of an aircraft carrier. He looked instantly at home, eager and friendly, and always a concerned, good listener. Oh, she did love him.

She looked up suddenly and found her grand-mother's eyes on her. Georgia said nothing, just inclined her elegant head, but Bella felt as if she had been given her grandmother's blessing. She hugged herself.

'You'll love him,' she said, suddenly certain that she was right.

'I probably will, dear. As I said, you and I are very alike.'

Richard met Bella at the station on New Year's Eve. Just him. No security officer, no Press Adviser. The station-master touched his cap in a friendly way and wished them both Happy New Year, and Richard drove the big 4WD off up into the hills, along an unmade track to the house.

'Best view,' he said, waving at folds of snow-covered hills to his left and a sparkling, darting brook in the white valley below them.

'It's gorgeous,' Bella said, truthfully.

'But freezing. Hope you brought plenty of warm clothes?'

'Yes, I came prepared.' Conscious of Georgia's Alternative Posh Frock in her suitcase, Bella said carefully, 'What will people wear to the ball tonight?'

Richard glanced down at her. 'Yes, OK. Don't rub it in. I'll be prancing around in a kilt with a lace jabot and a velvet jacket. And so will all the other guys. I don't get a vote.'

She was taken aback. 'No? Really? You mean, I get to see your knees?'

His eyes glinted. 'You've seen my knees, you baggage.'

'Not in public. Not to really stand back and admire

249

them.' She let herself dwell on the picture with pleasure for a moment. Then said, 'No, actually, what I meant was the ladies.'

He shrugged. 'It's easier for them. They wear their usual rig. With mountaineer's underwear underneath to keep them warm, of course.'

'Their usual rig?'

'Yes. Why?' he said puzzled

She thought of The Striped Horror. Puffed sleeves like a Michelin Man's biceps were nobody's idea of normal.

'I think I may have got the wrong end of the stick,' she said diplomatically. 'Look, do me a favour. I've borrowed a dress . . . well, actually, like your boat, it's more sort of inherited. Will you come and give me your opinion on it before we have to join the party?'

Richard agreed with enthusiasm.

And later he took one look at her in a Grace Kelly number, with a soft skirt of misty grey silk crepe, and, 'Very elegant.'

So that was all right. At least it would be until Lady Pansy caught sight of it. Her niece, the Honourable Chloe, was among the guests as well. It would be interesting, thought Bella with a touch of cattiness, to see whether Chloe's gown was out of the School of Striped Horror.

Richard took her down to the drawing room at Drummon House, at the cocktail hour. There was a handsome fire blazing in the great hearth, but a combination of stone walls and ill-fitting windows meant that the warmth did not permeate very far into the room.

The Queen, greeting Bella kindly, seemed not to notice that she had failed to curtsey.

Prince George, a taller, gawkier version of Richard, flapped a hand in greeting. 'Hi. The sooner the physical jerks start, the sooner the sound of chattering teeth will die away.'

A steward offered her a tray. Richard inspected it and explained its contents. 'You can have one of three sorts of malt whisky or a concoction of blended Scotch, amaretto and cointreau, which George invented last year. I don't advise it.'

'I call it Drummon Hell,' Prince George told her proudly.

He had the reputation of being a bit of a hell-raiser and Bella had been wary of meeting him, but she found she liked him. It was impossible not to; he was a Labrador puppy in human form.

Bella took one of the glasses, with a word of thanks, and they moved further into the drawing room. As soon as they were out of earshot of the Queen she hissed, 'I hate whisky.'

'Don't worry. I'll drink it.'

'And I forgot to curtsey to your mother.'

'She'll get over it.'

'But Lady Pansy won't. She looked really disappointed. You know, more in sorrow than in anger.'

'Pansy's an old fart,' he said brutally. 'Don't worry about it. Lots of people don't curtsey these days.'

'I have tried, honest. But I just can't get the hang of it.'

'No sweat. When you have to, it will come naturally.'

Bella was alarmed. 'When I *have* to? What do you mean, *have to*? You just said lots of people don't.'

Richard looked mischievous. 'Wait and see.'

Bella looked round the room. There was a smattering of dinner jackets but the men were mostly in kilts, worn with crisp white shirts, a frilled or lacy stock, and a waisted black velvet jacket with gold buttons. They looked very fine. The women were more varied in their dress. If they had had the same instructions as Bella, none of them had resorted to stiff shiny satin and puffed sleeves. Some of the older ladies were wearing long white gloves, above the elbow. The cannier ones kept pashminas to hand. Bella saw that Lady Pansy herself was in a stiff violet crinoline that she had probably been wearing in the eighties.

No black permitted, Bella remembered from Lady Pansy's notes, low necklines discouraged and sleeves were obligatory. Lottie had howled with laughter: 'Where do they think they are? In a cathedral?' she'd said. But now, looking at one of her fellow first-timers who had ignored the spirit of the notes and opted for festive décolletage, Bella felt sorry for the woman. Diamonds and gooseflesh was not a good look.

She did not have long to pity her, however. There were three mighty raps at the door, followed by an ear-splitting noise like an elephant farting. Then the doors were flung open and in marched a piper, kilt swinging.

At once there was a scramble to fall in behind him.

George hissed in her ear, 'We all march round the room after him, and divide so women go to the left and men to the right. Then we go down either side of the

252

room and meet in front of the doors and join up with a partner and go into a Grand March.'

The name was vaguely familiar but that was all. 'Sorry. My mind's a blank.'

'Don't worry about it. It's dead easy. Just do what everyone else does. All you need to do is make sure that nobody queue jumps when you go to meet your partner. It's a favourite trick.'

'I didn't realise it was so competitive.'

'Blood on the floor,' said George cheerfully. 'Keep your eye on Richard. You may need to make a grab.' And he waved cheerily as he peeled off in the other direction.

'I will.'

Bella nearly lost him, though, when Chloe, in a figure-hugging lacy dress that was only just this side of decent, darted in front of her at the last moment, just as Bella was about to step out in front of the big doors to meet him.

'Excuse me,' she said in a breathy, little girl voice that exactly matched her wide-eyed stare.

But Richard was too quick for her. With a nifty soft-shoe shuffle that Fred Astaire would not have been ashamed of, he slid momentarily out of his line and in again behind a grey-haired man, who at once stepped up to the place in front of the doors. The Hon Chloe had no choice. She gave the elderly party her hand and they marched off together down the middle of the drawing room, now cleared of furniture.

As they met and followed, Richard took Bella's hand and laid it gently on his velvet-jacketed arm,

'Fifteen love to us,' he murmured.

A terrible desire to giggle took hold of her, as they marched solemnly down the freezing cold, over-furnished room, and round the edge again to join up in fours. The servants just about managed to clear a wide enough path through the furniture for the column of four to pass. But Bella had begun to see what was going to happen next. And there was no way they were going to be able to march down that room eight abreast.

'Someone's going to get impaled on a suit of armour,' she said, half fascinated, half appalled.

Richard kept a straight face. 'It has been known. It is rumoured that someone forgot to clear away the piano one year and my Uncle Leopold marched straight over it, dragging his partner after him.'

Bella folded her lips tightly together. Her shoulders were starting to shake. Oh, God, I'm not going to be able to get through this lunacy without disgracing myself, she thought.

And then they did all join up in an eight, and the lady at one end of the line and the man at the other did indeed have to vault over occasional tables and slalom round chairs. Above the clatter of falling objets d'art and cries of anguish from those who had stubbed their toes, the King's voice could be heard saying testily, 'Keep time. Keep *time*, damn you.'

Richard bent his head sideways. 'Don't worry. He's almost certainly talking to the piper rather than my mother,' he confided in a whisper.

Bella's ribs ached. She moaned. Suppressing laughter was becoming agony for her.

'You're a swine,' she said conversationally, keeping her bright smile in place.

'Yeah. But I know how to do this stuff. So,' he went into a mobster voice, 'you need me, baby.'

That was when the double doors at the far end were flung wide and they progessed, eight by eight, into what Bella could only describe as a baronial hall: high ceiling, banners, serfs gathered round the walls watching, the lot. She gasped and would have stopped dead, but for the momentum of the group which kept surging forward. She stumbled but Richard and George between them half lifted her off her feet, keeping her upright and moving until she had regained her balance.

'Keep up. Keep up,' muttered Prince George in a very good imitation of the King.

Bella gave a strangled gulp and her ribs started to hurt again.

The piper got to the far end of the hall and turned to face them. The eights all peeled off and formed squares, and the serfs – who, now she came to look, were just as well dressed as the Royal party – bundled on to the floor too.

The piper started to tap his foot. You could feel the whole room counting. *One*, two, three, four. *One*, two, three, four. And they were off, circling round to the right, and then back, hell for leather, like a cavalry charge.

Richard said over his shoulder, 'Next, stick out your right hand, left round my waist. You're going round in a star with the other ladies.'

Bella was still trying to assimilate this when he put his arm round her waist, flung her into the circle and was galloping off, round again. And when they completed the circuit, he switched places with her and they went back and around the other way. Her head started to spin . . .

It seemed as if every time she learned how to do a move, and started to enjoy herself, the damn' dance did something different. And did it fast. There was a good bit in the middle where you were allowed to stand still while other people did their thing. But sometimes you had to do your thing and that was torture. Richard was really good at sending Bella off into the fray, with a gentle push in the small of the back. But the other people in the set all seemed to know what they were doing, and helped too, reaching out a hand to steer her when it was feasible, giving her good clear hand signals when it wasn't.

The music finally came to an end on a long chord and she and Richard were bowing to each other.

'Curtsey,' he mouthed.

'What?' But she looked sideways and saw what the women across the set were doing. Bella copied them and didn't wobble too much at all.

'I told you it would come naturally,' said Richard smugly, taking her hand as she rose out of the curtsey. He tucked it under the crook of his arm. 'I'm going to have to do lots of duty dances, but I've lined up friends and experts to take you through when I can't dance with you. Have you got your dance card?'

'A dance card? I'm supposed to have a dance card?' Bella shook her head, caught between laughter and dismay. 'What is this, *Gone with the Wind*? Georgia won't believe it when I tell her.'

'Pansy was supposed to have sent it to you. It has the list of dances in it and a small pencil.'

'Well she sent me a paper mountain, but I don't remember a dance card.'

'Not a problem. There will be spares.' He turned to his brother. 'George, would you—?'

'I'm on it.' George disappeared into the throng like an eel and returned with the prize.

Richard squiggled his distinctive black R beside several dances and made sure that her other partners were both kind and expert. 'You can dance with George,' he instructed, 'but not in the Duke of Perth, when he goes crazy, or the Irish Rover because he always gets lost.'

George agreed cheerfully. He didn't seem worried. 'Everyone has one dance that brings them to their knees. Actually, that's half the fun of reels – the catastrophes.'

Richard sighed. 'See what I mean? Dance with him if you must, but watch yourself.'

But it wasn't George who brought about the disaster. That was all Bella's own fault.

Her partners, briefed by Richard, got her through the figures by a combination of timely crisp instruction and sheer muscle power. She danced a thing called Postie's Jig with a gentle-faced, middle-aged man, who was clearly an expert.

'It's an interesting dance,' he told her in a soft Highland accent. 'Like a piece of paper that keeps being folded in on itself. Two couples dance at the same time, while the other four dancers stand still at the corners and help them round. Very pleasing when it's well performed. It has balance.'

'Um, good,' said Bella doubtfully. She just wanted to scramble through it without falling flat on her face or poking someone's eye out, but she didn't tell her kindly partner that.

And they would have been fine, she was sure, if they had joined one of the friendly sets she had been dancing in up until then, where the other dancers were happy to give her an informal push in the right direction. But unfortunately she and her gentle partner were summoned to join the Queen's set, in which Lady Pansy was also dancing. And Lady Pansy tried to help by shouting instructions at Bella across the set. Sometimes these conflicted with her partner's. It was a nightmare, with Bella turning right when she should have gone left, blundering too far down the set, grabbing the hand of the wrong man when they came to turn in the middle . . . And then real disaster struck. They were dancing in the middle of the set, towards the Queen and her partner, in full regimentals. One couple had to make an arch; one had to go under it.

'If you're going *up* the set, you put your arms *up*,' her kind partner whispered.

But Bella had no idea which direction was up. She thought she felt a tug and started to raise her arm, but Lady Pansy, standing at the top left-hand corner of the set, frowned and shook her head. So Bella snatched her hand back again – just as the Queen and her soldier lowered their heads to come through the arch they were expecting.

Well, Bella recovered but not fast enough. The Queen's priceless tiara slid over one ear and started to fall.

It lasted only a moment, less than a bar of music. Bella tried to look over her shoulder but her partner forced her to dance on. So did everyone else, including the Queen, who for the rest of the dance held her tiara in place with the hand that she should have been giving to other dancers. Lady Pansy looked as if she would cry.

Afterwards everyone apologised. The Highlander was mortified, he could not understand it, nothing like that had ever happened to him on the dance floor before. He begged the Queen's pardon again and again. Bella felt like a murderer.

Queen Jane, of course, could not have been nicer. 'These things happen, Henry. It's not the end of the world.' And to Bella, 'My dear, it couldn't matter less. Postie is always fast and furious. At least no one was hurt.'

Which didn't make Bella feel any better.

Prince George, when he heard, went into mourning. 'You knocked Mother's crown off and I missed it? Not even a photograph, since Father went and banned phones! Bugger, life's unfair.'

The Queen re-attached her tiara and they danced for an hour and a half. Then dinner was served, the serfs at long trestles which were put up in the baronial hall, the Royal party in the dining room. Formal dinner with the King and Queen was not fun. There were rules about when you could eat and when you had to stop. Twice Bella had her plate whisked away from under her nose before she had finished. Practised courtiers like Lady Pansy, she realised, hoovered their food in as soon as possible, to avoid exactly that.

'You could have warned me,' she said to Richard, on her left.

He grinned, unrepentant. 'My father hates long meals. He wants to get this over with and go back to his engines. You watch. He'll be out of the hall at midnight plus a nanosecond.'

'Really?'

'Maybe not quite a nanosecond. We all have to sing Auld Lang Syne and give three cheers for the King. But after that he legs it as fast as he can.'

'So the party ends at midnight?'

He looked startled. 'In practice, the King goes, the party gets going. Two parties, usually. The reeling will carry on till dawn but there's an alternative gig in one of the barns for anyone under thirty. George is usually involved. Dodgy lighting, crazy music, that sort of thing. Do you want to go?'

Bella smiled straight into his eyes.

'Do you want to?'

'Maybe for half an hour or so,' he said, his voice suddenly thickened.

He took her hand under the table and held it so hard she could feel the pulse in his fingers.

She said softly, 'Any chance of seeing you tonight?'

He looked so astonished that she caught herself saying, 'No, of course not, I'm sorry. Silly thing to say. Not under your parents' roof. Not with all those rules about when and where you can walk in the corridors . . .'

'What do you think all those rules are about, for God's sake?'

'Um – tradition?'

'Yup. A tradition that grew up so that everyone could get back to the right bedroom in the morning without being seen by anyone who could tell on them.'

'*What?*'

'Think about it. You spend the night with the lady of your heart. She may, or may not, be married. But anyway, you shouldn't be there. So what happens if someone sees you creeping back to your own room? Well, they shouldn't be there either, so it's mutual blackmail. Works like a dream.'

'You're not serious?'

'Trust me. No servant will set foot above the ground floor until eight o'clock, on express orders. Apparently, in my grandfather's heyday, it could get like the rush hour. Mind you, he had a particularly libidinous set of friends.'

Bella shook her head. 'So all these rules are just so you can behave disgracefully?'

'Behave disgracefully and not get found out, yes.'

She looked severe. 'It's not very honest. Not sure I approve.'

His eyes glinted. 'Tell me that and I'll go back to my own room, I promise.'

He silenced her by carrying their clasped hands to his lips and feathering a quick kiss along the knuckles of hers, before tucking them back under the table again.

Bella gasped.

But the servants were removing the plates and she felt

someone's eyes on her. When she looked up, she saw Chloe Lenane staring down the table at her with an expression almost of hatred. It was so unexpected that Bella blinked. Yet when she looked again, the previous ditzy vague expression was back. It was unsettling.

At a signal from the Queen, the ladies retired. Bella would have missed it if Richard hadn't hissed, 'Off you go, follow my leader.'

In the boudoir set aside for the female guests, Lady Pansy came up to Bella.

'I see you found a different dress.'

She murmured something about the difficulties of packing when you were coming by train.

Lady Pansy gave her a sweet smile that made her eyes glisten like flaming arrows. 'I do hope you're enjoying yourself, dear. Just a word to the wise.'

'Yes?'

'Do be careful not to put yourself forward too much. This is the big event of the year for these people. They look forward to it for twelve months. The young girls, and not just the young ones –' she tittered in a way that Bella suddenly found rather unpleasant '– all hope to dance with the Prince of Wales. Like a fairytale. Something to tell the children. It would be very selfish of you to monopolise him and spoil their evening.'

Bella was not going to tell her that it was Richard who had decided how many times they would dance together.

'Thank you. I'll remember,' she said tonelessly.

'I was sure you would.' And Lady Pansy's violet crinoline bobbed away.

Bella uncurled her fingers. Lady Pansy was seriously starting to get on her tits. Oh, Lord, she's the Queen's best friend and I want to slap the woman, Bella thought ruefully.

The rest of the evening passed as Richard had predicted. At two minutes to midnight the band finished a lively reel and someone switched on the radio. People began to look round for the person they wanted to be with at the turn of the year. The Queen, Bella saw, went to the King's side. George had acquired a stunning redhead, and Eleanor . . . but then Bella saw Richard powering his way towards her through the crowd and forgot Princess Eleanor and everyone else but her own lover.

He was standing in front of her. They smiled into each other's eyes. There might have been no one else there.

The room fell silent. The countdown started. One, two, three . . .

Everyone joined in, even the King. The Queen, Bella saw, was watching her and Richard. She looked unhappy.

Seven, eight, nine . . .

George had produced squeakers and was passing them round his immediate neighbours with an evil grin.

Ten!

There was the first boom from Big Ben.

Bella flung her arms round Richard's neck and kissed him fiercely. She didn't stop kissing him until the final boom was dying away. She fell back, startled by her own intensity. The light in his eyes made him almost unrecognisable.

'Oh, God, I love you,' she said under her breath, more to herself than to him.

His hands tightened on her waist. 'Never mind about that damned bop in the barn. I need to see you alone. OK?'

'Yes,' she said, shivering for the first time that evening. And not from cold.

George's squeakers went off in an appalling chorus. Even people inured to the drone of the bagpipes clapped their hands over their ears.

'Happy New Year,' everyone was saying to everyone else. 'Happy New Year.'

There was a lot of kissing. As Lady Pansy had warned, Richard came in for a good deal of it from female tenants of all ages. And, Bella saw, Chloe Lenane into the bargain.

'Auld Lang Syne,' cried the King, seizing a couple of hands and backing against the wall with his newly acquired partners. The Queen was not one of them.

There was even a protocol to 'Auld Lang Syne,' Bella found. She was used to a cheerful, drunken shambles with people hanging on to the person next to them and then diving into the middle, cheering. In Drummon House you sang the first verse (there are *verses*? she thought) standing upright with your hands by your sides. It was only the second verse – *And there's a hand, my trusty fiere, and gie's a hand o' thine* – that you were actually licensed to take hands. She began to long for a good old-fashioned bop where you could do anything

264

you wanted, with your own hands or anyone else's.

The singing done, everyone kissed some more, though more sedately. They cheered the King. The King waved a gracious hand and bolted for home. The Queen did not go with him.

'Uh–oh,' said Richard. 'Not good. Will you be OK? I need to dance with my mother. *Then* we're going to be on our own and nobody is going to stop us.'

He was gone for one dance only. When it was over, Bella saw him take his mother's hand. He seemed to be reassuring her. Then she saw a courtier hovering and turned away, dismissing her son.

Richard came back to Bella. 'Ready to return to the twenty-first century now?'

She looked at him. 'Is your mother OK?'

'You've got sharp eyes.' He was rueful. 'We had a slight difference of opinion, that's all.'

'And it's settled?'

'She's cool. Now, tell me, do you really want to go and dance in George's barn?'

She shook her head.

'Then come on, let's go sort out the rest of our lives.'

15

'Best and Worst Proposals' – *Girl About Town*

Richard made Bella bundle up in warm clothes and took her out of a side door. Nobody noticed them go. The big off-roader was standing there, its lights on and the engine humming.

'Thanks, Bill,' Richard said, as a tall man in Highland dress got out of the driving seat.

'You're welcome, Sir. Miss. Have a nice look at the stars.' And the man went off chuckling to himself.

'The stars?' echoed Bella, clutching the collar of her coat to her throat. 'I don't believe it.'

'Don't argue. Bill has been warming this car up for you for a good ten minutes. There's a car rug, too, if you're chilly.'

Richard helped her into the vehicle and it was indeed as warm as toast. Bella relaxed a little.

'Where are we going?'

'There's a painting hut on the hill. It's really good for looking at the stars.'

She looked at him suspiciously. 'Are you winding me up again?'

'I want to be alone with you without some member of

staff, or courtier, or bloody nosy member of my family getting in the way,' he said with sudden violence. 'It seems like for ever since we had some privacy.'

'I know.'

The painting hut was a small single-storey stone building. It might have started life as a shepherd's cottage but now it had expanses of glass set into the walls and the roof. More important, there was smoke coming out of its chimney.

There were vehicle tracks leading up to it and Richard stayed in them, so that the off-roader swayed and bumped but did not slide on the midnight ice that was forming over the impacted snow.

'In, quickly,' he said when they got there.

The place was not locked. It too was as cosy as could be, with a wood-burning stove glowing in the hearth.

But Bella did not look at the stove. She gazed at the stars. Walls and roof had been carefully replaced by glass, so no matter which way you looked, you saw only the night sky. It was like being suspended in space. The stars were so close you felt you could touch them, and the moon had a frosty halo.

'It's amazing,' said Bella, awed.

'Yes. I come here to think. I always have. I was up here this afternoon before I came to meet you. And that's when I realised I had to bring you here.'

'So I'm here. And?'

He drew a deep breath and turned to face her. In the moonlight, he looked handsome and passionate and deeply serious. But his voice was level.

'Bella, it's been three months. I know I've already told

you that I knew the moment I saw you . . . you must have thought that was crazy . . . but I did. I can't explain it. I saw you, with your feet in the air, covered in bits of ivy, and it was like everything in me clicked into the right place at that moment. I know I thought: so she's the one. That'll be all right then.' He stopped talking and she saw him swallow.

'Only, of course, it isn't. Anyone who marries me, marries the job, the family, the protocol.' He almost spat the last word.

'I think that's always true though, isn't it? I mean, if you marry a doctor, you end up answering the phone to an emergency in the middle of the night.'

What am I babbling about? thought Bella. I'm being proposed to, for God's sake. *Shut up, Bella Greenwood.* She closed her lips firmly, and waited.

Richard said, 'And then there's the public.'

She nodded.

'Bella, I know you don't want to be in the spotlight. We tried to keep out of it, both of us, didn't we? But you see – it can't be done, or not for long. You've been brilliant, all the time, funny and tolerant and kind and . . . oh, all the things I knew you'd be, the moment I fell in love with you. But—'

But? BUT? Hey, am I getting my marching orders, not a proposal at all?

He said very quietly, 'Bella, I love you. I want to marry you. But what you see is what you get. The job is me. I can't not be what I am. If you can't take that . . . and I won't blame you. Honestly, I won't. But if you *can't* . . . then please, will you tell me now? And we can say goodbye tomorrow, with no hard feelings.'

She almost bounced with indignation. 'No hard feelings? Are you out of your mind? Don't I get a chance to say yes before you write my refusal speech for me?'

He stared at her in the starlit dark. 'What?'

She calmed down somewhat. 'Ask me to marry you. Go on. Just ask.'

For a moment he looked almost frantic. 'Bella, I—' Then, typically, he drew a long breath and was calm again. It came out with the precision of a shopping list, and about as much emotion. 'I love you. I want to be with you. I want to make you happy. Please, will you be my wife?'

She had known what she was going to say; had known for days, been certain. Yet suddenly, all her doubts rose up and locked her tongue. she found she couldn't say a word.

Richard searched her face.

'Why?' she managed at last. It was not much more than a croak. I've got cold feet, she thought, appalled at herself.

Scrupulously, he didn't touch her. 'I go to a lot of weddings.' His voice was reflective. 'They're big promises. Heroic. In sickness and health. For richer, for poorer. They stop you dead in your tracks. You think: am I up to this? Can I really promise everything I have to give? And mean it, really *mean* it?'

'Everything I have to give,' Bella repeated slowly. 'Yes.'

'And that's what you want?'

'Only if it's mutual.'

269

Still she hesitated, suspended between everything she'd known up to now and the unpredictable future.

'Oh, God, Bella it's the one thing I'm certain of. I can do it with you.'

Still she waited, not quite trusting herself.

His voice suddenly ragged, he said, 'How can I explain? I *want* to make you those promises. It just seems right. Not easy exactly, but natural.'

'Yes,' she said, her doubts falling away as she recognised the feeling and the strength of it. 'The next big thing in my life. Our lives.'

He held his breath as if he couldn't quite believe what she was saying.

Bella leaned into him and kissed him, gravely and deliberately. It was acceptance and a promise, and they both knew it.

'Yes please, Richard. I would very much like to marry you.'

Afterwards he was in tearing spirits. They bounced down the hillside, with him singing 'Scotland the Brave' at the top of his voice. He was all for bursting in on George's barn and announcing their news at once. But Bella, remembering the Queen's unhappy glances in her direction, said, 'No, you have to tell your parents first.'

So he settled for a wild boogie instead.

'But I'm rubbish at it,' wailed Bella. 'I bump into things, you know I do. And I've got two left feet.'

But nothing could curb Richard's enthusiasm. 'I got you through the Eightsome Reel, didn't I? Stick with me, baby. You ain't seen nothing yet.'

270

The party was in full swing when they ran in, hand in hand. Grace Kelly style, Bella found, worked just as well for dancing in a barn as for reels. George and his team had hung tartan rugs over the walls of what must once have been a cow byre, and there were several glitterballs and a lot of blue lighting. Also a table full of drinks where you could have a simple beer or invent your own cocktail. Mothers had been baking for weeks and there were sausage rolls, sandwiches and a competitive selection of cakes. The dance floor was a patchwork of stone slabs and old floorboards but nobody seemed to care much.

There was no DJ but a local band could, and did, do everything from heavy rock to punk hop. The lead singer did a passable imitation of Springsteen, too.

'Dance, with you,' said Richard, not taking no for an answer.

And he was right, she didn't fall over or kick anything. In fact, it was while an astonished Bella was delivering some eloquent pelvic thrusts to 'I'm on Fire' that Richard stopped her dead and said breathlessly, 'Enough already. I've got a *bad* desire.'

Her smile was blazing. 'Let's go.'

The night, as she afterwards told Lottie, should have been torrid. They were both wracked with lust and had been behaving well all evening. And they hadn't seen each before that for what seemed like a lifetime.

Only it was very difficult to do torrid passion in a house with a frugal central heating system and draughts to make the North Wind slink away, outclassed. After

271

they twice lost the mountainous covers and Bella screamed for the wrong reasons – acute and agonising cramp in her right calf – they collapsed into laughter and put lust on hold.

'I'll take you to Barbados,' promised Richard. He got out of bed and brought her the sapphire kimono that she had left over the back of a chair. He tied a big bow at her waist and then got back into bed, cuddling her up to his chest and tucking the heavyweight blankets round her ears. 'Or the Sahara.'

'I'll hold you to that.'

They were asleep almost at once.

They were awoken by a discreet scratching on the door. Bella came awake to find Richard out of bed, shivering and swearing. She didn't blame him. She had no idea what time it was, but from the scrap of window she could see where the curtains didn't meet, the sky was still as black as a coal cellar outside. She put on the light.

'Take my robe. I'm warm now.' She pulled off the kimono and threw it towards him.

He pressed it appreciatively to his face, before pulling it on. Of course, it gaped across his chest, but it was better than nothing, thought Bella. The bedroom was icy. He thrust his feet into his dress shoes at the same time. 'Thank you.'

He opened the door, indifferent to the rules, scandal, or even his own dignity.

'What the fuck?' he said with pardonable asperity.

It was Julian Madoc. 'I'm really sorry, sir.' He even sounded it. 'But the King says, please will you join him in the study as soon as possible? There's been a development.'

'What sort of development?' demanded Richard disagreeably.

'More internet comment, I'm afraid. And an unfortunate photograph of Her Majesty. The Press will be here any time.'

'*Here*? You mean you've set up a Press Conference?'

Madoc was clearly shocked by the suggestion. 'Certainly not. But outside, you know. In the village. Asking people for their stories. Bringing their chequebooks. We need – that is, the King feels we need an agreed line.'

There was a pregnant pause. Then Richard said, 'Oh, very well. We'll be down as soon as we've climbed into our Arctic weather wear.'

He closed the door firmly. Bella pulled the covers up to her nose and watched appreciatively.

'I fancy you in blue silk.'

He grinned briefly. 'You fancy me in anything. Thank God. Damn, I'm so tired of worrying about the bloody Press. Oh, well, I suppose we'd better get dressed and join the Council of War. Have you got a good thick sweater, or shall I bring one back for you?'

She liked the idea of wearing his clothes. 'Almost certainly mine isn't thick enough.'

He nodded. 'Right. I'll bring you one.'

He went, leaving Bella to wonder dreamily whether any returning adulterer whom he met on the way would keep quiet about the fact that the Prince of Wales darted about Drummon House in a blue silk kimono.

273

By the time Richard returned, Bella had pulled on all the clothes she had brought with her, pretty well. He was wearing thick tweed trousers, double-knit socks and walking boots, and a green military jumper over several layers of natural fibre.

Bella purred. 'Love the combat gear. Not as swash-buckling as a blue silk kimono, of course, but you look ready for action.'

He eyed her consideringly. 'I can always take my Aran sweater away again.'

'No, no, please. Please. I didn't mean it.'

The big white thing was as solid as a horse blanket and just as cosy. Bella pulled it on over her stylish but inadequate cashmere and instantly felt her frosted muscles start to thaw. It was ludicrously too big, of course. The sleeves hung over her hands, but it smelled of Richard's shampoo and she knew that smell.

'Thank you,' she said, basking a bit.

He put his arm round her and they went to face the music.

The study turned out to be a relatively small room, so that the big fire there did actually have some effect. The Queen was sitting beside it, looking elegant as always but concerned. The King was reading a printout.

George had been wrong about the absence of mobile phones. There was a photograph of the Queen with her tiara over one eye. It had been all over the Twittersphere by midnight.

The King handed the print out to Richard.

'I don't understand some people. Don't they have any-thing to do except criticise others?' he said irritably.

Richard ran his eye down the messages Julian Madoc had printed out.

'Someone called LoyalSubjekt101 said Bella attacked the Queen last night and has posted a photograph of Mother with her tiara coming off at the party,' he sighed. 'And then a bunch of idiots who need to get a life started arguing about whether it was deliberate or an accident, political or personal, spite or a republican gesture.' He cast the sheets away. 'Oh, this is just ludicrous. Why are we wasting our time on it?'

'Exactly,' said the King with gloomy satisfaction.

But the Queen said, 'We can't just ignore it, Richard. These are very nasty allegations. Someone might actually try to hurt Bella, in retaliation. Pansy tells me there have been rumours for weeks.'

'Then let's kill the rumours,' said Richard calmly. 'Tell 'em we're getting married and they can bloody well like it or lump it.'

The Queen put a hand over her eyes.

Bella said frostily, 'Excuse me? Do I get a vote on this?'

The King gave a bark of laughter. 'You mean, he hasn't asked you?'

'Yes and no. Yes, he's asked me. No, we didn't talk about any public announcement.'

'Well, he mentioned it to me last week,' said the King, stirring it.

'Oh, really?' Bella narrowed her eyes at Richard.

'Thought you were running a bit of a risk there, lad,' said his father, starting to enjoy himself.

Even the Queen said, 'Good grief, what's wrong

with you, Richard? You go to war with me when I say I think it's too soon . . . and you still haven't asked Bella properly? I give up. I really do.'

'Shut up, Mother,' he said, still calm.

He went down on one knee in front of Bella. 'Please will you marry me and let me announce it to the world? There, we're sorted now, aren't we?'

She was outraged. '*Sorted?*'

'Mistake,' said the King.

'Shut up, Father. Bella, you know that dating a Prince of Wales isn't all joy. And you've spat on your hands and given it your best shot. If you've enjoyed it as much as I have, please, please, please, let me tell the world you'll marry me?'

She stared down at him, transfixed.

He said softly, 'I'm not complete without you. You know that. Why shouldn't everyone else know, too?'

The Queen said, 'You've only known each other three months.'

Richard did not stand up and he did not take his eyes off Bella's. 'Best three months of my life,' he said.

Bella felt as if she were in a high wind. 'You didn't like all of it,' she pointed out, trying to get her feet back on the ground. 'You stalked out in a huff.'

'And you got your revenge by not answering my messages.'

'You know that was an accident—'

'I know that it made me feel desperate. Hell, I even offered to write poetry to get you back.'

'Ho,' said the King. '*Big* mistake.'

'Father, we don't need audience participation. Shut up or go away.'

Bella said, 'Yes you did promise me a poem. A . . . a . . . a trillet or something. And you've never delivered. Don't you keep your promises? What sort of omen is that?'

She waited for a torrent of denials. She had underrated Richard.

'I was negotiating,' he said blandly. 'A triolet sounded good.'

'I'm holding you to it. If you love me.'

Their eyes locked. There was a long pause.

Richard looked very serious.

'What about a limerick?'

Bella was so startled she gave a shout of laughter and bent and kissed his nose. 'You are a shocking, devious man and I love you.'

At once he leaped to his feet and took her in his arms.

'So can I tell them you'll marry me?' he whispered, for her ears alone. 'It'll be good, I promise.'

'Yes,' she said blissfully. 'Yes.'

16

'It's Official!' – *Morning Times*

By the time the Press started pouring into Drummon Bridge there was a much bigger story than they had come for. The King sent Julian Madoc down to the gates to invite them in, while the staff set out chairs in the drawing room, Richard drafted what he would say and Bella telephoned her parents with the news.

Her mother was nearly silenced. 'My little girl. My dear little girl. Oh, Bella.'

Her stepfather took the phone from his wife. 'Your mother's weeping into some kitchen roll. What she means, of course, is that we're both delighted and we hope you'll be very happy. We liked him very much.' He lowered his voice. 'It would be nice if you could come and see her really soon, Bella. I think she needs to talk. And not on the phone.'

'Yes, Kevin.'

'And our very best wishes to Richard,' he said, surprising her. 'Tell him he's on to a good thing.'

She was misty-eyed when she put the phone down. Dear Kevin.

It was just as well that someone wished her well

because her father, predictably, went into a rant. He was on board a boat somewhere in the South Atlantic and he had to talk over howling gales from the sounds on the line. He managed it easily.

'. . . never thought a daughter of mine would be so feeble. Succumbing to celebrity culture, that's what it is. Celebrity and social climbing. God, you're just like your mother.'

'You stop that,' yelled Bella. 'There's nothing wrong with my mother. She's a better parent than you ever were.'

'At least I gave you ideas and some principles,' he shouted back. 'What happened to them, eh? What happened? A bit of discomfort on your first expedition and you're back in London chasing some parasite because he's got an outdated title. When I get back . . .'

'I love him, you moron!' she shouted.

Richard looked up from the desk where he was writing his piece and blew her a kiss.

'. . . we're going to have to have a serious talk about what you'll do with your life.'

'I've got news for you, Finn,' Bella said more calmly. 'You're not on the management team. *My* life. Note the adjective. Mine. Not ours. Now you can jolly well bog off! And don't call me until you're ready to be nice to Richard. God help me, he even admires you. You don't deserve it, you bigoted old freak!'

And she slammed the phone down with real fury.

Richard sat back and applauded. 'That told him.'

'Well, he is.'

'What did he call me, exactly?' Richard asked mildly. 'I might use it in my speech.'

Bella gave an impatient sigh. 'Don't. It will only encourage him. He was rude about my mother, too. After he wandered away and left her to sort out having two children and no money. Bastard.'

'OK, I won't mention him. Not if it's going to turn you spitting mad,' he said, amused. 'We're supposed to be giving the Press good news, after all. Do you want to say anything?'

'Do you want me to?'

'I quite like "I love him, you morons", but it's not very conciliatory, I suppose. Up to you.'

'I'm not a great speech-maker.'

'Fine. If you change your mind, pinch my bum and I'll hand the microphone to you.'

Just imagining it put her into a much better humour. Even Lady Pansy, bustling in to give her some helpful advice on how to dress for the momentous announcement, didn't disturb her equilibrium. Did she, asked Lady Pansy kindly, want to borrow something from Chloe?

'No, thank you.'

'But you can't wear—' Lady Pansy indicated Richard's Aran sweater and the jeans.

Richard said, 'This isn't a formal thing. We'll have a proper engagement session, with the ring, the wedding date, the lot. The gig today is just a warm-up. Bella should wear what she feels comfortable in.'

'Well, at least do your hair,' said Lady Pansy, despairing.

'That's fair,' agreed Bella.

By the time she came back, brushed and combed, there were a dozen or so journalists and rather more cameramen in the drawing room. The King was uncharacteristically chipper.

'The barbarians are past the gates then,' he said, and went off chuckling at his own joke, to await Julian Madoc's signal.

Richard said, 'The Press Secretary is going to be so *mad* about this.'

Bella cocked an eyebrow. 'You sound rather pleased.'

'I like justice. He went ski-ing with a lot of smart friends and sent the second team to Scotland. It's always so bloody freezing, he gets out of it every year. So he misses the juiciest story of the year. Serves him right.'

They lined up in the dining room while Madoc quieted the audience. Then a servant opened the double doors and the King, resplendent in kilt and a tweed jacket, marched up to the hastily erected microphone. Richard and Bella followed.

'Welcome,' said the King. 'Glad to see you. For once I really mean that.'

There was surprised laughter.

'Got some good news, which my eldest son will tell you all about.'

And he went and sat down, beaming. Nobody could doubt that he was delighted.

Richard put his arm round Bella's shoulders and they went to the microphone. He didn't look at his notes. Bella realised suddenly that he must have spoken to a gathering like this many, many times before.

'Happy New Year,' he began.

Several of the audience returned the greeting.

Richard put his hands in his pockets. 'This is a bit of a shock to me. As you probably know, I've been trying to persuade Bella Greenwood for a while now that I am a Good Thing. I'd got quite a nifty campaign planned out, to be honest. And then suddenly it's New Year and I don't see the point of waiting. So I asked her. And she said yes. So—' He turned to her and she put her hand in his and came in closer 'Ladies and gentlemen, may I introduce Miss Isabella Greenwood, who has agreed to marry me. I'm a lucky man.'

The applause was spontaneous and seemed genuine.

Julian Madoc stood up. 'His Highness will take a few questions.'

Bella suddenly felt terrified, but the questions were friendly and easy to answer.

The only difficult one was, 'And how has Miss Greenwood's father taken it?'

'From what I heard of the telephone call, he's not dancing for joy,' said Richard, with a great air of frankness. 'We're going to have to work on that.'

God, he's cool, thought Bella.

There were questions to her, which were easy too. Yes, Prince Richard had met her mother, brother and stepfather and they were all very pleased. A ring? Not yet. A present then?

Beside her she felt Richard stiffen. She knew what he was thinking: Damn, we never thought of that.

But she could handle it. She squeezed his hand to reassure him and told the lady journalist, 'Well, he's promised me a limerick. But I'm not holding my breath.'

There was a shout of laughter.

Before it had died down the King rose and Madoc made a sign to the stewards who had come in unobtrusively and were now lined up along the walls of the drawing room, bearing trays of whisky and champagne.

'I would like to invite you all to drink the health of my son, the Prince of Wales, and his intended wife, Miss Bella Greenwood.'

The glasses were handed out with amazing speed.

'Richard,' boomed the King, not bothering with the microphone and sounding as if he was about to break into a happy dance. 'Bella, my dear. Your health.'

Everyone drank to the toast and there was prolonged applause and Richard murmured, 'Smile. Wave. Exit right, right?'

They did.

As the great doors of the drawing room closed behind them, Bella broke into a tap dance.

'I did it! I did it! My first press call and I didn't knock anything over or poke anyone in the eye.'

'You were a model of decorum and stayed upright throughout,' he agreed gravely. 'You're a natural.'

Bella stopped dancing. 'No, I'm not. I'm a walking disaster and there are photos of tumbling tiaras out there to prove it. But just this time it went right and I didn't let you down.'

He hugged her.

She hugged him back. 'Life doesn't get any better than this.'

*

It didn't stay as good at that, of course. It was one thing to charm a group of journalists and photographers who were in the same room as you, especially when you were giving them free champagne. It was quite another to convince hostile editors. Or, for that matter, the wildly partisan blogosphere.

'Don't look,' advised Lottie. 'You'll drive yourself mad. The Palace will get the news alerts and pass on anything that you should see.'

But Bella knew that there were people who thought the news was wonderful and were bubbling excitedly about The Day, The Dress, The Honeymoon, as if she were one of their relatives. It was kind and friendly in one way, but in another it felt as if there were suddenly a load of people acting like they knew her. Only she didn't know them.

'It's a bit like being a polar bear in a zoo,' she told Richard. 'You don't get to stare back.'

'Public property,' he said with a sigh. 'I know. I'm sorry.'

'No, don't be. So many people wish us well, I feel rather buoyed up by it.'

She was not so buoyed up by the paparazzi. They scurried after her, breaking out of alleyways as she walked to work, or appearing round shelves at the Late, Late Market when she was buying milk.

'They're after the one iconic picture. You hitting a small child for one section of the press. You giving a puppy the kiss of life for another,' explained Lottie.

'You're joking?'

'No, I'm not. I've done my time, spinning these

things. It's part of what I do for a living. I know how it works.'

'How long are they going to chase me?'

Lottie shrugged. 'Until somebody more newsworthy comes along. At the moment, there's a big premium on the Princess-to-Be. Sorry. You're gonna have to live with it.'

At first Bella's new employers didn't like it. They wanted press attention, they said, but not on the celebrity pages. But as their website began to get more hits, they decided that maybe it wasn't so bad after all and became a lot less frosty.

'So that's all right,' Bella told Richard, when they were in the car going to a charity Ice Show. 'As for the media, as far as I can see there are two schools of thought. Those who think we're a lovely couple, wish us well and either don't care or are positively pleased that I'm not a toff. God bless them. Then there are those hate me *because* I'm not a toff. They write these nasty articles, pretending it's about all sorts of other things – I'm too fat; I'm too thin. I'm grumpy; I'm over-familiar. I'm a career woman and no support to you; I fawn on you sickeningly. And a whole raft of other stuff I forget.'

'Hey, I thought you weren't reading them,' said Richard in concern.

'I'm not now. But I wanted to know what all the noise was about.'

'And now you do?'

She shrugged. 'Nothing I can do about it. If someone hates you, they hate you. They're not going to change their mind.'

There was a pause. Then he nodded soberly. 'That's a tough one, isn't it?'

Bella swallowed. 'Yes, it is. There's one blogger who scares me bit, she's so spiteful.'

Richard was silent for a moment. Then he said, 'LoyalSubjekt101?'

'Yes. You've read it? Do you know who it is?'

'Not yet,' he said grimly. 'I've got people looking into it.'

Bella was doubtful. 'Can you do that? I mean, what about free speech?'

'I can't stop her saying anything, unless it's libellous. But I agree. There's something about the tone of that one that is disturbing. So we're digging a bit.'

'Oh.' A wisp of cold touched Bella happiness.

'Hey, don't look like that. It's probably some strange person who has fantasies about marrying me herself and wouldn't actually hurt a fly. Might not even be a woman. It's just a reasonable precaution to find out who it is.'

'Yes, of course.'

He gave her a comforting hug. 'Mostly these things come to nothing. They fall in love with somebody else, or go back on the medication, or win a story-writing contest or something.'

Bella smiled. 'I'll bear that in mind.'

'Do that. I'll keep you safe.'

But if Richard was sympathetic about the nasty blogger, he just laughed when the *Daily Despatch*, who had run the original falling tiara photographs for several days, called Bella a klutz and commissioned a

286

number of cartoonists to envisage things that she might drop, break or crash into.

'They're not as fervent as your father, but the *Despatch* has never liked us since my father had its editor-in-chief escorted out of the Royal Enclosure at Ascot for pinching a waitress's bottom.'

'Did he?' Bella was fascinated. It didn't seem in character with what she had seen of the absent-minded King.

'Don't get him wrong. He likes to play the old buffer, but when he gets the bit between his teeth, he really goes for it. And he doesn't like bullies.'

'I remember you saying your grandfather—'

Richard stared pointedly at the driver's head and Bella stopped.

'So, I'm afraid you'll just have to put with the *Despatch*. If they weren't calling you a klutz, it would be something else. Price of joining the family.'

She didn't care about the family. But it was a price worth paying for loving someone as special as Richard, she thought.

The more she knew of him, the more certain she was that he was right: they were made for each other. Nothing seemed to faze him. She regularly forgot to check out with the Guard House when she stayed overnight at Camelford House and he would receive calls from an irate security officer. He never lost his temper, not with Bella, not with the Guard House. Once she was late for a date because she got absorbed at work and he forgave her; more, he made a joke of it. Yet she *knew* how tight his schedule was and she could have kicked herself. Especially as she was surrounded by a self-appointed support group. She sometimes wondered who Richard had who was there for *him*, not just for the Prince of Wales.

She said as much to her grandmother.

Georgia, who had come to the flat for an evening with Bella and Lottie, looked thoughtful. 'He has you.'

'Oh, well, yes, obviously. But I meant someone of his own.'

'His own?'

They were in the kitchen and Bella was peeling potatoes. Georgia had a surprising weakness for English school food and had requested shepherd's pie for a treat. But at her last observation Bella put the peeler down and turned to face her.

'What does *that* mean?'

Georgia tried to dismiss the question. 'Oh, nothing.'

'Don't start with the Forest Wise Woman on me,' said her granddaughter crisply. 'I know it meant something. Give.'

'It's just that, I suppose this engagement has all happened very fast.'

Bella was nearly dancing with irritation. 'Don't be enigmatic. I've had a long hard day making sense of an illiterate PhD proposal. I'm in no mood for guessing games. If you think I'm doing something wrong, spit it out.'

Georgia laughed. 'I think you're doing just fine, dear.'

And then Lottie came in and they started talking about important things like saving the rain forest and how to get red wine out of a silk blouse.

Later, as they were finishing their coffee, Georgia said, 'Have you talked about dates for the wedding?'

Lottie cast her eyes to heaven.

Bella said hurriedly, 'Bit of a sore point, Georgia. The Government wants us to get married in the summer, for the tourists. But the Queen thinks we should wait until after next Christmas. Negotiations, as they say, are ongoing.'

Georgia's brown eyes were shrewd. 'And what do you want?'

'Richard's diary is the main constraint, really. He says a lot of people will be disappointed if he cancels engagements. So he's got his office analysing the forward plan.'

Lottie and Georgia exchanged looks.

'Not Richard,' said her grandmother. '*You*.'

'Me? I'll fit in with . . . What?'

Both Lottie and Georgia had shrieked in protest.

'What?'

'It's *your wedding*,' said Lottie. 'You know, the thing little girls dream of from the first time someone tells them the Cinderella story. Big white dress, centre of attention, flowers in the hair, walking down the aisle with a dreamy look in your eyes. It's *your day*.'

'Richard says it's everyone's day. We have to be . . . accommodating.'

Lottie snorted.

'We've been through this before, Lotts. It's a state occasion. There's no getting away from it. Richard and I aren't the only ones involved.'

Georgia always sat up straight, she said that was what

Southern Belles were taught to do, but suddenly she looked as dignified as the Queen herself. The shabby old armchair could have been a throne.

'That is true. And you are very right to remember it. I am proud of you.' She sounded as if she were summing up the case for the prosecution. 'But saying there are a lot of people to consider does not mean that you are prohibited from saying what you would like.'

Lottie bounced on the sofa. 'Right on, Granny.'

Georgia ignored that. She was very fond of Lottie and adored Bella but she never cared to be reminded of her grandmotherly status.

'Do you *know* what you would like, Bella?'

'Richard says . . .'

Bella found two pairs of beady eyes daring her to go on. She ground to a halt.

'I haven't thought about it, OK? There didn't seem much point.'

Georgia fixed her eyes on her granddaughter with terrifying intensity. 'Are you saying it doesn't matter what you want?'

'Not in the scheme of things, no.'

'And have you told Richard that you feel like this?'

Bella felt harassed. 'Well, no. I mean, he's got a lot on his plate. It's not such a big deal, after all.'

There was a silence. Even Bella could see that this was probably not an ideal way for a bride to think about her own wedding but she would never admit it. She put up her chin and broadcast dignified Keep Out signals right back at Georgia.

To no effect at all.

'While I do not agree with your father in all his anti-monarchical barnstorming, I am coming to feel that, in this case, he has a point,' announced Georgia. 'I don't know if it is the fault of the Royal Family, the Court or Richard himself. But I am very sorry to say,' she didn't sound sorry, she sounded brutal, 'that they have done a number on you, child.'

Lottie drew in a little hissing breath. 'Have at you, foul courtier!'

Bella sent her an impatient glance but Georgia ignored her. 'Marriage is a partnership, not a corporate venture, Bella. You and Richard need to talk about this. And soon.'

'I love you, Georgia,' said Lottie with fervour.

'When you have done so, you may bring him to dinner. I will telephone you tomorrow with dates when I am free.'

Bella gulped.

Georgia stood up and turned gracefully to Lottie. 'It is always delightful to see you again, Lottie. I so enjoy our talks. Goodbye. Thank you for a lovely evening.'

Subdued, Lottie stood up and they air-kissed.

Bella said, 'I'll call you a cab.'

'No need. I can always find one round here. If necessary I'll go to Victoria Station. There are always cabs there.'

'I'll walk with you,' said Bella firmly.

She helped Georgia into her warm coat – a chocolate brown, waisted, full-skirted thing, with a discreet fur collar and military buttons. Georgia set her big Russian hat at just the right angle and pulled on fur-lined leather gloves. It was all very warm and practical but, thought Bella, even for a domestic evening of shepherd's pie with the girls, her grandmother was catwalk elegant.

Bella shrugged on her own coat, stuffed her keys in her pocket and they went out into the night air. The street was deserted. Not a cab in sight.

They began to walk.

Georgia said, 'Honey, I know you're getting a lot of advice, from all over the place, and most of it is frankly crap. I don't want to add to that, I really don't. But I am certain that you and Richard need to work out what you want before everybody else gets to have their say. It's just so easy to be taken over by the rest of the world. I was. And it took me half a lifetime to get myself straight.'

This was news to Bella.

'I didn't know that,' she said cautiously.

'When you've made your bed, you lie on it,' said Georgia dryly. 'Old saying. No reason for you or anyone else to know. But, believe me, when I say talk to the man, I speak from experience. Oh, look, there's a taxi with its light on. I do so love London taxis! They're so big and solid and uncompromising, and you have room to spread out the skirts of your dance dress. Heaven. Just heaven. I have great hopes for you, Bella.'

On which gnomic utterance she raised an arm to hail the cab, kissed her granddaughter quickly, jumped in and was gone.

17

Bella did not act immediately on her grandmother's advice, not even when Georgia sent her a list of possible dates for bringing Richard to dinner. But she did think about it.

Richard was on a brief tour of middle European capitals, in support of trade promotion. After that he was going on to a ski-ing holiday in Andorra. He had asked Bella to go too, but hadn't argued when she said that she couldn't start a new job and take a holiday after only a month.

'I can't duck out of this,' he said apologetically. 'It's a family tradition. We go every year. We stay with my mother's cousins and take friends. Including, this year, my goddaughter, who has a birthday that week. I can't disappoint her.'

'Of course you mustn't cancel,' said Bella, shocked. 'Include me when you book the next one.'

'You got it.'

But later he rang and said, 'How would you feel about coming for just the weekend? I'd like you to meet everyone.'

So she left work at lunch-time on Friday and flew to Barcelona. She wondered if Richard would meet her there himself. She remembered how they had fallen into each other's arms that first time at Waterloo Station. But a uniformed airport official picked her out while she was walking from the plane and led her off through silent corridors to a waiting limousine, having her passport stamped en route.

'Thank you,' she said.

The official bowed. 'Our pleasure. We hope that you will be very happy, you and Prince Richard.'

'Good heavens! I mean, thank you for your good wishes.' I'm starting to sound like Georgia, she thought.

The car took her to a substantial villa behind an even more substantial wall. There were a few sightseers and the inevitable photographers waiting in the country lane that led to it. Bella had learned the form now. She leaned forward, so they could see her face, and gave everyone her best smile.

No waving, Lady Pansy had warned. Not unless she was accompanying the Prince. People wouldn't like her pretending she was Royal before she was. So Bella kept her hands locked tight in her lap and beamed for Britain as gates swung silently open and the limo drove out of their sight. The people in the road waved like mad. It was a real physical effort not to wave back.

Richard did come to meet her as the car arrived, though. He ran down the steps and kissed her, with a slight air of restraint.

'Lady P been getting at you too, huh?' muttered Bella.

'What?'

'Nothing.' She slipped her hand into his and they went into the house. 'Tell me who's here.'

'My mother is resting at the moment. Nell is on the slopes with the whole Lenane family and our cousins. George is sprawled in the rumpus room getting over a hangover.'

'*Still?*'

Richard grinned. 'He and the younger ones went into town last night. Most of them came back around midnight, but Chloe tells me that George got into some heavy salsa action. Don't ask me when he got home. I don't want to know.'

Bella smiled but said slowly, 'Chloe Lenane's here?' So the ditzy blonde who had looked at her with such hatred on New Year's Eve was included in the family party. Just great!

Richard was saying, 'She's a fellow godparent to The Monster, Tilly, which isn't really fair as she's a cousin and should cough up for a birthday present anyway. That's why I'm so important, The Monster tells me. All her godparents are relatives except me.'

'I look forward to meeting her.'

'You won't enjoy it unless you've brought her something,' Richard warned. 'But she's very entertaining.'

He was right on both counts. In fact, Bella was surprised to see how cool, courteous, dignified Richard got down and dirty with the make-up kit of Tilly Lenane's Suki doll.

'There is an irresistible appeal to a grown man sitting on the floor wearing pink lipstick and gold dust,' she told him. 'Do you think perhaps some rouge on his cheeks, Tilly? Nice round spots, about the size of a tenpence piece.'

His eyes promised vengeance but he sat calmly while the small girl polished his face to a shining carmine. The child's mother, coming in with the Queen to put Tilly to bed, was taken aback. Queen Jane, however, was as charmed as Bella.

'Very nice, Tilly. I think he looks very handsome. Don't you, Bella?'

'Stunning,' she said gravely.

His lips twitched. 'Do you think I ought to stay like this for dinner then?'

Even the Queen did a double take at that.

Bella, however, considered the suggestion, 'Could be a bit rococo for a simple family meal?'

He allowed his shoulders to droop. 'I'm really sorry, Tilly,' he told his goddaughter mournfully. 'You're an artist but supper is no place for your art.'

But she didn't mind at all. 'I can do it again tomorrow,' she offered generously.

Bella swallowed hard. 'Maybe it's time I changed for dinner,' she said unsteadily.

'Good idea, I'll come with you. See you later, Mother, Nicola. Goodnight, Tilly.'

They escaped together. 'How do you get this stuff off?' hissed Richard as they ran up the stairs.

Bella was bubbling over. 'No idea. That make-up is toy stuff, intended for dolls. They're plastic. I don't know whether ordinary make-up remover will take it off skin. You might have to use a blow torch.'

'Alternatively, a good long session in the shower with an expert might do the trick,' he said, whisking her inside their bedroom and locking the door. 'Let's go to it.'

They came down to dinner a little late but very, very clean.

The next day everyone went off to the slopes. Bella didn't really like ski-ing and had only done it a couple of times, so she was glad to see that there were lots of easy runs and a relaxed family atmosphere to the place. The cousins, a dispossessed Grand Duke turned industrialist and his wife, were hospitable and the Lenanes jolly. Prince George treated Bella in exactly the same way as he treated his sister, giving her his spare stuff to hold while he shot off to buy a burger to fill the gap between mid-morning coffee and late lunch.

'What? I'm still growing, you know!' he said when Princess Eleanor called him a greedy pig. 'I burn up a lot of energy.'

'Not on the ski slopes, you filthy porker,' she said, prodding him. They were clearly great friends though Bella suspected that they were both a little in awe of Richard. Of course, he was five years older than George, seven years older than Eleanor. It was a big gap, even if he wasn't also carrying all the responsibilities of being the Prince of Wales.

Eleanor was not as cheerfully accepting of Bella as George was. She seemed friendly enough but remained distant, almost as if she were embarrassed.

That afternoon the cause of this became clear.

'I'm glad that you're with Richard,' Eleanor said, awkwardly, when she and Bella found themselves drinking warming soup together while Tilly proudly showed off what she had learned that morning.

'It's been a bit difficult. Everyone thought he was going out with Chloe again.'

'Again?'

Eleanor looked surprised. 'You might not know but he'd been dating this Deborah person. We all knew it wouldn't last. She was always looking round for the cameras. When that finished, he took Chloe to some party and then they went on to a nightclub. I don't know the details. But he had a little walk out with her years ago, just after he left university and before he did his year in the Navy.'

Eleanor looked up at the mountain.

'I don't know how serious it was. You know Richard, he doesn't talk about his feelings, and I was only a teenager. But Pansy said that Chloe was waiting until he came back. And when he did . . .'

'Deborah?'

'No. Nobody for a long time. Then there was Anastasia for a bit.'

Bella looked blank.

'Princess Anastasia? Of Finland? She married last year. Big spread in *Royalty Watchers*.'

Bella nodded as if she knew what Eleanor was talking about. Whereas she had never heard of *Royalty Watchers Magazine* until last year.

Eleanor wasn't deceived. 'You don't know, do you? OK. She was an Art History major at Smith. Whenever he was in the States, he saw her. And then she came over here and worked for the National Gallery. Her father is on the Olympic Committee?'

Bella clicked fingers. 'Got it. King Edvard or something. One of the bicycling Royals, right?'

Eleanor choked with laughter.

Coming up behind them Richard took off his sunglasses and surveyed Tilly's composed run. 'She's not bad. What were you laughing about?'

Eleanor looked agonisingly embarrassed.

'Bicycling Royals,' said Bella crisply. 'It's rude to eavesdrop.'

'What's wrong with them? I'll have you know that some of my best friends are bicycling royals.'

He put his arm round Bella and pushed his woolly ski hat further back. She saw that he had got rid of his skis.

'Ready to go?'

'What about you? Don't you want another run?'

He shook his head. 'I've had my fresh air for the day. Anyway, Mother's tired. I thought we could go back with her?'

'Sure.'

He drove with that controlled competence Bella was coming to learn he brought to everything. The Queen sat next to him and she did, indeed, look tired.

'I will go and lie down for half an hour,' she said when they arrived at the house. 'Let's have tea together in the conservatory at half-past three. I want to talk to you both before everyone gets back.'

What she wanted to talk about, it turned out, was the

wedding. 'Your father tells me that the Prime Minister's Office has a list of possible dates, most of them this year. It is your decision, of course. But I want you to think about it very seriously.'

Bella looked at Richard. Did he know this was coming?

Richard was calm. 'I think we've got that, Mother. The PM sent the list of dates over in the second week of January. That's a fortnight ago now. Someone has been sitting on it. I know it's not me and it doesn't seem to be Father's office. So it had to be you. What exactly is going on?'

The Queen folded her lips together. 'Maybe I shouldn't have done that.'

'No,' Richard agreed, not angry but not very friendly either.

His mother flushed. 'I really wanted to get to know Bella . . .'

He said very coolly, 'No, you didn't. Have you even called her since the New Year?'

The Queen looked miserable. Bella felt sorry for her.

'So, I repeat, what's this about?'

The Queen drew a long breath. 'This engagement, this affair, it has all happened too fast. You're still starry-eyed about each other, I can see that. I think it's lovely. But it's no – no *foundation* for your future life.'

She turned to Bella.

'You don't come from our world. Don't misunder-stand me. I think that's a good thing, I really do. But it means that you have no idea what your life would be like if you married my son.'

300

'Will,' said Richard, with steely quiet. '*Will* be like. *When* she marries me.'

The Queen ignored him. 'All I'm asking is that you give yourself a year. You're his fiancée. It's official. You can be his companion anywhere you want. Just see what it's like.'

Bella leaned forward. 'I know he's public property. He told me so right at the start and I've seen it with my own eyes. We don't have to wait a year for me to learn that.'

The Queen shook her head. 'And do you realise what it's going to be like being Princess of Wales? It's a job, you know.'

'Richard will help me—'

The Queen drummed her fists on the arms of her chair. 'But that's just it! He won't. He can't. He'll be off doing his own programme. Do you know his diary already has events booked in for five years ahead? *Five years*. When his grandfather died, it took the Private Offices three months to rework everyone's calendars. My poor George was launching ships. He was *eleven*. My little boy, all on his own in front of a horde of men in uniform, throwing a bottle at a damn' great ocean liner. But his father said that someone had to do it and George was old enough and liked the sea. Liked the *sea* . . .'

She fought with herself, drew several calming breaths. Richard watched her with dawning concern.

'He enjoyed it, Mother. He still talks about it.'

'That's not the point. He was on his own.'

'No, he wasn't—'

'*I wasn't there!*' she screamed. And banged her hand

301

down so hard that dust flew out of the upholstered arm of the chair.

There was a shocked silence.

Bella said slowly, 'This is about the children, isn't it? You're worried about our children.'

Richard drew a sharp breath.

The Queen shook her head. 'Not just the children. It's hard on them. But you can't imagine what it's like when you can't stop them being pushed on to the public stage when they're little. You feel so helpless.'

Bella remembered Richard telling her that the Queen had been good at protecting the family from the old King and his schemes. She looked at him now. He was very pale.

She couldn't bear it. She said fiercely, 'Richard and I will take care of each other and our children. I *promise* you.'

'I know you think you will, dear. We all think that. But the pressures never stop. In the end, you get so tired. And lonely,' she added, almost imperceptibly. And quite suddenly the Queen's eyes filled with tears. She jumped to her feet.

'I'm sorry. This is your business. I should never have delayed that list. I'm sorry. Please talk to your father about it, Richard. Excuse me. I'm not well.'

She hurried away, leaving a shocked silence.

'Poor lady,' whispered Bella.

'Oh, Lord,' said Richard. He looked at Bella. 'What do you want to do, love? Sleep on it?'

She thought about what Georgia had told her. It made a lot of sense.

She took his hand. 'I think you and I need to work out what *we* want before anyone else gets a vote.'

'O – K. And that is?'

Bella looked at the little lines round his eyes which always deepened when he was worried about something. He was being so careful not to push, not to put her under pressure, to step back and let her take an independent decision. And yet she could see how desperately he didn't want to wait for a year.

Well, neither did she. She knew that without any doubt at all.

She slipped out of her chair and knelt beside him. 'I love you so much, it's like being soaked in sunshine. I'd marry you tomorrow if I could.'

She watched the lines disappear. He gave a long, long sigh as if he'd put down a great burden.

But all he said, in his practical way, was, 'What about June?'

18

'The Ring!' – *Royal Watchers Magazine*

It was the start of a whirlwind that Bella would never have believed. The next week, Richard talked to the King and the Prime Minister and they narrowed the date down to three possibles. Richard's office was on the phone to Bella every hour about some option or other until she longed to say, 'Just do it. I'll go along with whatever you want.'

But, mindful of Georgia's advice, she didn't. And they kept right on consulting her.

And then the date was finalised, a Press call scheduled, and the Queen called her at last. Summoned to an audience, Bella took another early departure from the office and recorded it carefully on the time sheets she had introduced when she took over. One thing she didn't need, she thought, was some journalist claiming that the new Princess-to-be skived off work!

The Queen was on her own. As soon as the flunkey had retreated and closed the doors behind him she said, 'I owe you an apology for our last meeting. I should never – all I can say is that it was with the best of intentions.'

'I'm sure it was,' said Bella. 'I'm certainly going to come to you for advice. I shall need it.'

'Yes, you will,' said the Queen sadly. 'So I suggest that Lady Pansy moves from her informal role as your friend and mentor to becoming your formal Court Adviser. You will want a Personal Assistant as well, of course. Maybe your little friend, Charlotte Hendred, is it?'

You're very well briefed, thought Bella.

Aloud, she said, 'I wouldn't ask her to interrupt her career. But thank you, that's a good idea. I will start to look for one.'

The Queen smiled. 'That's settled then. And, forgive me, I know that you young people like to be self-supporting, but this is rather exceptional. So the Palace will pay. In fact, I suggest your team should use an office in St George's Tower, where a lot of our staff are housed.'

More security, more forgetting to sign in and out, thought Bella, with a sinking heart. But there were some battles that were worth fighting and some that weren't. So she said, 'Thank you, Ma'am,' as if she were really grateful, and the office was set up.

But before she could make her first visit to her new team, she had a call from Richard.

'Can I take you to dinner?'

'Any time. When?'

'Tonight?'

' *Tonight?* I thought you were at some Trade Fair.'

'Yup.'

'Don't tell me, you're tired of admiring machine tools and want me to come and massage your back?'

'That would be a definite bonus.'

'All right then. Where shall I meet you?'

'I'll send a car,' he said mysteriously. 'It'll be at your office around four, if that suits.'

'I was looking forward to scrambled eggs on toast in front of a DVD . . . Of courses it suits! Lovely.'

It was driven by Ian, though she didn't know the car. More important, nor did the three or four photographers who now camped regularly outside her office. Bella waved to them as she went past, forgetting Lady Pansy's precepts. She was nearly skipping along, delighted to be seeing Richard on the spur of the moment.

I'm going to see my love, she thought. I'm going to see my *love*.

Ian was waiting for her round the corner, as he had promised. She slipped into the passenger seat and he took off, heading for the motorway.

'Where are we going?'

'Richard said something about a picnic.'

'A picnic? In February?'

Ian chuckled. 'You haven't noticed the date, have you?'

'What?'

He jerked his head towards the back seat. 'It's on the paper.'

Bella turned round and fished up his copy of the *Morning Times*. 'February the fourteenth. So?'

He sighed. 'Look in the Personal Column.'

'If Richard is sending me messages in the Personal Column he never told me,' said Bella indignantly. 'I hate this business of his office talking to my office. It's just so artificial, I – oooh!' as she saw the columns of fond messages that made up the page today. 'It's *Valentine's* Day.'

They drove for about an hour, then turned off the motorway and drove for probably another hour or even more deep into mysterious countryside, full of stone houses, abrupt hills, tiny single-track roads and thatched pubs.

'Are we going on a tour of Middle England?' asked Bella. 'This feels like Tolkien country to me.'

But Ian just shook his head mysteriously, glanced at his watch, and kept on driving. Eventually they turned on to an even smaller road, with a green Countryside Trail signpost.

There were fields on either side of them, completely dark. The lane was deserted, not a house or light to be seen. It ended at a cattle grid and a five-bar gate. Richard was leaning against it, dressed in a Barbour and jeans.

'Is that a spare pair of Wellington boots?' said Bella suspiciously. 'Jesus, he really did mean a picnic.' She got out of the car.

Richard met her, kissed her, handed over the Wellington boots as if they needed no further explanation, and said, 'Thanks very much, Ian. See you in the morning.'

Ian grinned. 'Fine. Er – well – good night.'

He drove off.

'For a moment there, I thought he was going to say "Have a nice night",' said Richard reflectively.

By then Bella was hanging on to him as she thrust a foot into the first Wellington boot. But at this she snorted and staggered and Richard had to pull her upright. He held her firmly.

'You are so rewarding to tease,' he said, deeply pleased.

She put on the other boot and he took her shoes, sticking one in each pocket.

Clouds scudded across a black sky. The landscape was lit only by occasional shafts of light from a watery moon. Richard was carrying a torch, small but with a powerful beam.

'We are going up the hill a little way,' he said. 'Hang on to me.'

She climbed over the five-bar gate and went with him. It was not long before she saw . . .

'Is that a tower?'

'I thought you'd appreciate an indoor picnic, given the wind-chill factor.'

'You think of everything,' Bella said politely.

It was quite a small tower. Just one room on each of the three floors. Inside, he had lit a fire already, so the place was warm as toast. There was a tartan rug on the old flagstones with a rush basket laid in the middle of it. Two folding picnic chairs were set either side of the fire. In one corner, at the bottom of the stairs, there was small desk with an electric till and an array of postcards on it.

'Should we be here?' said Bella uneasily. 'It looks very – municipal. We haven't climbed in illegally or anything, have we?'

He laughed aloud. 'I promise. The Administrator knows we're here. He gave me the key and permission to park my car in the next field.'

'And the fire?' said Bella, still suspicious. 'When was that chimney last swept?'

'Do you know, I didn't ask?'

She relaxed. 'Oh, all right then. If it explodes and burns us to a crisp, I shall blame you.'

'Do that. Champagne?'

She was surprised. Richard was a claret man normally but he knew she loved the lightness and sparkle of bubbles.

'Very spoiling. Thank you.'

She sat in one of the picnic chairs and he opened the bottle and brought two glasses to the hearth.

They toasted each other. It seemed as if he wanted to say something and didn't know where to start. This looked serious.

'Why are we here?' Bella said at last.

'I don't know if I've done the right thing. You may want to choose your own. But – I've never given you anything personal. Not really. And I wanted this to be from me to you. Sort of private.'

He reached into the pocket of his Barbour and removed: her right shoe, a checked cap, a tube of mints . . . and a jeweller's ring box.

He looked down at it, swallowing. 'If you – oh, hell, here it is. I hope you like it.'

And he stuffed it into her hands as if it were a ham sandwich.

Bella opened the little velvet box very carefully.

Inside was a swirl of silver metal like a curly 'S', with single lemon-coloured diamond set in the middle. It was very simple and yet, somehow, heartbreakingly beautiful. It was also completely *him*, like that gorgeous plain apartment with all the light and the wonderful inlaid wood.

'It looks like the wind,' she said, awed.

His breath came out in a rush. 'You like it? You really like it? It's by a young designer. I've admired his work for ages. We talked about the design for a long time and I said I wanted something that was free, that sort of flowed. This was the one I chose. We talked about gold but I liked platinum better for you. You really like it? You're not being kind? Because you can choose your own engagement ring, you know that.'

She got up and kissed him. 'I really, really like it. I love it. You're a genius.'

Richard beamed.

'Terrific. That's – terrific.'

He bounded to the stairs. 'Now come and look at the stars. And then I'll feed you.'

They ran up the rickety stairs. The tower, it seemed, had ramparts. From the top, you could see mountains, valleys, the sparkle of water in the moonlight, little sleeping towns and great fields. The lower clouds had lifted but there was still a dark roof of high cloud with a great gap punched through it leading to the universe beyond where stars twinkled. Moonlight flowed down in golden swathes Bella felt she could climb.

'Hello, Britain,' said Richard, taking her hand and holding it high. 'Here she is then. My lady and yours.'

19

'The Dress!' – *Royal Watchers Magazine*

Of course the ring had to be kept under wraps until the photocall at which they were due to announce the date and venue of the wedding. Richard suggested that Bella should take it home and wear it for a while, to make sure that it didn't need any adjustment. Lottie had stolen one of her gloves for him but the jeweller had warned that only gave an approximate size.

Bella was terribly tempted. But in the end she decided to be sensible.

'I'm such a klutz, I might do something terrible like drop it down the loo,' she said with a shudder.

'You'll have to get used to it some time,' Richard said, amused. 'But never mind. It can wait a week. I'll take it back and put it in the safe, if you like.'

She thanked him with fervour.

So when she paid her first visit to her new office in the Palace, she could honestly say that, no, she did not have a ring yet. Lady Pansy was put out.

'Haven't you at least chosen the stones? And have you decided what to wear for the engagement photograph?'

'Goodness, no,' said Bella.

She had been hoping to get in and out of the place in an hour but Lady Pansy had a list of decisions to be made that would take most of the morning. Bella considered rebelling but then thought better of it. It was not Lady Pansy's fault that she took everything at a slow march and paid attention to every detail. Besides, she was the Queen's friend and had been part of the arrangements for the King and Queen's marriage thirty-odd years ago. So she would know the traditions at first hand.

In the interests of harmony, Bella sat on a sofa and made notes on her smartphone while Lady Pansy worked slowly through several files.

Clothes had a big file all to themselves. Bella would need clothes for lunch, for dinner, for formal balls, for attending the ballet . . . Her head began to reel. And then, of course, there were the clothes for the official photographs: the engagement photograph; a relaxed session in the country – no doubt Prince Richard had somewhere in mind; the going-away outfit; the entire honeymoon wardrobe; and The Dress.

The way Lady Pansy said that, it sounded as if the thing was some sort of Alien Being out of *Dr Who*, thought Bella. *The Attack of the Mutant Wedding Dress?* She recognised incipient hysteria and calmed herself.

'I'm afraid I've not really thought about a wedding dress. I've never been terribly interested in fashion, and with my year away I lost touch with even what little I did know.'

Lady Pansy beamed at her in a motherly way. 'I am so glad you said that, my dear. It makes it easier for me to say – you will need a complete makeover in order to assume your royal role. I'm sure you realise that.'

'Er – do I?' said Bella, who didn't realise any such thing.

'Having accompanied Her Majesty on so many of her trips, I am sure I will be able to help. Now, for the engagement picture – a British designer, of course. Nothing too avant-garde. You have to appeal to all ages and sections of the population, many of whom are very traditional in their tastes. Would you like me to have some samples send round?'

Bella had a hair-raising vision of hours and hours spent trying on clothes, with Lady Pansy giving them marks out of ten, and said no, thank you, she thought she could probably sort that one out. Lady Pansy did not exactly look crushed, she was too well trained in assuming that frozen courtier's expression, but Bella felt bad for her.

So she said kindly, 'But if you would give me a list of the designers you think I should look at for the wedding dress, that would be a huge help.'

The woman inclined her head without cracking a smile.

'And perhaps you would tick any that you particularly like,' she offered.

Lady Pansy thawed and said she would be delighted to do that.

Bella made her escape before Lady Pansy could think of anything else for her to decide. She jumped into a taxi and called Lottie on her way to the office.

'Lotts, I need fashion advice. You know me.'

'I do indeed,' said Lottie. 'The best bikini collection in the business, but otherwise your wardrobe is pants.'

'I was living on a tropical island, for heaven's sake! Swimming was part of my job.'

Lottie gave a dirty laugh. 'Richard is still in for a treat I bet he doesn't expect.'

'I probably won't be allowed to wear them,' said Bella, suddenly depressed. 'They'll be too avant-garde for the British people.'

'Oh, God, don't tell me there's a Palace Advisory Note on bikinis too?'

Bella choked. 'Haven't seen it. Anyway, that's ages in the future. I need something for this damn' photoshoot next week. Where can I go? Any ideas?'

'Yes, but I've got a meeting two minutes ago. I'll pick up some mags on the way home and we can talk about it later.'

It turned into a perfect girls' night in. Lottie had not only picked up a bag full of fashion and celebrity magazines, she had bought each of them a super new organic face mask and the raw material for mutual manicuring. And chocolate.

'This is the life,' Lottie said, trying not to move her lips. She was lying flat out on the sofa in a towelling robe, with her newly washed hair wrapped in a towel and a mask scented with orange flowers slowly setting on her face.

'How do you know when it's cooked?' said Bella, wandering in from the bathroom in her blue kimono. She was still applying hers. It came in a pot, like cream, only with raspberry pips in it.

'It turns pink. Bright pink. About twenty minutes.' Lottie lifted her wrist. 'I've got another eight.'

Bella put the pot down, cleaned her be-pipped but sweetly scented fingers on a wet wipe, and settled herself in the armchair, with her feet on a leather floor cushion. She tipped her head back and stared at the ceiling.

'Do you remember when we were teenagers, Lotts? We used to talk about our weddings. You wanted to be carried off from the altar by Carver Doone.'

'A much-misunderstood man. Lorna Doone was a fool not to marry him,' said Lottie firmly.

'He was the villain.'

'He was sexy.'

'So basically you didn't want to be married, you wanted to be ravished?'

Lottie considered. 'No-oo. No, I don't think so. I think I just wanted to drive a man mad with lust. Preferably in front of all my friends and relations, including Jemima Crane from next door and Richard Gere in *Pretty Woman*. Of course, then they'd have to chase after us and rescue me. But, hey, I'm a drama queen. What can I tell you? I don't think it was anything more sinister than that.'

'I can't remember what I wanted.'

Lottie canted round on the sofa. 'You chopped and changed. You wanted to be married in a woodland glade, in secret, I remember that. Oh, and you always had that picture on your wall, with that woman with long flowing sleeves knighting a handsome young man in chain mail.'

Bella wriggled. 'Oooh yes, *The Accolade*, I can't

remember the artist, but the woman wore the most gorgeous dress, with those long flowing mediaeval sleeves and all that golden embroidery. Ah, I'd love a dress like that . . .'

Lottie nodded enthusiastically. 'Actually long mediaeval sleeves aren't a bad idea for a princess. Why not go with something like that.' She looked at her watch and swung her feet to the floor. 'That's me done. Back when I've excavated.'

When she returned Bella said reflectively, 'Neither of us was really into trailing down the aisle in a big white dress, with a piss-up afterwards, were we?'

Lottie peered at herself in the sitting-room mirror. 'The skin is definitely softer. And there aren't any shadows under my eyes. I think this is good stuff.'

Bella yawned. 'Good. I'm nodding off here.'

'You can't do that. We have Bridal Wear to nail.' Lottie turned round and put her hands on her hips. 'Is it time to open a bottle?'

Bella stretched. 'Mmmm.'

'Come on. You can't go to sleep. We must work.'

'I saw Richard last night,' said Bella dreamily. 'Got to bed *very* late.'

'Good for you.' Lottie had fetched a bottle and was applying a corkscrew with brisk efficiency. 'That's the idea. Concentrate on him. What do you think he wants to see walking down the aisle towards him?'

'The Curse of the Mutant Wedding Dress.'

Bella told Lottie about her fantasy moment when Lady Pansy was boring on, and they both cackled.

Lottie agreed. 'No, you don't want one of those giant

meringue things that looks as if it could walk on its own.'

'Walk, hunt, kill,' intoned Bella.

'Very probably. How much did you drink last night?'

'One bottle of champagne between us. Honestly, Lotts, I'm just tired. I've got three proposals which deserve funding and I've only got the money for two. I need some time to evaluate the comparison and bloody Lady bloody Pansy rings me all the time about what colour stationery I want to write my thank-you notes on.' She leaped up, looking at her watch. 'Hey, I've gone over time. I'll be burned to a crisp.'

She scooted down the hall into the bathroom and later could be heard swearing

Lottie poured herself a glass of wine and set about arranging the magazines round the floor, open at pictures she liked.

Eventually Bella came back, watery-eyed. 'I got some stuff in my eyes when I was getting rid of the sediment,' she explained. 'But you're right. My skin does feel softer.' She poured a glass of wine for herself. 'I shall tell Lady Pansy, so she can start another sodding file. Face masks, brides for the use of.'

She plonked herself down on the rug in front of the fire and crossed her legs. 'So, right, let's have a look at the meringues.'

But Lottie had opened all the magazines at photographs of day dresses. Tailored day dresses, floaty day dresses, knock-out cream wool belted day dresses. Skirts of all lengths. Waisted jackets; loose, unstructured jackets; almost-a-man's-dinner-jacket jackets. And silky cocktail trousers with piratical silk sashes and high-collared shirts. Even multi-layered grunge-with-attitude outfits where you couldn't tell which bit went where.

'What are these for?'

'The photoshoot next week? Remember?'

'Oh, God , Yes. OK.' Bella surveyed them all quickly. 'I like that,' she said, looking at the cream wool stunner with a sigh. 'But I'd spill coffee on it or something.'

Lottie choked. 'Yup. You probably would. Anyway, it's a bit too sophisticated. Touch of the cougar, don't you think?'

They both contemplated the worldly expression of the stick-thin model.

Bella nodded slowly. 'See what you mean. Anyway, I'm not really thin enough for it. Now I'm not starving any more, I'm back to my normal weight.'

'Good thing too. So forget cream wool. It's strictly for people who don't eat, don't move, and don't carry cups of coffee. Any idea which designer you would like?'

Bella broke off a corner of the giant slab of hazelnut chocolate Lottie had bought and sucked it thoughtfully.

'Lady P says they have to be British.'

Lottie snorted. 'Lady P is talking out of the back of her neck! Oh, maybe for the wedding dress or the . . . what do you call it? . . . Trousseau. That's the word – trousseau. Sounds very nineteen thirties, doesn't it? But in next week's photocall, the press will want to see the girl Richard fell for. You as you are. Cinderella before the ball. Trust me on this.'

Bella took more chocolate in her agitation. 'Bikini top, denim shorts and flip-flops?'

'Come on, you can do better than that. You've bought

some nice stuff since you got back. Have you looked through your wardrobe?'

'There's nothing there. It's either suits for work or jeans. Or party dresses, and they won't do. Lady P always looks as if she's going to an Ambassador's lunch. I reckon she thinks I ought to be the same. And I don't think I can.'

Lottie was bracing. 'Hey, you're a green-eyed blonde. You can look a million dollars when you put your mind to it. Any Ambassador would be proud. Do you actually *like* any of these looks?'

Bella picked up the whole chocolate bar and hugged it against her like a hot water bottle, rocking slightly. Lottie took it away from her.

'Chocolate and silk. Not a good look. Concentrate, Bel.'

Eventually Bella stopped panicking and decided that she liked the lace cut-out top and trouser combo, with fantastically high heels, and also a collection of very simple dresses in wonderful colours. 'The colour needs to be darkish to show off the ring,' she said thoughtfully.

Lottie gave a crow of delight. 'So that was what last night was about. You got the rock!'

'Mmm.'

'Come on then, give. Has he given you an heirloom?'

'Better,' said Bella dreamily. 'It's platinum with a yellow diamond, and it's beautiful. Designed for me. Just me.'

Lottie sat back on her heels, her eyes wide. 'Cor. I've never seen a yellow diamond. It's a good choice, though. You've got yellow flecks in those green eyes of yours. He must have noticed. Blue-whites are too harsh and emeralds would be too loud. Anyway some people think they're unlucky. But a yellow diamond . . . Yeah. He's got class, your Richard.'

'So point me at an outfit which returns the compliment,' said Bella, not dreamy any more.

'With pleasure.'

Lottie stabbed a finger at three. 'Not the lacy thing. Too predatory. Buy it for a party some time, though. Try the navy day dress, it's very elegant, a bit *Mad Men*, no? Or that green wrap-around chiffon dress with the kicky skirt. It's got a great neckline and the colour would be awesome for Little Miss yellow diamond.'

Bella agreed that both were worth looking at and Lottie was a star.

'And tomorrow I'm taking you shopping, before you lose your nerve,' said the star briskly. 'Sorted.'

After that they creamed each other's hands, and softened and trimmed cuticles, pared nails and then, ceremoniously, painted each other's nails gold. And finished the bottle.

The photoshoot was a breeze. She didn't know what *Mad Men* was and frankly it all sounded rather treacherous, so she had gone with the ivy-green number. With her height the skirt fell just on the knee, but was deemed demure enough by the powers-that-be. And it did show off the diamond beautifully. Bella loved her ring so much that she kept patting it and looking at it against different backgrounds. Each made it appear more perfect than the last. Richard was clearly delighted. The designer silversmith was there too, a shy self-effacing man who only came to life when he talked about his work.

'That man is coming to the wedding, isn't he?' Bella hissed to Richard, when drinks were served and the posing and snapping were over.

'If you want him, of course. Put him on your list.'

'Ah.'

'You have started a list?'

She winced. 'Not really.'

'But Pansy said—'

'It's not Lady Pansy's fault. She's given me a file and notes and everything. It's just that I'm struggling with competing proposals at work at the moment.'

Richard had that stony expression which she knew meant he disapproved.

'I'm really sorry, love. I'll do it next week.'

The stony expression did not lift.

'This week, I mean. I'll do it before Friday.'

'That would be helpful.'

'Ouch. Don't go Royal on me again.'

He looked down at her, startled.

She put her head on one side, looking up at him naughtily. 'Remember what happened last time.'

The stony expression dissolved.

'Which reminds me, you still owe me one limerick.'

He could not help himself. He laughed aloud.

It made a fabulous photo for the magazines, the two of them laughing together in a corner, when they thought no one was looking.

Tube Talk blew it up to a whole front page, under the

headline 'So Happy and So in Love'. And even the *Daily Despatch* said grumpily that clumsy Ms Greenwood must be doing something right.

Only LoyalSubjekt101 couldn't find anything nice to say about them. He or she thought the ring was a tawdry stunt, and buying an unbelievably expensive yellow diamond a slap in the face of the British people at this time of public austerity. The whole piece brimmed over with spite, particularly against Bella.

Richard was angry but Bella shrugged it off. 'You can't have everyone love you. Or even like you. On the whole, I think our hit rate's pretty good. Forget it. We're doing OK.'

Richard nodded. 'I suppose you're right. So far so good.'

But there was still the choice of the wedding dress to come and that was turning into a nightmare. For one thing, Lady Pansy had not understood that Bella wanted to look at pictures and get a general idea of the styles of the various designers, since she didn't know any of them. Lady Pansy had telephoned eight and commissioned original drawings.

'You mean, I'm paying for eight exclusive designs?' said Bella, hollowly. She couldn't begin to guess what it would cost but she was fairly sure that it would increase her student debt exponentially.

Lady Pansy waved aside the vulgar consideration. 'They won't charge. It is a great honour for them to be asked. Of course, they will let their clients know that they are in the running.'

'That doesn't seem very fair. I can only choose one and they will have done all that work for nothing.'

'Only in outline. They won't actually have bought any fabric or *made* anything.'

'You're clearly not creative,' said Bella. 'They will have worked on it, eaten, slept and dreamed of it. Raising their hopes like this is callous. It's not right.'

Lady Pansy stiffened. 'It's the way we always do things.'

'Don't tell me,' said Bella wearily. 'Tradition.'

But it was even worse when she looked at the drawings. They were all, every single one, huge-skirted, frilled and furbelowed, with swags of pearls or bows of lace in every conceivable crevice.

'I'll look like a duvet cover while it's being changed,' she told Lottie gloomily. 'Some right-thinking person will jump out of the crowd and try to beat the lumps out of me.'

'It can't be that bad. You're being paranoid again.'

But after she'd looked through the portfolio that Bella had brought home, Lottie had to admit that it was not paranoia. They truly were . . .

'Frightful,' said Bella.

'Not your style,' amended Lottie. She peered at the signature on a crinoline so huge that it could probably double as an air balloom. '*Lawson?* What on earth? He's the guy who usually sends brides down the aisle with the back of the wedding dress cut down to the bum. Known for it. It's his signature quirk. This thing has got a liberty bodice sewn in! He must have gone mad.'

Bella clutched her hair. 'It's almost certainly Lady

Pansy. She briefed them all. It has to be traditional, it has to please Middle England, and it has to make me look like the biggest laundry bag in the world.'

Lottie looked at the drawings again and made sympathetic noises.

'She's the Queen's best friend. She's known Richard since he was in the cradle. They all love her and they're certain she knows best. And I can't prove she doesn't, because I'm letting it all get on top of me. Oh, God, Lotts. What am I going to *do*?'

20

'Bridesmaids and Vikings' – *Morning Times*

Oddly enough, it was Janet who came up with the solution to the problem. She had come up to Town for lunch with Bella since it was, she said, the only way she got to see her daughter. Conscience-stricken, Bella booked a table at a small wine bar round the corner from the charity's offices. But, though her mother was in a determined mood, there were none of the reproaches that Bella was braced for.

'Look, Bella,' she said, 'Kevin and I have been talking. I know that your father has washed his hands of the wedding. Has he even spoken to you?'

Bella had to admit he hadn't. 'But that's happened before, Ma. You know what he's like. And I was pretty rude to him.'

'Good for you,' said Janet, surprisingly. 'It's your life. But anyway, Kevin wanted me to say, he would be delighted to help out in any way. For instance, neither of us feels quite comfortable with the way the Palace seems to have taken you over.'

Bella was startled. 'Doesn't sound like you, Ma.'

Janet pressed her lips together. 'I admire the Royal

Family. But it does seem that they are riding roughshod over you sometimes. Whenever I speak to you, you have to break off to take a call from Lady Pansy in the middle of it. And it seems to me you're rushing from pillar to post, trying to keep up with it all. So Kevin says what you need is a proper, trained Personal Assistant. He says that would take some of the strain off you. And he would like to pay for it.'

Bella was so touched that for a moment she could not speak.

Janet began to look nervous. 'Is that all right? We don't want to interfere. I just hate to see you looking so frantic.'

'Ma, you're wondrous. And Kevin is undoubtedly the best stepfather in the world. They did say they were going to employ me a PA. But in the end Lady Pansy just hired a couple of girls without consulting me, and they work for her in the office in the Palace. Lottie helps me think and keeps me sane, mostly. And there's Carlos and everyone at the hair salon. But . . .'

'I know,' said Janet. 'Everyone's busy. So is that all right then?'

Bella nodded. 'I'd be so grateful. I can't tell you.'

Janet looked delighted. 'I'll tell Kevin. He will be so pleased. Um – any chance of you coming to stay at all?'

Bella consulted her schedule. These days she downloaded Richard's week first and then fitted her own activities around his.

'Well, Richard's away on some Schools Sports thing this weekend. I could come though, if you don't mind just me?'

Janet brightened. 'That would be lovely. It's beautiful at the moment. The daffodils are all out and there are primroses along the river.'

For a moment Bella had such a pang of longing it was almost physical. She loved London but she was a nature girl at heart and it was a long time since she had smelled the damp of impacted leaves and the sharp clean scent of things pushing up through the warming earth. Spring was always beautiful in the New Forest.

'Oh, yes, Ma. I'd love that,' she said from the heart.

'Good. I'll ask Neill and Val, if they're free.'

'You won't get Neill. He's got his Viking thing on Easter Monday. He's training every moment he gets.'

'Well, Val then. She seems much happier these days. And Georgia perhaps. Oh, it will be just like old times.'

Bella put it into her schedule and copied it to Richard and his office.

He texted back at once: *Good idea. Wish I could make it. Give Janet my love.*

She passed it on, they finished lunch and her mother went back to Hampshire.

Kevin was on the phone within half an hour of Janet's departure. 'Don't know if you have anyone in mind as a PA,' he said gruffly. 'But the Head of HR here says they could probably help. Young woman with small children, delighted to work from home, that sort of thing. If you would like, I'll send you her email. Don't want to interfere, though.'

Don't want to interfere. That's what her mother had said too. How different Kevin and Janet were from Richard's family, thought Bella. And then thought, no, it's not his family. Apart from Queen Jane's outburst in Andorra, none of them had even tried to interfere, and that had been much more about the Queen's own life than Bella's and Richard's.

No, the interference, the plethora of petty details, the comments, the criticisms of anything she wanted to do, that all came from the blasted Private Offices via Lady Pansy, with Lady P herself putting her oar in at every opportunity. Were they making work to keep themselves important?

Bella squashed the thought at once. But could not quite banish it.

So she said to Kevin that she would be grateful for any help she could get.

Before the end of the week, she had a friendly human dynamo in the shape of Trudy, mother of two and hot-shot administrator, who was going spare at home while the children were busy with nursery school and play-group. Within two days she had set up a spreadsheet with a To Do list plus target dates and notes of people to be consulted.

She also gave Bella some shrewd advice. 'Lady Pansy is straight out of the quill pen era. Not her fault, but she needs managing.'

Bella gave a hollow laugh. 'But *how*?'

'You have to pre-empt her. Be pro-active. Set up meetings with her, put them in the diary, keep them short. Make her feel key to the whole process, but stop her picking up the phone every time she thinks of something else.'

It worked.

Of course, Lady Pansy didn't like it. To begin with she forgot to copy her messages to Trudy. But when she found that Bella re-routed all her text messages to her new PA and kept her telephone permanently set to voice mail, she gave in. There was a difficult little meeting when she suggested, with great sweetness, that Bella was finding her new role too overwhelming.

'Maybe you ought to move into the Palace? I can mention it to Her Majesty. We are having coffee this morning.'

The prospect was hair-raising. Bella knocked it on the head fast.

'That's very kind, Lady Pansy. But not necessary, thank you. I think I have worked out how to balance my *work* life with everything I need to do for the wedding. I'll review the situation with Richard in a few weeks. And this is how I see it working . . .'

She presented Lady Pansy with the new timetable. Bella would still go to the Palace to meet her, but she would do it on a regular timetable: at 2 p.m. on Monday to review stuff that had come in at the weekend and make any changes needed to the week; a quick catch up on Wednesday at 5.30 p.m.; the major review and planning meeting of the week to be two hours on Friday morning. With adjustment to her childcare manage-ment, Trudy thought she could generally manage to attend the Friday meeting. Lady Pansy was to pass any questions to Trudy who would prioritise and manage while Bella was at work.

Lady Pansy knew when she had been outmanoeuvred. Her phone calls slowed to a trickle.

Bella and Trudy spoke at lunch-time every day.

'You need to pace yourself,' Trudy advised. 'Plan to do one thing at a time and stick to it. Wedding dress this week. Bridesmaids the next.'

'Oh, God, bridesmaids! I haven't thought about bridesmaids.'

'*Next* week,' said Trudy firmly.

Yet it was Richard who found the solution to the wedding-dress problem.

'Of course you can't have a dress you hate,' he said vehemently. 'You'll be looking at photographs of it for the rest of your life.'

'But tradition . . .'

He took her left hand and looked at the ring. 'We can set some of our own traditions.'

She searched his face. 'You're sure?'

'Of course.'

'Your mother had the full meringue, and so did your grandmother.'

He snorted. 'And my great, great ever so great grandmother wore a dress of total bling. Your point is?'

Bella was stunned. 'Bling? How do you know? I don't believe you.'

'Would I lie to you? Look, I'll prove it.'

They were in his flat, padding around in early-morning disarray. He went over to his desk and switched on the laptop.

'Look. Here.'

Bella went and peered over his shoulder. He had called up a Regency sketch of a man in knee breeches and an elaborate jacket leading a girl in a slim, high-waisted, low-cut dress, with puffed sleeves trimmed with lace. Her hair had been screwed into a knot on top of her head and she was not wearing a veil. Bella peered closely.

'Silver lamé on net over a tissue slip,' she read. 'It was embroidered at the bottom with silver lamé shells and flowers. The manteau – oh, I see, that was the train – the manteau was of silver tissue lined with white satin, with a border of embroidery to answer that on the dress and fastened in front with a splendid diamond ornament.' She looked up. 'Heavens, she must have looked like a Christmas tree.'

Richard's lips quirked. 'Especially when you think of all the candles they'd have needed.' He flickered his fingers. 'Glitter, glitter, glitter. What about going the whole hog and reviving the traditions of 1816, then?'

Bella kicked him, not very successfully as her feet were bare.

He held her off, looking injured. 'Only trying to be helpful.'

'No, you weren't. If you were really being helpful, you'd tell me who I should get to make the dress,' Bella said with a sigh. She looked fondly at her ring. 'You have a really good eye. Haven't you got a favourite young dress designer as well?'

'Well, I suppose I could ask around,' he said doubt-fully. 'But it's terrible bad luck, isn't it? I don't care, but a lot of people do. No point in giving the insects some-thing else to exercise their mandibles on.'

'You're probably right. I think my mother would worry too. She's quite superstitious. Oh, well. Back to the drawing board.' Bella glanced at the screen again, and said wistfully, 'Did you see that they got married in Carlton House? Family and fifty guests, that's all. Those were the days.'

They had decided to marry in the Cathedral. It was beautiful, of course, but not, as Bella said, human-sized. Besides, there was a huge echo. It made their footsteps on the marble floor sound like Death treading ponderously up from the vaults to claim a soul. That was something she did not say.

Richard knew she wasn't comfortable with it. He also knew – they both did – that there wasn't really an alternative.

So now he gave her a quick hug and said, 'Look, what about a Working Party?'

'What?'

'OK, you can't see off the Meringue Party without support. So get some.'

'What do you mean? How?'

'Think who you would have asked if you hadn't been marrying me.' He winced a little at the thought. 'I just bet your grandmother has ideas about wedding dresses.'

He had responded to the summons to meet Georgia far better than Bella had dared to hope, especially as her grandmother had grilled him with ladylike thoroughness and there had been several dodgy moments.

The turning point had come, though, when Georgia, ramrod straight and acid sweet, said, 'Are you saying that you knew you would get my granddaughter the moment you saw her? Like buying a painting?'

Richard smiled down at her and said, very gently, 'I love her, Mrs Greenwood. I don't own her and I never will.'

Georgia's eyes snapped and Bella held her breath.

But in the end her grandmother said grudgingly, 'Ah. You see that. Good.'

And in the car home, Richard said, 'It's not a word I normally use but that woman is truly awesome. A Southern Belle with fabulous manners and an inter-rogation technique that MI5 could learn from. *And* she looks like one of those classy old movie stars, Lauren Bacall or someone. *And* she's out saving the rain forest in person.' He drew a long, astounded breath. 'I thought your father would be great to meet. But – wow. Just – *wow!* I think I'm in love.'

So now Bella said teasingly, 'You just want to meet my grandmother again.'

He nodded enthusiastically. 'If we work the schedule right, I could even give her, I mean all of you, lunch.'

'Machiavelli.'

He laughed, not denying it, but said soberly, 'Call her, Bella. Your mother too. Every girl wants to consult her mother about her wedding dress, doesn't she? No one could criticise you for that. Maybe Lottie, too? Get them all in a room together, schmooze a bit, and come out with a better brief for the designers. Include Pansy and whoever she wants to bring along. Just make sure she's outnumbered. She looks like a sweet little old lady, but Pansy can be quite an operator when she wants to be.'

333

'Thank you,' said Bella, surprised and grateful. 'That sounds like a plan. Er – have you any ideas about bridesmaids?'

'Out of my league,' he said with feeling.

But Bella found an unexpected ally on the bridesmaid issue and she didn't have to go looking for her.

Princess Eleanor wandered into the Wednesday catch-up meeting with Lady Pansy and said, 'Have you seen the daffodils by the lake, Bella? Do you fancy a walk? It's so lovely and fresh outside now that the rain's gone.'

Bella leaped up with alacrity and, as they wandered along the banks of the lake, her soon-to-be sister-in-law said, 'Have people started lobbying you about being a bridesmaid yet?'

Bella bit her lip. 'Yes. It was a bit of a shock, actually.'

'Well, this is a bit of a cheek. But I'm lobbying, too.'

'Eleanor—'

'Call me Nell, like the boys do. I've been thinking about bridesmaids since I was at school. All my little friends fancied being mine.' She pulled a face. 'So I've got some theories. Wanna hear them?'

'Very grateful,' said Bella, touched.

'You need your best friend. Plus a sister or cousin or whoever. And a sister or cousin from the bridegroom's family. One small attendant. One to mind the small attendant. But the important thing is that they're *your* bridesmaids. Not your husband's. Not your mother's. Not your mother-in-law's. Yours. These women have to get you through the day, so you need to *like* them. Don't be blackmailed into asking anyone you don't want. If there's someone you absolutely have to include but can't face on the day itself, you can always ask her to your Hen Night.'

'Hen Night,' murmured Bella, committing it to memory. Something else she had forgotten.

However, when Lady Pansy produced her big file labelled Bridesmaids, and started to run through the daughters of the country's senior aristocrats, along with their family's service to the Crown over the last two hundred years, Bella was able to say that she had already decided who she was going to ask to be her bridesmaids, thank you.

Lady Pansy stiffened. But Bella had run her choice past Richard who had not only approved but said, when he stopped laughing, 'And you called *me* Machiavelli!' So she knew she was on firm ground.

'Princess Eleanor. She's already said yes. My second cousin Joanne. So has she. Tilly Lenane, because she's Richard's goddaughter and I think she's a sweetie. Chloe, because I know how big a part she's always been of the Royal Family's life, as you are yourself.'

Lady Pansy inclined her head graciously. She seemed taken aback but pleased, definitely pleased.

So while she was preening, Bella slipped in the news that would make Lady P as sick as a parrot when she started to think about it. 'And my best friend Charlotte Hendred will be my Chief Bridesmaid, of course. So if you would just find out from Tilly Lenane's parents and your niece whether they're happy to trot down the aisle after me, we're sorted I think, Lady Pansy.'

'Of course,' said Lady Pansy. She looked sandbagged. *Yes!* Result.

With that, the arrangements went swimmingly. After consultation with the King, the Press Office organised a bunch of interviews and think pieces.

'I told them to leave you alone to get on with it, my dear,' the King told Bella, when she and Richard joined the rest of the Royal Family for supper, one cool spring evening. 'I said to Julian Madoc, "I like her style. She's got a good head on her shoulders and she's very well behaved." Unlike some,' he added with a dark look at Nell, who pretended not to see.

'We'll send a minder along, of course. And you must ask for any advice you want. But basically be yourself. Ver' charming. Ver' charming.'

With the Royal seal of approval, it seemed Bella could not go wrong. Even Lady Pansy stopped arguing. Though the High Level Talks on the wedding dress nearly changed that.

It was Lady Pansy, of course, who arranged the conference room and the coffee in the Palace. So she decided to take the initiative and invite four of her favourite designers to come too, in the afternoon, to present their ideas.

'You did *what?*' said Bella aghast, arriving before her support group.

Lady Pansy was affronted. 'Time is ticking away. You need to assign the contract today. Having the top four here will save time. Not all together, of course. You can talk to them in turn,' she said kindly.

Bella was tight-lipped. 'You knew quite well that this was to be a planning meeting only. This is *not* helpful. Get rid of them.'

But even her grandmother, when she arrived, said that it would be bad form to uninvite them at such short notice. So Bella gave in. She was still seething, though.

However, the discussion itself was very useful. Everyone had a different perspective. Bella realised she wouldn't have thought of half the points on her own.

Janet said the most important thing Bella needed to think about was being comfortable. She would be standing a long time, she would have to move a fair amount, step backwards, go round corners, up steps, kneel and stand up again.

'You have to feel that you can move in the dress without having to brace yourself every time, pet,' her mother said earnestly. 'There's so much to do at a wedding. You want to be able to put your dress on and forget about it.'

Lottie was the self-appointed Look of Now expert. She set up her laptop and delivered a PowerPoint presentation of some of the options, given current fashions. She had cleverly produced images of Richard and Bella which were to scale and transferred dresses across to slot on to the Bella figure.

Every time anyone stopped speaking, Lady Pansy broke in with what the Queen had worn at her wedding, the Dowager Queen, Richard's aunt the Princess Royal . . . She described the dresses in loving detail. They were all clearly meringue on the grand scale.

Bella said clearly, 'Thank you, Lady Pansy. We have understood the precedents very clearly now.'

She was not seething any more. Her indignation had cooled to an icy determination to stop Lady P in her tracks. She stood up.

'So let's get this out of the way now. I will *not* go down the aisle to meet Richard wearing some vast crinoline that makes me look like the Dame in a provincial pantomime. It's not my style. Please, everyone, strike that option *now*.'

She sat down. Lottie applauded. Lady Pansy was temporarily hounded out of sweet superiority and glared with fury. Bella ignored her and turned to her grandmother on the other side of the conference table.

'Georgia? You haven't said anything yet. What do you think?'

Georgia considered. 'A wedding dress makes a big statement. And you need to remember what the back of it says. The photographs will all show the front. But in the church—'

'Cathedral,' put in Lady Pansy loudly.

They all ignored that.

'In the church everyone will be looking at your back throughout the service. That young man who likes to design backless wedding dresses seems to me to be asking the congregation to join the bride in – well, almost deceiving the bridegroom. Sneering at him, even. I'm sorry, Lottie. I don't think they're very kind.'

'Hadn't thought of that one,' said Bella cheerfully, her temper restored. You could always rely on her grandmother to come out of left field. 'OK, Georgia. Dress must be kind. What else?'

Lady Pansy snorted audibly.

'Of course, it's all about the way line and colour are combined. Something very white and severe could say "I'm not for touching", for instance. Myself, I think that some of those boned tops, which cut into the flesh, look as if the bride is constrained. In a straitjacket, if you will. Not comfortable and not . . . free.'

Lottie laughed aloud. 'Well, that's knocked out the collections of at least three designers I know, Georgia. That's narrowed it down.'

'If you want my advice, Bella dear, I think you have to consider the message you want to give the congregation. And, more important even than that, the message you want to give your husband. He's the most important person there for you, after all. Isn't he?'

'Yes,' said Bella, feeling her ears go pink and knowing there was not one single thing she could do about it. 'Yes, he is. Good thinking, Batwoman.'

But if the discussion was a success, the beauty parade of designers was not. Once they grasped that meringue was out, they pitched hard for their own most recent collections. Bella sat there with a frozen smile on her face, feeling it was more and more hopeless, until eventually one man said, 'Everything happens around the Bride. A wedding is a picture, with the church and congregation as the frame, and the Bride the blank canvas to which I apply the image of the Day.'

There was a brief flurry. Suddenly Georgia was on her feet, elegant and deadly.

'May I clarify something?' she said, very courteously. 'You just said that my granddaughter is a blank canvas?'

He did sense danger but not enough to sidestep it. 'Just for the purposes of the Day . . .' he began airily.

He was stopped dead in his tracks.

'You are a very silly man. You do not know how to do your job. Please leave.'

That was when things changed, Bella thought afterwards. Up till then, the Press had either loved her or given her the benefit of the doubt. Even the grumpy *Daily Despatch* hadn't actually attacked her. But soon there was a rumour that Bella had told favourite-of-the-stars designer Jonas Krump that he was a silly man who did not know how to do his job. And the backlash started.

It wasn't all bad. The *Morning Times* did a very nice piece about her family, including Neill's upcoming appearance as a Viking, and ran a profile of her bridesmaids in their weekend supplement. A charities magazine did an evaluation of her first three months at the forestry project and said she was hard-working and inventive, with really sound hands-on experience from her time in the Indian Ocean. The women's pages were generally pleased when she chose a younger British designer, Flora Hedderwick, to design The Dress.

But LoyalSubjekt101 said she was a control freak with an ego problem, who didn't care about British trade, the Royal Family or even the Prince of Wales. And other bloggers started to creep out of the ether, repeating the same story.

'Bloody nonsense,' said the King, storming into Lady Pansy's office while Bella was there one Wednesday. He was in a fine temper, and knocked over a small table stacked with files as he fulminated.

Lady Pansy, leaping to her feet, did not know whether to curtsey or rescue the files, so did a sort of wild salmon writhe until the King said, 'Oh sit down, woman. Sit *down*.'

This grumpiness was so unlike him that Bella was astonished. His colour was high, too.

'Are you all right?' she asked him.

'Bastard reptiles, he said, not answering directly. 'All they want to do is tear into people. Never mind who gets hurt. You carry on, my dear. You tell the truth – and if they don't like it, tough.' He turned on Lady Pansy. 'And if any of them ask you, it's no comment. Right?'

And he stamped out, leaving Lady Pansy curtseying behind him.

'I do think,' she said in the soft, patronising voice that Bella was coming to loathe, 'that it would be a lot easier if you were to move into the Palace, where you could be *guided* more, Bella dear.'

'Bastard reptiles,' floated back down the corridor.

Bella's lips twitched. 'I think I've got it about right as far as His Majesty is concerned,' she said.

And left, with a spring in her step.

If only she had known.

She spent Easter with the Royal Family at the Castle and, after lunch on Sunday, she and Richard drove down to Devon to cheer on Neill and his fellow Vikings the next day. The fields were full of green shoots and a brilliant spring sun made the budding trees look as if they had been studded with tiny emeralds.

They had a perfect evening in the grounds of a small village pub tht led down to the river where the longboat was due to land the next day. In fact they were sitting there in the scented dark when Neill arrived, looking harassed.

'We've got a problem, Sis,' he told Bella. 'Our celebrity has broken his hand, careless bugger, and we're one oarsman short. Can you call Lottie? She said she'd try and get one of the Richmond lot to come along. At this stage, we can live without a celebrity. We just need someone to pull an oar.'

Richard stretched lazily. 'I can pull an oar,' he remarked.

Neill said, 'I haven't got her number. I've looked everywhere. I—' He did a double take.

'I can pull an oar. I was in the second eight at college. Of course, it wasn't quite Viking style.'

Neill said eagerly, 'But you were pretty good when we were playing around that weekend.' And then, 'No. No, you can't. We haven't got a costume for you.'

'What happened to the celebrity's costume, then?'

'I mean we haven't got a costume for *you*.'

'I don't think Viking raiders had Prince of Wales feathers on their sea coats,' said Richard dryly. 'I'm up for it, if you are.'

And of course, he did brilliantly. His springy hair kept pushing off his Viking helmet, so it had to be held on with elastic, but otherwise he looked the part fantastically. And when they came to land, he swaggered up with the rest of them, bare-chested and with a distinct glint in his eyes.

'Sexy swine,' said Bella, going to meet him along with all the other wives and girlfriends. 'God, you smell good.'

There was a lot of laughter and making faces at the camera but the wind had got up and soon enough the mighty oarsmen decided they could do with tee-shirts. And the tee-shirts, carried the logo of the sponsor, a hand-crafted biscuit manufacturer.

It was on the internet by nightfall. *Prince of Wales in Advertising Scandal*. And there was Richard, in the green-and-white tee-shirt, with a tankard of ale in his hand and one arm round a laughing Bella, advertising Morgan's Ginger Thins.

Some said he was stupid and drunk. Some said he was stupid and calculating. Some said he was stupid and did what his bride-to-be told him to. Of course, every version of the story started with the fact that his fiancée's brother was the reason Richard had become a Viking in the first place.

Bella's phone rang all the time. It felt as if the thing was vibrating with rage. Richard was inclined to shrug it off.

'It's bad luck about the sponsorship. But as long as Morgan's don't try to cash in – which would be very silly of them – I don't think anyone will care, for long. The proceeds go to Sailing for the Disabled, after all. And I had a bloody good time. End of.'

Only then his Father heard about it.

By midnight the King was in hospital with a suspected heart attack.

Richard suddenly went very quiet. A helicopter was scrambled to take him to London.

'I'll come with you,' said Bella.

But Richard shook his head. He looked pale and drawn but he was his usual calm self, contained, in control. Bella had never felt so far away from him, not even when they fought.

'Better not,' he said, as politely as if she were a stranger. 'Someone has to drive the car back to London.'

'You want me to do that?'

'If you wouldn't mind?'

'Oh, my love.' She went to put her arms round him but he evaded her embrace without really seeming to see it.

'I'll call you.'

He doesn't want me, Bella thought. He blames me. And he's right. It's my fault. Neill would never have agreed to let him in the boat if it weren't for that silly game, rowing on the carpet at home, before Christmas.

She swallowed. 'Yes, do. Please. Call me as late as you like. I won't go to sleep until you do.'

'Yes. OK,' he said, only half with her. 'Got to go.'

A kiss – barely a kiss at all, really – and he was gone.

21

'When One Thing Goes Wrong . . .!' – *Tube Talk*

Bella drove back very carefully the next day. She hadn't slept much.

Richard had rung to say that his father was in the King George IV Memorial Hospital for Officers and seemed to be stable. The doctors weren't really sure what was going on. They'd done a blood test and results suggested a minor heart attack.

'According to his valet he fell asleep over the television last night and then woke up and suddenly started talking scribble. That could have been because he was still half asleep. But it just might have been a small stroke, which is what's worrying them. Madoc said he's been short of breath a lot lately. And also there were a couple of odd episodes this week, when my father seemed very anxious about something. But Madoc didn't press him and it seemed to pass. Classic symptoms of a mild heart attack, apparently. He's being monitored round the clock at the moment. Anyway, the quacks say it isn't life-threatening, though he needs to be careful.'

'How are you?'

'Me?' Richard sounded drained but impeccably polite, as always. 'I'm fine. The emergency was all over, pretty much, by the time I got here. My mother is shaken, though.'

Bella just longed to be with him, to hold him. Somehow she couldn't quite bring herself to say it. She did say, 'What can I do?'

He puffed out his breath as if he were trying to think of something for her to do, to make her feel better. 'Bring the car back to Camelford House. I'll make sure the Guard House are expecting you and don't play any of their stupid tricks.'

She knew he would too. Even when he was so tired he couldn't see straight, even when he was desperately worried about his father, he would make sure that she did not have to lock horns with some jobsworth who wanted to show her she didn't belong there. She thought her heart would break.

'I'll see you tomorrow then.'

'What? Oh, yes. Tomorrow. Thank you.' He was obviously about to put the phone down and added conscientiously, 'Good night. Thank you for waiting up.'

She did not know how long she sat there with tears falling silently. She loved him with all her heart but in his distress she could not get near him. It was like walking into a wall.

Bella did not know Richard's big car very well. Had only driven it a couple of times before, to move it in car parks and so on. But she was a good driver, steady and unflappable, and the tears had dried towards dawn. She delivered it safely to Camelford House by mid-afternoon.

It was Fred, one of the nicer security men, in the Guard House when she put her head round the door.

'Afternoon, Miss Greenwood. How's His Majesty?'

'On the mend, we hope, Fred. Has Prince Richard got back yet?'

'Been and gone, miss. He's over at the Palace with the Private Office. They'll be rearranging diaries, I reckon.'

'Yes.' Yes, of course. She shouldn't have needed a security officer to tell her that. 'I'll – just go then.'

'Right you are, miss.'

He took the keys from her and Bella wandered blindly out into the London streets. Should she join Richard? Would he want her? Or would she be just another burden that he had to carry and be polite to, in addition to everything else?

There was only one way to find out. She half expected it to go to voice mail but he answered his phone after only three rings.

'Bella. Where are you?'

'Back in London. They tell me you're at the Palace. Shall I come over ? Or—'

'Yes,' he said with urgency. 'Yes, come now. That would be – yes.'

A flunkey escorted her to a room she hadn't seen before. It was long and thin, with several desks with slightly outdated computer screens on them, and wall-mounted clocks showing the time in Ottawa, New York, Kingston Jamaica, Paris, Rome, Delhi and Canberra.

Richard was standing at a long folding table – it

reminded Bella of a pasting table she had seen decorators use in her mother's house – with three other men, looking at a huge roll of paper.

He glanced up when she came in and surged towards her, almost lifting her off her feet with the strength of his hug.

'I'm glad you're here,' he said, too quietly for anyone else to hear. 'So glad. I wished I hadn't gone off last night the moment I got into the helicopter. I wasn't thinking straight.'

'You were worried. We both were. What's this?'

He took her hand and led her towards the table. 'My father's schedule. He doesn't hold with computers. He likes to see it mapped out in front of him.'

It resembled nothing so much as a giant campaign plan. It was even colour-coded. One of the blocks of colour started in three days' time. She looked at it hard.

'But that's—'

'Australia,' said Richard levelly. 'Yes. My father and mother were due to fly out on Thursday on the first leg of an Asian Pacific Tour. Six weeks away. They'd get back just over a month before our wedding. It's out of the question now. The King has to be under medical observation for at least a month.'

'You're going to cancel?'

He held her hand very tight by his side. 'No. Can't do that. I will take over their schedule. Nell will accompany me to Australia and fulfil my mother's programme there. My mother may join us later, depending on my father's rate of recovery.'

'So you don't want me there?'

348

'Oh, I want you all right,' he said, with such bitter weariness that she had to believe him. 'I just can't have you. It's not *done*. It's not protocol, God help me. You're not Royal yet.'

'They'd be getting a substandard product?'

He gave a snort of laughter and immediately looked better for it. 'Yeah, I s'pose.

'So I take over my father's diary. George is supposed to be studying, but he doesn't have another exam this year, so he can take over mine. He's cleared it with his supervisor. Maybe you'll help out?'

'Me? Even though I'm not Royal?'

'Always helps to have a bit of skirt, though,' said a voice from Richard's other side, and Bella realised that her future brother-in-law was among those present.

He lurched round Richard and gave her a hearty kiss. 'We'll keep the world on its toes while you're away, Magister.'

That was when she realised, truly realised, that Richard was going away and she would be left on her own. And knew that she could not make a fuss. It would only make things worse for him.

'Yes, sure. I'll stay here and keep on with the pre-Royalty arrangements, counting down to the wedding.'

'And I'll phone you every night.'

'I'm banking on it.'

They spent Richard's last two nights in England together. He sat up late at his desk, working through things. Sometimes typing at the computer. Sometimes staring into space, thinking. Bella brought him a drink or coffee or, once, cocoa because he said he couldn't remember what it tasted like. So she pulled on her outdoor clothes and slipped out to the Late, Late Store attached to the big local garage and came back with a tin of cocoa, sugar, because she had never seen any in his kitchen, and enough milk to sink a battleship. She made it carefully and then frothed it up as a treat.

He was writing again, but turned at her arrival by his desk. 'What?'

'Cocoa.'

He stared at the mug in her hand. 'But we haven't got any cocoa. I've never seen any in the Palace. I didn't even know it was still made.'

'Late-night garage shop,' she said smugly. 'And it is made by me. Taste it and see if it's sweet enough.'

He inhaled the aroma first. 'Oh, heavens, yes. I must have been about six the last time I had this.' He tasted and a look of bliss came over his face. Then he lowered the mug.

'What is it?' Bella said. 'Too hot, too cold? Needs cream? What?'

'You,' he said in an odd voice.

'Me? Yes?'

'You – think about me.'

'So?'

'You don't understand. Lots of people take care of me, smooth my path, give me things. But that's their job, or else they're being polite to my father's representative. You – think about me and then go and do what you see I want. *Yourself.*'

She stood quietly in front of him, her hands by her sides.

350

'Of course,' she said softly.

He leaned forward and rested his head against her. Bella stroked his hair. She could feel all the worry and effort and alertness drain out him, and he stayed there, just being in the moment, for the longest time. Eventually he stirred.

'You're wonderful,' he said in a matter-of-fact voice, as if it were so obvious, it was just something you said to remind yourself. Like, check door key, or turn off iron.

Bella felt her heart would spill over, it was so full. This, she knew, would carry her through the next lonely six weeks without him.

It would have to.

22

'The Hen Night!' – *Daily Despatch*

Richard was due out on a mid-morning flight from Heathrow on Thursday. He and Princess Eleanor were travelling on a scheduled flight, albeit first-class of course.

Neither Richard nor Bella slept very well the night before, though neither of them mentioned it – nor did they know that the other was in the same state. They were both awake early, though Richard's manservant had packed his bags and sent them over to the Palace the day before, from where the whole party would leave.

'Walk with me before I go?' Richard said quietly.

There was a hazy mist over St James's Park and the lake was as still as a mirror. Office workers were already striding through the walks, on their way to their offices in Whitehall or Piccadilly or the Strand. It seemed that only Bella and Richard had time to stop on the bridge and look at the ducks.

'I'll take you to Sydney another time,' he said with sudden passion.

'Any time you say.'

They wandered on, beneath cascading fronds of

young willow, catching the faint warm scent of crocuses in the air.

'You will be all right. George will help. He can be a prune but his heart is in the right place.'

'Of course I'll be all right. I'm an independent woman. If I can survive Francis and the fish, I can survive anything.'

His fingers almost crushed hers.

At last Bella said reluctantly, 'We're going to have to go. You know what the office is like about punctuality.'

'My poor love. You're learning the hard way, aren't you?'

They turned their back on the fantastic skyline of Whitehall and the London Eye and strode out for the Palace.

Queen Jane had insisted she was going to see her children off at the airport. She had dressed very carefully in a trim scarlet coat worn with a black pill-box hat. This was a cheerful woman, you would have said, who had no fears at all for her husband's health. But when you got close, you saw how thick and careful the make-up was, how strained her eyes.

'You look very handsome,' Bella said involuntarily. 'My grandmother Georgia would say that coat was giving a message of good cheer.'

There was an indrawn breath from Lady Pansy and a couple of others in the assembled entourage. Oh, bother, thought Bella, remembering Lady Pansy's folder on how to address Their Majesties. Page one said, among other things, don't address them unless Their Majesties speak to you first. Page two covered subjects which should never, ever be raised with Their Majesties. High on the list was their personal appearance. So five minutes here and she'd broken two rules. Well done, Bella.

But, although the Queen looked surprised, her tired eyes smiled. 'Thank you, my dear. How kind of you. I certainly hope so.'

Bella was all set to travel in the second car with Princess Eleanor, and was even moving towards it, when the Queen stopped her with a gloved hand on her arm.

'No. You go with Richard, Bella. Stay together as long as you can.'

They drove in a convoy through Central London. As well as the two Royal cars there were also security cars in front and behind them, and motorbike outriders. All through the city traffic stopped and drew to one side to let them through. Six months ago Bella could never have imagined such progress. Now it didn't seem to matter. She held Richard's hand tightly all the way there. The journey didn't take long. They didn't speak.

At the airport they were driven to a small VIP room, where quiet, efficient officials completed passport and flight formalities painlessly. And then the two limousines drove out on to the tarmac and came to rest beside the waiting plane.

Everyone got out. Bella could feel her throat thicken with tears. This was crazy. It was six *weeks*, for God's sake. And Richard had much more to worry about than she had; not just the trip and all the briefings he would have to catch up on as he went along, but his father's health, too. She had seen how genuinely fond he and his father were of each other, though neither of them ever expressed it of course.

I must not make a scene and make this harder for him, she thought.

She said brightly, 'I want lots of photos and a kiss a day.'

He kissed her formally. But there was a smile in his eyes that was worth all the repressed sobs in her chest. 'You've got it.'

He and Eleanor went up the steps. Turned at the top and waved. But not to me, thought Bella, suddenly desolate. This one is for the cameras.

When they had disappeared and the cabin doors were being closed, the Queen turned to Bella. 'Ride back to Town with me?'

As soon as they set off, the Queen pressed a little button and a soundproof glass partition slid up between them and the chauffeur.

'My dear, I wanted to say how grateful I am for the support you have given us all, especially Richard, over the last few days. It cannot have been easy.'

Bella did not think she could say anything without blubbing like an idiot, so she just made a vague you're-welcome gesture.

'Quite,' said the Queen, understanding. 'You behaved beautifully back there. I was very proud of you. Proud of you both. I know this is the worst time for you to be apart. I'm just so sorry that circumstances—'

Bella couldn't take any more. 'How is His Majesty?' she said swiftly.

The Queen smiled. 'Not very pleased with life. He

feels fine. But the doctors won't release him until they know what happened. He says he's become a lab rat and is being difficult about blood tests. The doctors have all my sympathy. He's on fighting form.'

'That's good news.'

'Yes. Now, I wanted to ask you whether you would like to move into the Palace soon? With Richard away and the wedding approaching . . .'

Oh, Lord, thought Bella. Is this my punishment for encouraging him to play Viking and promote Morgan's Ginger Thins?

She said in a small voice, 'I'm very happy sharing a flat with Charlotte Hendred.'

The Queen looked as if that surprised her. 'Are you sure? Don't the paparazzi make a nuisance of themselves?'

Bella grinned. 'They stood around outside the block of flats for five days and saw Lottie and me leave to go to work every morning and come back from work every night, except for Saturday when we bought food and went to our parents'. They got bored.'

The Queen smiled perfunctorily. 'That might change now.'

'Now? Why?'

'While Richard's away. They will be watching to see who you amuse yourself with.'

For a moment Bella didn't understand. 'Catch me two-timing him, you mean?'

'Not necessarily. They will be more interested as it gets closer to the date anyway. And with this unfortunate business of the promotional tee-shirt—'

'I knew it! This is my Ginger Thins punishment.'

Queen Jane smiled. 'No question of punishment. That was entirely Richard's own fault and so I told him. But we thought that after that incident, especially with him away, you might find yourself a little – exposed.'

Bella was certain that 'we' included Lady P. Interfering old bat.

She said carefully, 'You may be right. Can we see how it goes?'

'Of course, my dear. I only want to help. Just remember that if the pressure becomes too great, there are always rooms at the Palace for you. We can protect you, you know.'

The only pressure, thought Bella, was from Lady P and the Meringue Party. But she did not say so. She thanked the Queen warmly instead.

'I narrowly escaped incarceration today,' she told Lottie that evening. 'With Richard gone, Lady P made her move. The Queen invited me to live in the Palace.'

'Cardiganville?' said Lottie, who had rather taken against Lady Pansy at the Great Wedding Dress Round Table.

'Oh, worse than that. It's cold and dark with acres of corridors, deserted except for some pictures of men in uniform or killing animals. The Cardigan Sphere is quite cosy by comparison.'

'Cardigans can suffocate you though,' said Lottie darkly. 'Now listen. I need to talk to you about the Hen Night. What do you want to do?'

Bella cheered up. She hadn't had a really good

session with her girlfriends since they all went off to Greece the summer after college. She had seen a couple of them since she got back from the island but she had been so absorbed, between Richard and job hunting, that there were at least half a dozen girls she had still to catch up with.

'Going back to Greece would be nice,' she said now, wistfully. 'Do you remember that terrace?'

'Yeah. Brilliant. But I'm not sure it's practical for a weekend. Don't forget, Nicki and Sarah are on first-year teacher salaries.'

Bella nodded. 'I know. And it would be a hassle banging through airports and things. Besides, Lady P would probably set the Press on me if went outside the UK. We must support British trade.'

Lottie chuckled. 'Well, I can do you a very nice cowboy bar in Newcastle, complete with bucking bronco and a rugby club down the road.'

Bella's eyes popped. 'You're not serious?'

'Yup. Girl from work had her Hen Night there. We all took turns on the bronco. Fell off. Threw up.'

Bella, who had been on four Hen Nights so far and thought she knew the form, was impressed. 'One hen always throws up. But the whole flock?'

'Every last woman. And then they cleaned up, came back and tried again. And then danced till dawn with a couple of cowboy strippers. They make 'em tough in the North.'

They were both silent, contemplating the enviable stamina of other people.

'So do you fancy it? Bronco busting?'

'Maybe not.'

'Thought not. I'm getting together with Joanne sometime this week to sort things out. Anywhere you really want to go? Anything you want me to veto?'

Bella smiled. 'I trust you.'

'OK then. A judicious combination of silly and togetherness. I can do that.'

And so she did, or at least tried to do.

It all started very well. Joanne had found a small spa in West Yorkshire. Newly opened in a down-at-heel not-quite-stately home, it was inexpensive enough for even the tyro teachers to afford and fifteen of them turned up on Friday night. They had a lovely morning walk ending at a local pub, then lay around talking and taking massages and facials. Bella had been given the master suite, which was pretty impressive with a fourposter bed and balcony, and they all congregated there. Three of them sprawled on the bed with the others dispersed about the room while they advised Joanne on the use of a borrowed set of hair straighteners and discussed the evening to come. And then the whole event was overtaken by an irresistible force, in the form of the Honourable Chloe and Princess Eleanor.

For form's sake, Lottie and Joanne had had to ask along the two bridesmaids from Richard's side. For form's sake, they'd had to accept. But Nell had only just got back from New Zealand, where Queen Jane had taken over by Richard's side, and Chloe had a Friday night party to go to. So they said they would drive down together on Saturday afternoon, in time to hit the local town for dinner. And when they arrived it rapidly became clear that these two were going to party to the max and were absolutely determined to take everyone else with them.

'Right, people,' said Nell, for whom three weeks of enforced good behaviour had been too much. 'Let's get the rules straight here. The photos will be incriminating. You will be drunk. You will be sweaty. You will wear false eyelashes.' She said to Chloe, 'Anything else?'

Chloe said, 'RM?'

'RM. Right.' Nell tapped the side of her nose. 'How could I forget him? Anyone who doesn't snog a random man gets locked out.'

They both collapsed in giggles.

'Oh my Lord,' muttered Bella, sitting bolt upright against the fourposter bed's rich crimson bolster. 'What have they been drinking?'

'Let's hope it's just drink,' said Lottie grimly.

Whatever it was, its effects didn't abate. Instead of going for an Italian meal, followed by a spot of karaoke, the group found themselves whisked through some rudimentary tapas and on to a whistle-stop tour of every club and dive in the place. There were more than Bella expected and some of them were pretty rough, the sort of places where you went in and danced and kept your nose carefully blocked against the prevailing smell of last night's clientele.

Eventually they ended up in a dungeon of a nightclub. Chloe, who was barely coherent by then, ordered vodka with Sambuca chasers for everyone. Bella had looked forward to the prospect of trotting around town with brightly dyed feathers in her hair in the company of friends in a similar state, but now she was stone cold sober and starting to feel seriously uncomfortable. She managed to lose her drinks behind a giant cocktail card and signalled Lottie.

'I'll give it thirty minutes tops and then I'm off.'

'Nell will pass out before then,' said Lottie knowledgeably.

And, indeed, she was wobbling dangerously on her platform heels and grabbing any man who passed, almost certainly more for support than RM reasons.

'I can't stand much more of this,' muttered Bella. 'It's no fun. And Joanne looks as if she's going to cry.'

But Lottie was made of sterner stuff. 'Don't be a wuss, Bella. Someone *always* cries on a Hen Night.'

That was true. And Joanne had one or two of the three classic reasons to cry: she had just broken up with her boyfriend, and she had been at Bella's christening.

'You were a lovely baby,' she said, smearing her mascara terminally on Bella's handkerchief. 'A lovely, lovely baby. I so wanted a sister. You're as good as a sister to me. I love you, Bella. I've always loved you like—'

'Like a sister. Yeah, you said. Thanks, Jo. I love you too.'

'Beautiful baby,' said Joanne, who was at that stage of inebriation where the sufferer thinks that if they keep on plodding round the same track again and again they will find the slip road off and get away.

There was a stag do at the other end of the club which now decided to join forces with the girls. Chloe Lenane announced that she was going to snog all of them, and did. It took some time. The guys accepted the challenge enthusiastically. A tall hockey player came over, plucked Bella out of her corner, danced her round in a fast latin number and ended up throwing her over his arm, trying to suck her face off. Bella extricated herself.

'Thanks for the dance. I'm just going.'

'Oh, come on! The night is young . . .'

But Bella had caught sight of a commotion at the bar. Nell, having run out of snoggable men in the stag party, had wriggled round behind it and was trying to grope the hot young bartender. He was nice about it, but put her firmly out of his way by sitting her up on the counter. Only, from there she scrambled to her feet and strutted along the top of the bar. Already unsteady, she skidded in the spilled drinks and shot the entire length of the bar on her bottom, skirts and huge platform shoes flying. Then she fell off the end, landing in a tangled heap and lay there, laughing like a maniac.

Bella said, 'Right. That's it. I'm taking her back to the spa.'

Lottie had a fleet of taxis on standby. She called one up and between them she and Bella bundled Nell home.

When they got there, Nell flung herself flat on the bed and passed out. She was terribly pale and there was a sheen of sweat over her face.

'I'd better stay with her,' said Bella, worried. 'In fact, I might even call a doctor. That doesn't look normal to me.'

Nell opened her mouth and began to snore.

'That's normal,' said Lottie. 'But sit up with her if you

362

must. She was mixing her drinks like a sailor. And she must still be jet lagged, too. What a numpty.'

Numpty indeed, thought Bella, sitting with her as the night grew colder and the snores did not abate. She was so tired and her head hurt. She was also angry. She had been looking forward to her girls together weekend. It wasn't fair that these two idiots should mess it all up.

She was even angrier when she came down in the morning to find two unshaven photographers perched on the low wall round the car park. The nightclub had not been dark enough. The entire stag party had taken photos of the goings-on with their phones. The *Sunday Despatch* had completely changed its front page to print them.

Bella didn't know which made her feel more sick: the one of Eleanor, skidding along the bar; or the one of her bent double over the arm of a very fit bloke being, apparently, kissed senseless.

She stamped upstairs to Eleanor's room. The Princess was sitting on the edge of the bed, looking as if she would not easily move.

'Get dressed. We're going. You're a pain in the butt!'

Eleanor moaned, 'I'm going to be sick.'

'That's the least of your worries.'

The stately home owners did their best to keep the marauding flocks of photographers and journalists at bay. In fact, one of them came upstairs and said, 'There's an underground passage to the gatehouse. We cleared it for the children, so we know it's safe. Do you have someone you trust who could pick you up there?'

'George will help you,' Richard had said.

'I'll see,' said Bella.

She called George.

He hadn't seen the papers. He was barely awake. But he grasped the situation at once. 'OK. I'll be there. Directions?'

Fortunately he was less than an hour's drive away, staying with friends.

Lottie was her usual practical self. 'Leave the packing to me. Stay in Nell's room. I'll tell everyone you were worried about her colour last night and took her off.'

'Won't Chloe Lenane come to see her?'

'Bloody Chloe never came home last night. *If* she turns up, which I doubt, I'll get her off the premises. Confiscate Nell's phone, by the way. You don't know what she might send.'

'Good thinking. I don't trust her. She was out of her skull last night.'

Bella found Nell's phone in her tiny pink crystal-studded handbag and pinched it. Nell was sitting in a chair with a wet towel over her face by then and didn't notice. It was a bit of a struggle to get her down to the kitchens in order to access the passage because she kept saying she wanted to go home. But in the end, Bella managed it.

George called them when he was approaching the gatehouse and barely had to stop while Bella pushed Eleanor into the back seat and got in beside him.

'Drive,' she said between her teeth, 'before I kill your sister.'

From the back seat, Eleanor moaned.

Bella's sense of humour returned momentarily. 'Or before she throws up all over your motor.'

He drove like the wind.

23

'Will He Call It Off?' – *Sunday Despatch*

Bella was still in the car when Richard called. She expected fury, or that deadly Royal chill, but it was worse than that. He just sounded tired.

'How could you be so thoughtless?' he said. 'How could you? Nell is barely more than a child, my mother and I are out of the country, my father has a heart murmur . . . You just don't *think*.'

Bella looked over her shoulder at Eleanor, now slumbering heavily. She looked about twelve. 'It just got out of hand, that's all. I know it's a mess but these things happen . . .'

'Well, you'll have to clear it up,' he said flatly. 'Julian Madoc is talking to the Press Officers. The internet has gone crazy and there's some very nasty stuff out there. He'll be in touch with you. I strongly advise you to do what he says.'

'Of course.'

'Where are you now?'

'On the road back to London. With Nell. George is driving us.'

'Well, that's something, I suppose. Don't go to

366

Camelford House. Take her straight to the Palace. I'll call Pansy.'

Bella flinched.

'And when you get there—'

'Yes?'

'I know you don't want to, but this is non-negotiable. You move into the Palace and you stay there. Or I'll issue a statement that the engagement is off. I mean it, Bella.'

She felt numb with shock. 'I can hear you do,' she said through frozen lips.

'So do it.'

He rang off without saying goodbye.

It was dreadful. Julian Madoc was quite kind, to Bella's surprise, but Lady Pansy could barely contain her triumph. It came liberally coated with more-in-sorrow-than-in-anger, but triumph was what it was. Eleanor kept to the room that had been prepared for her and a nurse sat with her. Nobody told Bella what, if anything, was wrong with the Princess. Nobody told Bella anything much, until George came over to see his sister before dinner and dropped in to see Bella afterwards.

She was sitting in the window seat, trying to read a mystery and failing to keep her mind on the blood-spattered corpse.

'How's it going?' said George, sliding round the door like a murderer himself.

Bella wondered if he had been told to keep away from her contaminating presence. She wondered if Richard had told him that.

367

'I'm fine. How is Nell?'

'She's thrown up. Just as well or I think old Jones would have stomach-pumped her. She's lying in bed with the duvet over her head sulking. Which means she's ashamed of herself.'

He wandered round the room, which looked as if it had been furnished by Lady Pansy. There were pictures of men with guns, coupled with china cabinets full of King Charles spaniels and pirouetting Columbines. It made Bella feel crowded and faintly ill. But George seemed completely at home in it.

He said, 'She's a pill. But it's not all her fault. When people give you a role, you sort of play it. You know?'

'A role?'

'The three of us. Good Boy, Bad Boy, Wild Child. They've been calling her that since she was thirteen. People *believe* it.'

'But surely . . .' And then Bella remembered the cartoon she had seen, before she even met Richard. The Royal Family as the Seven Dwarfs, that was it. What had they called the children? *Dim, Ditzy and Dull.* She'd believed it, hadn't she? 'I'm sorry,' she said, ashamed of herself.

He shrugged. 'I get to play the Clown. Not a problem. It's tougher on Richard who does all the dull stuff and never, ever gets drunk, or goes on the razzle, or even does his own thing. At least, not until he met you.'

'Me?'

'You have no idea what a bid for freedom you were. For all of us, including Nell and me. You gave us hope.'

'But why? Surely Richard does everything he wants to? The Queen says he's very strong-willed.'

'The Good Boy?' said George. 'He'd give up anything, if he thought it was his duty. He was a fine sailor, you know. Really gifted. Might even have had trials for the Olympics if they'd let him carry on with it. Only Mother said it was too dangerous. So he gave it up. My father didn't stop him. He *gave it up*. It's as if he's trying to kill off everything about him that isn't . . .'

'Public property?' said Bella in a small voice.

'Yup, maybe. Then he started parkour. Do you know what that is?'

She shook her head.

'Sort of free running. You try to cross the city without touching the ground. Very gymnastic. Lots of vaults and springs and swinging from your hands. He was really good. He still watches it on YouTube sometimes. It makes me so mad. He should be *doing* it.'

'He told me he liked climbing buildings,' said Bella, enlightened.

George cocked an eyebrow. 'Really? As if he still does it?'

She said carefully, 'As if he still plans to do it, certainly.'

'That's the best news I've heard in years. Let's hope he sticks with it.' He brightened at a thought. 'If you can get him into a horned helmet, hauling an oar with a bunch of weirdos, there might still be hope for him. Power to your elbow, Bella Greenwood. Power to your elbow.'

*

369

But there was no sign of Richard breaking out. Even when he and the Queen came back from their tour, he and Bella never got their old intimacy back. Partly, of course, it was because he insisted on her living in that barracks of a place. It didn't feel quite right, sleeping together in the great echoing Palace, with servants popping out of doors when you least expected them, and the King at one end of the building and the Queen at the other. But he could have kissed her as if he meant it, talked to her properly. Even taken her out somewhere.

He didn't. He was just courteous and considerate and desperately busy. Whenever he saw her, he made it clear that he was on his way somewhere else. He couldn't even spare half an hour to walk round one of the parks with her.

The only sign of emotion he gave was when she said quietly, 'Richard, I don't know what's gone wrong. This *can't* just be about the Hen Night. Do you want to end the engagement?'

He looked at her as if she had stabbed him. It was the only hopeful sign she had seen.

And at once he said tonelessly, 'If that's what you want, then of course.'

Bella said, 'No, it's not what I want. How can you think that? Remember what we used to be like?'

She went to him. His hands came out to her for just a moment. Then they fell to his sides and he stepped back.

It was like a slap in the face.

She stood very still for a couple of seconds, mastering

herself. Then she said quietly, 'What has happened to us? Is it something to do with your father? Surely he's better? He seems terrific.'

The King, alone of the family, seemed to be in tearing spirits. He had lost a stone and a half, started jogging round the Palace grounds, and had thrown himself back into his official engagements with a will. He looked, in fact, like a man who has been on holiday. Unlike his elder son, who looked so fine-drawn, you could see the skull under his skin.

Richard said formally, 'He is very well indeed. The doctors are very pleased with him.' He looked at his watch. 'Now, I'm sorry, I'm overdue at the Cathedral. The Prior is talking about a rehearsal but I'm saying it's too soon.'

And he was gone before Beth could stop him.

It was only afterwards that she thought, *he* is going to the Cathedral? Without me? What is going on?

Of course, it was probably because of the paparazzi. The tell-tale photographs had come from cellphones and the newspapers had tweaked and enhanced them in-house. But the paparazzi didn't find her boring any more. Whenever she stepped outside, they homed in on her like wasps round a jam jar.

'Do they think I'm going to throw myself into the arms of some passing hunk?' she asked Lottie irritably, having run the gauntlet of their cameras in order to have her hair done by Carlos, followed by supper with her friend. 'What do they think I am?'

'Desperate,' said Lottie frankly.

'What?'

'That's how you look. Tense and haggard, as if you hadn't slept for a month. And you're losing weight again, too. Have you been dieting after that silly photo?'

'What? No. What are you talking about?'

Lottie blushed and apologised. 'I was thinking of that photo the mad person put up on their blog. Loyal Subject or whatever they call themselves. It was you standing on the cliff, when the boys were doing their Viking thing. There must have been a stiff breeze because you're leaning backwards but it blows the front of your waterproof out, as if you've got a bit of a tummy. A few of the nastier bloggers were calling you podgy.'

Bella shrugged. 'I didn't see it. I don't look at the internet much. The Press guys send printouts to Trudy, but she says it's just depressing how badly written it all is. So I don't see it.'

'Oh, well, good. So you're not dieting to look like a skeleton? It just happened?'

Bella flushed. 'I know. I'll do better. But it's almost like being in prison, Lotts. They want me to work at home, too. Well, I can do that. Project evaluation is a solitary activity. I don't have to go into the city to sit at a desk and do it. But I liked the desk and the office and going round the corner to meet Ma at the pub for lunch.'

Lottie made sympathetic noises. She said she couldn't envisage a life in which you couldn't go round the corner to the pub.

Bella smiled, but her smile swiftly died. 'Everywhere I go I have a palace minder in case I get drunk and fall over and a security officer in case somebody else does. I said I wanted to buy some new knickers and they asked Marks and Spencer to stay open 'specially for me.'

'I'm impressed.'

'Don't be. A great shop like that, with nobody but me and a few Palace watchers in it. Creeped me out.'

Lottie said awkwardly, 'Bel, do you think – could they be trying to scare you off? Freak you out by showing you what it's going to be like being Mrs Richard?'

Bella nodded slowly. 'I thought of that. But I don't see the point. I told him we could break it off and . . .' She drew a long breath. 'He didn't want to. He looked horrified. No, the one thing I'm absolutely certain of is that he still wants to marry me, Lotts.'

But, in her heart, she wasn't certain at all.

24

'Good to Go!' – *Tube Talk*

And then, out of the blue, her father rang.

'Bella?' he yelled. He always yelled as if he were in the midst of the Siberian wastes, even if it was only Clapham Common.

Bella felt her heart lift. Finn was a meteor, whizzing at top speed and possibly destructive, but he always sizzled with energy. 'Hello, Finn. Where are you?'

'I'm staying with your brother. He's worried about you. We're coming to see you. Time we broke you out of the Bastille.'

Maybe it was Finn's renegade influence, but quite suddenly Bella had had enough of being a ladylike prisoner, with Lady Pansy vetoing her every choice and all her own friends unreachable on the other side of the Palace's curtain wall.

'No, I'll meet you,' she said decisively. 'St James's Park. On the bridge. Today at four.'

Lady Pansy, a creature of habit, took tea with the Queen at four on Tuesdays and Thursdays.

And while Lady Pansy was away, Bella just walked out. Nobody stopped her. The policeman on the gate didn't even question her, just tipped his hat.

Why didn't I think of doing this before? she thought. I must have been going stir crazy in there. I could have walked out any time I wanted.

She walked gently round the park, smelling the honey and musk of the early roses, savouring the great blowsy displays of annuals in the beds, and the lush green grass. It felt good to have the warm air on her face again. At last, Bella felt she could breathe.

She got to the bridge at four o'clock exactly. Finn wasn't there. Par for the course, thought Bella tolerantly, and leaned over the railing watching a family of ducklings show off their prowess at swimming in a straight line – except for the tail-end Charlie, who kept getting distracted and was endlessly chivvied back into line by his father. She laughed aloud.

'That doesn't sound too bad,' said a voice.

And she turned and there was Finn: disreputable holed jeans, appalling old lumberjack shirt, open to the waist, several days' worth of beard and an Akubra hat. He raised his a hand, which was the closest he ever got to giving anyone a hug.

'Live long and prosper.'

He was also a fan of cult TV. How could she have forgotten that? Bella was so pleased to see him, she grinned from ear to ear.

Her phone started to ring. She switched it off. This was Bella time. No one else was muscling in on that.

'Finn, it's good to see you. You look a complete down and out.'

He took it as a compliment and preened like one of

the ducks. 'Got back two days ago. Went straight to Neill's. That Viking stunt of his looked good fun. Sorry I missed it.'

'Well, stick around. He may do it again.'

'I might. I might stick around to see you married, too. How do you feel about that?'

Bella thought about Finn slouching into the Cathedral and coming face to face with Lady Pansy. She could have danced with glee. 'Oh, yes, *please*, Dad.' Suddenly her eyes were brimming over.

He blinked. She never called him Dad. 'Hey. No need to cry. If you want me there, I'm up for it. I'll even walk you down the aisle if you want.' His tone said it would be an enormous sacrifice.

'You don't have to go that far. Kevin has offered and he actually doesn't mind wearing a morning suit.'

Finn gave a sigh of relief. 'Great chap, Kevin. Always said so. Now walk round this pond with me and tell me what's wrong.'

To her amazement, she did. Finn, who normally found human relationships both difficult and boring, listened with unusual attention. In the end he said, 'You know, something seems to have happened to this chap of yours. He hasn't had a blow to the head or anything, has he?'

'No,' said Bella, with a tearful chuckle.

'Well, then, you'd better ask him what's going on,' said Finn. 'Because sure as hell, something is.'

'I don't see what it could be—'

Finn raised his eyes to heaven. 'God, this is why I can never live with women. They go off into corners and think, maybe it's this, maybe it's that. Ask, woman. *Ask*.'

Bella hesitated.

'Call him now and I'll buy us both an ice cream.'

She laughed. 'Oh, all right.'

She switched the phone back on and at once texts started whizzing across the screen. Well, tough. She called Richard.

He picked up so fast, it was like a cat pouncing. 'Bella. Oh, thank God! Are you all right? Where are you?'

'I'm in St James's Park,' she said. 'Looking at the ducks. In front of the ice-cream stand. Look, you and I need—'

'Stay there. Stay *there*,' he said urgently. 'Don't move. I can see you. I'm coming to get you.'

Bella let the phone drop, her mouth open.

Her father called out something.

She turned to him, shaking her head. 'What?'

'I said—'

And out of the bushes pounded Richard, Prince of Wales, and hit him. Actually, he felled Finn by the unscientific but effective method of knocking him behind the knees and then jumping on him.

'What the fuck?' gasped Bella.

'It's OK,' said Richard, with a knee in Finn's back. 'I've got the bastard. You're safe.'

Safe?

Bella glugged but no words came . Finn made some protesting noises.

'Shut up,' said Richard, so fiercely that even Finn shut up.

Richard pulled out his phone. 'It's OK, I've got her.

377

She doesn't seem to be hurt.' He looked at Bella, his face haggard. 'You're not, are you?'

She shook her head.

'She's safe. Now come and arrest this bastard before I wring his neck!'

Bella got back the power of speech. 'What are you doing, you, you thug?' she shouted. 'Get off my father! Get off my father *now*.'

Richard stared at her blankly. 'Your father?'

Bella calmed down somewhat. 'The man you are sitting on,' she said, very precisely, 'is my natural father, Finn Greenwood.'

Richard got off his victim automatically. 'But he shouted at you. Abuse . . . I heard him.'

Bella turned to her father, who stood up, spitting grass and rubbing the back of his hand across his mouth. 'What did you shout, Finn?'

His eyes crinkled up at the corners. Say what you like about footloose and irresponsible, Finn was good at riding life's punches. 'I said, "Chocolate, vanilla or coffee flavour?"' he repeated mildly. 'I take it you're my intended son-in-law? Good to meet you.'

Richard shook hands on auto-pilot.

Down the path came two security officers. One, Bella saw, was Ian.

'What's going on?' she said.

He came panting up to them. 'Are you out of your mind?' he yelled at Richard, entirely forgetting the respect due to the Prince of Wales. 'For all you knew, he could have been armed.'

'Exciting,' said Finn, mildly interested. This was the

378

sort of human interaction he could handle, thought his daughter fondly, plenty of action, none of the soppy stuff .

Richard rubbed his hand over his face. 'I thought I'd lost you,' he croaked.

He pulled Bella into his arms, heedless of his prospective father-in-law, security officers, ice-cream vendors and a tribe of interested mothers and children who entirely forgot to feed the ducks.

He became aware at last that everyone was staring. 'Oh, God. Let's get out of here.'

'I still have Lottie's key,' said Bella. She was torn between bewilderment, relief and sheer spitting fury. She definitely didn't want to go anywhere Royal, just at the moment, and was quite prepared to say so. Nobody asked.

So they went back to the Pimlico flat and Bella brewed tea. Richard went into the kitchen with her.

'God, I've missed you,' he said.

Looking at his face, Bella could believe it. He had dark grooves around his mouth and his eyes looked haunted. Much of her fury dissipated. She touched his poor tense mouth and he seized her hand, kissing the palm and holding it against his cheek as if he could not quite believe she was there.

Bella lost the urge to yell at him. On the other hand . . .

'You've been keeping me in the dark,' she said levelly. 'You've got to stop that, you know. I'm a grown-up.' She tugged her hand away.

'I know. I know. But you were in danger, all because

of me. If you hadn't met me, if I hadn't chased you, it would never have happened. You'd have had a safe and happy life. So it was my fault. Besides, I *had* to keep you safe. Do you see?'

Yes, she saw. She went on making tea, putting mugs on a tray. 'But why didn't you just *tell* me?'

'I didn't want you to be afraid,' he said simply.

She snorted. 'Great! Just great. So you put me in prison instead?'

He winced. 'I didn't think.'

'No. You didn't. And you don't seem to think that I can either. Marriage is a *partnership*, Richard.'

She took the tray through to the sitting room, while he held the door for her.

'Right,' she said. 'I want to know what's been going on. All of it.'

Ian and the other security officer looked at Richard for guidance. Bella could have screamed. But he nodded quickly and she decided to let it go.

'There's a blogger we've been watching for a while. He's particularly hostile to you, Bella,' said Ian. 'The profilers say he is fixated on Richard. The threats get worse every time you two are seen together in public.'

So that's why Richard had been keeping away from her. Idiot! But she didn't say it aloud. Not yet. It could wait.

Richard said, 'I thought if you went to live in the Palace, you would be safe. And you *were*. But it's made you look like a ghost. And so sad. When you asked me if I still wanted to marry you, I nearly stopped it. But –

well, LoyalSubjekt101 was still out there. Still is, since this hobo isn't our man.'

He gave Finn a complicated look, somewhere between apology and irritation. Well, at least he'd got over hero-worshipping her father, thought Bella, suddenly amused. That was a good sign.

'What sort of things does the blogger say?' she asked.

Richard recoiled. 'You don't want to know.'

She just looked at him.

'Oh, very well. Some of it's vile and some of it's just stupid . . . like saying you looked fat because the wind was blowing up your windcheater, or that you dressed like a frump because you wore some terrible striped dress to the New Year Ball, which you didn't even wear . . .' He tailed off. 'Bella?

She had sat bolt upright. 'He said I was going to wear a striped dress?'

'Yes.'

She went into her old bedroom and brought out The Striped Horror. 'This one, I imagine?'

Everyone stared at it.

'I never saw you in that,' said Richard slowly.

'No one did except Lottie. She was here when it was delivered. Some dressmaker must know about it, since she made the damn thing. But the person who gave it to me was Lady Pansy.'

There was a moment's silence, as they all assimilated the implications.

Then Richard surged to his feet. 'And that – that – *Judas* is having tea with my mother right now. Come with me!'

He seized the dress as they went.

When Bella and Richard burst in to her sitting room, the Queen was looking tired. Not surprisingly, thought Bella, who recognised one of Lady Pansy's interminable monologues when she walked in on one.

'Shut up,' said Richard ferociously.

Lady Pansy did.

'Richard dear,' said the Queen, alarmed.

He flung The Striped Horror into the middle of the carpet. 'Trapped by your own spite, Pansy. If you hadn't tried to make my Bella wear the ugliest dress in the world, you would never have given yourself away. Mother, this loyal lady-in-waiting of yours is LoyalSubjekt101.'

The Queen went pale. It was clear she knew about the mad blogger. But she said bravely, 'That has to be nonsense. Pansy . . .'

Lady Pansy said nothing. She didn't have to. Guilt was written all over her face, as soon as she saw the dress.

Ignoring the Queen, she turned on Richard, the horse face suddenly ugly.

'You had no right to marry *that*,' she said. 'You had to marry someone with breeding, with dignity, with a history of . . .'

'Service to the Royal Family? Yadda, yadda, yadda,' said Richard, suddenly a lot less dignified than Bella had ever seen him in front of other people. 'Shut up, you poisonous parasite. Shut up!'

Lady Pansy screamed then and went on screaming. It took a couple of the security officers, waiting in the corridor, to subdue her, and then a doctor to sedate her ravings.

The Queen was distraught. Richard called his father. When the King came hurrying in, Queen Jane was standing in front of the fireplace, wringing her hands in agitation.

'How could I have been so mistaken? How could I? She always seemed to be my friend. Why didn't I see? Your poor Bella, Richard. I've been so blind.'

The King stepped over to her, stilled her frantic hands and said, 'It's not your fault, my dear. If it's anyone's it's mine.' He drew a deep breath. 'I don't like unpleasantness or I would have got rid of Pansy a long time ago.'

'*What?*' said Richard. 'You *knew?*' He looked very grim suddenly.

Bella put a hand on his arm instinctively.

The King said steadily, 'My father did not treat Pansy well. I knew it. And I never said.'

'Oh,' said Bella, enlightened. 'So when she kept on about service to the Royal Family, what she really meant was that she was in love with the late King.'

'He couldn't marry her, of course. Not that he would have done anyway. Not a *loving* man, my father. But we didn't marry commoners in those days.'

'Commoner?' echoed Bella faintly. Lady Pansy of the horse face and ancestors who had served the Royal Family for a hundred years was a *commoner*?

'A technical term,' said Richard dryly. 'My father means not of the blood Royal. Bicycling Royals count. Daughters of an earl don't. Pansy would never have been a candidate for a Royal wife and she knew it.'

'And then you wanted me, without any sort of title in my family! No wonder she hated me!'

'Poor woman,' said the Queen. 'No husband and children of her own. Just us and that flaky niece. And none of us really *seeing* her properly. She used to drive me mad, and I was so determined to be *nice* to her . . .' Her voice trailed off.

She turned to the King then. For the first time since Bella had known them, she saw the King put an arm around his wife. He did it awkwardly. But it did not look insincere.

'Right,' said Bella, 'I have something to say. Please listen. You've got to stop trying to live other people's lives for them,' she said, first to the Queen and then to Richard.

'I know you do it with the best of intentions. It's very sweet. I really appreciate it. Richard was willing to throw himself in front of an assassin's knife for me and I don't take that lightly, I really don't. And the very first time we met, he took care of me. It's very good of you, my darling, but it has to stop. If I can't make my own mistakes, I'm not human. You ought to know that if anyone does.'

She turned to the Queen next. 'And you have to stop trying to prevent him from taking risks. He's so tender of you and his father, always trying to spare you worry. But he shouldn't. He's a grown man. He knows his own abilities. He needs to test himself, without thinking about you and the country and everyone else all the time.'

Nobody said anything. But the Queen rested her head against the King's chest.

'Now . . .' Bella went to the door. 'I am going back to stay with Lottie. Richard and I will go out, in public, whenever and wherever we want. I will come to the Palace the night before the wedding and not before. I'm taking my life back.'

25

'The Day!' – *Morning Times*

It was the morning of Bella's wedding day. In the courtyard of the Palace, a golden coach awaited the new Royal bride. In her borrowed boudoir in the Palace, she sat in a gold-embroidered cream dress, with flowing mediaeval sleeves. Brilliant sunlight shone into the window, illuminating a tall mirror.

Janet Bray stood back and smiled dreamily. 'You're beautiful, my darling. Just like the woman in your picture. Happy the bride the sun shines on.'

Bella would have been just as happy if she had been stomping up the hill in Wellington boots to marry her Richard in the pouring rain in front of their tower. But she didn't say so.

In fact she didn't say anything at all. Because she thought she was hearing something that should have been impossible. A scraping at the brickwork, a sharp and probably profane exclamation, the rending sound of a creeper being ripped from a wall.

No, she told herself, it was her imagination. It couldn't be happening. Not on her wedding day. Not with everything timed to a nanosecond. The Prince of

Wales, in scarlet regimentals and a gleaming sword, would be getting ready to go to the Cathedral even now.

'I so want you to be happy, my love. Even Finn says you two were born to be together.'

'Yes, I know, Ma. He said the same to me. Mind you, he's impressed that Richard has read all his books. Finn says it's more than he has.'

Janet looked momentarily shocked. 'Finn hasn't read his own books? No!'

'He puts them on tape and then forgets about 'em apparently.'

Bella tried to shift her position without actually craning round her mother too obviously. Was it possible that a face had just bobbed up outside the window?

No, of course not. It had to be her imagination.

Janet half turned to look out.

Bella said hurriedly, 'I can't tell you how grateful I am to Kevin for walking me down the aisle.'

Janet beamed and faced her again. 'He was so touched that you wanted him to do it.'

Bella breathed out in relief. 'He's a wonderful man. I . . . oh my God!' she cried, jumping to her feet.

'Darling, what is it? Are you nervous? Tell me?'

'Yes. No. I don't know,' said Bella, who had definitely seen the face bob up, a hand wave – in greeting? Desperation? – and both of them disappear again.

There had been no loud cry and thud of a falling body. So he was still there.

'No need to be. I remember my own wedding. . .'

Bella passed her options under rapid review. She could call in someone to help now. Richard wouldn't like that, unless he was hanging on by a fingernail. No, come to think of it, he would *particularly* dislike it if he was hanging on by a fingernail. So calling for help wasn't an option either way.

In which case, she had to get rid of her mother.

'And two lovely children,' finished Janet, misty-eyed.

Bella hugged her, said she was wonderful, and walked her backwards to the door.

'Um, yes, Mother. Do you – do you think you could leave me on my own for a bit now? I want to think. Yes, that's right. I want to be alone with my thoughts. It's such a big step, marriage.'

'Of course, love.'

As soon as the door had closed behind her, Bella flew to the window and flung the sash up.

'Are you mad?' she scolded, leaning out to find her beloved hooked on to the stone window sill and swinging gently in the breeze.

He grinned up at her. His face was dirty and he looked as happy as a schoolboy. 'Nope. Pretty good mood actually.'

'Stay right there.'

'Aren't you going to let me in?'

'Not until I've protected myself,' said Bella grimly.

She was absolutely not going to mention bad luck with him hanging outside her third storey window. She was not even going to think about it. On the other hand, she was not taking any chances either. This bridegroom was not going to get a glimpse of the wedding dress until the appointed hour, just in case. She pulled the pretty chintz coverlet off the bed and wrapped it round herself.

'OK then, Spiderman, in you come.' She leaned over the window sill and helped him haul himself into the room.

Once he was there, she breathed again. Though she did not let him see her anxiety. You can't tell someone they should be free to try any dangerous stunt they feel like and then freak out when they do, she thought. Damn it!

She still couldn't stop herself saying, 'You could have killed yourself.'

'Nah,' said Prince Richard, dull, stuffy, conscientious, dutiful, unemotional Prince Richard. He stamped some brick dust and paint over the priceless Aubusson and tidied his climbing axe away neatly. 'I told you. I've been looking at this wall for ages, my love. I knew I could do it.'

'But why today?' she wailed, backing away from him, chintz clutched to her bosom.

He leaned forward and kissed her. 'Because today I'm marrying you. Today I can do *anything*.'

'I'm flattered.'

'No, you're not,' he said seriously. 'You know me and I know you and we both know we're stronger together than we'll ever be apart. And we'll have a hell of a lot more fun too.'

'I'll hold you to that,' said Bella, unbearably moved and absolutely determined not to cry and mess up the work of art that was her make-up. 'But if you get dust on my wedding dress, I will *kill* you. After all the effort it cost. And you still owe me a limerick, you waster.'

'Ah,' he said. 'Glad you mentioned that. Here it is.'

And from inside his climbing suit he produced a neat piece of parchment with the five-line verse written out in a hand that would not have shamed Shakespeare. 'Enjoy. See you in church.'

'*Cathedral*,' she shouted after him.

But he had already shut the door behind him.

So she sat down in front of the mirror and looked at herself, in her fairytale dress, with her fairytale tiara and the bouquet of soft summer flowers, with the trails of ivy that Richard had insisted on. And then she looked at the ring he had designed for her. And read his poem.

And blushed.

And laughed.

And blushed and read it again.

And dabbed, terribly, terribly carefully at the corner of her eyes.

Then picked up her lovely skirts and went to promise her love everything she had to give.

Confetti Confidential

Holly McQueen

Isabel Bookbinder dreams of pearly white weddings, happy brides, handsome grooms. And champagne towers that don't topple over. She dreams of the perfect wedding. But not for herself . . . For her clients, of course.

It's all about bride management as far as Isabel's concerned. Even when she misplaces a couple of brides and loses her job working for wedding guru Pippa Everitt, Isabel isn't disheartened. She throws herself straight into launching *Isabel Bookbinder, Individual Weddings*.

But, nothing in Isabel's life is ever straightforward, and despite her best efforts, things don't go quite according to plan . . .

Praise for Holly McQueen

'I quite fell in love with Isabel. Funny, charming and accident prone, she is the perfect heroine for today' Penny Vincenzi

'Like catching a snippet of gossip in the girls' loos and deciding you want to carry on listening . . . As frivolous deckchair escapism . . . it certainly does the job' *Daily Mail*

'I think Isabel and I were twins separated at birth. I love her!' Katie Fforde

arrow books

A Perfect Proposal

Katie Fforde

It's time to live a little . . .

Sophie Apperly has spent her whole life pleasing others – but when she realises her family see her less as indispensable treasure and more as general dogsbody, she decides she's had enough. So when an old friend offers her the chance of a lifetime, she decides to swap Little England for the Big Apple, and heads off to the land of opportunity.

From the moment Sophie hits the bright lights of Manhattan she's determined to enjoy every minute of her big adventure. And when fate throws her together with Matilda, a spirited *grande dame* of New York society who invites her to Connecticut for Thanksgiving, she willingly accepts. English-born Matilda is delighted with her new friend – though her grandson Luke, undeniably attractive but infuriatingly arrogant, is anything but welcoming.

When Luke arrives in England a few weeks later, Sophie hardly expects him to seek her out. But Matilda has hatched some complicated plans of her own – and so Luke has a proposal to make . . .

Praise for Katie Fforde

'Great fun ... had me hooked to the end' *Daily Mail*

'A funny, fresh and lively read' *heat*

arrow books

THE POWER OF READING

Visit the Random House website and get connected with information on all our books and authors

EXTRACTS from our recently published books and selected backlist titles

COMPETITIONS AND PRIZE DRAWS Win signed books, audiobooks and more

AUTHOR EVENTS Find out which of our authors are on tour and where you can meet them

LATEST NEWS on bestsellers, awards and new publications

MINISITES with exclusive special features dedicated to our authors and their titles

READING GROUPS Reading guides, special features and all the information you need for your reading group

LISTEN to extracts from the latest audiobook publications

WATCH video clips of interviews and readings with our authors

RANDOM HOUSE INFORMATION including advice for writers, job vacancies and all your general queries answered

Come home to Random House

www.rbooks.co.uk